AS ₿/p

HIDDEN
BONES

BOOKS BY RITA HERRON

PROLOGUE
RIVER BEND

Blood dripped down the side of her mother's face, tears rolling from her eyes. She lurched forward to help her, but Mama shook her head and pointed to the closet door.

"Run and hide, honey. Don't make a sound."

For a minute, her feet were frozen. She couldn't leave Mama like this. Her clothes torn, black and blue bruises on her face, crying.

Footsteps thundered as the monster stomped back from the kitchen. Terrified, she darted into the hall closet and shut the door. But she could see through the cracks. Her heart raced even harder when she saw he had a kitchen knife.

He waved it above her mother's face and jabbed it toward her chest. "I told you to keep your mouth shut. It's your fault I have to do this."

Pressing her fist to her mouth to keep from sobbing, she pulled her knees up to her chest and hugged them hard. She wanted to help her mama, but the monster was so big he could crush her with his hands.

Then he grabbed her mother by the hair and dragged her down the hall toward the back door.

Mama screamed and kicked at him. "Let me go!"

"Shut up, you tramp."

Her mother threw her fists at him, but they bounced off as if he didn't even feel them.

Then he flung her against the wall, raised the knife and slashed her throat. Her mama gasped and blood spurted everywhere, running down her throat and soaking her shirt.

The little girl covered her mouth with her fist to hold back a scream, but the sound slipped out anyway.

The man jerked his head up and peered down the hall.

Shaking, she hunched into her mother's winter coat and slid behind the box of junk Mama had gathered for the Goodwill donation.

Holding as still as she could, she listened again. Somehow Mama had to get away.

Suddenly the monster yanked open the door. She hid her face in the coat that smelled like mothballs and the perfume she'd given Mama for her birthday. She bought it at the Dollar Store, but her mother said she loved it.

Two beefy hands pulled her from the closet. She kicked and screamed as he dragged her into the kitchen, but the sight of the river of blood on the floor around her mother's body made the scream die in her throat. Her mama's dark brown eyes stared at her, lifeless and empty. One hand reached out as if clawing for help. Blood soaked everything in sight.

"You say a word, you die, too," he growled.

Seconds later, he shoved her to the floor. She couldn't move. All she could do was stare at Mama's pale skin blotched in crimson.

A minute later, he tied her hands and feet, carried her outside and tossed her into the trunk of his car. He killed her mama. What was he going to do to her?

1

CROOKED CREEK, GEORGIA

Present day – thirty years later

DAY 1

Detective Ellie Reeves couldn't shake her dismal mood as she entered the Corner Café. A quick glance in the mirror and she winced at her reflection. She looked as glum as she felt. Her ash-blond hair was falling out of its ponytail, dark smudges rimmed her blue eyes and her T-shirt was torn and smeared with dirt.

Damn. She was bone-tired tonight, headache threatening. Spring break always sparked pranks and kids joyriding, just as it kicked off the season for hikers to begin their 2200-mile trek on the Appalachian Trail from Georgia to Maine.

The chaos had already started. Young kids had been breaking into houses for fun and she'd had to bust them. She hated having to make arrests like that, but the high-schoolers had to be stopped before they escalated to more serious crimes. Worse, their parents had been defensive, pressuring her to let them off with a warning. She had, but only because they hadn't hurt anyone or stolen anything of value. Still, she'd warned them if it happened again, she'd throw the book at them.

She slid onto a bar stool beside Ranger Cord McClain just as the café owner Lola Parks handed him a beer. Cord worked Search and Rescue and knew the sprawling Appalachian Mountains better than anyone. He was also part of the task force established by the governor a few months back to investigate the growing number of crimes in the area.

He and Lola had been dating for a while now. Ellie wondered where that was going. Cord had had a rough childhood and was close-lipped about it. She hoped he was happy with Lola – he deserved it.

The bell over the door tinkled as a family rushed in, chattering about their camping vacation. "Tomorrow we'll go to the Native American festival," the mother said.

The little girl bounced up and down on her heels. "I wanna do arts and crafts. They teach you how to make jewelry!"

"And there's ghost stories," the boy said.

The little girl wrinkled her nose. "There's no such thing as ghosts."

"Is, too." The boy pouted. "I just saw *Ghostbusters!*"

The little girl shivered, reminding Ellie of the first time she'd attended the yearly Native American festival and listened to the myths and legends passed down through the ages. There was so much tragedy in the stories about the Trail of Tears, where tens of thousands of Native American were forced off their land in the area.

Cord's thick brown brows rose, his whiskey-colored eyes focusing on her as he thumbed his fingers through his shaggy hair. "Hey, you okay?"

Ellie shrugged. "Long day. Spring break madness has begun with a bang. Had to bust up some kids on a B&E."

"Tell me about it," Cord said. "I ran some college kids off from the Native American burial grounds."

Ellie motioned to Lola that she wanted a beer, too. "Didn't they know that area is sacred?"

Cord took a sip of his IPA. "Yeah, some damn TikTok challenge has gone viral. Thought they'd catch sight of some of the spirits and post about it."

"Damn social media's dangerous," Ellie muttered.

And all the talk about ghosts was stirring the ones from her own past. Hard as she tried, she couldn't outrun them.

2

HAWK HOUSE

"Dead people don't talk." Nineteen-year-old Mandy Morely juggled her backpack on her shoulder as she trudged through the woods behind her friends: eighteen-year-old Sherry, nineteen-year-old Walker who she had the hots for, and his brother, sixteen-year-old Porter who'd first shown them the TikTok Challenge. Then Walker and Porter had the great idea to come to this old orphanage that was supposedly haunted.

Mandy's chest pounded as she looked up at the dilapidated structure. It had been abandoned – shut down – years ago. Over the years, teens and college students had challenged each other to spend the night on the property, and some claimed that ghosts roamed the house.

Sherry paused by a boulder, uncapped her water bottle and stopped to look at her. "If you don't believe, why are you coming, Mandy?"

No, she didn't believe. She'd lost her mother to a brutal killer last year and as crazy as it sounded, she'd tried to talk to her from the grave – to ask her why she never told her about her father, local sheriff Bryce Waters.

But her mom never answered. She didn't even appear in

Mandy's dreams. But she wanted to impress Walker. He was obsessed with all things paranormal.

"If we don't see anything, we can debunk all this nonsense," Mandy answered, shivering as the wind whistled through the tall pines and hemlock trees. She hated the woods almost as much as she hated the dark. Too many things lurking in the bushes.

Sherry rolled her eyes. "Ha. You just want to be close to Walker. If you get scared, you can crawl in his sleeping bag."

A frisson of nerves tickled her belly at the idea. She was a freshman at the local college but she'd never slept with a boy. Her mother would have been proud but it was just plain lame. And the past year, she'd been too upset dealing with her mother's death to even think about boys.

But the idea of kissing Walker made it almost worth hiking three miles and sleeping on the ground. *Almost.*

The boys called their names, and Sherry yelled back, "Coming!"

Mandy huffed and climbed the hill, and she and Sherry ran to catch up. Weeds clawed at her legs and she pushed away low branches, stumbling over a tree root as they reached the clearing. Ahead, the boys raced toward Hawk House, its spooky gray silhouette illuminated by the glow of the full moon. The *No Trespassing* sign looked battered and was tilting sideways, the tape roping off the property torn and flapping in the wind.

Her pulse jumped, and she dug her nails into her backpack.

"Hey, Mandy," Walker said. "Let's set up camp beneath that big oak tree. Then we'll explore the old house." His eyes fired a challenge at her and he grabbed his camera with the night lens. He and Porter had bragged about being modern-day ghostbusters, and Walker wanted to document whatever they found to prove they'd survived the demons dwelling on the property.

Sherry rushed ahead and dropped her backpack on the

ground beneath the tree, and Mandy sucked in a breath and joined her. A gusty breeze picked up again, and she fought a chill as she looked up at the sharp turrets of the ancient stone house. The windows looked foggy, coated with years of grime, and kudzu climbed the walls and trellis.

Bats flew through the treetops. Trembling, she set her backpack by Sherry's then spread her sleeping bag on the ground.

The boys placed theirs a few feet away, then Walker set the six-pack of Miller Lite he'd crammed in his backpack down. He and Porter found some stones and arranged them to make a firepit, while she and Sherry gathered twigs and a couple of logs, and stacked them in the center. The chilly wind nipped at her, and Mandy was grateful when Walker lit the twigs, adding a glow to the dark area and a burst of heat that she warmed her hands over.

While Porter began to tell them accounts of ghost sightings over the years, Mandy huddled in her windbreaker and Sherry hovered near her, chewing her nails.

"According to one story, some teenagers saw a headless boy wandering the yard of the orphanage," Porter said. "They say you can see a trail of blood where his head was chopped off."

Mandy shuddered, then curled her fingers into the palms of her hands as she scanned the neighboring woods. The house sat on a hill overlooking a sharp ridge so thick with trees you couldn't see past them.

Porter made a ghoulish sound and Sherry jumped. Mandy scooted closer to the fire and Walker, who poked at the embers with a stick, stirring the flames. The wind blew smoke around them, the smell of burning wood mingling with the scent of her own fear.

A growling sound echoed from near the house, and they all jerked their gazes toward the spooky structure. Mandy could have sworn she saw a shadow in the tiny attic window.

"Come on, let's check it out," said Walker, gesturing toward the house.

Porter leaped up and took off running, his phone poised to capture a video. Walker snatched his camera too, and Sherry pulled her flashlight from her bag.

Terrified at being left alone, Mandy grabbed her torch, nerves clawing at her as she and Sherry followed Walker and Porter. Walker tried opening the door, but it was shut tight. He motioned for them to follow him, and they walked through weeds, brush crunching beneath her boots as they trekked from one window to the other. Finally, he found a side window with the glass shattered.

He waved a hand toward the opening. "Who wants to go first?" Mandy shook her head, but Porter piped up. "Me."

Dark clouds moved across the moon, and the wind howled, leaves tumbling across the ground. Again, Mandy thought she saw the silhouette of a large figure behind the foggy window. All around her, the air felt stagnant with the scent of death.

Porter was climbing through the window when he shouted that someone was inside. Icy fingers of fear trailed up Mandy's neck and she turned to run. Porter dropped back to the ground with a grunt, and Sherry's eyes widened.

Walker rushed to help his brother, but Mandy acted on instinct and ran back around the side of the house. Shadows hovered everywhere, eyes piercing her from the darkness of the woods. Behind her, she heard footsteps closing in.

Chest tightening with panic, she picked up her pace but tripped over a layer of branches spread on the ground and lost her footing. The branches snapped and caved in, sticks and weeds stabbing her. She screamed, reaching for something to hold onto and snagged a vine. But her fingers slid down it, thorns pricking her, and she felt herself falling.

The darkness swallowed her, and she grabbed thin air as she hit the bottom of what must have been a pit. Her hand twisted, pain shooting up her arm. Sharp rocks and sticks stabbed at her palms and back, and something crawled across her leg as she collapsed into the dirt.

Shaken and terrified, she flipped on her flashlight and panned it around the inside of the hole. Her heart hammered in horror as the light illuminated the ground.

She couldn't believe what she was seeing.

Bones... There were bones down here.

3

CROOKED CREEK

Hushed whispers and laughter rumbled from a side table and Ellie spotted Maude Hazelnut, aka Meddlin' Maude, and her brood deep in gossip. Lola set Ellie's beer in front of her, and she ordered a burger and fries to go.

"Gonna be a bunch of crazy ghost hunters coming in because of that show about haunted places in the South," Ellie heard Maude muttering.

"Already a woman named Crystal Marrs has opened up some kind of magic shop selling witchcraft potions," Carol Sue from the Beauty Barn added.

Maude tittered. "We need to put a stop to this nonsense."

Ellie gritted her teeth. Leave it to Maude to make trouble out of nothing.

The door opened again, and old Ms. Eula hobbled in, leaning on her cane.

"Speaking of ghosts," the mayor's wife Edwina said with an eye roll.

Ellie barely resisted stalking over to the women and telling them to shut up. Ms. Eula was strange, no doubt about that, and everyone thought she talked to the dead, but Ellie had a fondness for her.

The wind suddenly picked up, rattling the windows and making the lights flicker off and on for a brief second. Cups on the table clinked and the wind whistled through the café, adding a chill in the air.

Lola approached, cutting her eyes toward Cord then back to Ellie. "I'll grab your order so you can get on home."

"Thanks." Ellie sensed Lola was rushing her off. Still, she needed a shower badly. And some sleep. Although she felt restless – the last time she'd had this twisted feeling in her stomach, a little girl had been kidnapped.

She caught sight of Lola looking through the open window from the kitchen, watching them, and she frowned. "You two okay?"

Cord gave a quick nod, then took a long pull of his beer and drummed his scarred fingers on the bar surface. Just as he was about to answer, his phone buzzed. Hers rang at the same time.

He answered immediately. "Ranger McClain."

Ellie answered her own.

"9-1-1 call came in," her boss Captain Hale said. "Some kids at Hawk House. One of the girls fell into a pit and is in trouble. She found bones."

Ellie inhaled a deep breath. "I'm on my way."

When she hung up, she turned to Cord. "I have to go. Trouble at Hawk House."

"I got the same call." Cord jangled his keys. "I'll drive."

Lola appeared from the kitchen, brows furrowed as she handed Ellie her food. "Burger and fries."

Ellie snagged the bag. "Thanks."

"We got a call," Cord said.

Lola glanced between them, her lips pressing into a thin line. "Cord, come by my place when you're finished."

"It may be a while," Cord said. "Talk later."

Lola flipped her hair over her shoulder with a sigh, then disappeared into the kitchen. She was obviously upset about something, but Ellie didn't have time to dwell on it.

Instead, she and Cord hurried outside to his truck. That damn old orphanage was off limits just like the other abandoned properties in the mountains, but that didn't stop kids breaking in every year.

Ellie dug into her food as Cord drove. The moon glowed bright and full, stars glittering in the inky sky. February had been rainy with the creeks flooding, but tonight the bright yellow moon shimmered off the sharp ridges and steep cliffs.

As Cord punched the accelerator and climbed the hills winding up the mountain, Ellie saw a flock of black crows hovering on power lines and circling in the distance. Folklore touted that crows symbolized death, an omen of the end of life. Ellie tried to dismiss the idea, but more than once when she'd seen the crows, she'd been working a murder case.

Hopefully, the bones the kids had found were an animal's, not human. Still, if someone was hurt, they might need medical treatment, so she phoned for an ambulance to meet them at the property.

"Have you been to Hawk House before?" Ellie asked Cord.

His jaw turned to steel. "Long time ago."

Cord had always been secretive about his past, but she knew he'd been dumped in more than one foster home. His last foster father, a perverted mortician, had been abusive.

"Want to talk about it?" she asked softly.

A firm shake of his head indicated the subject was closed.

They lapsed into a tense silence, though Ellie desperately wanted him to open up. But Cord was private and kept his pain to himself.

She understood that. She had her own demons to conquer. And scars that she didn't want to talk about either.

Crystal Marrs lined the essential oils on the shelf, the soft lavender scent of the incense wafting through the shop. Ever since she was little and her daddy had brought her to the mountains to pan for gold in Dahlonega, she'd been interested in crystals.

Natural stones were abundant in the area and she'd collected them as a child, then studied the various properties associated with each one, along with natural herbs and plants in the area which could be used for medicinal purposes.

Through the picture window where she'd displayed her favorite candles and soaps, she spotted the nosy biddies who'd been protesting her store. They'd called her a witch, a charlatan and other names she refused to say even in her mind.

She was none of those things, just a businesswoman who believed in holistic treatments and finding peace in nature, and she wanted to share her love with others.

If she was a witch, she'd cast a spell and turn those busybodies into real squawking hens who had to scratch in the dirt for their dinner.

Laughter bubbled in her throat. Some would say that was naughty, not to think such things, but she couldn't help herself.

She moved from the essential oil display to the corner where she'd arranged colorful scarves, handmade jewelry, and quilts handsewn by the quilting club. She also sold beaded purses, Native American baskets and pottery by a local potter, all on a consignment basis.

The bone windchimes tinkled as the door opened and that woman called Maude came tottering in, her brows bunched in a scowl. The others flocked behind her, chicken necks flapping, tongues wagging.

"Look at this." One of them pointed to a section of herb pouches, lowering her voice as if they thought she couldn't hear them. "She thinks she can come to our town and breed evil with her potions."

"She'll never last," Maude said staunchly.

Crystal rubbed the bone necklace around her neck and bit back a smile. That old rooster had no idea who she was dealing with. She'd been run off from places before. Ostracized.

But she'd bounced back stronger each time.

Crooked Creek had trouble flowing through its rivers and streams, embedded in the red clay soil.

She was here to help fight it.

6

HAWK HOUSE

Mandy couldn't stop screaming. She squeezed her eyes closed.

"Try to stay calm," Walker called to her from above.

Stay calm? He had to be kidding. She was sitting in a black pit with what felt like bones next to her. Was someone buried down here?

"I called 9-1-1. Help's on the way," he said. The light beamed across the dirt and then onto her, then he made a strangled sound and cursed. Walker never cursed.

"Please get me out of here," she cried. Trembling, she pulled her legs up around her and wrapped her arms around them, folding herself into a tight ball. But the images bombarded her, and in her mind she began to see faces of the dead.

The scent of something rotten floated in the damp cold air and the sound of a rodent skittering brought another scream from her. Each second felt like an eternity. Above her, the wind whistled. Sherry was freaking out, but Porter sounded pumped.

"Take pictures," Porter shouted to her. "We'll go viral!"

Mandy squeezed her eyes closed again. "No, I can't look."

"I'm right here, Mandy." Walker's voice sounded so far away that tears trickled from her eyes and slid down her cheeks.

Her hand was throbbing. She tried to flex it and realized it might be broken.

Something stabbed at her hip as she shifted. Another sharp rock – or a bone? She shivered and rocked herself back and forth. Were the ghosts of the dead trapped down here, reaching for her?

Cord's truck bumped over the rutted road leading to Hawk House, gravel spewing as he wove along the narrow one-way road winding through the wilderness. Ellie surveyed the scene, her pulse hammering as shadows danced across the moon. Wind whipped at the trees, March rolling in with a vengeance.

Thanks to her own traumatic past, she struggled with her fear of the dark and couldn't imagine these kids alone out here in the woods.

This place was originally a home for wayward boys, but it had evolved into an orphanage that housed girls as well. The headmaster had supposedly used cruel punishments to steer the kids back on track. Like the telephone game, the truth was probably buried somewhere in the midst of the stories that had passed from one generation to another.

"It's up there a few thousand feet," Cord said as he pulled up the long oak-lined drive.

At one time, the house was probably stately and impressive, but now cobwebs, layers of grime from weathering and fog-coated windows made it look spooky. The grass was brown, barren in places and tangled weeds climbed the front of the house.

Cord cut the engine, and Ellie spotted a young boy of about fourteen running toward them. She and Cord got out, hurried to him and identified themselves.

Behind him, she saw sleeping bags and a makeshift firepit. They'd obviously set up camp beneath the cluster of red oaks.

In spite of the breeze, the kid was sweating. He motioned toward the rear of the house. "Come on, the pit's back here."

Flashlights in hand, they jogged after the teen. An older boy and girl hovered near a pile of brush, the blond-haired girl cowering in a red parka, rocking herself back and forth. The older teen's dark brown hair looked mussed, and he was on his knees, talking down into the pit.

She and Cord crossed to them and introduced themselves.

"I'm Walker and that's Sherry." He gestured toward the younger kid, "And that's my brother Porter. We were running away from the house when Mandy fell through the brush."

Ellie's heart thundered. "Mandy?"

He nodded. "Mandy Morely."

Dear heavens, Ellie thought. Mandy was her niece – and now she was in trouble.

Mandy's mother Vanessa was Ellie's half-sister – although Ellie hadn't known that fact until Vanessa had been killed. After her death, Ellie had promised to be there for the young girl.

Mandy was also the sheriff's daughter.

A second later, Mandy's shrill scream catapulted her into motion.

"Careful, El," Cord warned as she rushed toward the underground hole. "We don't know how solid the ground is or how wide the hole is."

"Help is here!" Walker called to Mandy.

Cord grabbed a large tree branch, then moved slowly toward where Walker was kneeling, testing the ground as he treaded carefully. He walked around the edge, gauging the distance. "Looks like it's about three feet wide, two feet long."

Ellie clenched her hands by her sides. Mandy had been through so much the past year and a half. Losing her mother. Then learning her father was the sheriff, Bryce Waters. They'd only begun to forge a relationship.

"Mandy, it's Ellie," she said, then knelt beside Walker.

"Ellie!" Mandy screamed. "Ellie, help me!"

"I will, honey," Ellie shouted. "Are you hurt?"

A sob escaped the girl. "I jammed my wrist. And I think there's bones down here..."

"Let me grab a harness from the truck," Cord said. "I'll be right back."

"We'll get you out of there, Mandy. Ranger McClain is getting equipment from the truck. Just hang on." She angled her head toward Walker. "What happened?"

He scrubbed his hand through his hair. "We were doing that TikTok challenge, going to spend the night and try to get pictures if we saw anything."

"Did you?" Ellie asked.

He shrugged. "Not really, but we heard a noise. Then Sherry thought she saw someone in the house and screamed and we all started running, and... Mandy fell."

Ellie narrowed her eyes. "So it was an accident?"

His eyes widened in alarm. "Yeah, I mean we didn't see anyone around."

Ellie scanned the area and realized the opening had probably been covered with fallen limbs and leaves. In the dark, Mandy wouldn't have seen it.

Sherry's blue eyes swam with tears. "We shouldn't have come, Mandy didn't really want to," she said in a tiny voice.

Walker's jaw tightened. "It's my fault. Porter and I talked the girls into the challenge."

Ellie studied the kids. They looked and sounded sincerely upset. Considering the situation, Ellie let it slide that they were trespassing.

Cord rushed back, carrying a harness and thick heavy cable.

"Let me call for back-up, then I'll go down, harness Mandy and they can haul her up," he told Ellie.

"No need." Ellie grabbed the harness. "I need to take a look myself. I'll go down, help her into the harness and you can pull her up."

Cord halted. "Are you sure? I know you're claustrophobic."

She choked back her paranoia. She was and she hated the dark, but Mandy needed her.

"Ellie," the girl cried again.

"I'm right here, honey," Ellie leaned over the opening. "Ranger McClain is going to lower me down, then pull you up. How much room is there? Enough to stand?"

"Y... es, but it's not very wide," Mandy whimpered.

The panic in Mandy's voice made Ellie summon her courage, and she allowed Cord to help her into the harness. When she glanced down at the hole, she kept thinking about the old wells in the country and the folklore of Soap Sally, an old hag who lived in the wells. Legend claimed that if you got too close, her gnarled hands would drag you down into the well and eat you.

Cord touched her hand. "You okay, El?"

She gave a quick nod. "Yes, let's do it."

"Can we help?" Walker asked.

"I'll secure the end of the cable around that tree," Cord told him. "You can help me pull Mandy up once Detective Reeves secures the harness around her." The young man nodded eagerly, his concern for Mandy obvious.

After attaching the cable around the tree, Cord hurried back to her. Ellie hooked her flashlight on her belt, clutched the cable and held her breath. A second later, she dropped to her knees, and Cord slowly lowered her into the darkness.

Each second that passed felt like an eternity as the rancid odor of damp dirt, moss and death engulfed Ellie. Though the opening was fairly narrow, she guessed the pit was about fifteen or twenty feet deep.

Mandy's terrified sobs ripped through her.

"I'm coming, honey," she said softly. "Almost there."

She touched the wall with her hand and felt dirt and rock crumbling. Dust fluttered down into her face as her body hit the side and she brushed it away, trying to focus. Hollow emptiness echoed around her.

Mandy hovered against one wall, knees pulled to her chest, arms wrapped around them. She was shaking so badly Ellie heard her teeth chattering.

"Hold me still!" Ellie yelled to Cord. "Let me see what's down here."

The cable snapped tight, and Ellie illuminated the interior with her flashlight. Horror washed over her. These were not rocks. They were bones. Tiny slivers of alabaster shimmered on the ground and a couple of larger pieces of bones jutted through the dirt. She spotted a skull with empty eye sockets, and thin fragments that might have been fingers...

"Okay, lower me the rest of the way!" Ellie shouted.

The cable began to drop, and Ellie forced herself not to think about the small, cramped space and what was hiding down here.

When her feet touched the ground, something crackled beneath her boots. Ignoring the stab of panic, she carefully stepped over to Mandy, then stooped in front of the girl. "Hey, honey, I'm here."

Mandy's eyes were glazed with shock, tears staining her face. Ellie drew her into a hug. "Listen to me, sweetie, we'll have you out in a minute." She brushed Mandy's hair from her cheek. Her arms were scratched, her face dusty and dirt and debris clung to her hair.

"Let's get you in this harness. Just hold onto the cable with your uninjured hand and Ranger McClain will do all the work."

Ellie unsnapped the hook and harness, then helped Mandy slide into it. The girl swayed, clinging to Ellie. "Hang in there, honey," she murmured, then she secured the harness and yelled for Cord to lift Mandy.

Ellie held her breath as Cord and Walker helped the girl from the pit. Now Mandy was safe, she forced herself to assess the situation.

Up above, the sound of a siren wailed announcing the ambulance's arrival. "You ready to come up?" Cord yelled.

"Not yet." Ellie clenched the flashlight with clammy hands as the she spotted what appeared to be a skull bone embedded in the dirt. "I see other bones, too. I think there's someone buried down here. With decomposition it's hard to say how long." She checked her phone but had no service. "Call Captain Hale and ask him to send the ME, a forensic anthropologist, the recovery team and ERT. I'll take some pics then come up."

Anxious to escape this underground hellhole, she began documenting the scene.

Seconds ticked into minutes. Sweat trickled down the back of her neck and her lungs strained for air.

What exactly had happened? Was more than one body buried here? Had a killer used the pit as his dumping ground?

She surveyed the space, looking for weapons, but if there was any, they were buried in the debris. Rocks, leaves, sticks, dirt. Strands of something that could have been hair were stuck to a large stone. Or was she just imagining that?

Remembering this place had been a home for children, her mind went to dark thoughts, and she leaned over, pressed her hands on her knees and forced herself to absorb the horrible possibilities.

"Ellie, you okay?" Cord shouted.

No, hell, no. She understood why Mandy was so freaked out. "Yes. Bring me up."

Cord lowered the harness, and she quickly secured it, allowing him to haul her up. Voices drifted to her, and the bright lights of the ambulance twirled against the dark.

Her legs felt unsteady as Cord coaxed her a few feet away. Walker, Sherry and Porter were crowding around Mandy where she sat trembling on a stretcher. The medics were taking her vitals and working to calm her, but it would take time for her to overcome the trauma.

Cord rubbed Ellie's arms with his hands, his voice gruff. "You okay, El?"

She gave a little nod although she was lying. How could she be okay knowing there might be a child's body down there?

"Detective, the girl is asking for you," one of the medics said as he approached her. Ellie crossed to Mandy who sat wrapped in a blanket, her eyes glassy with shock.

"I'll call your aunt and have her meet you at the hospital," Ellie said, placing a gentle hand on Mandy's shoulders.

The girl nodded and reached for her hand, and Ellie squeezed it. "What happened?"

Mandy rubbed at her wrist. "I thought I saw someone through the window, and I ran. I heard him following then lost my balance and fell and... then I saw the bones," Mandy whispered.

"It is a pretty gruesome sight. I'm sorry you had to see it," Ellie said softly, rubbing the girl's back. "Hang tough. I have to wait here for a forensic team, but I'll check on you later. Okay?"

"'Kay," Mandy said in a tiny voice.

Walker, Porter and Sherry stood beside Mandy, their anxiety palpable. Ellie offered them sympathetic looks.

"You guys should talk to your folks about what happened," she said. "Do you need rides home?"

Walker dug his hands into the pockets of his jeans. "I have my car," he said. "But I want to go to the hospital."

Sherry wiped her eyes. "Me, too."

"All right," Ellie said. "But promise me you'll let your families know where you are." The kids agreed and while the medics loaded Mandy into the ambulance, Ellie phoned the girl's aunt, Trudy Morely.

"Trudy, it's Ellie," she said when Trudy answered. "It's about Mandy."

The woman made a strangled sound. "What happened?"

"She's all right, but she and some friends came to Hawk House. Mandy took a fall and her wrist may be broken. The medics are transporting her to the hospital."

"Good grief, I told her not to go to that place. But she doesn't listen to me," Trudy said.

"She's a teenager, Trudy. At least she wasn't alone." Ellie plucked a leaf from her hair. "Listen, she's pretty shaken. She discovered bones when she fell."

Mandy's aunt gasped.

"She should see a counselor," Ellie suggested.

A tense silence followed. "She has been through a lot this last year. Maybe I can convince her to talk to Emily Nettles."

"That's a good idea," Ellie said. Emily was a counselor and head of the Porch Sitters, the local prayer group.

The sound of a motor broke the night, and Ellie realized the ME and the ERT team had arrived. Another van brought the recovery team and equipment.

"I have to go, Trudy."

After they hung up, Ellie called Bryce. "It's Ellie. It's about Mandy," she said to the sheriff, then relayed what had happened. "I thought you'd want to know."

"I'll head to the hospital. That is unless you need me there."

"No, you should be with your daughter. I'll handle things here."

"Okay. But I'm available," Bryce said. "This is still my county."

"I know, Sheriff," she said, irritated at his attitude. Ever since he'd taken over the office, he'd lorded his power over her.

Ellie hung up then studied the dark woods. This place had always had a mystery about it. Tonight, she was sure they'd found skeletal remains. What other secrets would she find when she dug into the orphanage?

Ellie met the forensic recovery team by their vehicles and explained the situation. "We need to preserve any skeletal remains as best as possible. Also look for teeth, clothing and other items that might help us identify the remains."

"This is going to be a process," Abraham Williams, the head investigator, stated. "In order to preserve the bones and evidence, I suggest we come back in the morning. That underground hole is pitch dark and with it being already midnight, we might miss something or accidentally contaminate evidence. It's too late to set up the special lighting we'll need."

"Understood," Ellie agreed.

The ME, Dr. Laney Whitefeather, stood in silence, her pallor slightly gray as she stared at the pit then back at the house.

"Laney?"

Laney jerked her head toward Ellie, her voice cracking. "Sorry, something about this place gives me the creeps."

"It does have an eerie vibe," Ellie agreed.

Laney took a couple of deep breaths, then seemed to pull herself together. "We'll have to estimate how long the remains have been here based on weather, temperature, and soil conditions, then match DNA to identify the victim."

"I know it's complicated," Ellie said. "While your teams work to put together a rough time and cause of death, and the age and sex of the victims, I'll start investigating Hawk House and search the premises. Maybe I can find a roster of the kids so we can pull medical and dental records for DNA comparison."

Laney tugged her dark reddish-brown hair into a ponytail, then quickly braided it. "You think the remains belong to a child?"

Ellie gave a small shrug. "I don't know. It's possible."

"Do you want to lower me down there and let me take a look before they start the excavation?"

"That's not necessary," Ellie said. "I photographed everything. Whoever is down there has seriously decomposed and may have been there for years."

Laney's body went rigid again as she looked up at the flock of hawks soaring above. The silhouette of their sharp beaks and wingspan were outlined in the glow of the moon.

"Growing up on the reservation," Laney murmured, "I heard stories about the hawks. In Native American folklore, the hawk is a symbol of power, courage, strength and leadership. In the Cheyenne tribe, they're seen as protectors from enemies."

Ellie pursed her lips. "Odd, since in politics being a hawk means using force and violence instead of diplomatic methods." Leaves fluttered down from a gust of wind. "From what I've heard, the headmaster of the orphanage, Horatio Blackstone was that type of man." Which made her stomach twist at the possibility of who might have been dumped in that hole.

Laney wrinkled her brow, while Ellie showed Laney the photographs she'd taken.

"Judging from the size of the skull I saw, I think the remains belong to a child," Ellie said.

Laney folded her arms across her chest. "I'll set up tables at the morgue to sort any bones we find for analysis and call in the forensic anthropologist."

With a plan set in motion, Williams started erecting crime scene tape around the perimeter of the pit. The next two hours dragged as the teams searched the exterior of the house for other bodies or bones but found nothing. Still, the woods went on forever and they would have to return at daylight to continue.

Ellie stepped aside and phoned her captain, explaining their findings. "We should station a guard here tonight. Once news of this hits, curiosity seekers may flood the place."

"I'll send Deputy Landrum there," Captain Hale agreed.

Ellie ended the call, her blood pumping. This case would draw attention from all over the state.

It was time to call in Special Agent Derrick Fox.

12

The sleazy woman had gotten off easy today.

Tonight, she'd pay for that.

He led her blindfolded inside the mountain cabin, his heart stuttering as the anticipation built. His urges had kicked in the moment he'd seen her today.

She called herself Sugar because she worked at the Sweet Tooth in town.

Laughter bubbled in his throat. She was anything but sweet. He'd seen a hint of fire today which had intrigued him even more and triggered his dark desires to surface. Then he'd known he had to have her.

"Where are we?" she murmured as she clung helplessly to his hand.

"A cozy romantic cabin by the creek." He put one hand at her waist to steady her as they crossed the room. Although, if he removed the blindfold and she saw what he had waiting for her, she might not describe it that way. Then again, she'd agreed to the blindfold. Had said she was open to anything. She didn't mind it rough.

As long as he paid upfront.

He pushed her toward the bed where thick ropes were secured to the bed posts waiting for her. The leather straps and toys he needed hung on the wall in full display, making his cock harden as he imagined using them on her.

Smiling at his wall of treasures, he grabbed her and threw her on the bed. Her legs parted as she settled back on the mattress, stirring his blood to a feverish heat.

She made a small, surprised sound as she hit the mattress. "What do you have planned?"

"Fun and games," he said in a deep voice.

She giggled and reached out her arms. "Then come here, lover boy."

He took a knife from the table, the shiny steel glinting in the dim moonlight filtering through the room, then crawled on top of her and pressed the tip to her neck.

She made a shocked sound, her breath wheezing out. "What are you doing?"

"Undressing you," he murmured, then he moved the blade beneath the skimpy top and ripped it away. Her breasts jutted up, nipples stiff peaks. Licking his lips, he traced a circle around each one with the knife. She moaned, half excitement, half fear. Breath quickening, he cut away the sliver of what she called a skirt.

"Put the knife away and let's get to it," she murmured, reaching for his shirt.

He shoved her hands away, then dragged her up to stand, pushing her into the wall. His breath came in quick pants as he jerked her hands into the leather straps hanging above and secured them.

"Let's go back to the bed," she whispered. "I'll do whatever you want there."

"Oh, you'll do whatever I want all right." He took a feather and traced it along her bare back, smiling as goosebumps shimmied across her skin. She parted her legs again in anticipation and he shoved them father apart with his knee.

Then he grabbed the whip from his wall of horrors, raised it and slapped it across her back.

Her first scream made his cock jump, then he swung it again. She screamed again and yanked at the binding, her soft cries of shock and pain sending him over the edge.

13

CROOKED CREEK

By the time Ellie reached her bungalow, her eyes felt gritty and her shoulders ached. After being lowered in that dark pit, she was grateful she'd left the porch light on outside and her kitchen was lit. With dirt and debris still clinging to her hair and the smell of rotten earth permeating her skin, she desperately wanted a shower.

But first, she'd call Derrick.

The sound of a coyote howling from somewhere deep in the woods sent a frisson of nerves along Ellie's spine as she let herself inside.

Derrick's voice sounded thick when he answered as if she'd awakened him. "What's going on, Ellie? It's one in the morning."

Damn, she hadn't thought about the time. Just that she needed his help. "Sorry. I just got home. We have a crime scene." She quickly relayed their discovery at Hawk House.

"You found remains?" Derrick asked.

"Yes. The team is meeting early in the morning to start recovery. Cord is organizing SAR to comb the woods in case there are more."

"How long have the bones been there?" Derrick asked.

"Hard to say. We'll know more once Laney and the forensic anthropologist get to work. But judging from the decomposition, I'd say a long time." Ellie picked a leaf from her jeans. "Tomorrow I'll search the interior of the house. Hopefully we'll find something to tell us more."

"Wait for me," Derrick said. "I'll meet you in Crooked Creek and we'll go together."

Ellie agreed then hung up, grateful to have Derrick working with her again. She'd seen very little of him since Christmas and the few times she'd spoken with him he'd sounded distant. Almost troubled. She had a feeling something was bothering him, but she hadn't pressed him to talk about it.

Then again, maybe she was imagining it. He had been visiting his mother which had to stir memories of the loss of his sister, murdered when they were just children.

Mentally, she made a list of where to begin in the morning as she stripped and showered. The orphanage had been shut down for almost three decades. That complicated the investigation. Had the allegations of violence and abuse regarding the headmaster been looked into?

Her father – who had once been the sheriff – wasn't in office at the time, so she'd need to speak to his predecessor. Still, Randall might know something, might have discussed the case with his predecessor.

She'd call him first in the morning then she'd meet Derrick.

Her phone buzzed as she dried off and dressed in sweats, and she walked to the kitchen to make a cup of hot tea. The call was from Angelica Gomez, the reporter who'd covered previous cases.

The fact that she'd called this late indicated Angelica knew about the discovery tonight. Ellie rubbed her temple, then decided to switch the tea for a finger of vodka before she returned the call.

Tomorrow, a shitshow would probably start. The town would be thrown into a tizzy over the discovery of the bones and the fact that more children had died in Bluff County.

Hopefully, the search inside Hawk House would yield some answers.

14

SOMEWHERE ON THE AT

Images bombarded him as he played out his dark fantasies with the woman. He'd whipped her and forced her to pleasure him on her knees. The photographs he took were stunning, of her begging for him to stop.

Hour after hour he punished her until she lay exhausted, and he was spent. She curled into a ball on her side, and he wrapped her in a blanket then carried her to his car and tossed her inside. She moaned, a little sob escaping her, then he started the engine and drove away.

The rumble of the car must have lulled her to sleep, and he maneuvered the twisting mountain roads, silently replaying the evening in his mind.

He hated himself for the dark cravings that seized him, making him go insane with lust, stirring insatiable desires that he couldn't deny.

And shame. Shame for them. Shame for himself.

But he couldn't stop.

The first time he'd watched... No, he couldn't let his mind go there. It had been disturbing. But he hadn't been able to drag his eyes away.

A misty rain began to fall, and thunderclouds gathered above, the sky blue-gray as the stars disappeared into a fog. The moon was barely visible now, darkened by the night just as his soul was black with forbidden cravings.

He weaved down the mountain until he reached the outskirts of town and the corner of the trailer park. Cutting his lights, he eased to the end trailer where he'd picked her up. He walked around and opened the door, then scooped her into his arms and carried her inside.

The place reeked of booze, stale food and some cheap cloying perfume. She stirred slightly then moaned, and he deposited her on the sofa. She didn't look so pretty now.

He tossed the cash he owed her on her naked body then placed one of the photographs he'd taken on her chest. His insurance policy.

The door of the trailer screeched as he let himself out.

15

CROOKED CREEK

DAY 2

The next morning Ellie massaged the kinks out of her neck from tossing and turning all night. She'd finally gotten up at sunrise, showered quickly, pulled her hair into a ponytail then blotted on a little powder to disguise the dark circles beneath her sleep-deprived eyes.

After quickly dressing in a T-shirt and jeans, she poured herself coffee and snagged a bagel, smothering it with cream cheese. Settling at her computer, she nibbled on it while she looked for police reports involving the orphanage. But the digitized files didn't go back that far – the downside of working in a small-town police department.

Next, she studied NCMEC data bases, the National Center for Missing and Exploited Children, looking back thirty-five years in search of a possible victim, maybe a child reported missing from Hawk House. There were numerous children's photos, and it took another hour to weed through ones reported in the Appalachian area.

A handful had been foster kids, but none referenced placement at Hawk House.

Frustrated, she finished her coffee and poured herself another in a to-go mug. Time to meet Derrick.

Her stomach fluttered slightly at the thought of seeing him again.

It's all business, Ellie. For cripes' sake, he's only coming back because of the bones.

Her phone buzzed as she strapped on her seatbelt. It was Deputy Shondra Eastwood, her coworker and friend. Starting the engine, she connected, "Hey, Shondra."

"Break-in off Route 9. Teens again. I'm on my way. Do you want to meet me?"

"Sorry, I can't." She filled Shondra in on the discovery of the skeletal remains. "I'm on my way to the station for a press conference now."

"Oh, geesh. Let me know if you need back-up."

"Will do. Agent Fox is meeting me to search the house today and the ERT team will be there along with recovery teams to excavate the bones."

"Just when we thought things were settling around here, you catch a cold case," Shondra said wryly. "At least it's not another serial."

"I'm not so sure about that. If there was one body, there might be more." Something sinister had happened, she was sure.

She ended the call and passed the Corner Café, surprised to see Lola wasn't there yet. Maybe Cord had gone by her place last night and they'd slept in, she thought, her stomach churning.

A minute later, she parked at the station, checking herself in the mirror to make sure she didn't have food on her face. She hated going on camera but couldn't avoid it today and the news van was already on site. It was important to get on top of the story before the rumor mill ran with it.

As they'd discussed when they'd talked the night before, Angelica was waiting for her in the press room when she arrived, her cameraman Tom juggling his equipment as he prepared for the press meeting. Captain Hale was speaking with Bryce whose grass-green eyes looked troubled, his dark-blond hair tousled as if he'd forgotten to comb it.

She threw up a hand in greeting to Angelica and signaled she'd be there in a minute, then rushed over to Bryce. "How's Mandy?"

The sheriff heaved a weary breath. "Except for a broken wrist, she's physically fine. But she's really shaken up." Concern thickened his voice. "Trudy's taking her for an appointment with Emily Nettles today."

"Good," Ellie said softly. "Emily will be good for her."

Bryce shifted and looked down at his boots. "Thanks for calling me."

"I know you're trying with her, Bryce. It can't be easy."

He shook his head. "It's not."

"Just be patient," Ellie said. "She's been through a lot."

"I know." The door opened, and Derrick entered the station, his broad shoulders squared, dark hair rumpled, eyes steely. Dressed in dark jeans, a white shirt and boots, he looked handsome as hell but all business.

Angelica motioned that she was ready to begin, and Ellie walked over to join her.

"This is Angelica Gomez, Channel Five News, at Crooked Creek Police Department with this breaking story." She angled herself toward Ellie. "Last night human remains were found in the mountains. Detective Ellie Reeves is here to fill you in."

Ellie licked her dry lips. "Late yesterday afternoon, a group of teenagers stumbled on bones buried on the property that was once an orphanage called Hawk House. Teams will be working today to recover the remains, then the identification process will begin, although we expect it to be a lengthy process." She paused and took a breath. "If anyone has information about the remains or the people associated with the orphanage, please contact the police."

Angelica cleared her throat. "There have been rumors that Hawk House began as a home for wayward boys, that some children who were sent there didn't survive. Do you believe the bones belong to one of those children?"

Ellie gritted her teeth. Angelica knew better than to put her on the spot, but the tenacious reporter would do anything for the scoop. As much as Ellie admired that trait, it was infuriating at the same time.

She lifted her chin, forcing herself not to react. "At this time, I can't speculate one way or the other. As a detective, I analyze facts and will be working in conjunction with the FBI to collect evidence and investigate. Again, anyone with information should call the police." She offered a small smile to instill confidence in the viewers. "I do ask that people please stay away from the property. It is considered a crime scene. Anyone who comes around could contaminate evidence and will be charged with trespassing and interfering with a police investigation. Please cooperate and let us do our jobs." She thanked the reporter, then stepped away.

Leaving Angelica to wrap up with the phone number for Crooked Creek Police Department and the sheriff's office, Ellie gestured for Derrick and Bryce to meet in her office.

"Deputy Landrum guarded the crime scene last night," Ellie told them both before turning to Bryce. "Special Agent Fox and I are headed there to search the interior of the house. Ranger McClain and a team are bringing dogs to search the woods and property in case there are more bones. Bryce, your family seems to have been in Bluff County the longest. Maybe your father knows something about the allegations regarding the orphanage."

Bryce's shoulders went rigid. As sheriff, he ran the county and balked at the feds' interference. But his father was mayor and had contacts in the town. Still, his face crinkled with distress. "It's possible but my folks and I aren't exactly in sync right now."

"What's going on?"

"Don't sweat it. I'll handle it," he said, closing the subject. "I'll talk to Randall, too."

Ellie stiffened. Although she understood his motivation, she still detested the fact that her father had endorsed Bryce as sheriff instead of her. Obviously, Bryce was the son Randall had always wanted...

"Start with your father and the townspeople," Ellie replied. "I owe my dad a call, so I'll ask him. Also, check on Mandy. Maybe she or one of the other kids remembered something else."

Bryce's gaze darkened, and he gave a quick nod, then strode from her office.

"I see he's still as pleasant as ever," Derrick muttered.

Bryce disliked having the feds in his county so it was no surprise that the two men had clashed from the start. Still, she had to cut him some slack today. "He had a rough night. The girl who fell in the pit, Mandy Morely, is his daughter."

Derrick's brows shot up. "What?"

"Don't mention that I told you. He only found out a few months ago, after Vanessa died. He's trying to get to know her."

Derrick's frown deepened, but he didn't comment.

"Let's go." She grabbed her keys. "I'll call my father on the way."

16

QUAIL RIDGE, BLUFF COUNTY

Seventy-two-year-old Edgar Ogden's hand shook as he lifted the Marlboro to his lips and took a long, slow drag. The orange glow of the ashes flickered like burning embers as the sweet burn of nicotine bled through him. His body zinged with tension, muscles and limbs old and achy, mind struggling to stay clear-headed when the memories were running at him like an eighteen-wheeler barreling off the side of the road and crashing into the mountain.

Typically, a smoke calmed his nerves, but he poured himself a Jim Beam straight up and carried it to his back porch.

Nothing could calm him right now though. Not after seeing that news story about Hawk House.

A cold sweat broke out on his neck as he looked up toward the mountains where the orphanage stood. The wind carried the scent of fear that had dogged him every day for the last thirty years.

Randall Reeves had been a decent sheriff. But lucky for him, all those years ago, Reeves had been sidetracked with that missing Fox girl case and put his focus there. With everyone pre-occupied with the little girl that had vanished into thin air

one summer, the questions surrounding the headmaster's disappearance had fallen by the wayside.

But Randall's daughter, Ellie, was different. A rare breed.
The kind of detective who didn't give up until she dug the truth
from the bowels of whatever tomb it was buried beneath. Once
she sank her nails in, she'd keep clawing until she sifted out all
the dirty secrets of everyone associated with that place.

He threw back the bourbon, savoring the burn, then
lumbered down the steps holding onto the rail to steady himself.
Dammit, he hated getting old and weak. His hip throbbed as he
tossed the cigarette butt to the ground and stomped it out.

Chest heavy, he walked past the shed, the memories
swirling through his mind. He'd done what he had to do back
then, and he wasn't one damn bit sorry.

Just as he'd do what he had to do now to keep his secret.

17

CROOKED CREEK

Ellie clenched the steering wheel, driving past the fliers advertising the Native American festival. Storytellers would be featured at Books & Bites, sharing myths and legends of the Indians. Native American arts and crafts were being sold at Crystal's, and at Bear Mountain, shows were planned for spectators interested in the cultural dances, language and history.

Derrick was unusually quiet as she drove through town. Just the mention of including her father in the case must have bothered him – her father had been the sheriff when Derrick's little sister disappeared decades back. But she had a job to do, and she couldn't ignore the fact that Randall might be an asset.

Using her hands-free, she called him as she wound around the mountain. He answered on the second ring. "Hey, Dad, it's me. I'm driving with Agent Fox. Putting you on speaker."

He hesitated for a tension-filled moment, then said, "I saw the news this morning. What can I do to help?"

"Tell me what you know about that old orphanage."

He released a long sigh. "Mostly just the rumors. We hadn't been in Crooked Creek long, and Sheriff Ogden was retiring. I'd heard rumors in town that there was some trouble up at that orphanage and the headmaster had disappeared about three months before, then the place was shut down. When I asked Ogden about it, he said he didn't find anything nefarious. And you know how gossip is. You have to take it with a grain of salt."

That was true. "Did he keep files on his investigation?"

"If he did, they wouldn't be digitized yet. He may have left them in storage. I'll see if I can find them."

"Thanks, Dad. That would be helpful." Ellie glanced at Derrick. His jaw was set so tightly she was surprised he didn't crack a tooth. "We're headed to the property now to conduct a search," she said. "Call me when you find the files."

He agreed, and she hung up and pulled on her sunglasses as the bright morning sun slanted through the windshield. The March winds picked up, battering the car, and a steady stream of traffic slowed her way as she maneuvered the switchbacks. SUVs and pick-up trucks carried rafts and canoes, and vans were loaded with families and rooftop carriers.

By the time they arrived at the site, Cord and his men, the ERT and the forensic recovery team had already erected lights and tables, and set up their equipment.

Cord met her and Derrick near the pit, his expression grim. "My guys and the dogs are ready."

"Keep us posted," Ellie said.

Nodding, Cord strode back to his men, organizing them into teams and search grids.

Laney and the forensic anthropologist approached. "We set up tables for the bones as they're recovered," Laney said. "Depending on the decomp, we'll do our best to piece together the remains. As the pathologist, I'll look for cause of death while Dr. Chi works in forensic taphonomy and will help determine what happened to the body at death and postmortem."

"How long do you think they've been down there?" Ellie asked.

"That's hard to say. Bones can sometimes last years or

fossilize over time. Some of these may have been preserved due to the temperature underground. In the mountains, it's colder and the pit was covered so somewhat protected from the elements."

"If you have names of any of the children placed there, we can request dental and medical records to expedite the process," Dr. Chi added.

"I'll work on that," Ellie said. "I checked NCEMC but didn't find anything. Age of the bones and how long they've been there will help me narrow down the search. Agent Fox and I hope to find a roster of the kids inside the house."

If the bodies belonged to one of the children. She couldn't discount another serial who'd used the place after it was deserted.

18

HAWK HOUSE

The wind picked up, bringing the scent of wildflowers and acrid odors from the woods as Ellie and Derrick approached the house. A dead animal. Damp grass. Wild mushrooms. Decayed timber from fallen trees that had lain wet and were rotting from recent winter storms.

"You ready for this?" Derrick asked as they walked toward the dilapidated house.

"I don't know," Ellie said with a shiver, but the victim or victims – whoever they were – needed her to be strong.

Grime coated the fifty-plus year-old windows, and parts of the stone that might have glistened in the sun when it had been built were now black. When she looked up at the small oval window in the center of the house, Ellie thought she saw shadows floating past.

Looking at this place, she almost believed the ghosts of the dead were trapped inside. waiting for someone to free their spirits so they could finally move on.

Wind whined around her and screeched off the mountain. The sound of Derrick opening the heavy wooden door jarred her back to the present. She had bodies to identify.

Murders to solve.

Families who might have waited decades for answers. Who'd given up hope.

They entered through a large entryway that felt as cold as a prison. Relieved they'd brought high-powered flashlights, she and Derrick shined them across the space that led to a big common room. Cobwebs dangled from the corners, dust motes fluttered in the air and rodents skittered somewhere in the house. Wind wheezed through broken windowpanes and even though it was early spring, there was a chill in the space that reeked of abandonment and death.

Derrick aimed his light to the right of the staircase. "I'll search down here. Looks like a study for the headmaster and an adjoining master suite."

"I'll check the kitchen and living area," Ellie offered.

Derrick nodded then headed toward the study, and she passed the staircase into a large kitchen with more cobwebs, dark cabinets, a workstation in the center and a long, battered steel table that looked as if it belonged outside. Nothing homey about this place.

The cabinets were empty except for rodent droppings and shelf paper that had yellowed to the point of disintegration. The stove was industrial-sized with ancient grease stains, thick and dried. A window that overlooked the back of the property offered a view of towering mountains and sprawling woods that looked daunting even in daylight. The sense that bad things had happened in this place echoed through the halls and ten-foot ceilings.

Ellie searched the cabinets, where a few rusted pots and pans and utensils remained. The pantry held assorted canned goods in industrial size cans, all outdated, some dented and covered in dust.

Satisfied there was nothing telling in the kitchen, she went to meet Derrick. He sat at the desk in the large room that must have served as the headmaster's office, head bent as he searched the drawers.

"Nothing in the master bedroom," Derrick said. "Clothes cleaned out. Closet empty. Nothing personal. Thought we might have better luck in here."

The man's study would have been where he kept records. A bank of shelves ran along the far wall and a giant mahogany desk dominated the room. Dark paneled walls, heavy gray drapes and cold black tile floors gave it a mausoleum feel.

Derrick looked up at her with a frown. "Not much here. A few papers, old bills," he said. "But there has to be more, records of the kids placed here."

"Unless someone destroyed them." Ellie crossed the room to the wall of shelves. She studied the contents – there were old textbooks, books on Native American history, human anatomy then another focused on forensic anthropology. She picked one of the books and flipped through it; drawings of animal skeletons filled the pages, including detailed descriptions of the bones. There was one written by a medical examiner determining cause of death and one about animal husbandry.

An odd collection in a home for children.

A cold draft blew through the room, and she chose another book which held photographs of animals that had been mauled and birds of prey feasting on the remains. Shivering, she shoved it back on the shelf, but her finger brushed something that felt like metal. Using her flashlight, she realized it was a lock. She tried to open it, but it was rusted.

"Derrick, I think there's something behind these shelves."

His boots pounded the floor as he crossed the room. Derrick leaned close to examine it, then pulled at it with his fingers, but it wouldn't budge. He removed a Swiss army knife from his pocket and used the blade to pry open the lock. It snapped open and Ellie pushed at the shelf. It screeched as the shelves parted to reveal a hidden room.

Goosebumps skated across her skin as a stench clouded the air. A large wooden filing drawer sat in the corner and dust and dark stains covered the floor.

A single cot with a thin mattress was pushed against the wall, a heavy chain attached to it and the wall above. Ashes covered the mattress – ashes that looked like crumbled bones.

19

Ellie shuddered at the images that flashed through her mind. Children punished in here, tortured? Maybe even murdered.

Derrick grimaced then yanked open the top drawer of the filing cabinet. It held nothing. Neither did the second. "Looks like someone cleaned out the files."

Dropping to his knees, he ran his hands across the bottom of the cabinet then lifted a false bottom. Beneath it, he pulled out a thin Manila envelope.

Ellie looked over his shoulder. There were photos inside: old, grainy black-and-whites. The pictures were so old they were blurry, and she squinted to discern the images. They were topographical maps of the forest and the property.

"Why hide pictures of the woods yet take the files?" Derrick asked.

"Maybe whoever took the files didn't realize these photos were here," Ellie said with a shrug.

Derrick's gaze met hers. "But if Blackstone put them there, he would know."

Ellie quirked her mouth sideways in thought. "True. Maybe

he forgot about them." Her mind took a leap. "Or someone else stole the files after he left."

"That would mean someone else knew what was going on here and was responsible."

And that crimes had occurred under Blackstone's watch. "Could have been one of the employees."

"True."

They had to dig deeper.

Derrick tapped the envelope. "I'll send these to the lab. Maybe they can recover the faded images."

Ellie nodded, snapping photos of the room, focusing on the cot, chain and forensics. Scanning in all directions, she noted scratch marks and dark stains which could have been blood. "Forensics needs to go over this. Let's move on through and see what else we find in this house of horrors."

After Derrick tucked the envelope inside his jacket, Ellie followed him through the door. As they climbed the staircase to the second floor, a sense of trepidation filled Ellie. Her fears were confirmed when she glanced inside the first room.

Six cots were lined along one side with several inches in between. Faded, threadbare blankets covered the thin mattresses. Metal hooks were attached to the wall above each bed with chains attached that must have been used to restrain the children.

She turned away for a moment to compose herself.

Derrick crossed the room and paused at the row of metal lockers on the far wall. Together they searched the lockers. Most were empty although a few pieces of clothing – boys' jeans and T-shirts – were stored inside. Once again, she noticed scratch – or claw – marks on the wall, along with dark stains. The stench of urine, blood and mold permeated the air, triggering her disgust.

"We need forensics in here." Maybe they'd find DNA or

fingerprints that would help identify the kids who'd suffered. DNA that might match the slivers of bones...

Stomach twisting, she moved to the next room. Six more cots, with chains and hooks, threadbare blankets. This time, the lockers held girls' clothing, skirts, thin cotton dresses and hair ribbons.

Images of the little girls restrained, crying in bed, alone and terrified, taunted Ellie.

20

Ellie forced the disturbing images at bay as she and Derrick moved on to the basement. Stone steps dove into the darkness, the cold seeping all the way to Ellie's soul.

If horrors had occurred in that bedroom, what the hell would they find down here?

The thick concrete and stone walls would have worked as soundproofing from anyone upstairs, which had probably served well for Blackstone, especially if social workers or outsiders visited.

The distant ping of water trickling down the wall echoed in the silence, along with the sound of her own choppy breathing.

At the bottom of the steps, a rat skittered in front of her, and Ellie jumped back. Her own flashlight spanned the interior, and she spotted a steel table in the middle of the room, next to a sink and chemicals lining on a shelf above it. The acrid odor of death mingled with mold, bleach and formaldehyde, made her gag. Garbage bags were piled in a corner and a big barrel sat in the corner. Dear God. What could be inside them?

Nerves gathered in her belly as she walked over and opened

a freezer. Multiple containers were stacked inside. She picked the first one up with a shaky hand to examine it.

Tiny bones filled the container, bones that looked as if they came from a small animal. Another one contained slightly larger bones. The feet looked like a chicken's.

"What is it?" Derrick asked.

She angled the container so he could see the contents. His brow furrowed as he studied it, then he reached for a container and opened it. More bones.

A tense silence ensued as they searched through the remaining containers. Each one held bones of various sizes, all cleaned and bleached, preserved by the cold. They hadn't found guns in the house though, not a rifle, nor a bow and arrow to suggest Blackstone had been a hunter.

A taxidermist might have a workstation similar to the steel table, but a taxidermist would preserve the entire skeleton. If Blackstone was responsible for collecting the bones, what had he done with the feathers and animal remains?

Her gaze flew to the barrel and the trash bags, and her stomach roiled.

21

Derrick must have read her mind. With gloved hands, he untied a bag and opened it. Covering a cough with his hand, he looked inside.

Holding back, dread balled in Ellie's stomach. She hoped to heaven human remains weren't inside.

Using a tool he found on the wall, Derrick poked around inside. "Not sure. Looks like feathers and God knows what. Contents have disintegrated pretty badly. The lab will have to determine the source."

Ellie breathed out a sigh, relieved that he hadn't mentioned human body parts.

"Let's let forensics open the remaining barrels and bags," he said grimly.

Ellie gave a clipped nod. With thirty years having passed since the orphanage closed, anything inside would have decomposed until it was unrecognizable.

After they catalogued the scene, they climbed the stairs in a thick silence. Cold cases meant no immediate rush to solve the case, yet knowing the bones probably belonged to children made Ellie want to push hard.

Like Derrick and his mother, the families of those children might have waited decades for answers.

Dust clogged the air, and Ellie covered her mouth and nose to keep from breathing it in as they made their way through the house. Outside, she gulped in the fresh air, but the sight of rangers and forensics teams combing the woods intensified her anxiety. Voices and shouts echoed through the thick trees and flashlights flickered across the terrain.

One of the CSIs approached. "There's a metal trash can around back that was used as an incinerator. Looks like ashes inside."

"Someone burned evidence," Ellie said.

He nodded. "You want to see?"

No, she didn't. But Ellie had a job to do so she and Derrick followed the crime investigator around the monstrous building to a fenced area housing several large containers.

"There's evidence of accelerants in each of those," the investigator said. "The contents have been burned to smithereens, but the lab might be able to sift through the ashes and determine the contents." He gestured toward a rusted, smaller charred metal trash can with soot stains.

Ellie held her breath as she peered inside. Using a stick, the investigator dug into the can and lifted a piece of partially disintegrated cloth. "Looks like part of a man's jacket," the man said. "Found a couple of brass buttons inside and a piece of fabric that looks like it came from a uniform."

Derrick straightened, eyes dark and troubled. "A military one."

"Blackstone was described as running a military-type school," Ellie said. "Let's get it to forensics."

Maybe it would lead them to some answers.

22

Derrick couldn't erase the haunting images from his mind as he stared at the woods. He understood the military mindset. Knew how tough and brutal commanders could be. And the training...

But he'd been an adult when he'd enlisted. And still, he'd come out scarred on the inside.

The woods here were a graveyard just like that damn village of innocents who'd died when he and his military buddy had gotten wrong information. The powers above deemed it collateral damage.

But he could never overcome the guilt. He'd only learned to live with it by diving into work and committing his life to saving others.

And by not talking about it. He never had. He never would.

Even though Lindsey wanted – no, begged – him to.

For a moment he was back there. To the order that had them flying over that village. The bomb dropping. The whooshing sound as it zoomed to the ground and hit the target.

The explosion... The small village bursting into flames, screams as they watched people go running, falling to their deaths.

He balled his hands into fists, unable to erase that damn moment. Their information had been wrong. They'd killed innocents. Women. Children. The government had covered the truth.

He couldn't change that.

Someone had covered up what had happened here, too. And he would find out who and make them pay.

23

Cord grimaced as his gaze scanned the acres of forest. He'd found another pit about seventy-five feet from the first. Judging from the way the ground had been covered with plywood and brush, it had been intentionally covered. But the strong wind coming in from the predicted Nor'easter had tossed some of the brush aside, exposing it.

A quick look indicated there was another body down there. Maybe more, but he'd have to go down to see. Although that was above his pay grade. Ellie would want a forensic specialist on the recovery team to do that to preserve the evidence.

His handheld radio vibrated. "McClain," he answered.

"We found more bones scattered in the woods," Milo, another of the SAR team, reported. "Looks like they might have been buried but some animal dug them up."

Cord shifted. "I think there's a body in another hole in the ground. Let me talk to Detective Reeves."

"Copy that. We'll mark the areas to make it easier for the forensic teams to locate."

"Good work."

Cord disconnected, placed a marker beside the pit, then

headed back toward the house. Ellie raised her eyebrows in question as he approached. He gave a shake of his head to indicate she wouldn't like what he'd found.

"There may be more remains here, El," Cord said as he joined them where the forensic anthropologists were working. "But it's hard to tell. Some have fossilized. There are piles of what looks like ashes in other places."

"Which means they've been here a while and were more exposed than the ones in the underground pit." Ellie shaded her eyes as she scanned the woods. In her mind, she saw children running and screaming from the monster who'd done this. "God. They may be kids, Cord."

Cord scrubbed a hand over his beard stubble, his expression as dark as his permanent five o'clock shadow. "I also found a second pit. I think there's a body down there."

24

God, this was bigger than she'd originally thought. "I'll tell the excavation team." Stomach knotting, Ellie gazed at the thick trees starting to bud with new life, and the bushes starting to flower. Mountain laurel and black-eyed Susans dotted the terrain amidst dried brush and limbs that had fallen in the winter storm. Yesterday, the area had looked hopeful with spring.

Today everything looked dreary and as daunting as the storm predicted to blow through.

What in the hell had happened at this place? And why hadn't anyone discovered what was going on before the bodies had piled up? She still didn't know just how many and wouldn't until the remains were sorted through.

The next few hours, the tension grew as they confirmed that at least one more body was in the second pit. Dusk had set in, the shadows of night casting a dreary gray over the dilapidated house and mountains. Vultures soared and swooped over sections of the forest as forensic workers carefully photographed and documented the bone sightings, and recovery workers worked diligently to remove the bone fragments to transport to the lab.

Forensic teams collected samples of the dirt and searched for loose fibers, clothing, buttons, anything that might offer clues as to the identity of the victims or the killer.

Had the bodies been left here while Blackstone was in charge? If so, why hadn't an employee come forward?

Her mind took another leap. Until she got a firm timeline for how long the bones had been here, she couldn't discount the possibility that the remains had been dumped here after the orphanage had closed. Although what she'd seen inside the orphanage suggested otherwise.

An engine rumbled, and the Channel Five News van rolled up. Dammit, she'd hoped she'd given Angelica enough to keep her satisfied. But the reporter wouldn't stay away. She thrived on exposing the truth, believed people had a right to know.

Sometimes Ellie thought they'd be better off not knowing. Living in innocence. Seeing the ugly got under your skin.

Agent Fox went to talk to the head of the ERT team, who was about to call it a night and suggest reconvening at daylight. Angelica slid from the van, her red stilettoes digging into the cobbled drive as she spanned the area. Ellie wasn't yet ready to reveal the depth of this case yet and braced herself for the interview.

Angelica's cameraman Tom trailed her, surveying the area around for the best vantage place to capture the unfolding scene.

Determined to protect the integrity of the investigation, Ellie cut Angelica off before she got too close. "You can't film the excavation or any of the forensic workers."

Angelica planted her hands on her hips. "Understood. We'll only take distance shots. Faces will be obscured. But my boss is on my ass to cover this and people in town are already starting to gossip."

"The facts are sure as hell not going to give them comfort." When they saw the magnitude of what they were dealing with here, panic would spread.

"Still, sometimes what people imagine is even worse."

"What could be worse than children being murdered?" Ellie's stomach twisted.

"People deserve to know the truth," Angelica pointed out. "Besides, perhaps someone knows what happened, and when they see the story air, they'll finally come forward."

A valid point. Ellie couldn't solve the case without questioning residents in town, especially ones who lived in the area thirty years ago. In fact, she needed them to talk.

"All right, let's do it," Ellie said.

Angelica pasted on her professional smile, her polished red lips tilting into a smile as she motioned to Tom to roll the camera. "Angelica Gomez here at Hawk House, the orphanage that was shut down thirty years ago where what's believed to be human remains were discovered by a group of teens. Forensic teams are here searching the property as we speak. Detective Reeves, what can you tell us about this mysterious discovery?"

That the case was mindboggling. But Ellie refrained from declaring that statement. "At this time, we are in the recovery process," Ellie said. "It will take time for our medical examiner and forensic specialist to analyze the remains and determine who they belong to, along with how long they've been here."

Angelica cleared her throat. "But you believe they were children?"

Ellie spoke through clenched teeth. "Considering the place was once an orphanage, it's possible although we have no confirmation of that at this time." She had to control the narrative. "If anyone has information regarding Hawk House, Mr. Blackstone, employees of Hawk House, the names of children who were placed here or the social workers in charge of their cases, please call my office or the Bluff County sheriff's department. Thank you."

She hoped to hell the phone would start ringing. Someone in the area knew what had happened here.

And they might be hiding in plain sight.

25

CROOKED CREEK

Damn that reporter. Damn the detective. They were going to be digging into everything.

But they'd never find him.

Body teeming with tension, his dark hunger mounted. Fantasies burst behind his eyes, and he was tempted to take care of himself while he showered.

But no... he wanted the fun. The anticipation of watching the woman squirm. Of seeing her eyes morph from pleasure to pain. Of hearing the tremble of fear in her voice. Her breath fading to nothing.

Stepping from the shower, he dried off as the urges summoned him to take action. He knew who he'd take tonight. He'd been watching her for days. She suspected nothing.

He yanked on jeans and a clean shirt, then grabbed a whiskey. Turning it up, he tossed down a shot then checked himself in the mirror.

He pasted on a charming smile and smiled at the image. He wasn't *GQ* handsome, didn't stand out in a crowd. He was one of those men who could move among the masses and no one thought anything of him.

That was their mistake.

26

CROOKED CREEK

Aunt Trudy told her not to watch the news. But like a rubbernecker, Mandy couldn't help herself. She was glued to the screen during the news report. It was like a bad horror movie that grabbed you and wouldn't let go.

She hated horror movies.

But she wanted to know what had been down in that pit. She chewed on her nails. She *needed* to know.

Ellie had very few details and no real answers – except she suspected the remains belonged to children.

What kind of monster would kill kids and dump them in the ground?

Chill bumps skated up her arms, and she checked the lock on her door again. Then the windows. Last night she'd thought she'd seen someone looking in. Watching her. Eyes peering at her in the dark.

That she'd heard the window lock jiggling.

She'd turned on all the lights and stared through the window until her eyeballs hurt and her head was busting. Every time she blinked, in her mind she saw the slivers of bones poking through the dirt. Felt them jabbing in her legs and back. Heard the brittle sound of them crunching when she'd moved.

Her phone rang and she jumped, then glanced at it. Walker calling. Again.

Tears blurred her eyes as her mind bounced all over the place. She wanted to see him. She didn't want to see him. It was his fault she'd gone to that awful place. She'd seen Porter and Sherry and her other friends posting on Instagram and TikTok. Ghoulish pictures of ghost sightings. Photos of the creepy dark woods surrounding Hawk House. Pictures of skeletal remains they'd pulled off the internet.

Her social media pages were blowing up with them. Some teens were even making up stories about what they thought had happened there. Who might have died. Some thought the killer was still lurking around, hiding and laughing that he'd gotten away with multiple murders.

Her friends were probably laughing at her, too. Calling her a wimp. But what if the killer was still around? What if he came after her?

A knock sounded at the door, and she rocked herself back and forth on the bed.

"Mandy, honey, please come out and eat something," Aunt Trudy called through the door. "I'll order a pizza if you want."

Her aunt had been trying to push food on her ever since she'd come home from the hospital. But Mandy couldn't stomach food right now.

"Mandy, please. I'm worried about you."

"I'm not hungry," she said, her voice weak.

"But you haven't eaten anything—"

"I said I'm not hungry," she snapped. "Leave me alone."

Her aunt was silent for a minute, but Mandy pictured her hovering by the door, waiting, fretting, brows furrowed with worry. Hoping she'd come out.

"How about you invite some friends over?"

"I said I want to be alone." Why couldn't her aunt get it? Her room was safe. She was safe alone. She didn't want to eat or talk or be with anyone right now.

She crawled in her bed and pulled the covers over her face. She wanted to disappear so that monster couldn't find her.

27

TWISTED BRANCH

Mama always said not to get in the car with strangers – or in their bed.

But Kelly Louise Hogan stopped listening to her mama a long time ago. In fact, she'd run off from their double-wide mobile home years ago and hadn't bothered to say goodbye.

"You'll never amount to anything, Kelly girl," Mama had told her. "You ain't got the smarts God gave a dog."

"I'm going to be somebody one day," Kelly had yelled.

Her mother had just laughed. "Ha. You got shit for talent. Don't come crawling back to me when you don't make it."

Now, Kelly dotted Chanel No. 5 behind her ears. Maybe Mama was right.

She had tried and failed. Then she'd decided to give Mama's way a try, and she'd met Mike. She'd tried to be the perfect wife. A good mother. Had even joined the PTA. But... she just didn't fit. When she'd told Mike about her dream, he'd shrugged it off.

He didn't believe in her either.

It doesn't matter, she told herself. She reminded herself of the affirmations she'd read in the dozens of self-help books she'd bought. *If you say something and believe it, you can make it happen.*

And she would make it happen. She'd never crawl back to Mama. Not after the things she'd done. The person she'd become. The lows she'd stooped to.

And her marriage... She wouldn't crawl back there either.

But at least now she had a plan. A quick check in the mirror, and she fluffed her long dark hair, mussing it to add a sexy flair. Ruby-red lipstick curved her lips, and she added a hint of rouge to accentuate her cheekbones.

All her life she'd felt homely. In school, the boys had picked the prettier girls. The ones with the big boobs. The perky blonds. The ones with nice clothes and highlights in their hair.

Then she'd met Mike and knew Mama would have been pleased. They had a decent life. But something was missing. When she mentioned she wanted to sing, he'd laughed at her just like Mama. Told her to stay home and take care of their son.

Her heart gave a pang. Her son was the one she missed. But it wouldn't be forever.

She was going to get *out* and prove everyone wrong.

Willie Nelson crooned "Hello Darlin'" in the background as she opened the drawer where she kept her cash. She'd been saving for a year now. One more night and she'd have enough.

She'd buy a guitar and head to Nashville. She'd take singing lessons and record some of the songs she'd been writing.

She lifted her head and smiled at herself in the mirror as she pictured herself on stage belting out a love song. She would prove Mama wrong.

And her son would be proud. Then she would get him back. "Who'll be laughing then, Mama?"

Standing, she grabbed her handbag and phone. One more night and then she'd be finished with this life.

And she'd begin a new one.

28
CROOKED CREEK

As Ellie left the boneyard and drove back to town, fear wrapped its icy tentacles around her.

Derrick said nothing, lapsing into a brooding quiet that unnerved Ellie. Not that he was much of a talker, but he definitely seemed disturbed by what they'd found. More disturbed than on other cases.

Either that or something else was bothering him.

"You okay?" she asked him as she drove onto Main Street.

He mumbled yes then glanced at his phone as they passed through the one light in town which was swaying in the gusty breeze.

"What's going on, Derrick? Something wrong?"

"No," he said, although his gruff tone sounded less than convincing.

"You want to talk about it?"

He shook his head and looked out the window as they passed the Corner Café. Cord's vehicle was already there. He deserved a hot dinner after his hard work today. So did they. Lunch had come and gone without a thought by either of them. "Want to get something to eat?" Ellie asked.

"No, thanks. I need to settle back into the cabin."

Though he worked out of the main field office in Atlanta, when the governor had asked him to create a task force to work the Appalachian Mountain area, Derrick had secured a small cabin on the river.

But Ellie sensed his refusal for dinner was more about being alone. She felt a distance between them that she hadn't felt in some time and wondered if something had happened back in Atlanta. He'd spent time with his mother. Maybe she'd discouraged him from getting close to Ellie. She must blame the Reeves family for her daughter's death.

A commotion on the street caught her attention, and she grimaced. A smattering of women, led by Maude, had gathered to protest the opening of Crystal's, the new gift shop. Signs boasted their distaste: *Stop the Magic. No Witches in Crooked Creek. Charlatan!*

Shondra stood on the sidewalk keeping the protest civil. In the window, Ellie spotted windchimes and shelves filled with crystals. Native American pieces were being featured in honor of the festival at Bear Mountain.

Crystal had told Ellie that in a separate room, she held performed Reiki healing, a Japanese form of energy healing, an alternative medicine, which was also called palm healing or hands-on healing.

Ellie didn't know if Crooked Creek was ready for it, but the young woman seemed to truly believe in its effectiveness.

She rolled her aching shoulders to alleviate the tension, but it did no good. She was wound tight with the gruesome images of that boneyard.

"Just drop me at my car," Derrick said.

Ellie pulled in front of the station and parked by his sedan. "You sure you don't want to grab a bite and talk? Work through some theories?"

His dark, impenetrable gaze met hers. "No use speculating

until we dig into that place. Let's start with the former sheriff tomorrow."

Ellie wanted to say more but she simply watched him go. Maybe he was just disturbed by the case.

A case which might tear this town in two again.

Her phone was ringing as she headed toward home. Captain Hale.

"Ellie," her boss said when she answered, "sorry to ask this of you after the day you've had, but I just got a call. A break-in. Eastwood's at that crystal shop and Deputy Landrum is directing traffic at an accident out on the highway."

"Where is it?"

"Storage unit. Steve's on Butt's Boulevard."

"I'm on my way." She punched the accelerator and sped toward the address. If it was the same kids she'd busted earlier, she'd come down hard on them this time and put an end to this nonsense.

29

SOMEWHERE ON THE AT

A frisson of alarm shot through Kelly as the man hauled her from his Lexus. The cabin where they'd stopped was dark and set in the middle of nowhere. It reminded Kelly of the horrible serial killer stories she'd seen on *Dateline*.

"I've changed my mind," she said. "Let's go back to town."

A deep laugh rumbled from him, and he jerked her bound hands and shoved her forward. She dug her feet in and tried to turn back to the car, but the sudden sharp prick of his knife against her back made her move forward. The door screeched open and she blinked against the shadowy corners of the room, then quickly surveyed it. A metal bed. Ropes. Chains. Whips.

Dear God, this looked some kind of torture chamber.

"Please don't hurt me," she said in a choked whisper. "I have a son."

"I'm sure he'd be proud of you," the man whispered as he pushed her onto the bed. "And don't bother screaming. No one can hear you out here."

Panic seized her, and she struggled to loosen the ropes around her wrist.

Her eyes pleaded with him to release her, but his look was

crazed, his cold calloused hands roaming all over her, his husky voice sending chills up her spine. "You're mine tonight, slut."

She kicked and flailed, but she was weak from whatever drug he must have put in her drink and her limbs felt heavy. Then he yanked the ropes tighter and secured them to the bed posts.

She tugged her arms to free herself, but the metal rattled and the ropes cut into her wrists. The acrid scent of whiskey, sweat and anger railed off him.

"You like it rough, don't you, baby?" he growled against her throat.

She tried to scream but he stuffed a rag in her mouth and the sound was muffled. He climbed over her and she closed her eyes, trying to block out what was happening.

It would be over soon. Then she'd be free and she'd buy that guitar and prove to the world she was somebody her son could be proud of.

Suddenly the man went still. He bellowed like a sick mad animal, and she realized he'd gone limp.

His thick lips quivered as he cursed and he shoved her deeper into the bed, holding her down by the throat, her teeth biting into the rag.

With a bellow of rage, he grabbed the knife from the side table.

God help her. He was big. He was mean. And he was going to kill her.

She opened her mouth to scream again, but choked on the rag, then he jerked her head backward and slashed her throat.

She tasted blood and felt it dribble down her neck as her body fought and shook. Her own scream echoed in her ears. The sound of bones tinkling from the windchimes she'd seen on the porch cut through her wailing.

A second later, ice swept over her. Then the world turned black and there was nothing.

30

STEVE'S STORAGE UNITS, STONY GAP

Night hugged the corners of the row of metal buildings as Ellie swung the Jeep into the parking lot for Steve's Storage Units. Her senses were on alert as she cut the engine. Holy hell. The only car in the parking lot belonged to her father. What was he doing here? She knew he kept a police scanner. Had he responded to the call as some kind of citizen cop?

Pulling her service weapon in case the intruders were armed, she slowly opened the car door, her gaze sweeping the dark alley between the block of storage units. Two rows of six each sat inside a chain length fence, with a patch grass in between, dotting the graveled dirt alley.

A noise sounded, then footsteps and she caught sight of a figure in a dark jacket and black ski cap running down the alley. The fence rattled as the intruder grabbed it to climb over. Gun at the ready, she slipped through the gate opening, then darted along the units, scanning each one and bracing herself for an ambush as she gave chase.

Her mind raced. If this was a burglar, he'd need a vehicle close by to stow the stolen stuff. But she didn't see another car around.

"Stop, police!" she shouted as she raced after him. But when she neared the fence, the man had disappeared into the bushes. A second later, an engine fired to life and roared away. Dammit, he'd escaped.

A groan made her jerk and turn around and she peered inside the last unit.

Her father lay on the cement floor face-down, half unconscious, blood pooling beneath his head.

31

Fear choked Ellie as she ran to her father. They'd had their differences, but she'd idolized him growing up. He'd fallen off that pedestal she'd put him on as a little girl when she'd learned she was adopted, but maybe it had been unfair to put him there in the first place.

No one could survive idolism without a fall from glory at some point.

"Dad?" She shook him gently, pressing her fingers deeper into his throat and finally felt a low pulse. He moaned and stretched out his fingers, digging at the gravel to try to push himself up.

She patted his shoulder. "Just lie still. You have a head injury. I'll call an ambulance."

Another moan, then his body went slack again, sending her heart into another panicked flurry. She pulled her phone and dialed 911. "Man injured, head wound. 556 Butt's Boulevard, Steve's Storage Units. Please hurry."

Her father always carried a handkerchief, so she dug in his pocket, then lifted it and wiped at the bloody gash on the back of his head. Sticky blood matted his thick brown hair, and she parted it to assess the wound. A gash about three inches long, not too deep, but it would need stitches. There was a lot of blood, but she reminded herself that head wounds bled easily, and that he was breathing and one of the toughest men she'd ever known.

He rolled his head sideways. "El?"

"I'm here, Dad," she said, her voice a rough whisper.

"Files... Ogden's... Came to get them... Someone else..."

"Was here, too," she said filling in the blanks. "He assaulted you and got away. Did you see who it was?"

He shook his head.

Using her torch, she scanned the cement floor and found several boxes shoved into a corner. She hurried over to them and saw they were labeled by year.

The stacked boxes were closed, apart from one. That box was labeled January 1992 – the same date Hawk House had closed.

Pulse hammering, she shuffled through them but the file on Hawk House was gone.

32

As the ambulance arrived to transport her father to the hospital, Ellie called a crime team to process the storage unit, then Steve to report the break-in. The medics indicated that Randall would be okay but needed stitches and had a possible concussion.

As she headed to her Jeep, she phoned her adoptive mother Vera. "Mom, Dad's on the way to the hospital with a head injury."

Her mother shrieked. "What in the world happened? Is he okay, Ellie?"

"He will be. Meet me at the hospital and I'll explain." Ellie paused, her mother's shaking breathing filling the silence. "Or do you need me to swing by and pick you up?"

"No, just go with him. I'll be there as soon as possible."

Ellie hung up, flipped on her siren and chased the ambulance, wishing like hell she'd caught the bastard who'd assaulted her father. If only she'd been a few minutes sooner.

The ambulance peeled around traffic, weaving in and out for the next fifteen minutes, then finally skidded into the hospital ER parking lot, blue lights twirling. Reminding herself that her father would be okay didn't lessen her fears, and she threw the Jeep into a parking spot, jumped out and jogged toward the hospital entrance.

By the time she reached the ER, a nurse was rolling her father to an exam room. She rushed to the nurses' station and identified herself. Before she could go to him, the doors swished open and her mother ran in, looking terrified and disheveled in a pale green jogging suit and her bedroom shoes, a sharp contrast to her usual coiffured look.

"Where is he?" Vera asked shrilly.

"They've taken him to an exam room," Ellie said, guiding her mother to the waiting room.

Vera's eyes turned cold. "What happened?"

Ellie took a deep breath. "It's about those bones we found at Hawk House. Dad went to the storage units to look for the files covering the investigation years ago."

"Ellie, listen to me. I've always hated you working with the police and you know it." Her mother's mouth tightened.

"Mom—"

Vera held up a hand to silence Ellie. "I tolerated your father's job, but every day was a living nightmare. I constantly worried whether or not he'd come home at night." Her voice cracked. "Now he's retired, I can finally breathe again. I know he'll be there, that we can have a life without all that fear." She gripped Ellie's arms. "The last two years you've almost died several times. Sometimes I think you have a death wish." Animosity laced her tone. "I have horrible dreams of you being beaten and tortured, of burying you. Sometimes when I close my eyes, I see you lying in a casket, your eyes staring up at me, blank and empty." Tears trickled down her cheeks. "I realize you won't quit, that you're stubborn and somehow you like all this horror, but from now on leave your father out of your investigations. If you can't, I'll insist that we move away from Bluff

County so we can finally have some peace." Vera pushed away from her. "Now I'm going in to be with your father. Go home, Ellie, and leave us alone."

Her mother's words hung in the air as she disappeared into the ER.

33

HAWK HOUSE

Thirty years ago

Giant stone hawks stood along the path as he pushed her toward the front door. The big old building looked like the haunted house in town at Halloween. She'd been scared then.

She was so terrified now she could hardly breathe.

The big metal door slammed shut as he dragged her inside. The hall was dark, long, filled with dust motes swirling around. A long staircase wound up to another floor that smelled like must.

She tried to make her feet work to run, but a big beefy hand clenched her so tight she felt weak.

Another man, tall and wide-shouldered, stood in the shadows of the room. His black eyes looked like a black bear's, but he said nothing.

Giant bookshelves towered behind him, brown wood on the walls. Brown everywhere. He opened a door behind one of them and the man who'd brought her here shoved her inside. The tiny room was pitched in darkness and smelled like something rotten. Then he tossed her on a hard cot in the corner and shut the door.

She trembled, the walls closing around her. Tears blurred her eyes, and she curled up on the cot against the wall and stared into the scratchy blanket he'd wrapped her in when he'd thrown her in the trunk.

Who was he? Where was she? Why had he hurt her mama?

She closed her eyes and replayed the scary night in her head. *"Run. Hide."* Mama's voice sounded like a faint whisper now, lost and far away. She willed her to speak again. To tell her she was coming for her.

She couldn't be dead.

But she knew people did die. They went away just like Mama said her granddaddy did.

Dark red splotches of color sparkled behind her eyes and she felt like she was back at the house hiding in the closet...

Her mama's blood was everywhere. She crammed her fist against her mouth so he wouldn't hear her, but she must have whimpered and then he was there looming over her.

She tried to run but her feet hit the red stream of Mama's blood, and she slid and slipped then he yanked her up and dragged her away.

The voices grew louder outside the room, jolting her away from the heartbreaking memory. Footsteps hammered, and the big men were talking. "I had to get rid of her."

"I'll take care of it," the other man said.

She buried her head in the blanket. Were they going to kill her now?

34

CROOKED CREEK

Cord stared at the ceiling, counting the cracks, willing himself to sleep. Lola was nestled to him, her body curled around his, a slender hand on his bare belly, her breathing tickling his neck.

But the room was too bright and she wasn't Ellie. Ellie who had been in his head ever since she was a teenager and had followed him on search-and-rescue missions. Ellie and the one night they'd had together before she went off to the police academy.

He'd known it was wrong then. It was still wrong. He could never be anything more than her friend.

Lola slid closer, but he was too distracted to focus on her. Instead, his mind turned back the boneyard behind Hawk House. His own childhood of barely surviving on the AT gave him a glimpse of what might have happened at that place. Children tossed away. Unwanted. Hoping each day someone would come for them. Would give them a forever home. Losing hope each day that life would get better.

He'd felt that way himself. Had been beaten and tortured as a kid. Forced to do unspeakable things. Made to feel he was nothing. That no one loved him. That no one ever would.

He still felt that way sometimes. How could anyone love him when he still harbored secrets that tore him up inside? Secrets that would send Lola running.

And Ellie... God, he didn't know if he could face her if she knew.

His breathing grew rapid and sweat trickled down the side of his face. The longer he lay there the more restless he became. Lola rolled toward him, her hand on his scarred chest. The scars that hid the truth. He didn't want anyone to see the man he really was.

Slowly, he eased her fingers from his stomach and tried to slip from bed without disturbing her. She reached for him and her eyes fluttered open. "Don't go, Cord."

He cursed a blue streak in his mind. He didn't want to hurt her. She was so good to him. Better than he deserved.

But he was what he was. And she deserved a man whose mind was not someplace else.

"Sorry, but I have to go."

She pulled at his arm. "Why? It's late."

He gave her a quick kiss. "Can't sleep. And I have to be up early to help search the woods behind that orphanage."

"That's horrible, what they found," Lola said softly. "But maybe someone else could go. It upset you being there."

Hell, yeah it had. But that subject was off limits. Let her fantasize he was a good man. "It's my job," he said gruffly.

"If it keeps you awake at night, maybe you should step away." She tugged him toward her. "Find something else to do with your life."

Cord stiffened. She'd never understand. Working SAR had *saved* his life. It was *who* he was, his salvation, not just some job. "I can't. I have to help."

"Why?" Lola asked, her tone annoyed. "Why does it have to be you? Because of Ellie?"

"Don't start," Cord said curtly.

"If it's not Ellie, then tell me why it's so important that you go instead of letting some other SAR workers take this one."

Cord couldn't explain it. But he felt a kinship to those forgotten kids. He'd been one of them once.

They needed someone to speak for them now. And he damn well would whether Lola liked it or not.

35

COYOTE CANYON

Damn tramp was a bleeder. All over her. The floor. His hands. He'd clean up his place later. But now, he had to get rid of her.

Rage eating at him, he stuffed the bitch into a garbage bag to keep her blood from staining the trunk of his car then slid into the driver's seat. His knowledge of the law worked in his favor. He knew how to cover his tracks and how not to get caught.

It was the little things that tripped people up. Details like a stray hair or button. A partial fingerprint. Skin beneath the victim's nails.

But he'd made sure that wasn't a problem. Then he'd decided to take a piece of bone to add to his collection. Easy peasy. Snip, Snip. The little bones cracked right in two.

How dare she plead with him that she had a kid, as if she was a good mother?

Where to leave her now though? Cops were all over the woods on account of those bones they'd found. He sure as hell couldn't go anywhere near there.

These mountains and woods had been his hunting ground as a boy, and he decided on Coyote Canyon. He could still see the predators' eyes piercing the dark when he'd hunted there as a teen, their growls punctuating the night as they stalked back and forth. Hungry for their next meal.

A freezing rain splattered the windshield as he drove deep into the mountain, weaving around the switchbacks. He passed the turn off for the Native American burial ground and veered right onto the narrow road leading to the ridge that jutted out over the hollow. Raindrops pelted the windshield, running off the leaves of the cypress trees as he parked. He tugged on his raincoat and hat, scanning the area for other cars, but the bad weather and late hour meant no one was around.

He hauled himself from the car, then opened the trunk and lifted the body from inside. She was dead weight in his arms as he dragged her across the wet ground. Mud and leaves clung to the garbage bag, the sour odor of her body swirling around him.

Sweet satisfaction filled him as the body thumped over the rocky edge of the ridge and plunged into the hollow below.

DAY 3

The next morning Ellie couldn't shake her mother's harsh words as she hurried into the hospital to visit her father. She and Vera had butted heads over the years, but the last few months she thought they'd reached a better understanding.

Yet seeing Randall injured had obviously triggered Vera's worst fears. How could Ellie blame her mother for being upset? When she'd first seen her father lying on the floor with blood pooling around his head, fear had paralyzed her.

Then all night, she'd heard children screaming from the dark pit. Seen them running into the woods to escape Black-stone and whatever was happening in that orphanage. Seen the monsters that snatched children's lives and left their bones scattered over the land.

The people who'd turned a blind eye were culpable too. Someone should have spoken up, and she intended to track each and every one of them down.

As she walked down the hall, the sound of someone crying over a loved one drifted from another room. Two nurses ran along with a crash cart, shouting orders and running to another room where a red light blinked. The scent of medicine and antiseptic and sickness permeated the walls.

Nerves flitted through her when she reached her father's room and saw her mother in the recliner by her father's bed. His head was bandaged, his pallor gray, and he was sleeping. So was her mother who looked pale herself, her cheeks still stained from crying, body slumped uncomfortably in the chair.

A twinge of guilt rippled through Ellie. But she refused to give up her job. Chasing down bad guys and protecting the town was her calling.

Resigned, she eased open the door and slipped inside.

Her mother opened her eyes and looked up at her warily, then patted her fingers over her hair to feather her bob back in place.

"How is he?" Ellie asked.

"Resting," her mother said. "Ten stitches and a concussion."

And it's all your fault.

Their voices roused her father. For a moment, he looked confused then he touched the bandage around his head. "Did you see who attacked me?"

Ellie slowly approached him, well aware that her mother was ready to pounce if she upset Randall. "Afraid not, Dad. He disappeared down the alley, then I saw you."

"You should have gone after him instead of stopping to take care of me," he said gruffly.

Her mother's sharp intake of breath made Ellie swallow hard. No matter what she did, it was wrong.

She cradled her father's hand in hers, unwanted tears pricking her eyes. His skin was clammy. "Of course, I had to stop and take care of you, Dad. I love you."

Her mother wiped at her damp cheeks while Randall rolled to his side, wincing as if the movement hurt his head. "Did you find the f... files?"

Ellie shook her head. "No, the man must have taken them. I'll talk to Sheriff Ogden. Maybe he kept copies."

"Hand me the phone and I'll call him," her father said.

Sensing Vera's disapproval, Ellie squeezed his hand. "No, Dad, you aren't going to do anything but rest. I can handle this on my own. Well, with my team of course. Agent Fox is here to assist."

Randall's mouth compressed into a tight line. Because she'd mentioned Derrick? The two men could never be friends – Derrick could not forgive Ellie's father for withholding important information when he'd investigated his little sister's disappearance.

"Fine," he snapped then turned his head away to stare at the wall.

Ellie sensed she'd hurt him or angered him – she didn't know which. But one look at her mother's worried face and she knew she'd done the right thing.

Reluctantly, she lowered his hand, then headed to the door. Vera followed her into the hall. "How long will he be in the hospital?" Ellie asked.

"At least another day. They want to make sure there isn't any cranial bleeding."

Ellie hoped to soften Vera's anger. "Take care of him, Mom. And call me if you need me."

Vera crossed her arms. "The only thing I need from you is to leave him alone. Go chase these lunatics on your own."

Ellie tamped down her hurt. "Don't worry," she said between clenched teeth. "I won't bother you two anymore."

Heart aching, she turned and walked down the hall.

Her mother was right. Randall had sacrificed for years to protect the town.

Her father's time for investigating predators had passed.

She would leave them alone. But she'd do her job. And she'd make whoever hurt her father answer for what he'd done.

37

CROOKED CREEK

"No! Get away. Get away!" Mandy thrashed at the covers, *kicking and throwing her fists. The bones crackled and jabbed her as she fought.*

The sightless eyes of the children dripped blood-red tears. The monster gnashed his teeth and tossed another screaming child into the pit.

Mandy pushed at the body, willing the child to be alive, but then the skin melted away and it was all bones.

She jerked awake, kicking away the comforter and clawing to get away. Suddenly the door burst open, and a big man stood towering over her. She scrambled backward, to hide, tossing a pillow at him.

"Mandy, honey, it's Aunt Trudy and Bryce." She heard footsteps, then heard the voice again. "Shh, shh, honey, it's all right," Aunt Trudy whispered. "You're safe now."

Slowly, the fog of her nightmare began to fade and she realized she'd been dreaming. She was in her own room in her own bed, not in that pit of bones.

She blinked, wiping away tears and trembling as she pulled

her childhood teddy bear up against her. God, she was lame. She had started sleeping with it again when her mother died.

"Mandy, Trudy is right, you're safe," Bryce said in a low voice.

Her blurry eyes made out the concern in his face. Her father was in her room, seeing what a nervous wreck she was and she didn't like it.

"Get out," she choked out. "I don't want you here."

"Mandy," Trudy scolded softly.

Mandy glared at her. "I told you I want to be alone."

"Let me help you, Mandy," Bryce said.

She whirled on him, tears and rage and shame washing over her. "I don't want you here," she cried. "I wish you'd died instead of my mother!"

Aunt Trudy gasped, and Bryce went very still. She didn't know her dad very well, but his jaw tightened. His throat muscles worked as he swallowed, and he turned and strode from the room, his boots pounding.

Her aunt ran after him, and she heard voices but couldn't make out what they were saying.

Then the door slammed and she heard his car engine burst to life. He tore from the driveway, tires screeching.

38

CROOKED CREEK

As she drove to the police station, Ellie phoned Edgar Ogden. The phone rang four times then went to voicemail. "This is Detective Ellie Reeves from Crooked Creek Police Department. I'm investigating skeletal remains found at Hawk House and need to talk to you. Please call me ASAP." She left her phone number then hung up as she passed the Cat Café. She smiled as she watched Ms. Eula, Ms. Ivy and two other older ladies entering, grateful the women had found each other.

Signs advertising that Chief Thunderhawk was going to be sharing Native American tales at Books & Bites that evening flapped on the lightpost. The garden club led by the mayor's wife had gathered in front of city hall and were planting flowers in the flower boxes out front. Crepe myrtles were budding pink now, but the impending storm could hinder their blooming.

She parked, pulled on her windbreaker then headed into the station. The coffee pot was empty, so she brewed a fresh pot of her favorite dark roast, then carried a mug to the conference room and tacked photos of the property at Hawk House on the white board.

She heard a low whistle as the sheriff entered.

"How's Mandy?" she asked Bryce.

"I don't want to talk about it," he said bluntly.

"She just needs time," Ellie said.

Bryce clenched his hands into fists, but pain flickered in his eyes. Had something happened?

Shondra sauntered in, sipping coffee from a travel mug, her black braid wrapped in a colorful turban. Deputy Heath Landrum followed, his dirty-blond hair standing in tufts as if he'd just crawled out of bed.

"What happened with the break-in?" Ellie asked Shondra.

"I busted the little smart asses and threw them in a cell for the night," Shondra said. "They were vandalizing some abandoned cabins on the river and in possession of drugs."

"The same two kids I warned the other night?" Ellie asked.

Shondra nodded. "I told them they'd spent their get out of jail free card. Parents are throwing fits, but little arrogant twits gotta learn a lesson."

"I agree. Captain Hale back you up?"

"I did," he said as he loped into the room, chewing on a mint. "They had enough Molly for a felony charge."

"Which meant they were probably into distribution," Ellie surmised.

"Let's nip that shit in the bud," Captain Hale said. "Throw the book at them." He gestured toward the whiteboard. "Wanna fill us in, Detective?"

"Sure." Ellie glanced at the door wondering where Derrick was – they needed to get on the job. "The team is working on recovering each and every bone and documenting injuries sustained," Ellie began. "Ranger McClain and SAR teams are widening the perimeter."

Agent Fox poked his head in the door, his shoulders squared. Ellie noticed dark circles beneath his eyes, and he'd also forgotten to shave this morning, giving him a rough-around-the-edges look. Something was definitely off with him.

But she wouldn't broach that subject in front of the others, so she turned back to the whiteboard. "We also found bones stored inside the house," Ellie continued. "Most appear to belong to small animals." She pointed out the pictures of the secret room, the dorm rooms and chains attached to the wall.

"Unbelievable," Deputy Landrum muttered. "How did this happen without anyone knowing?"

"Good question. I'm waiting on the former sheriff to return my call." She angled her head toward Bryce. "Did you talk to your father, Bryce?"

His gaze didn't quite meet Ellie's. "I left a message, but he hasn't returned my call yet. Guess he's busy being mayor."

His sarcastic tone suggested he and his father were not getting along.

But she had to focus on the case. "If the bones were on the property before Blackstone left, why wouldn't Ogden have found them?"

"Maybe he just ran a shoddy investigation," Shondra said.

"Or the bones were dumped there after Blackstone left," Landrum suggested.

Ellie scratched her forehead. "It's possible, I guess. But my father was assaulted trying to retrieve the files. They were stolen which suggests to me they contained incriminating information that someone didn't want revealed. I'll talk to Ogden."

She gestured to the deputy. "Find out everything you can about the orphanage, the employees, records of the names of kids placed there and any social worker affiliated with it."

"Copy that," Landrum murmured.

Captain Hale's phone trilled, and he stepped out to take the call.

"Deputy Eastwood, canvass the old-timers who lived here back then. See what they remember. Even the slightest detail might give us a lead."

Shondra nodded. "Will do."

Her captain poked his head back inside. "Detective Reeves, woman was found dead at Coyote Canyon. You and Agent Fox need to get up there now."

"But, Captain, what about this case?" Ellie asked. "I need to talk to Ogden."

"He and the bones can wait another hour. We have a current murder to solve."

Ellie didn't like to feel splintered, but he was right. As long as Landrum and Shondra were hunting down info on Hawk House, she wasn't abandoning that investigation. There wasn't much she could do until Laney finished and she learned more about the people associated with the orphanage. Hopefully Ogden could enlighten her with that information, and she could take it from there.

Ellie gestured for Derrick to follow and they hurried outside to her Jeep.

"Cause of death?" Derrick asked as they buckled their seatbelts.

"He didn't say. Guess we'll find out when we get there. Meanwhile, I'll try Ogden again."

Connecting to her hands-free, she punched his number as she started the engine. Once again, the phone rang several times then went to voicemail. She left another message, this one more terse. "This is important. Please call me ASAP."

"Maybe he's on vacation," Derrick said as she drove from the station through town.

"Or he's avoiding me because he saw the news," Ellie said, veering off the main road.

Derrick rubbed his hand over his jaw, his beard stubble rasping. "If he did and he's hiding something, that would make sense. But why cover for a child abuser?"

She couldn't think of a reason to do so. "Good question." And one she wanted the answer to.

"I'll call my partner Bennett, see what he can dig up on Blackstone," Derrick offered.

Ellie nodded agreement. The FBI had resources and access to databases the police department didn't have.

They lapsed into silence as he made the call, and she noted rain clouds gathering in the distance above the rising peaks and ridges. She'd never been to Coyote Canyon, but on a hike with her father at Bear Mountain, he'd told her stories of the coyotes that swarmed the canyon. The mangy animals with their shifty eyes and screeching howl always unnerved her.

Sharp rocks jutted between the boulders, creating pockets for the animals to hide. The wind tossed loose brush across the brittle grass which, according to her father, seemed to always be brown here as if life could not exist in this area.

It was not a popular tourist spot. But it was a good place to dump a body where it might never be found.

The killer had probably counted on that. And the fact that the coyotes would ravage the remains and destroy any evidence left behind.

Cord was standing by his truck near a small ravine when Ellie pulled up. A group of boy scouts sat in a van to the right, the leader standing strategically in front of it to block the preteens' sightline.

"Will the coyotes attack?" Derrick asked, his tone wary.

"They usually don't attack humans unless provoked, but they do prey on smaller animals."

"Then we don't provoke them," Derrick said sardonically.

The two of them climbed from her Jeep and walked toward Cord who faced them, hands jammed in the pockets of his jeans.

"What do we have?" Ellie asked.

Cord gestured toward the ravine. "Body left in a garbage bag. Coyotes were about to rip into it."

Ellie's breath stalled in her chest at the grisly sight. A black garbage bag, partially torn, a woman's limp bloody hand sticking out.

"Those kids found her?" Ellie asked.

"Their leader did. They came for the Native American festival. Took a day trip to hike. One of the boys spotted the coyotes prowling and the leader got curious. He made the boys stay in the van while he checked it out. Shot a round into the air and the coyotes ran off. When he saw the bag, he called us."

Frown lines creased Derrick's forehead. "This is one trip those guys won't forget."

"Not the kind of life lesson they should get at their age," Cord muttered.

Ellie heard an engine and looked up to see Laney drive up. The ERT was close behind. She waited on them before she took a closer look.

"I'll check around, see if I can find anything." Derrick glanced up. "It's possible the killer parked by the ridge and threw her over the edge."

"Tell the crime investigators to divide up and search up there and down here. Laney and I will examine the body."

While Derrick went to meet the investigators, she and Laney approached the victim. "Let me get some snapshots before we move her," Ellie said.

She captured the scene at different angles, then zeroed in on the garbage bag. Blood, dirt and leaves clung to the bag which appeared to be damp and soggy. Ellie covered a cough at the rancid odors.

She gestured to Cord. "Let's move her out of the ravine so we can examine her."

"Course. Stand back." He was already wearing gloves, and with his muscular physique dragged the corpse to more level ground. Ellie and Laney stooped beside her, and Ellie snapped another picture of the bag where it was torn, then the protruding hand.

Using scissors from her kit, Laney cut away the plastic and exposed the body.

Ellie tasted bile at the grisly sight. A brunette, she guessed to be mid-twenties. She'd once been attractive, but now lay mangled in her own blood. Multiple stab wounds covered her chest and throat, deep and vicious. Her fingertips were also bloody where the killer had cut off the tips.

"I don't like to speculate, but I'd say she died from exsanguination." Laney lifted the woman's arms. "Defensive marks, but also those rope burns indicate she was restrained first."

"How long do think she's been dead?"

Laney sighed. "Judging from rigor, I'd say hours. She probably died sometime last night."

"No ID on her." Ellie pulled her phone and first took a close-up picture of the woman's face from different angles, texted the photo to Shondra then called her.

"Female found dead. Multiple stab wounds. Run this through missing persons reports and DMV records and see if we can get an ID," Ellie said. "If that doesn't work, we'll try facial rec."

"Got it. I'll get back to you," Shondra agreed, and Ellie hung up.

Laney narrowed her eyes as she examined the remainder of the body. The victim's chest had been sliced with the knife, gashes marring her arms and legs. Rolling her over revealed whip marks on her back.

"Looks like she either had rough sex or was sexually assaulted," Laney said. "There are bruises on her thighs and torso. Look at her ankle. See that raised reddening, it's fresh. He marked her with a symbol. It looks like a pentagram."

Ellie considered the MO. The violence of the kill suggested deep rage and now a symbol – were they dealing with another ritualistic killer?

TWISTED BRANCH

An hour later, as Laney was supervising the body being transported to the morgue, Shondra phoned Ellie with an ID. "Ran that pic through facial rec. Woman's name is Kelly Hogan," Shondra said. "She's twenty-seven, married to an accountant named Mike Hogan. I'm sending you the address."

"Thanks." Ellie hung up, then informed Cord and the chief ERT investigator they had to make the death notification.

"We did find evidence someone was on the ridge above," the investigator said. "Partial boot prints. Large, most likely a man's. Took a cast of them if you find someone to make a comparison to."

"Any tire marks or sign he brought her there via a sled or ATV?"

"Not that we've found. But we'll have men search the woods for a trail or path he could have taken."

"Ranger McClain knows the area better than anyone. Have him lead the search. If you find a button, piece of clothing, anything, log it in. We need to nail this sicko."

Judging from the fact that the killer had had to park and carry the woman to the ledge to dump her body, he was strong.

The depth and sheer number of stab wounds indicated he was out of control. That something might have set him off.

The big question – did he know the victim or was she a crime of opportunity?

Ellie and Derrick tossed around possible scenarios as she drove to Twisted Branch, a new gated community in Bluff County with walking trails, a pool, tennis courts and majestic views of the mountains. The ancient trees were huge, the twisted branches entwined like long fingers creating natural canopies by the river.

"The Hogans look like they've done well for themselves," Ellie commented.

"Looks like," Derrick agreed. "Yet the wife still fell prey to an animal."

"Unless the husband was the animal."

Tension stretched between them as she stopped at the gate and identified themselves. The guard waved them through, and she drove passed estates on acre lots with houses so big her bungalow would fit inside the garages. The Hogan's two-story Georgian home looked stately.

Ellie noted a bicycle and soccer ball in the drive, and her heart squeezed. "They have kids. Or at least one child."

"Ahh, damn." Derrick opened his door and climbed out, his expression grave.

Ellie followed him along the brick paver pathway. She rang the doorbell, and they surveyed the property as they waited. A pristine manicured lawn, flowerbeds starting to flourish, the sweet scent of honeysuckle wafting around her.

Derrick punched the bell again, and finally they heard footsteps. A boy of about ten opened the door, his eyes widening when he saw Ellie's badge clipped to her belt.

A wave of sadness washed over her. She was about to destroy this poor kid's life.

42

COYOTE CANYON

Leah Gentilly's stomach cramped with nerves as she scoured the internet for more information on the recent discovery at Hawk House. Angelica Gomez had reported the story on the news which she'd watched like a rabid dog.

She'd followed the fiery go-getter reporter's work for the past two years, keeping up religiously with the crimes in Bluff County. Gomez's skills and perseverance made Leah miss the work and want to come out of hiding. After all these years, surely she was safe...

When the orphanage had been shut down and Sheriff Ogden had closed his lame investigation without digging for the truth, she'd thought he had his own agenda. But then the threats had come. And then the attack.

Thirty years had passed, but her leg still throbbed when it was cold and rainy. She'd almost given up hope that some smart cop or reporter would finish the story and expose Horatio Blackstone for the sadistic monster she believed him to be.

After the attack, she'd retreated to a cottage while she'd healed from the assault that had left her near dead in the woods.

A hunter had found her and carried her to his cabin where he'd nursed her back to life.

She'd fallen in love with the big tough mountain man while he kept her safe. By the time she'd recovered, the story had died and she'd decided she didn't want to die too, so she'd tried to put the story behind her and married the man who'd rescued her.

He'd been patient and loving with her. Except lately when she mentioned resurrecting her investigation. He claimed he didn't want her to endanger herself again.

But sometimes she thought he liked isolating them up here to control her instead of to protect her. Just yesterday when she'd mentioned contacting Angelica Gomez, he'd gone ballistic. They'd argued and he'd stormed out and hadn't come home last night.

Wind picked up, battering the shutters where they lived on top of the ridge that overlooked Coyote Canyon. Her husband enjoyed watching the coyotes roam the land below, but sometimes at night she swore she heard them nipping at the back door trying to get in.

43

TWISTED BRANCH

Ellie swallowed hard to tamp down her emotions as she faced the little boy. "Hi, there. My name is Detective Reeves and this is Special Agent Fox. Is your father here?"

The boy nodded, his eyes darting back and forth between them. Then he turned and ran down the hall. "Daddy, cops are here!"

Derrick pinched the bridge of his nose. "Poor kid."

"I know," Ellie murmured. It would be even worse if the husband was involved. But she had to consider him a person of interest until proven differently.

Footsteps echoed on the hardwood floors and a tall thin man with clipped brown hair appeared, worry darkening his pale green eyes. He tugged at his tie, and behind him she noticed two suitcases by the staircase. "I'm Mike Hogan."

Ellie cut her eyes toward the son. "Mr. Hogan, may we speak with you in private?"

His jaw tightened. "Todd, go upstairs and work on your Legos while I talk to these people."

"But, Dad—"

"Please, son, just do what I said," Hogan said, his voice edgy.

The boy's shoulders slumped. "All right." Todd dragged his feet as he climbed the steps and Hogan led them into his study.

He indicated two chairs facing his desk, and they all seated themselves. A frown pinched his brows and he steepled his hands together on the cherry wood surface of his massive desk. "What did Kelly do now?"

Ellie raised a brow. 'Why would you ask that?"

He hissed between his teeth. "Because this is not the first time she's been in trouble with the law."

Derrick removed his phone from his pocket. "Excuse me, I'll be right back."

Ellie narrowed her eyes. What the hell? He was taking a phone call during a death notification?

"What kind of trouble are you talking about?" Ellie asked, forcing herself to focus on the matter at hand.

The man stiffened. "Never mind. Just tell me. Did you arrest her?"

"No, Mr. Hogan, we're not here because of an arrest."

He drummed his finger on his desk. "Then what is this about?"

Ellie licked her dry lips. "I'm sorry to have to inform you, but your wife's body was found this morning."

Hogan rocked back in his chair, his mouth gaping open. "What? Kelly's dead?"

"I'm afraid so," Ellie said softly.

Emotions clouded his expression, and his breathing became labored.

"I know this is a difficult time," she continued, "but I really need your help."

"Wh... what happened?" he rasped.

A tense second passed, then Ellie delivered the rest of her news. "I'm sorry to say that your wife was murdered."

He shot up from his seat and paced across the room, hands rubbing the back of his neck. Ellie gave him a few moments to absorb the news. His polished shoes clicked on the wood floor, his movements agitated. "Good God, what am I going to tell Todd?"

Knowing he didn't expect an answer, Ellie simply waited.

He scrubbed a hand over his face, then exhaled. "How? Who killed her?"

"She was stabbed, sir," Ellie said, scrutinizing his reaction. "Multiple times. Where were you last night?"

Hogan sank back into his chair, pale-faced and trembling.

Pain wrenched Ellie's heart, then she heard Derrick come back in the room, his expression stony.

"Again, I'm so sorry, Mr. Hogan. But please answer the question. Where were you last night?"

"With Todd," Hogan said. "All night."

Hopefully that was true. "Tell me about your wife, sir."

He closed his eyes for a minute, then looked up at her again, and Ellie thought she detected anger or... maybe shame in his eyes.

"At first when we married, Kelly was a sweet girl. She didn't grow up with much and wanted to make something of herself. But I guess she got bored being a stay-at-home mom and... and..."

"And what, Mr. Hogan?"

"I wasn't enough," he said, disgust tingeing his voice. "I gave her everything, too. This nice house, let her stay home with Todd. Made good money and took care of all the bills."

"But she wanted something else?" Ellie asked softly.

His mouth thinned. "She started talking about having a career, singing. I... didn't think she'd ever make it and worried that rejection would destroy her."

Had he been judgmental or concerned? "She wasn't talented?"

He shrugged. "Maybe. But do you know how hard it is to make it in the music industry?"

"I'm sure it's difficult." Especially without support, Ellie thought. "Tell me more."

"So she got mad and then started going out all the time. She claimed she was taking singing lessons, but that was a lie." He heaved a weary breath. "When she came home smelling like men's cologne, I realized she was cheating on me."

Ellie schooled her reaction. "She told you about it?"

"Not in the beginning. But one night I saw bruises on her arms and when I asked about it, she admitted it. Said the guy had gotten rough with her." Hogan stood, his chair rocking back. "But she did it again and came home one night with an expensive necklace the guy gifted her."

"What happened then?" Ellie asked.

"I gave her an ultimatum." Pain slashed his face. "End the affair or I'd take Todd and leave. I couldn't have my son raised by a slut."

Ellie heard the torment in his voice. Had his wife's betrayal driven him to kill her?

44

Derrick studied Hogan's body language, but genuine emotions tainted his eyes. Hurt, shock, grief, anger.

Although that didn't mean that he hadn't murdered his wife in a fit of rage over her infidelity.

"Mr. Hogan," he said calmly. "How did your wife react to the idea of a separation and your threat to take Todd with you?"

Hogan released a long-winded sigh. "She was pissed." He clenched his hands into fists. "Can you believe that? She was cheating on me, and she got mad when I called her on it."

"Where were you last night, Mr. Hogan?" Ellie asked again.

"I told you, with my son. I took Todd to the movies then we got pizza and came home," he said, although his expression changed as he realized why the question had been posed.

"You can't think I'd actually hurt Kelly?" His gaze shot to a photo of the two of them on the mantle. "For God's sake, I loved her. I warned her that if she loved Todd she should stop."

"But she wasn't going to?" Derrick asked.

Hogan's shoulders fell. "No. That's why I was packing to leave."

Ellie felt for him. But he was digging himself deeper into a hole as far as motive went.

"And before you ask, yes, I was angry and hurt." He swiped a hand across his teary eyes. "But she is... was... the mother of my child. I would never take her away from him by murdering her."

"But you were taking him away from her," Ellie pointed out.

"Only to try to shake some sense into her," he said, his tone thick with disgust.

A tense silence passed, then his voice hardened to stone. "You do think I killed her, don't you?" Before they could answer, Hogan pulled out his wallet. "Here are my receipts from last night. Movie ticket stub and pizza receipt."

He tossed them on the desk. Ellie glanced at them and gave Derrick a nod, confirming they were legit.

"What time did you get home?" Ellie asked.

"About eleven," he said. "Since it's spring break, I wanted to treat Todd. He was upset about us moving out and I was trying to make it up to him." His voice shook. "Trying to be a good father and protect him." He sat down again and rubbed his hands over his face once more. "Jesus, God. Now he has no mother."

Another heartbeat passed, the man's anguish palpable.

"We are sorry, but it's procedure to ask these questions," Derrick said. "If you didn't harm her, we need to eliminate you as a person of interest."

"It was probably her damn boyfriend," he growled.

Derrick shifted. "Did you ask who she was seeing? Or who gave her those bruises?"

He shook his head. "I didn't want names," he muttered. "Hell, I didn't want to know any details. I just wanted her to be the sweet woman I married."

But she wasn't. And most likely that had gotten her killed.

45

Hogan knotted his hands. "It's my fault, isn't it? I should have made her tell me who did those things to her. I should have found the creep and beat the hell out of him."

"We're not here to pass judgment on you or your wife's lifestyle," Ellie said gently. "We just want to find out who's behind this."

"Mr. Hogan," Derrick said. "Did you go anywhere after you and your son got home last night?"

"No. We played video games until about midnight then Todd fell asleep, and I did some paperwork in my office."

"You didn't leave him alone and go out for a while?"

While she waited on Hogan to answer Derrick, Ellie studied his hands. Smooth nails, flawless skin, a paper pusher. Not a hunter. No scars or wounds from the night before which she expected with such a crime of rage. Her killer might still have blood stains in his skin or under his nails. Scratches on his arms where Kelly had fought to escape him.

Ellie couldn't picture the man in the polo shirt and khaki pants stuffing his bloody wife into a trash bag and hauling her into the woods. If he'd killed her, he probably would have hired someone or found a more civilized place to leave her body. After all, as he said, she was his child's mother.

Then again, desperation and betrayal made people do things they wouldn't normally do.

Both of those were bursting from him.

"You're sure you were here all night?" Derrick interjected.

"Yes," he said, teeth gritted. "Todd is ten. I would never leave him alone. There are bad people out there." His voice broke as if he realized what he'd just said. A heartbeat passed where he seemed to be reining in his temper. "I set my security system when we got home. You can check with my provider."

"We'll need that number," Ellie said, although she was leaning toward believing him. He might be an angry, frustrated, hurt and humiliated husband, but he seemed like a good father.

He opened his phone, checked his contacts then scribbled a number on a sticky note and shoved it toward them.

Ellie leaned toward the man. "Mr. Hogan, didn't you think it was odd or worry when Kelly didn't come home last night?"

His eyes shot to her. "Of course I did. But she'd stayed out before so I figured she was with *him*. Now, I need to be alone. And..." He glanced at the door where Ellie turned to see his little boy staring through the French doors. "And figure out a way to break this horrible news to my son. He's... going to be devastated."

"May I see your phone and computer?" Derrick asked.

Hogan's nostrils flared. "My phone but my computer files contain confidential financial information. I won't jeopardize my business by sharing it with anyone."

Derrick folded his arms. "If you have nothing to hide, you won't mind."

"I don't have anything to hide," he said with a bite to his tone, then he handed Ellie his phone. "But my clients trust me. If I allow anyone access to their financials, they won't come to me anymore. And they'll spread the word. That's the kiss of death for a CPA." He sighed. "But I can assure you that no one I represent would do anything to hurt my family or wife."

"Were you having financial problems?" Derrick asked.

"No." He clicked a few keys on his computer and hit print. A second later, he handed Derrick a copy of his bank statement. "You can see my savings and checking accounts along with my investment portfolio. My records are an open book, but my clients' are not."

Derrick skimmed the print-out. "Is there anyone who might want to get back at you for something? Maybe they thought you lost them money?" he asked.

"No, talk to my assistant at my firm if you need to. My wife was the one with the colorful lifestyle."

Ellie found nothing suspicious on his phone so she handed it back to him. "One more thing before we leave. Did Kelly have any tattoos or markings on her body?"

Her husband's head jerked back in confusion. "No, why do you ask?"

"We found a strange marking on her ankle. It looked like a pentagram."

"If she had one, I didn't know about it," Hogan said. "Then again, apparently there was a lot I didn't know about her."

Grief and disappointment vibrated in the man's every word.

"Did she have a personal calendar on her computer or phone?" Ellie asked.

"Probably on her phone. But her computer is upstairs if that would help."

"It might," Ellie said, hoping they'd find the name of the man she met the night before on it.

"I'll get it," Hogan said. "Then I really want you to go. Todd needs me."

"Certainly," Ellie replied.

They both followed him into the foyer where his son stood, twitching nervously, his freckled face looking confused.

"I thought you were gonna help me with my Lego set," Todd said with a pouty look.

"Let me get something for the detective," he told Todd. "Then we'll spend the rest of the day together."

Hogan disappeared up the steps and Ellie and Derrick were left in an awkward silence with the boy. Seconds ticked into a minute with Todd staring holes through them. Ellie's heart ached for him. His day with his dad was not going to be the fun day he anticipated.

Hogan bounded down the steps with a laptop in his hand and handed it to Ellie.

"We'll be in touch." Ellie laid her card on the foyer table. "If you think of anything else, please give us a call."

She headed toward the door, then turned back to face him. "And please, Mr. Hogan, don't leave town. We might need to talk to you again."

46

BEAR MOUNTAIN RIDING TRAILS

The ancient drums of her ancestors beat inside Dr. Laney Whitefeather's head as she mounted Scrappy, her favorite quarter horse, and rode onto the trail. Whenever she was stressed, she saddled up and rode for miles and miles into the hills. The fresh air, the wind whipping her braid around her face, and the scent of pine helped erase the ugliness of her day.

And there was much ugliness there.

The image of that poor woman's bloody body made her stomach turn. Who could do that to someone?

She shivered, the stories of the Trail of Tears haunting her as they always did this time of year when the festival began. She ran her finger around the silver circle dangling from the chain around her neck. The Native Americans believed that the world existed in circles. The sky was round. The wind's powers came in circles as it did tonight with the storm brewing. Birds made nests in circles. The sun was a bright yellow circle and the seasons always circled back. The life of man came from a circular pattern, that when one dies it is not an end but the beginning of a new life.

The cries of her people were stronger tonight than most,

images of the sweat lodges and poverty and children running shoeless and hungry on the rez making her heart ache for their suffering.

Yet her memories were as blurred and as broken as the families who resided there.

As broken and splintered as her own mind was.

Scrappy's hooves sent dirt flying as she climbed the hill, and Laney closed her eyes and listened to the babbling creek and the sound of birds cawing.

Fleeting snippets of being a tiny child floated back as if the wind itself stirred her memories.

The wind gives life, her grandmother said. *When it ceases to blow, we die.*

But do not fear death. It is part of the circle of life.

Her mother's warm hand clutched hers, reminding her she was alive. Her soft voice sang lullabies to her at night, murmuring more wisdom from her ancestors as she kissed her goodnight – *A single twig breaks, but the bundle of twigs is strong.*

But her mother was gone too soon. And when she'd probed her grandmother about the father she'd never known, she'd warned her not to ask.

Scrappy halted at the top of the hill, and Laney breathed in nature. The grass, the trees who her people believed had spirits. The whisper of voices telling her not to be afraid.

She gripped Scrappy's reins, uneasy with her thoughts. Why was she thinking about her past now? About all the questions that had plagued her? The question that haunted her the most – what exactly had happened to her mother?

All she knew was that there were lost years. A time she remembered her and a time she didn't. Going back to the rez and everyone being hush hush.

"She's different," the others had whispered about her when she returned.

"She might have seen the dead."

Laney gasped for air as she crested the hill. In her mind, she saw the Ghost Dance where the dead lived in a village of their own. Some believed that if they came and obeyed the priest and the Messiah, they could be reunited with their loved ones who'd passed.

But the reality of her job had taught her differently. The lost children crying to be released from the grave at Hawk House might be reunited with their families in the afterlife.

But she had to speak for them now.

While Ellie drove back to the police station, Derrick called the security company to verify Hogan's story. True to what he'd said, he'd activated his alarm at eleven and records confirmed that no doors or windows had been opened after that.

Angelica was waiting in reception when they arrived, her cameraman poised for a report.

"Derrick, why don't you look at Kelly's computer while I give a statement?" Ellie said.

"On it." He went straight to Ellie's office as if grateful to avoid the press.

Sheriff Waters strode in, his body rigid, stare honing in on Ellie. At the sight of Angelica, he halted at the door. Odd. Typically, he enjoyed the spotlight.

Angelica smoothed her hair. "Ready to fill in the public?"

"I can't tell you much," Ellie said with a shrug, "but sure, let's do it."

Tom signaled to start rolling and Angelica gave her intro. "We're here with Detective Ellie Reeves who has another murder to solve." She angled the mic toward Ellie. "Detective, what can you tell us about the latest crime in Bluff County?"

Ellie inhaled a calming breath to dislodge the image of little Todd Hogan's wary look from her mind. The poor kid had known something was wrong. "Unfortunately, the body of a young woman named Kelly Hogan was found this morning. Police are ruling her death as a homicide. If you have any information regarding her or her murder, please call the police department or sheriff's office in Bluff County."

"Do you have cause of death?" Angelica pushed.

"Not at this time. But I can tell you she died a violent death. Again, we need your help, folks."

"Any suspects?" Angelica asked.

"Not yet. But as I said, we are just beginning to investigate." She gestured that the interview was over, and Angelica motioned for Tom to shut off the camera.

"*Do* you have any idea who killed her?" the reporter asked.

Ellie shook her head. "This is off the record, Angelica. She was married to an accountant named Mike Hogan. He seemed genuinely upset and claims he was home with his son all night. But he and his wife were having marital problems."

"What kind of problems?" Angelica asked.

"She was having an affair." Ellie made a low sound in her throat. "We're looking for her lover now."

"You said her death was violent?"

"Yeah. She sustained multiple stab wounds, showed signs of rough sex, bruising, and possible bondage. Consent or not is the question. Could have been S&M gone wrong or some pervert who lost control."

"Maybe he wanted her to leave her husband for him?" Angelica suggested.

"That's possible. Although the husband was planning a separation."

"That points to him then," Angelica said.

Ellie nodded although she was not convinced. She needed

to find that lover. If he was guilty, maybe they could tie up this case quickly, and she could get justice for Kelly.

"Dammit, dammit, dammit," he muttered as the news anchor recited the number for the police department.

Anger churning through him, he crushed the charred bones into a pile of black ash and tossed them aside. He had no use for the burned bits, so he'd sorted them out by size, type of bone and animal.

They would fit nicely on his wall, the patterns emerging as he placed them artfully in the shapes of the animals they'd once been a part of. He'd started the collection years ago, had grown it over the years until it was a spectacular display from all species in these mountains.

Why the hell was that bitch ass cop talking about the stupid woman? She was insignificant.

Detective Reeves hadn't even mentioned Hawk House. *That* was the important news, not some tramp's death.

Mixed emotions warred inside him. Part of him wanted the secrets to stay buried just as the bones had. But some deep-seated, enraged part of him wanted justice. Wanted the world to know and to suffer for ignoring the sadistic horrors that occurred in their own backyards.

He just had to make sure no part of it was traced back to him.

49

CROOKED CREEK

Ellie braced herself for Bryce's condescending attitude as he approached. His thick hair looked mussed and windblown, his angular face set in stone.

"That was short," he said. "You didn't release details – was that to hold back from the public or because you don't have them?"

"Both." She filled him in on the crime scene, the manner in which they'd found Kelly Hogan and cause of death.

"You think it's the husband?" Bryce asked.

"Not sure yet," Ellie said. "They had problems – she cheated on him, and the husband was leaving her because of it, but he was home with his son last night. He admitted seeing bruises on Kelly from her lover. Agent Fox is searching her computer now." She softened her tone. "How's Mandy?"

His labored breath was heavy with frustration. "She hates me," he said between clenched teeth.

"I'm sure that's not true, Bryce. She's just frightened and traumatized right now."

Bryce's green eyes flickered with hurt, but he clamped his jaw tight.

"You remember what it was like to be a teenager?" asked Ellie. "Teens are struggling, hormones are running rampant and so are insecurities. Everyone's looking for a way to belong. Teens rebel. It just happens. And it's to be expected after all Mandy's been through."

He pulled a hand down his chin but merely grunted.

"Let's see what Agent Fox has got." She gestured for him to follow, and they found Derrick at his laptop.

"I caught the sheriff up to speed," Ellie said. "Anything on Hogan's computer?"

"His financials check out. His assistant claims he was well liked. Most clients bragged that he saved them a boatload of money when tax time rolled around."

"How about his coworkers?"

"His assistant was unaware of the affair. Said she liked his wife at first, but the last few months Kelly changed, had stopped dropping by, and Mike complained about her not being home with Todd. She sensed they were having marital issues, but Mike never went into detail."

"Was anything going on between the assistant and Mike?"

Derrick chuckled. "Not unless Mike was into grandmothers. She mentioned her six grandkids a few times."

Ellie smiled. "Anything on the affair?"

"Not yet. Her account is password-protected. I called Hogan and he gave me a list of possible passwords. I've tried her maiden name, birthday, childhood pet's name and the anniversary but none worked."

"How about the son's birthday?" Bryce suggested.

Derrick tried it and it worked.

While Derrick started his search and Bryce answered a phone call, Ellie scrolled through Kelly's personal phone, and found messages from the elementary school about activities and events. The tennis team captain asking if she wanted to rejoin for the summer. Another from the head of the PTA.

She wondered if any of the mothers were aware of Kelly's affair. With two cases demanding her attention, she needed to delegate so she phoned Shondra and asked her to question the PTA moms and members of the tennis team.

Women had a way of confiding in one another. Someone had to have known who Kelly was seeing.

50

Derrick cleared his throat just as Bryce returned. He didn't look happy, but Ellie couldn't worry about him right now.

"I don't think this was just a simple affair," Derrick said.

"What do you mean?" Ellie asked.

Derrick thumped his foot. "There are messages to multiple men on her computer."

"So she was cheating all over the place?" Ellie said.

"I think it's more. She seems to have connected to them through a site called Arm Candy."

Ellie leaned over Derrick's shoulder. "Is that some kind of new dating site?"

"Supposedly a modeling site," Derrick answered.

Bryce shifted next to her. "Some of the guys at Haints bar were talking about it. Women post pictures of themselves, like pin-ups. You need a membership to have access."

"Let me guess," Ellie said. "It's not just about modeling."

"Judging from Kelly's correspondence, it's a front for an escort service," Derrick said.

He pulled up the website for Arm Candy, and Ellie read the slogan: *Empower yourself.*

But this side gig had likely been anything but empowering for Kelly in the end.

"We need to know who Kelly connected with," Ellie said.

"Working on that."

Bryce cleared his throat. "I'll set up a fake account. Maybe connect with some of the girls and see if any of them knew Kelly. They might give us insight into her clients."

"That might work," Ellie agreed.

But they had to be fast. If one of Kelly's clients had killed her and it wasn't personal, he could target more girls from the site.

51

While Derrick researched Arm Candy, Ellie contemplated the way the killer had left Kelly and the disturbing pentagram on her ankle. Studying the photograph, she noticed a small raised puckered circle inside the pentagram. What did that mean?

Researching the meaning behind it, it was as she thought – the pentagram was a symbol of witchcraft. The five-pointed star converged into a single upright point which represented spirit above matter. Inverted, it represented matter above spirit, and was associated with gain.

From there, it got more interesting. Other names for the pentagram included the Devil's Star, the Endless Knot, the Goblin's Cross and the Witch's Foot.

Why would the killer mark Kelly with a symbol of witch-craft? And what did the raised marking in the center mean?

Thinking she might be onto something, she searched cases for ones with a similar MO. A female vic, multiple stab wounds, unique markings. A half hour later, she discovered three sex workers had been murdered in the Atlanta area two years before, all bearing a tattoo of the letter S, but the perp had been caught and was serving a life sentence now. The S had marked them as sinners. Another woman had been killed in South Georgia marked with a cross on her chest, but police had arrested the women's husband, a religious zealot who claimed she'd sinned, and he'd confessed.

Ellie stood and stretched, still needing more.

52

The door to Crystal's opened, the windchimes above tinkling as a light breeze blew in, and she looked up to see Jonas Timmons, one of the artisans she'd bought jewelry from. With his shoulder-length hair, long beard, wire-rimmed glasses and fringed suede jacket, he looked like a throwback from the seventies.

"Crystal, I have some new pieces if you're interested," he said, yanking at his baggy jeans as he set a box on the counter.

Crystal tugged her long wavy brown into a messy top knot, her moon-shaped silver earrings reflected in the mirror wall behind the sales counter. "What do you have today?"

A sheepish look flushed his face, and he lifted the lid of the box. "More jewelry and windchimes."

Crystal stared in awe at the assortment – a deer antler necklace, coyote molar teeth earrings and a vial pendant holding a small bone that looked like it had come from a bird.

"How do you get them to look so polished?" Crystal asked.

"I use a fine-toothed saw to cut the ends off the deer bones to expose the marrow, then clean out as much marrow as possible with pipe cleaners. Then I boil the bones in a dilute acid, usually sulfuric acid to get rid of the greasy texture. After that, wash and dry them, then soak in diluted bleach."

"They're stunning," Crystal said. "How did you get into using bones in art?"

His thin shoulders tensed slightly, his jaw clenching. "Grew up hunting," he said tightly.

Odd, but he didn't look like a hunter. Usually she pictured them as big, burly mountain men. He looked more the drifter type.

Next, he carefully unwrapped a set of windchimes from the box. The tinkling of the bone fragments and pieces rang like music.

"It's beautiful. What kind of bones are those?" she asked, noting some were larger than others as he removed a second set.

"Animal bones I found in the woods. Squirrel, raccoon, beavers, birds," he said.

"So you don't kill the animals yourself?"

His hazel eyes darkened, and he shook his head. "Why all the questions?"

Crystal shrugged. "Just curious. Always been that way about nature. Reason I opened the shop, to showcase locals' work along with selling natural remedies."

He tapped the box. "Do you want them or not?" he asked, his tone sharpening.

She seemed to have upset him but didn't understand what she'd said wrong. "Sure. I've already sold most of what you brought before. Same commission on these all right?"

With a clipped nod, he took the envelope holding his payment for the pieces she'd already sold. As he stuck it in his jacket pocket, his shirt sleeve rode up. She barely stifled a gasp at the jagged scars running up and down his arm.

53

HAWK HOUSE

Thirty years ago

The big mean man had scars. On his hands. His arms. A jagged one on his forehead that made one of his cheeks sag lower than the other.

He looked like a monster.

She covered her eyes when he came into the dorm room so she didn't have to look at him. But that only made him madder and he took her to that dark, scary room with the bones on the bed.

"This is your home now," he said in a dark voice. "You have to learn to be tough. To play the game."

A cold sweat covered her body as she curled into the blanket and tried not to move so she wouldn't feel the bone splinters. She didn't want to play a game.

She wanted to go home to her mother.

Squeezing her eyes closed, she tried to picture her mom's face in her mind. But it was blurry.

"Run. Hide," her mother had told her.

She had run and hidden, but he'd caught her anyway.

And now she was here.

At night she heard the other little girls crying. Heard the boys next to them whispering.

Listened to the wind outside and the screams that came to her from the dark.

Hugging her legs to her chest, she pretended her mommy was coming to save her. *"I love you, sugar,"* her mother whispered.

But sometimes now she could barely hear her voice.

Then she remembered the blood, so much blood, and knew her mother was never coming.

54

The moment Ellie entered Crystal's, the tinkling windchimes drew her attention. Three sets hung in various areas of the store, the breeze from the door lifting the fragile pieces and triggering the musical notes.

The smell of lavender and rosemary filled the air, along with incense and a myriad of scented candles.

Crystal, dressed in a floral kaftan with a dozen bangled bracelets on arms, threw up a hand in greeting. Two teenagers were browsing a display of candles and a young woman was checking out the silk scarves.

"Are you looking for something?" Crystal's nose ring glittered beneath the lights.

"Yes, some information." Ellie pulled a close-up shot of a pentagram on her phone and showed it to Crystal. "I'm looking for the meaning of this symbol. I understand the pentagram is a symbol of witchcraft. But look at the center, that raised red puckered circle. Do you know what it means?"

Crystal pursed her lips. "Hmm, let's take a look over here." She led the way to the book section and plucked a book titled *The Salem Witch Trials* from the shelf. Ellie watched, studying the pages as Crystal thumbed through them. "Here it is." Crystal's eyes sparkled. "In the Salem witch trials, witches were marked with symbols to indicate they'd made a dark pact with the devil. The pentagram is sometimes used for protection although some associate it with evil." She pointed to the raised red circle. "This one represents a teat. It was used to mark suspected witches because they believed that witches had a teat from which familiars suckled. The markings were often found on hands, wrists, shoulders, breasts and sometimes genitals."

Ellie sucked in a breath. Why would the killer mark Kelly as a witch?

The door opened again and the windchimes tinkled. Ellie glanced over at them and shivered as she realized they were made of bones.

55

"Where did you get those?" Ellie asked, suddenly cold all over.

"An artist named Jonas Timmons," Crystal said. "He crafts jewelry and art out of bones, crystals, feathers and arrowheads." She gestured for Ellie to follow and led her to a table display. "His work is being featured at the festival."

Ellie's mind raced. "Are those animal bones?" she asked.

"Most of them are," Crystal said.

"Where does he get them?"

"He said he collects them from the woods where larger animals have ravaged smaller ones. He skins what's left himself, then cleans and bleaches them. He described the entire process." She gestured toward a delicate pair of earrings. "He's very detail-oriented."

"I can see that." Ellie scanned the other pieces, recognizing wolves' teeth used in a necklace. "I'd like to talk to him. Do you have his contact information?"

"Sure, but I think he may live outside town. He seems like the reclusive type. Not sure he likes people much."

Had he become a recluse because he was hiding out?

56

HELEN, GEORGIA

Armed with Jonas Timmons's address, Ellie walked back to the police station, the wind gaining momentum and tearing her hair from her ponytail. In light of their case, the idea that Jonas used bones in his art seemed too uncanny to dismiss.

She redid her hair quickly, then filled Derrick in on what she'd learned about the pentagram.

"Any progress here?" Ellie asked.

"Kelly rarely posted on social media, but she had two Instagram accounts. One family- oriented with pics of her son. The other features risqué pictures of her in sexy lingerie. For that account, which was associated with Arm Candy, she used the name Ebony Rain."

Ellie rolled her eyes. "So cliched."

Derrick's phone dinged with a text. "My partner Bennett has info. The woman running Arm Candy is named Willow Rodgers. I have an address."

Ellie grabbed her jacket and keys. "Let's go."

Thirty minutes later, Ellie parked at a Victorian home on a quiet street outside Helen, Georgia, a tourist town set in the midst of the mountains near Anna Ruby Falls. Today, the town was busy with visitors combing the streets, enjoying the crisp spring air, and filtering into the tiny shops. Although weather predicted a Nor'easter blowing in from North Carolina, promising heavy winds and rain, maybe more flooding, for the moment the sky was clear.

The scene was so picturesque that it was hard to believe that a Madam lived in this quaint town. Dogwood trees were starting to blossom, and daisies and tulips peeked through the damp soil with a regal excellence befitting the turrets and angles of the Victorian. A welcome wreath comprised of eucalyptus leaves adorned the butter-yellow door.

"Doesn't look like a business," Derrick said as they walked up the cobblestone drive.

"People hiding in glass houses." Ellie rang the doorbell, scanning the property in case the woman inside saw them and tried to leave.

But a minute later, a slender brown-haired woman, maybe forty, answered the door. Her simple black tunic and leggings gave her the appearance of a yoga instructor, but her angular face was almost austere.

"Ms. Rodgers?" Ellie said.

A faint tightening of the woman's unpainted lips indicated she was disturbed by their presence. "Yes. And you are?"

Ellie flashed her credentials. "We need to ask you some questions." Not bothering to wait on a response, Ellie elbowed her way past the woman, and Derrick entered behind her.

"Would you like some tea?" the woman asked as she led them to a living room boasting antique furniture and a collection of vintage typewriters, all at odds with a woman who ran an escort service.

"Thank you but this is not a social visit," Ellie said. "We're aware that you run a site called Arm Candy. Is that correct?"

Another pinching of her lips. "Yes. The site features models showcasing lingerie and underwear and is only available to members." She crossed her slender arms, a picture of elegant innocence. "Is that the reason you're here? You want to shut me down? Because I can assure you that my company is legit."

"A legitimate cover for prostitution," Derrick bit out.

"I am not running a prostitution ring." She lifted her phone from her pocket. "But if I need to justify that to you, I'll call my attorney."

Ellie reached out and covered the woman's hand. "Before you do that, you may want to hear the reason we've come."

Alarm darkened her expression, and Willow crossed her arms. "All right. You have five minutes."

Ellie bit back a retort. If Willow Rodgers thought she was running the shots, she was dead wrong. "It's about the murder of one of your models," she said bluntly. "A woman named Kelly Hogan."

Willow's brows rose. "Kelly's dead?"

At least she hadn't denied a connection to Kelly. "Do you know her personally?"

"No, but I recall her name." Willow sank onto the velvet sofa and stared at her perfect French tips. Ellie and Derrick seated themselves in wing chairs facing her.

"The business is run remotely from here, all handled online. I never meet the girls or clients in person," Willow continued.

"Do you vet the clients first?" Derrick asked.

She flattened her hands on her legs. "My security team runs background checks, looking for prior arrests, drugs, instances of violence or sex crimes, et cetera. If we find something suspicious, we deny the person membership."

"I assume most of your clients are male," Ellie said.

Willow gave a non-committal shrug. "The majority are although we have a few members of the LGBTQ community."

"How are the girls paid?" Ellie asked.

"Payment is directly deposited into their private secured accounts."

"Once you take your cut," Derrick added.

She nodded.

"And tips?"

Willow crossed her arms. "That's up to the individual clients."

"How about extra services?" Ellie added.

Willow's shoulders tensed. "Arm Candy provides modeling and yes, some escort services. You'd be surprised at what some men would pay to have a pretty lady on his arm for business functions."

"What happens if you receive a complaint?" Ellie asked.

"Our legal team investigates. If allegations are founded, the client is dropped and no longer allowed to use our services."

"But you don't report this to the police," Ellie said with an eyebrow raise.

A heartbeat of silence passed. "If I thought one of the girls was in serious danger or had been assaulted, I would encourage her to go to the police." Willow tapped her nails on her leg. "That is up to them, of course."

"Have you had complaints?" Ellie pushed.

Indecision warred in her eyes. "A couple of minor instances of a client getting too rough. But nothing serious."

Ellie stared at her, long and hard. "Yet one of your models is dead."

"I can assure you that if I knew who hurt Kelly, I would tell you. But I don't."

"I'm going to need a list of her clients." Ellie gestured to the woman's computer.

Willow lifted her chin. "My clients' information is confidential. I can't divulge their names or contact information."

Ellie gritted her teeth. She hated being stonewalled with red tape. She flipped her phone around so Willow could see. "That is how we found Kelly Hogan. She was butchered to death then her body was stuffed into a black garbage bag, and she was thrown off a ravine into the brush to be eaten by coyotes."

The color drained from Willow's face.

"She left a little boy behind without a mother," Ellie said, her voice seething with injustice. "And we strongly believe that one of your clients, a man who paid for Kelly for the night, did this to her. Don't you want to find him?"

"Yes, of course," Willow said. "But if you interrogate my clients, we'll lose business. And some of these young women are doing this work to escape bad situations."

"How much worse can their situation be than hooking?" Ellie asked bluntly.

"You really are naive, Detective," Willow said icily. "Not all of the girls engage in physical relationships. I encourage them to save up money so they can further their education and be independent, not have to rely on a man."

Oh, the irony. "Yet they're doing that by selling their bodies."

"But this way they're in control," she argued.

Ellie tapped the picture in front of Willow again. "Kelly Hogan was not in control last night."

"I'm trying to help them," Willow argued.

"If you want to help find her killer, give us a list of her clients, including the one she was with last night."

Willow rubbed her forehead, obviously torn. "You won't reveal where you got his name?"

"Seriously?" Ellie slapped her hands on the coffee table. "You're still more concerned about your business than you are a woman's life. Hell, I should shut you down."

Willow moved behind her corner desk, clicked a few keys on her laptop, then looked up at them. "You have to be mistaken about her killer being a client. There's nothing on her calendar here about an appointment with anyone last night."

"You're lying," Derrick said.

"No, I'm not." Willow's tone was chilly.

"Who are you covering for?" Ellie asked.

"No one," Willow replied. "If you don't believe me, get a warrant."

"We intend to," Derrick said.

Ellie decided to try another tactic. "What about a regular customer? Maybe one of them became obsessed with her and wanted more than she would give."

"I'm sorry. There's nothing here to indicate that."

Ellie shot holes through the damn woman with her eyes. "This man was sadistic, Ms. Rodgers. He brutally stabbed Kelly dozens of times. Is that someone you want to protect? Because if he did this to Kelly, he may do it again."

The blasted woman stood, arms folded, although she chewed on her lip as if Ellie's statement had gotten to her. "I'm not protecting anyone. Now it's time for you to leave before I speak with my lawyer and file harassment charges against you, Detective."

The woman was all steel, Ellie gave her that. But she refused to back down. "Hide behind your lawyer for now. But if I learn you withheld information and are covering for a cold-blooded murderer, I will be back. And I'll not only shut down your business, I'll arrest you for accessory to homicide."

Derrick cleared his throat. "You'll regret this, Ms. Rodgers. And if I were you, I'd warn your other girls. You can't make money off them if they're dead."

Ellie bit back a smile at his blunt warning. Leaving the woman to stew over what they'd said, they strode to the door and outside.

"She's hiding something," she said as they settled in her Jeep.

"Oh, yeah." Derrick slammed the door. "We'd better get that warrant."

Gray clouds shuddered across the sky, robbing the late afternoon sunlight as Ellie drove toward Ogden's house. Derrick had found his address – the former sheriff lived in a cabin on the river in Quail Ridge, an area known for bird-watching and hunters. Although most quail hunting in Georgia was done at a reserve, wild quail thrived in some parts of the mountains and hunters were notorious for tracking them.

The pines and red maples quivered in the wind from the impending rainstorm as Ellie wound around the switchbacks. The land was mostly untamed, a few cabins interspersed amongst the secluded land, offering privacy.

Derrick glanced at his phone as it buzzed, and Ellie noticed the name Lindsey on the screen. He silenced the call without answering, triggering her curiosity.

"Don't you need to get that?"

He shook his head. "Let's focus on work."

His clipped reply told her not to push. "That's all I can think about," she said. "Last night I had nightmares about being trapped in that pit with dead bodies."

Derrick gave her an understanding look. "Sorry, Ellie. I

know you went through hell as a kid. And on the last few cases. Have you considered giving it up?"

She squared her shoulders. "No. And don't you dare start acting like Vera."

"What? Is she trying to convince you to change career paths?"

"She's always wanted that. She ordered me to stop consulting my dad about my cases. She's tired of seeing him injured or in danger."

"She cares about him," he said, surprising her with his understanding.

Ellie stared at him for a second, wishing he'd say more. That he'd tell her what was going on in his mind and who Lindsey was. But he remained silent.

The tires ground over gravel, and her brakes squealed as she rounded a curve and spun onto a narrow road leading to Ogden's. She climbed higher and higher, the wind picking up and banging at the Jeep as the clouds darkened and rumbled. Conditions were ripe for storms and tornado season was on them.

By the time she reached the top of the ridge, her hands ached from clenching the steering wheel. The rustic cabin looked at least forty years old. A propane tank used to heat the home sat beside the wood structure, and smoke drifted from the chimney rising into the heavens.

A black pick-up truck was parked by an old shed with a metal roof, and she saw a beefy white-haired man in jeans and a flannel shirt lumbering up the hill. His face looked ruddy, his hands dirty, his clothes spotted with mud.

After parking, she and Derrick got out and walked toward him. He tugged a fishing hat over his eyes as he looked up at her, then tossed the shovel in his hands toward the shed and wiped his hands on a handkerchief. On a pole in his other hand, he held a string of dead quail.

"Sheriff Ogden," Ellie said, her voice catching in the wind. "I've been trying to reach you. Why haven't you returned my calls?"

He propped the line of quail against the shed. "No cell service. Been out on the boat but fish weren't biting so decided to get some bird for dinner."

"Nice property," Derrick said.

Ogden's brows pinched together. "I like it."

Derrick walked down to the river edge, eyeing up the shed before stopping and looking out over the water.

Ellie raked her gaze over Ogden. Judging from the dirt on his hands and clothes, he might have been doing more than hunting.

59

Edgar Ogden had known Ellie Reeves would show up sometime. Randall always said she was stubborn as a mule and her nose-to-the-grindstone work ethic proved it.

He hadn't bragged on her intellect though, but Ogden saw smarts in her eyes. She knew how to read people. That was an asset for her.

And a threat to him.

Worse, she had a damn fed with her. He didn't like the way the man had looked at him – or his shed. He'd better not go poking around.

He'd lived alone for so long now in the peace and quiet up here, away from town and the old biddies who stuck their noses in everyone's business. He hated anyone encroaching on his territory. Once he'd retired, the casseroles had started showing up, then the pies. He rubbed his stomach at the memory. He'd gained twenty-five pounds the first two months. Then that Maude Hazelnut had started drilling him about the rumors over Hawk House and he'd known he'd had to cut bait and run. Otherwise, he'd slip up and hang himself. So he'd become a recluse, his only friends the Shadow people who lived on the trail, others like him who'd sought solace in the isolation.

"Mr. Ogden," Ellie said. "I assume you saw the news about Hawk House."

Logic worked through his mind. Lie and pretend he hadn't seen it? No, he wasn't stupid. "Yeah, I saw that story. Kids shouldn't have been up there trespassing. Probably shook 'em up, stumbling on something like that."

"Yes, it did," Ellie said. "It shook the entire town up. I understand you talked to the people at the orphanage when it was open and when it shut down. What can you tell me?"

Ogden stuck a toothpick in the corner of his mouth and chewed on it. "Just that the headmaster up and quit one day. Reckon he got tired of taking care of a bunch of delinquents and decided to wash his hands of the whole lot."

"What makes you think that?" Ellie asked.

"Didn't take much to figure it out. Kids and the teacher said he was gone when they got up that morning. Took his clothes and everything with him. Teacher called the social worker and she went out and took over."

"Why did they think he was wasn't coming back?"

"Teacher said he'd been talking about leaving for days."

"There were allegations of abuse by Blackstone," Ellie said. "Did you investigate?"

This was the tricky part. "I did," he said. "But none of the kids confirmed anything bad happening. Said he was tough, was teaching them to be men."

"Did you see the children's bunk rooms?" Ellie asked.

He heaved a breath, forcing himself not to wipe at the sweat beading on his neck. "Didn't see no reason to. The teacher Ms. Henrietta supported what the kids said and so did the cook."

"The cook?"

"Yeah, can't remember her name," he mumbled. "Neither one of them mentioned abuse. Hearsay didn't give me enough for a warrant. I warned Blackstone that if I heard anything else, I'd be back. Maybe that's why he left."

An odd look flashed in Ellie's eyes, then he saw the questions teeming there.

"Didn't that seem suspicious to you?" Ellie asked.

He shrugged. "Hell, I figured if he was gone, wasn't nothing to worry about. Kids got sent to other homes, staff all left and no one wanted to reopen the place."

"If the kids were sent away and Blackstone was gone, how do you account for those bodies we just found?"

Ogden shifted the toothpick with his teeth. "That place has sat abandoned for nearly thirty years. You know how criminals like to hide out in these parts. Maybe some other predator used it as a dumping ground?"

60

Ogden had obviously dismissed the allegations against Blackstone without thoroughly investigating.

And he seemed too quick to point her in another direction.

"Mr. Ogden, you said the teacher left when Blackstone did," Ellie said. "Do you know where she went?"

He wiped dirt from his hands on his dusty jeans, jeans that hung low below his pot belly, and looked over at Derrick who was walking up and down the riverbank as if he was searching for something. "No, figured she got another teaching job somewhere else or retired. She wasn't exactly a spring chicken."

"What was Henrietta's last name?" Ellie asked.

The man scratched his hair with a beefy hand, a hand scarred with knife wounds. From hunting or from an altercation of some kind?

"Think it was Stuckey."

Ellie made a mental note to track her down. "What about the cook?"

"Like I said, don't remember her name. No idea where she got off to."

Derrick looked lost in thought as he joined them.

"What about files from your investigation?" she asked. "I need a list of everyone who worked at the orphanage, the children who were placed there and the social workers who handled their placements," Ellie said.

"Would be in those files I left in the storage unit where we moved them when the police station was being redone. Reckon they're still there."

Ellie ground her teeth. "I'm afraid not. My father went to that storage unit to look for them. He was assaulted and the files taken."

Ogden threw his shoulders back. "Hell. Is Randall all right?"

"He has a concussion and several stitches, but he'll be fine," Ellie said.

Ogden hitched up his britches. "By God. Did he see who assaulted him?"

"No. But obviously someone didn't want whatever was in those files to fall into the hands of the police."

"How would anyone know Randall went to get them?" Ogden asked.

"They might not have," Ellie said. "With the airing of the news, they could have become nervous, gone to retrieve the files and found my dad at the storage units. They attacked him, stole the files and got away."

Derrick cleared his throat. "What you got in that shed?" he asked Ogden.

Ogden jerked his head toward Derrick. "Just some tools, fishing gear, canoe."

Derrick pointed toward the river and the hills climbing in the horizon. "How much of this property is yours?"

"Ten acres," he said. "Borders the trail which you know is a National Scenic Trail." He turned back to Ellie. "Shame 'bout your daddy. Reckon I'll stop by and see him."

Ellie shook her head. "No. My mother doesn't want him disturbed."

Ogden's gaze settled on her face then he coughed. "Whatever you say. This pollen's getting to me, bad allergies." He indicated his string of quail. "Now I need to get to these. Wish I could have been more help."

Grunting his irritation, he lumbered toward a worktable near the shed where tools hung on a pegboard. Ellie recognized fish skinning tools along with fillet knives and other tools for dressing animals.

Derrick nudged her toward the Jeep, his expression troubled.

"He's hiding something," he said quietly. "Maybe that's why he lives out here."

"A lot of mountain people or retirees live off the grid or have acreage," Ellie said.

Derrick quirked a brow. "Then you believe him?"

Ellie released a tired breath. "Not for a minute. He was too quick to dismiss the allegations against Blackstone and shut down the investigation. And he tried to steer me into thinking that those bones were put there after Blackstone left." Her keys jangled in her hand. "Maybe Laney and Dr. Chi can tell us if that's true."

61

CROOKED CREEK

Dammit to hell and back. That detective wouldn't give up.

And now the new life he'd built might crumble around him.

He had to do something. Protect the past. Make sure his secrets stayed buried. Had someone decided to talk?

Who the hell would do that? They'd made a pact and so far, everyone had kept silent. Had been too afraid to tell.

Worry pinched at his gut, and he popped an antacid, then paced to the cabinet in his study.

He'd worked too hard to establish himself. To overcome those years at the prison, as he'd called the orphanage.

No one could take it away from him now.

A chuckle caught in his throat as he picked up the tiny black book where he'd stored information on all those who'd once known him. Those who threatened his present life with their knowledge. Those who would no longer be a threat.

62

Derrick's conversation with Lindsey echoed in his head as Ellie drove them back to Crooked Creek. Needing privacy, he'd taken the call down by the river while she'd questioned Ogden.

Dammit, his past was threatening to destroy his sanity.

Ellie seemed curious about the interruptions, but he wasn't ready to tell her about Lindsey. Not yet. But she was part of his life now, and he would have to.

"When are you coming back?" Lindsey asked, her voice wavering.

"I don't know. As soon as possible," Derrick said.

"I need you now more than ever," Lindsey choked out. "Please, Derrick. You can't abandon us."

He pinched the bridge of his nose. Was that what he was doing by burying himself in another case? By running back to Ellie every chance he got? By renting a place in Crooked Creek and leaving Atlanta and his family and those who needed him behind to fend for themselves?

Lindsey's soft crying taunted him. "I'm sorry, Lindsey. As soon as I tie up this investigation, I'll be there."

"I'm going to hold you to that, Derrick."

"I promise." Although they both knew he'd failed her before. His heart hammered and he silently made a vow to himself.

He could not fail her again.

63

FIERY GROVE

Seventy-eight-year-old Yolanda Schmidt punched the off button on the television with her cane and cursed, vile words that she'd relegated only to the likes of the evil men she'd encountered in her life.

The day she'd left Hawk House was the best day of her whole sorry life.

She'd finally been free. Free of debt. Free to leave. Free to forget the horrid things she'd seen and done.

Only she'd never forgotten. Those days had tormented her for thirty years. There were just some ugly things you couldn't unsee. Some that went so deep they stole your soul.

Now she'd been tied to them and the lies so long that she'd wondered if she'd get past the pearly gates when she passed. And that would be soon.

She was ready. As ready as an old woman could get.

The arthritis made her fingers stiff and her knees crack as she hobbled out onto the front porch and stared at the row of Wildfire Black Gum trees on the hill, named for the dark fiery red of the flowers that burst to life. Already the deep ruby-red color was popping through the greenery, red that reminded

Yolanda of blood. So much blood that had been shed that sometimes she woke thinking she was drowning in a river of it.

She shivered.

The reporter's words about the bones at Hawk House echoed in her head. That Detective Ellie Reeves was the kind of tough woman Yolanda wanted to be.

She ran her fingers over the heart-shaped locket she always wore, then opened it and soaked in her daughter's face.

"I'm sorry, baby," she whispered. "All I ever wanted was to give you a good life."

But her daughter's life had not been good. And neither had Yolanda's.

A stiff wind gust slammed across the yard, shaking trees and tearing the Magnolia blossoms from the trees. *It's okay, Mama.*

Yolanda heard her daughter's sweet voice floating to her and knew her precious child was in heaven. At peace now.

But there would be no peace for Yolanda. And now she might not even see her girl in the afterlife.

God gave forgiveness. He also had his wrath. She deserved the wrath.

Ogden's comments weighed heavily on Ellie as she returned to the police station. Why would the damn sheriff cover up a crime?

Derrick answered another phone call, and she went to the conference room then studied the whiteboard. Two different cases. She couldn't make sense of either.

But Kelly Hogan's murder was more recent so she pulled up her laptop and decided to investigate the woman more thoroughly.

Rolling her shoulders to alleviate the fatigue from the long day, she scoured her social media again.

The one account Derrick had mentioned where she posted about her family, showed Kelly had stopped posting about two months ago. Curious, she looked back through her emails and found one to an attorney named Gilbert Lawrence.

I need your services.

Curious, Ellie clicked on the website address and was surprised to see he didn't handle divorces. He was a criminal defense attorney.

Knowing the lawyer would cite attorney-client privilege,

she ran a search for police reports and waited.

Shondra poked her head into the room. "I talked to the PTA moms and the tennis team members. They all claimed they didn't know Kelly was having an affair. Just that she'd grown apart from the group and had started dressing provocatively."

That wasn't a crime, Ellie wanted to say in the woman's defense.

But she and Shondra had had this discussion multiple times, about how prosecutors crucified victims of sexual crimes and painted them as the guilty parties, so she didn't need to preach her opinion.

"Thanks, Shondra."

Shondra nodded, then left the room just as Derrick returned, scratching his head.

"Mike Hogan's comment about Kelly's arrest got me thinking so I looked into it. She was picked up for solicitation."

He showed Ellie the police report and she skimmed it.

"She was arraigned in Judge Alexander Karmel's courtroom but released. No fine or jail time."

"Most states don't even arrest for prostitution anymore," Derrick said. "Could be the reason."

"All the more reason we find out who she was with the night she died."

"I'll take a look at her computer again," Derrick said. "See if I can find her calendar."

Ellie turned back to her computer and decided to take a deeper dive into the judge who'd let Kelly off. The background search revealed that he attended law school at the University of Georgia, then worked as a court-appointed attorney for three years before moving to a law office specializing in criminal defense.

She accessed the firm's website and learned Judge Karmel

had made a reputation defending misdemeanor crimes then after fifteen years ran for a position on the bench.

Next, she looked at records of his court dockets and realized he dealt mostly with drug cases and charges related to sex workers and sex trafficking. According to what she found, he had a tendency for being lenient.

Not one charge of solicitation had stuck.

Interesting. Maybe Derrick was right. Perhaps he didn't see the benefit of enforcing an antiquated law.

Just out of curiosity, she checked to see if any of the women charged had come through Karmel's court more than once and found one woman who had, a girl named Lynn Swinson.

"Derrick, see if you can find out if a woman named Lynn Swinson worked with Arm Candy."

"On it."

She looked up the woman's phone number then called it but received a message that it was no longer in service. Next, she tried the number for the hair salon where Lynn worked.

A friendly voice answered, "Daisy's Do's," the woman said. "How can I help you?"

"I'd like to speak to Lynn Swinson," Ellie said. "Is she working today?"

A strained beat passed. "Sorry, hon. But Lynn left town six months ago."

Ellie's pulse jumped. "What happened?"

"Don't know but I had a feeling it went sideways with some guy she was seeing. She just called in sick and said she had to get out of town. I stopped by to check on her, but all her things were gone."

Suspicions mounted in Ellie's mind. There could be a hundred reasons Lynn had left town, none of which had to do with her case.

Unless the man Lynn had been running from was the same man who'd killed Kelly...

65

FIERY GROVE

The wind cascaded from the mountains, blowing strands of Yolanda's brittle gray hair around her wrinkled cheek, and she brushed it back with a gnarled hand. The strong gusts were ripping plants from the ground and yanking at the trees by the roots as if Satan was rising from the bowels of hell to spread his wrath. Or maybe God had finally answered and sent a storm to loosen the soil and expose the bones.

Maybe it was time she broke her silence. The truth could set you free, they said.

Or it could land you behind bars. Or end up killing you.

Didn't matter now.

She rubbed a freckled hand over her plump belly then spread her fingers and stared at her hands. Hands spotted with age and hard work. Hands that had cooked many a meal for the children at that place. Hands that bore the scars from the biscuits she'd burned and the few times she'd tried to intervene between Blackstone and the children.

His threats and punishments had been harsh and she'd relented. Still, she'd tried to find some pleasure in feeding the children.

Oh, dear lord, how Yolanda liked to cook. And eat. Her plump frame was a testament to that. She'd taken solace in giving those little ones a decent meal, at least with what she'd had in that paltry pantry.

She'd never understand the skin and bones mentality of some of the young girls these days, thinking their protruding ribs and concave bellies made them attractive. Some of them looked like sick chickens who didn't have the good sense God gave them to scratch for grain in their own yard.

Lord, those little girls at Hawk House had been thin and frail and had been terrified of that monster. And then Blackstone's boys – his cruelty to them had known no bounds.

The images of them digging for bones taunted her. Every time she saw one of the poultry trucks go by on the country road, their cages rattling and birds squawking as if the scrawny animals knew their fate and were giving one last screeching cry for mercy, she saw the children fighting for their lives.

She hadn't protected them back then. And she hated herself for it.

She reached for the phone her nursemaid had left her, one with the big numbers that she could see with her old eyes. The cataracts had near made her blind.

Maybe it was time she did what was right.

66

CROOKED CREEK

Jonas Timmon's unusual artwork intrigued Ellie. His penchant for using bones was so odd that she decided to find out more about him so she checked DMV records for an address. As Crystal had mentioned, he lived off the grid, but she knew Cord could help her find his place.

First though she wanted to learn all she could about him.

She searched for a rap sheet but found no record he'd ever been arrested. His birth certificate indicated he was thirty-eight years old, born to a couple named Marlena and Don Timmons. Mother passed away in childbirth and father raised him somewhere in the mountains.

From there, information was practically non-existent. She found no record of him attending high school or college or ever being married. She found no deed for his property.

All she had to inspect was a website showcasing his art and offering online sales.

She studied the various pieces and names for his art which were categorized according to type of animal bone used, and knew she had to talk to him in person.

His address was not too far from Hawk House. He could have confiscated bones from anywhere in the woods – or from the orphanage.

67

FIERY GROVE

A rustling suddenly sounded from the side of the yard near the jack-in-the-pulpits and in the moonlight, Yolanda saw the bloodroot flowering. Heard breathing panting. Footsteps smashing foliage.

Her heart stuttered once, twice, then the silhouette of a man emerged from the shadows, the silver glint of a knife blade shimmering in the dark. His bulky body was blurry, his face distorted by the lack of light and her practically useless eyes.

She'd thought Blackstone might be dead by now. But what if he hadn't just run off? What if he'd seen the news and come to shut her up for good?

She turned and hobbled inside, praying she could hide until the police could come, but her knees ached and she was trembling so hard her vertigo kicked in, and she had to grab the wall to stay on her feet. She heard the door slam as an intruder entered, heard his footsteps steady and strong as he stalked after her.

She barely made it to the living room when she felt his breath on her neck. She turned and gasped at who it was. She hadn't seen him in years and he'd changed, but she knew that face.

She raised her cane to fight, but he swung the knife at her, and the blade slashed the wood in two. A sliver flew back and hit her cheek then he growled like one a mad dog. Instinctively, the will to survive kicked in, the determination to tell the world the truth so strong that she threw up her hands and feet to fight, but the force of the man jumping her made her bones snap and then she felt the knife plunge into her mouth. She gurgled up blood and knew she was going to drown in a river of it, just like in her nightmares...

68

CROOKED CREEK

Mandy pulled her knees up to her chest. Wrapping her arms around them, she stared at the door.

Walker was on the other side. "Mandy, please let me in. I'm worried about you."

She choked back more tears. She hadn't been able to stop crying since she'd woken up screaming with the nightmares again. "I'm tired," she said, and she really was. She had no energy to get up, to eat, to shower.

She just wanted to shrivel up and disappear so *he* couldn't find her. He being the monster in her dreams. The one who killed those children.

"I just want to hang out," Walker said. "We don't have to talk. Or maybe we could take a walk."

"I don't feel like it. Just go away, Walker."

"You can't stay locked in there forever," Walker said with a huff. "Let's grab a burger. Or I'll go get one and bring it here and we can eat on your deck."

Mandy buried her head against her knees. Part of her wanted to come out. To see Walker. To forget that there were monsters out there.

But she glanced in the mirror and saw her reflection and shuddered. She looked gaunt and hollow eyed. Cheeks splotched from crying. Eyes bloodshot from lack of sleep. Hair tangled and ratty. Her pajamas smelled like sweat. Her voice was hoarse from sobbing into her pillow.

She swallowed hard so she wouldn't sound as pathetic as she felt. "Not tonight, Walker. Just go away."

Silence stretched awkward and painful. She heard him sigh again, then his hand pushed at the door, but it was locked. Finally, he grunted. "All right, I'll go. But you can't shut out everyone forever. We were there, too. We should stick together."

Mandy bit her lip to keep from screaming that they couldn't understand. She'd lost her mother. Was drowning in grief and the nightmares.

Seconds later, she heard footsteps and Walker was gone.

69

FIERY GROVE

Ellie had planned to track down Jonas Timmons and talk to the judge who'd seen Kelly in court, but it was getting late and she might call it a night.

Then her boss called.

"Got a call, Detective. A murder at a place called Fiery Grove. Get up there to the scene now. Will text you the address."

"Copy that," Ellie said. "Who's the victim?"

"Older retired woman named Yolanda Schmidt. Her nurse called it in. Caller said it's pretty bloody."

Ellie's stomach knotted. "On my way." She hung up and went to tell Derrick. Dammit. Three months of peaceful quiet and routine calls and now bodies turning up everywhere. It was as if the Grim Reaper had unleased its anger on the mountains.

A few minutes later, she and Derrick were on their way. Night had set in, the sun long gone, the moon struggling to shine through rain clouds. As she turned onto the curved dirt road leading to the address for Yolanda Schmidt, she spotted the Wildfire black gum trees lining the drive and dotting the property. With so many trees clustered together, they resembled a forest on fire.

Derrick was trying to hack into records for Hawk House as she drove, but so far had no luck.

She parked behind an older beige sedan, the only vehicle there other than the ambulance, and she and Derrick got out and walked up the pebbled drive to the front door. The house was a small ranch with clapboard siding that desperately needed paint and shutters dangling sideways, loosened from a winter storm. The grass was patchy, weeds choking what might have been a flowerbed flanking the three steps to the shabby front porch.

The front door stood ajar, and she spotted two medics, one guarding the front door. Another knelt beside a middle-aged woman perched on the edge of a rocking chair on the porch. Her head was bent, body shaking, soft sobs drifting toward Ellie as the medic consoled her.

Ellie and Derrick identified themselves. "She's in the living room," the man at the door said in a deep voice. "Home health care nurse called it in."

"She was ill?" Ellie asked.

"According to the nurse she was seventy-eight, had an autoimmune disease but nothing terminal. Name's Yolanda Schmidt. Nurse stopped in every couple of days to check on her and bring her supplies."

"What happened?"

"DOA, body was cold. I checked for a pulse, but she was gone so called you. Didn't touch anything."

"Cause of death?" Ellie asked.

He pressed a hand over his stomach as if battling nausea. "Not my job to say, but it's a bloodbath. Looks violent."

"Crime team's on the way," Ellie said.

Just then, a car engine rumbled, as Dr. Whitefeather drove up and parked. Grabbing her kit, Laney tossed her braid over one shoulder and looked up at Ellie with a questioning expression.

"Medical examiner's here," Ellie told the medic. "We'll go in together."

Derrick indicated the pale-faced woman in the rocker. "I'll talk to the caregiver."

Ellie nodded, leaving Derrick to speak to the distraught woman.

"What do we have?" Laney asked as she joined Ellie.

"Older woman, DOA. I haven't been in yet."

Laney breathed out. "Let's take a look then."

A dank heaviness filled the air as they walked through the small foyer. Ellie saw a tiny kitchen to the left and the living room adjoining it. The scent of death, body wastes and blood suffused her, blending with the smell of dust and sour milk.

She paused at the doorway, where she and Laney slipped on foot covers and gloves before moving forward. The older woman lay face down on the soiled carpet, blood soaking the rug and her house dress, hands and arms outstretched. A broken cane lay on the floor, drops of blood caught in the shards of wood.

Kneeling beside the woman, Ellie and Laney examined the scene more closely. Definitely a lot of blood, but no visible wounds in her back. Ellie gently rolled the victim to the side, then gasped at the blood drying on the woman's face, her mouth, chin. Blood that had trailed down her chest and soaked her flowered house dress.

Laney turned gray, and for a moment swayed.

"God," Ellie murmured. "He cut out her tongue."

Laney's breathing turned to a pant, and she suddenly stood, hurrying to the door. A minute later Ellie heard the screen shut as she rushed outside.

70

Laney gasped for a breath as she stumbled onto the porch. On some level, she knew others were around, but her vision was so blurred, she gripped the stair rail and blindly staggered toward her van.

What was wrong with her? At medical school, her instructors had raved that she was the coolest med student in pathology classes, that the gruesome bodies didn't get to her. That had paved the way for her career.

But not tonight.

Black spots danced behind her eyes, the wind rolling off the mountain sending an iciness through her already chilled body. Images assaulted her, of that poor old woman, her mouth and lips and chin bloody, her tongue...

The saying her grandmother and the Cherokees used often rolled through her head. "Pay attention to the whispers, so we won't have to listen to the screams."

When she'd looked at this woman, the screams had filled her head. Like her ancestors, she knew death was part of life. But seeing it ended by violence shouldn't be.

Sweat trickled down her back, and she forced her feet to

move forward and open the van door. Reaching inside the glove compartment, she dug out her anti-anxiety medication. She hadn't had a panic attack since the Native American festival last year.

Hand shaking, she grabbed her water bottle and washed down two pills. Trembling, she leaned against the side of her work van, closed her eyes and inhaled deep breaths. She quietly hummed some of the chants that consoled her when she was troubled.

But a coldness swept through her, and the chants failed, the whispers turning into screams in her head as if ghosts were stampeding around her now.

71

Ellie had never seen Laney thrown so off-kilter by a crime scene, and they had uncovered some disturbing murders together. Of course, this scene was gruesome. And like everyone else, Laney was only human.

While she waited on Laney to return, Ellie captured photographs of the body and surroundings. The close-up of Yolanda's bloody mouth nearly made her gag. She had to turn away a moment herself and take long breaths to steady herself.

The heart-shaped locket around the woman's neck was stained with blood. Her heart squeezed at the photograph of a young woman in a wheelchair inside it. Who was the girl? Was she still alive?

Laney returned, although the ME's olive skin still looked deathly white.

"You okay?" Ellie asked.

"Yeah," Laney said. "Had to get my inhaler. Allergy season always triggers my asthma to flare up."

Ellie nodded. Ogden had also mentioned his allergies were bothering him. "He cut out her tongue," Ellie said. "Someone is sending a message. Someone who wanted to silence her."

Laney's breathing sounded choppy as she pulled on her glasses. She moved the body slightly checking for other injuries. "Clothes are intact so hopefully no sexual assault involved."

"Surely not at her age," Ellie murmured.

Laney's dark eyes flickered with disgust. "You'd be surprised at what some will do."

Ellie's gaze fell on a photograph of a teenager on the mantle. The same one she'd seen in the locket.

Another picture showed the victim with the girl, and she spotted the resemblance in the slant of their noses and the eyes. They had to be mother and daughter.

While Laney recorded her observations into her microphone, Ellie noted the blood spatter on the floor and walls.

"Any idea time of death?" Ellie asked Laney.

"I'd estimate a few hours ago. Body is not in full rigor mortis yet."

Ellie mentally catalogued the contents of the living room. An old oak coffee table, a plaid threadbare sofa, an armchair in a floral print that was now streaked with crimson red from blood spatter, an empty tea cup beside the chair along with a pair of reading glasses, and a prescription bottle of Naproxen. The lamp was overturned, drawers in the desk rifled through, as were the kitchen cabinet drawers. What was the intruder looking for?

She crossed the room to the desk in the corner and rummaged inside but found nothing but bills, papers and junk mail. Bank statements revealed that Yolanda had deposited social security checks, and that she had less than five thousand dollars in her account. Judging from her furnishings, she didn't have much of value.

In the bedroom, at first sight the room appeared neat. There was a chenille bedspread on a primitive metal bed and dresser drawers held only clothing items, although again she sensed they'd been searched.

If the woman had valuable jewelry, bonds or cash hidden beneath the mattress, it was gone. Yet the sheer violence of the killing suggested this was a crime of passion – or rage – and robbery was not the motive.

So what had this seventy-eight-year-old woman known or done that had gotten her killed?

72

HAWK HOUSE

Thirty years ago

She pressed her hand to her mouth to stifle a scream as he led her through the corridor to the basement door. She dug her feet in. Didn't want to go down there. She'd heard the other girls whispering about the horrors.

The floorboards squeaked as he opened the door and dragged her into the darkness. The air was cold. Something smelled rotten. She heard a low whine from somewhere.

She was so scared her knees were shaking. A banging sound echoed from a room to the right.

She looked down and saw fingers reaching below the closed door. The whine was coming from inside.

Someone was in there.

"Help," a voice cried. "Let me out of here." The monster pulled her arm and pain ripped through her. She stumbled but he held her tight and ignored the crying child inside that room.

Who was the boy? Was this place another punishment like the bone room?

Was he going to lock her down here and leave her in the dark?

73

FIERY GROVE

Derrick did his best to console the caregiver before beginning the interview. Judging from the brief glimpse he'd seen of the blood in Yolanda's living room, he could easily understand why she was in shock. Even a seasoned cop might not be able to handle it. The medical examiner herself dealt with death on a daily basis and had run out looking faint.

And this woman knew Yolanda personally.

"My name is Agent Derrick Fox," he said gently. "I know you're in shock, but it's important I ask a few questions so we can find who did this to Yolanda. Is that okay?"

She dabbed at her eyes with a tissue and sniffed. "I can't believe someone killed her. She was a kind old woman, church-going, at least when she was able to get out, never bothered a soul."

Derrick clenched his jaw. "What's your name, ma'am?"

"Shirley Ford," the woman answered.

"Were you friends with Yolanda?"

Shirley twisted her hands together. "Yes, we met at church about six years ago. Lately her rheumatoid arthritis got the best of her and after she lost her daughter, Hilary, she seemed to just quit on herself."

"What happened to her daughter?" Derrick asked.

"MS," Shirley said. "Medical bills ate all Yolanda's money, but she did everything she could to give that girl as normal a life as she could."

"Did Yolanda have other family?" Derrick asked. "Someone we should contact?" Or question.

"No, no one," Shirley said in a whisper.

"How about close friends or someone who visited?"

"Not really. A couple of the ladies from the seniors group brought meals a few times a month," Shirley said, tearing up again. "But Yolanda stopped wanting to socialize when her daughter died. She tolerated me stopping by to check on her cause I brought her medication."

"You're doing great, Shirley," Derrick said softly. "Did Yolanda mention having trouble with anyone?"

Shirley worried her bottom lip with her teeth. "No one that I can think of. For heaven's sakes, she stayed here by herself all the time. No one ever comes out here."

"How about a handyman or someone who did yard work?"

"My son, Frankie, mowed the yard for her. But he moved away before Christmas. I told Yolanda I'd find someone from church to take over this summer."

"How about valuables?"

Shirley gave a nervous laugh. "Heavens, no. Material things meant nothing to Yolanda."

"When did you last see or talk to her?"

Shirley pursed her lips in thought. "Yesterday," she said. "I stopped by around lunch. Told her about those bones being found up at that orphanage."

"You talked about that?" Derrick's pulse hammered.

The woman nodded. "It seemed to upset Yolanda though. I asked her why, and she said she lived around here when that orphanage was open. Then she clammed up, so I changed the subject real fast. She said she needed some groceries. Told her I'd bring some back the next day." A sob caught in her throat. "But when I got here..." Her voice cracked. "The door was wide open, and I... I called her name. When she didn't answer I went inside and then... Oh, lordy, I found her on the f... floor." She dropped her head into her hands and sobbed.

74

Ellie's mind raced. Kelly's fingertips had been cut off. And Yolanda's tongue. The cases couldn't be related, could they?

"The nurse mentioned Yolanda was upset about the Hawk House story," Derrick said, as she entered the house. "Maybe she knew something."

Ellie's heart stuttered, and she reached for her phone and texted Deputy Landrum.

Find out all you can on Yolanda Schmidt. Look for a connection to Hawk House.

He responded:

Copy that.

Laney stared at them, her face gaunt. "He cut out her tongue while she was still alive," she said with a shudder.

"Poor woman," Ellie said. Although the fact that Yolanda had been upset about Hawk House made her wonder...

"Laney, are you making progress on identifying the bones?"

"Nothing conclusive, but we managed to find enough remains that hadn't completely fossilized and analyzed them. We believe they belong to three males and one female, all between the ages of nine and eleven. Still have to analyze the remains from the second pit."

"What kind of monster are we dealing with?" She didn't expect an answer and Laney didn't offer one.

"I think I'll head out." Laney tucked her glasses in her pocket.

Ellie rubbed her arms to ward off the chill. "Before you go, do you have any idea how long the remains were in the pits?"

"That's hard to pin down. Exposure to weather, especially heat, can speed up decomp and then there's the problem with animals ravaging the bones. But the underground temperature in the mountains and the fact they were covered helped preserve enough for us to work with."

"I just need an educated guess," Ellie said. "What was cause of death?"

"Not certain. But judging from our analysis, I'd say the children were starved and dehydrated." Laney wiped a hand over her face as if to clear her head. She really did look ill, and her voice cracked as she spoke, "The forensic team also recovered numerous bones from animals and a couple of human bones on the property. We're working as fast as we can to sort them out."

Ellie ticked over the possibilities. "Request medical and dental records for the teacher who worked there, Henrietta Stuckey. And for Blackstone and the janitor." Although she hadn't found any death certification for Blackstone – so she couldn't rule out that he might still be alive.

75

ROSE HILL

After she and Derrick left the crime scene, they picked up a quick pulled pork sandwich from Soulfood Barbecue, then drove to Ms. Eula's house. The older woman had been around these parts longer than anyone Ellie knew in town.

Storm clouds gathered above the mountain as she parked, the wind shaking the tree branches, yet the blood red of the roses in Ms. Eula's garden looked an even deeper crimson tonight, flourishing with the spring showers and sunshine.

Ms. Eula sat in her porch rocker, the wood slats creaking.

"I figured you'd be coming, Ellie girl. Come sit a spell and let's talk. Can I get y'all some sweet tea?"

"I'm good but thanks," Ellie said.

Derrick rubbed his stomach. "Thank you, ma'am. But I just filled up on Soulfood Barbecue."

"Oh, my how I love that place," Eula said. "They make the best collards this side of the mountain."

Derrick murmured agreement, and he and Ellie settled in the porch swing.

Ms. Eula clucked her teeth. "I suppose you came to talk about those bones you found."

Ellie nodded. "Yes, we believe several of the remains belong to children."

"What they say about that place is true then. I always suspected so." Eula gazed out over the mountain, her face pinched.

Ellie filled her in on her conversation with Ogden and the missing files. "I hoped you might remember something helpful, Ms. Eula," Ellie said. "Did you know Blackstone?"

Ms. Eula fidgeted with the worry beads around her neck. "I only saw him a few times in town. He looked austere, unapproachable."

"Did you know anyone else affiliated with the orphanage?"

The rocking creaked as she pushed back and forth. "The cook. Yolanda Schmidt," she murmured. "She made some mighty fine biscuits."

Ellie went still. "Yolanda Schmidt worked at Hawk House?"

"Sure did. Course that was after she left the school cafeteria. Her daughter's medical bills piled up and she took a job at that place for better money. Gave her a place to stay and her girl got to go to a private facility for care." Eula rubbed her beads again. "Did something happen to her?"

"I'm sorry to say that she's dead," Ellie said quietly.

A sadness settled in Ms. Eula's eyes. "Poor Yolanda. She always seemed troubled, so worried about her child all the time. That takes a toll on a mama."

"I suppose so," Ellie said softly, as the wind blew the scent of the roses. "Did Yolanda ever talk to you about her work at the orphanage or about Blackstone?"

"Just that they gave her room and board. Never saw her much after that. 'Cept in town when she was taking her daughter to the doctor. But she was all button-lipped and kept to herself."

Exactly how Yolanda's caregiver had described her.

Had she been close-lipped because she'd known something bad was happening to the children there and was too afraid to tell?

76

The screech of a bird echoed from the cover of the trees.

"How did she die?" Ms. Eula asked.

"I'm sorry to say she was murdered," Ellie said. "And it's possible her murder is connected to those bones."

Ms. Eula tightened her shawl around her shoulders as a stiff breeze blew through, fluttering through the pines. "I can't imagine her letting anyone hurt those children."

Derrick cleared his throat. "Ma'am, did you know any other staff there? The former sheriff mentioned a teacher named Henrietta Stuckey."

Ms. Eula shook her head. "Never heard of her."

The wind scattered more rose petals across the porch, the color of blood droplets.

"But I did hear tell of a woman who sent her boy there."

Ellie straightened. "Who was that?"

Ms. Eula's rocking chair thumped on the wood floor as she rocked back and forth. "Ruth Crane. She was a strange one, heard tales about her working the streets. Claimed the boy was a bad seed and needed discipline."

Ellie swallowed hard. "Do you remember his name?"

Ms. Eula picked up a rose petal and rubbed it between her gnarled fingers. "Abel, after Abel in the Bible. Odd since she described him as the devil."

"She spoke that way about her own son?" Ellie asked.

"Sure did."

"What happened to him?" Derrick asked.

"Heard her say he ran away from Hawk House. Don't think she looked too hard for him though."

A picture began to form in Ellie's mind. "Did she report his disappearance to the sheriff?"

The rocker slowed as if Ms. Eula was thinking hard. "No idea, hon. But right after I heard about the boy, the place shut down."

"And Blackstone disappeared?" Ellie said.

Ms. Eula's thin shoulders lifted in a shrug. "Always thought that was a good thing. All the rumors about that place and him beating the boys into being men." She tssked. "That don't make a man."

Ellie agreed with that.

Questions nagged at her though. Why hadn't Ogden mentioned the runaway boy?

77

CROOKED CREEK

Although she was exhausted from the long busy day, Ellie felt as if her mind was a ping pong ball bouncing all over the place and slamming into a brick wall. First the case of the bones and inquiries into the past. Then Kelly Hogan's murder and now Yolanda Schmidt's.

What the hell was going on?

None of them seemed connected.

By the time she reached her bungalow, she was bone-tired but still restless. The temperature had dropped to the high thirties and was dipping lower every minute. The azaleas which had just started to bloom pink flowers were drooping.

Hurrying inside, Ellie locked the door. Chilled from the rapidly dropping temperature, she set her laptop on the breakfast island, booted it up and made herself a cup of hot chamomile tea.

Considering what Ms. Eula said about Ruth Crane, she logged on her computer to search for the woman. If she had been a prostitute thirty years ago, she was probably retired from that life by now.

In minutes, she found five female Cranes. One was deceased, three of them did not have children.

She checked police records dating back thirty years and finally located a Ruth Crane who'd been arrested multiple times for prostitution. Her child Abel was placed in temporary foster care. It had to be the woman Ms. Eula mentioned.

Curious as to what happened to the son, she ran a search on the name Abel Crane, but hit a dead end. She checked county then state death records but didn't find him or Ruth, suggesting they might be alive.

She plugged the address she'd found for Ruth Crane into her phone. A trip up there in the morning might yield more information. And if Abel Crane had been at Hawk House, he might be the key to telling her what happened to the other kids there.

Unless... he was one of the boys whose remains had been buried in that pit.

Leah was obsessed with the case again and couldn't sleep.

She took hold of the file she'd kept from years ago and laid the photographs she'd taken on the kitchen table. Her husband had gone hunting again and would probably camp out for the night, so she had some time to analyze the information she'd collected.

The picture of Horatio Blackstone gave her the chills. He was over six feet, wide-shouldered with thick dark hair cut military style. His face was chiseled with a sharp chin and eyes the color of coal. He looked imposing and spoke with an icy voice, thick with disapproval and judgment.

Her conversation with him had been short and terse, but she remembered his menacing attitude as if she was back there now.

"Mr. Blackstone, what do you have to say to the allegations of child abuse?"

"Spare the rod, spoil the child. That's how I was raised." His eyes pinned her with a threat. *"Come back on my property again and you'll be sorry."*

He slammed the door in her face. She knocked again and again but the door remained shut.

Sensing something was off, she slipped back to the van she'd parked outside the property. She sat for hours, drinking coffee and eating the snacks she'd brought until night fell and the sun disappeared behind the storm clouds and thick rows of trees.

Shrouded in night shadows, she snuck through the woods until she reached a hiding spot nestled behind a boulder. Voices and shouts echoed from the house then a stream of flashlights filled the sky, and children marched out single file, shoulders straight, heads bent.

She raised her camera and snapped shot after shot.

A loud wind outside hurled a branch against the house, startling her away from her memories. Footsteps pounded outside the door.

Her husband was home.

Panicking, she stuffed the photos back inside the envelope, but the door swung open before she could take them back to their hiding spot.

He shook damp leaves and twigs from his coat at the door, then spotted her. A growl erupted from his throat.

"What the hell are you doing, Leah? I thought you got rid of all that stuff the other night when we talked."

Nerves fluttered in her belly. "I can't help it. I have to know what happened. Maybe I can help if I show these to the police."

His footsteps thundered on the pine floor as he crossed the room to her. He gripped her chin with his gloved hand and tilted it, so she had no choice but to look into his eyes.

"You're not calling anyone," he said in a command. "It's too dangerous."

"But if I can help—"

"I said no." He reached for the photographs, but she snatched them back and stood. He grabbed them, strode to the fire and tossed them into the burning flames. The pictures began to sizzle and melt, the fire crackling as it sparked.

Leah stared at him, pure rage splintering through her. He'd just destroyed evidence. Thank goodness, she had duplicate copies.

Copies she kept in a safe place, one he knew nothing about.

79

BEAR MOUNTAIN RV/CAMPER PARK

DAY 4

The next day, Ellie woke to a dreary morning, a headache budding. Needing caffeine and food, she and Derrick met at the Corner Café for breakfast. Cord sat at the bar eating while Lola was setting out more pastries.

"Any updates?" Cord asked as they joined him at the counter.

"Working on a few things, but nothing concrete," Ellie said. "I want to talk to an artist named Jonas Timmons. He lives out of town. I was hoping you'd show me the way while Agent Fox explores other clues."

"Sure. You want to go now?"

Lola set coffee in front of them, and she and Derrick ordered food to go before she turned back to Cord.

"I have to question someone else first," Ellie said. "I'll give you a call when I'm ready."

"Sure."

Lola brought their food and she and Derrick walked out to the Jeep. Rain drizzled down, making the windows fog up as she drove. They ate in silence, but Derrick kept checking his phone, a frown deepening the lines around his eyes.

"Did you find any information on Abel Crane?" Ellie asked.

"Nothing. No driver's license, employment record or death certificate." Derrick sipped his coffee. "If he was murdered and someone covered it up, there wouldn't be a death certificate."

"Right. Unless he just disappeared into the system," Ellie said. "He could have been adopted and assumed his new parents' name."

"True."

They lapsed into silence again, and with the wind howling off the mountain, Ellie concentrated on the road, careful on the corkscrew turns with the wet streets. A few tree limbs had blown down and debris littered the asphalt as if the storm of the crime she'd just uncovered had crushed spring. The Jeep's tires chugged over wet pavement as she turned left at the fork in the road toward Ruth Crane's.

Signs advertising the Native American festival and honorary memorial adorned the town. A service would be held tomorrow at Bear Mountain, but nothing could undo the savage treatment the Native Americans had suffered.

She passed the turn off for the resort and the rental cabins, then onto another road that led into a more rundown area and a trailer park catering to campers and people passing through. Beyond it, one section was designated for mobile homes and long-term campers.

"This is it," Ellie said as she turned into the entrance. Campers, RVs and trailers were parked, with stone pitted fireplaces for grilling and cooking interspersed. The small plots of land backed up to the river where fishing, kayaking and canoeing were popular.

Had Ruth Crane lived here the past thirty years or was this

a temporary address she'd given the police when she'd been arrested?

"Look for number thirteen," she told Derrick as she wound through the park.

All around, families were rising for the morning, firing up camp stoves, kids bundled up in coats and running through the woods in search of sticks and brush to fuel the fires.

The parents looked tired and rumpled but rummaged up smiles. Ellie's mind strayed to her own childhood... Randall had been patient with her when she was young and they embarked on adventures in the woods. She still remembered how much better the food tasted and smelled in the open air, how the scent of her father roasting hotdogs over the grill had made her mouth water.

She was damn lucky that Randall and Vera had adopted her or no telling what might have happened to her.

She could have ended up at Hawk House never to be seen or heard from again.

80

Ellie pulled into the short, graveled drive-in front of a rusty mobile home that looked ancient. Patches of weeds flanked the cement steps leading to the mud splattered door and a junky orange Pinto sat in front. "I know this is a long shot, but let's see if she's here." Derrick climbed from the Jeep and she followed, the scent of rain still clinging in the air. Droplets fell from the leaves, pinging off her jacket and she shivered in the wake of the freezing temperature. More turbulent gray clouds hovered over the ridges, ready to unleash as the barometric pressure changed.

She headed up the concrete steps first, and Derrick glanced around the property. Ellie banged the door knocker, peeking through the curtains at the living room which held a faded pea green couch and an outdated TV playing reruns of *The Golden Girls*.

She knocked again and heard a voice yell, "Coming. Hold onto your drawers."

Derrick's mouth quirked into a crooked grin, and Ellie fought one herself. Southerners often had colorful expressions.

A shuffling sound echoed from within, and the door opened to reveal a gray-haired woman in sweats, a cigarette dangling from her parched lips. Her skin looked sallow, wrinkles fanning her bloodshot eyes.

"Are you Ruth Crane?" Ellie asked.

The woman puffed her cigarette. "Who wants to know?"

"My name is Detective Ellie Reeves and this is Special Agent Derrick Fox," Ellie said.

"I don't got no trouble with the law anymore." The woman pushed at the door to close it in their face, but Derrick slid his foot into the doorway to prevent her from shutting it.

"You are Ruth Crane, right?" Ellie asked.

The woman shrugged. "So?"

Ellie took that as a yes. "We just need to ask you some questions. We won't take much of your time." She glanced at the sitcom on TV. "I'm sure you're busy."

The woman tapped ashes onto the porch floor at Ellie's feet. "I am busy. And I ain't done nothing wrong. Just here minding my own business."

"We aren't here to accuse you of anything," Ellie said quickly. "And you're not in trouble with the law."

"It's about the bones discovered at Hawk House," Derrick cut in. "We heard your son was placed there."

Smoke curled from the woman's nostrils as she took another drag of her Camel. "I ain't thought about that damn place in years."

Ellie elbowed her way inside and Ruth stepped back, but her glare cut through Ellie like a laser. Still, Ellie moved past her, sizing up the small living area as she made her way to the tiny kitchen.

The woman followed and stubbed her cigarette butt into a Mountain Dew can.

"But your son Abel was there?"

"Yeah, little shit wasn't nothing but trouble. Mean as a rattlesnake."

Ellie's stomach twisted. "Do you know where he is now?"

"Don't know. Don't care."

"Mrs. Crane..." Ellie said.

"It's Ms.," Ruth said curtly. "Ain't never been married. Had enough sense not to let some old man tie me down and push me around."

Derrick's jaw tightened. "You don't know where your son is now, but what about when he was young? We know you were arrested and he was placed in foster care. What happened from there?"

"They was supposed to turn him into a man." Ruth rolled her shoulders. "But that was a big fat bust and he ran off."

Only from what Ellie had heard, he'd had no chance at all. "You must have heard about the allegations of abuse," Ellie said. "Weren't you worried about your son?"

Ruth's eyes pinned Ellie with a murderous look. "Listen to me. I never asked for that kid, it just happened. I couldn't do anything with him. 'Sides, he ran away from that place one night. Didn't bother to come home and I never heard from him again."

Ellie bit her tongue. Ruth Crane hadn't cared enough to look for her son. "You reported this to the sheriff at the time?"

Ruth shook her head. "Headmaster did, I reckon." She grabbed her Camels from inside her pocket, tapped out another cigarette, then lit it, took a drag and blew smoke rings into the air.

Ellie struggled not to cough as smoke clogged the musty air. She could feel her eyes burning, her nose stuffing up.

"Now, that's all I have to say. Get out," the woman muttered. "Betty White's funny in this next episode. I don't want to miss her."

Her comment told Ellie all she needed to know about what kind of mother she'd been.

"Well, she sure as hell won't win a Mother of the Year award," Ellie muttered as they stepped outside.

"More like Mommy Dearest," Derrick said.

"She didn't seem bothered that he might have been abused or that he ran away."

"*If* he ran away," Derrick added. "If something happened to him at Hawk House, they could have just told her that."

"True. And if she had this attitude back then, maybe the people at Hawk House knew she wouldn't report it if he ran away." Disgust filled Ellie. Her gaze swept the small cement stoop, and she spotted a cigarette stub on the concrete. She pulled a plastic bag from her pocket, then yanked on a latex glove, retrieved the cigarette butt and bagged it.

"DNA," Derrick said. "Good thinking."

Ellie sealed the bag then put it in her pocket to send to the lab. If there wasn't a familial match to any of the remains, they'd keep looking for Abel Crane. But if there was, she'd know he was one of the poor children left in that pit.

As they seated themselves in the Jeep, she phoned Angelica. "I have a name I want you to run on the news as a person of interest in the Hawk House investigation. Abel Crane."

"He's a suspect?" the reporter asked.

"He was sent there as a boy. Please ask him to get in touch with us."

"You got it." Angelica hesitated. "By the way, I may have another name for you. I've been poking through archives of articles covering the town back then. I found a couple written by a reporter named Leah Gentilly. It looks like she was investigating Hawk House and Blackstone, but then she disappeared. I called the paper where she worked and was told she had an accident and just quit one day. I thought I'd go talk to her."

Hope jumped inside Ellie. "I'll find her. See what you can uncover about that accident."

"On it. And I get the scoop," Angelica said.

"Of course. Let's just hope this reporter did a better job of investigating than Ogden."

"I'll dig into Yolanda Schmidt," Derrick said as they arrived back at the station. "See if I can tie her to the Hawk House case. And the warrants for Arm Candy came through so I'll work on that."

"I'm still waiting on Ogden to call me back. Meanwhile I want to talk to Jonas Timmons."

She and Derrick agreed to stay in touch, and Ellie called Cord.

"Pick you up in five," Cord said.

"Perfect." She tugged her jacket on over her holster and left her office to meet him outside.

Cord pulled up front and had another hot coffee waiting.

Ellie's mouth watered at the nutty aroma and thanked him. Cord knew she loved the southern pecan flavor and was always thoughtful enough to bring her a cup when they had work to do. She took a long sip, then explained what they had so far. "Bones of kids and animals, a dead escort possibly unrelated, and the cook who worked at the orphanage. Hoping Laney has news tomorrow on the identity of the remains."

"What about Blackstone?"

"Nothing on him yet." Ellie massaged her temple. "The killer cut out the cook's tongue which suggests he wanted to keep her from talking, but the sex worker doesn't seem connected."

"Could be two different killers," Cord suggested.

"True," Ellie agreed. "But the timing seems too coincidental. Still, we're exploring all options." She explained about the witch's symbol. "When I was in Crystal's shop, I noticed windchimes made of bones. Crystal said an artist, Jonas Timmons, designed the pieces. That made me wonder if he could have been placed at the orphanage as a child. That's who I want to talk to now. It occurred to me that Able Crane might be using a different name, Jonas Timmons, for his work."

She sent Deputy Landrum a quick text asking him to look into Jonas.

"Sounds plausible," Cord grunted as he parked at the beginning of the trail leading to Eagle's Landing. The March storm had gained strength along the coast and the winds had picked up to gusts of nearly thirty mph.

Ellie had to hold onto the side of the truck to maintain her balance as she got out. "How far is it?"

"Just a couple of miles north," Cord said. "Better bundle up."

She yanked on her gloves, glad she'd worn boots. The ground was still muddy where the sun hadn't reached it yet, and bursts of cold air ripped through her.

Using his flashlight, Cord led the way and she shined hers along the ground as she hiked, praying she didn't lose her footing on the sharp incline. Dirt and pebbles skittered below her feet, brush clawing at her legs. She pushed through briars and climbed over broken tree limbs, dodging one that was ripped from its trunk by the force of the wind gales.

Cord moved cautiously, pausing to point out dangerous drop offs and uneven terrain. Her foot slid on damp ground, and she grappled to hold on. He steadied her with a hand and their gazes locked. For a moment, tension stretched between them.

"Promise me you'll be careful on this one," he said in a gruff voice.

Ellie looked into his serious whiskey-colored eyes and saw the worry. "I'm always careful."

"Being careful isn't always enough," Cord said.

"That's why I have a partner and the reason I brought you," she said. "Now the storm's gaining momentum. Let's keep moving."

The next mile sent them winding along the ridge overlooking the river where the bald eagles fed. She heard the peal call from the trees where they nested as she and Cord approached the rustic cabin practically buried in the thicket of brush and trees. The high-pitched cry sounded like a gull with several rapid notes following, and she spotted three perched on the limbs of the tall pines.

Smoke curled from the stone chimney and floated toward the darkening clouds, a single light burning through the front window. A German shepherd lay sprawled on the front stoop of the cabin, licking its paws.

Cord lowered his hand and spoke softly to the animal as they approached. The dog sniffed him then licked his hand, and Cord ruffled his fur.

Her phone dinged with a text from Deputy Landrum. She skimmed the info he'd found on Timmons. His mother had died when he was nine, and there was no record of him in high school or college.

Ellie knocked. "Mr. Timmons, police, we'd like to talk to you." She pulled her coat tighter around her and knocked again. A shuffling sounded from inside, then the door opened. A tall, thin man with a goatee and scruffy hair stood on the other side, his shirt smeared with paint.

"Detective Reeves and Ranger Cord McClain," Ellie said. "May we come in?"

The man's slender jaw tightened to the point that his cheekbones nearly poked through his skin, but he stepped aside and motioned them in. "What's this about?"

Ellie swept her gaze over the room and noted a small couch facing the fire and an art studio to the right. Except for the firelight and the light in the art studio, the place was dark and chilly, an eerie feeling emanating through the space.

Canvasses lined one wall while a worktable sat beneath the window. Shelves held assorted paints and art supplies and an odd machine occupied the corner. Cord walked over to look at it while she spoke.

"I was in Crystal's shop and saw your artwork, the bone windchimes," Ellie began.

His eyes glinted in confusion. "You came all the way here to buy my art?"

"No, not to purchase it." Ellie got a sudden whiff of bleach and cleaning chemicals. "I just wanted to ask about it. You incorporate bones into your art?"

"Yes," he said. "I collect them in the woods, clean and bleach them, then use them to create unique jewelry and the windchimes."

"They're animal bones?" Ellie asked.

He shrugged. "Mostly from small animals in the forest that the larger animals and raptors have preyed on. I also incorporate feathers and arrowheads, designing Native American pieces." He indicated a display cabinet, housing various pairs of earrings.

Cord cleared his throat. "This machine here. It's a crusher, right?"

Jonas shuffled from one foot to the other. "Yes. I use it to crush some of the larger bones into seashell size, then make abstract collages."

"What is your fascination with the bones?" Ellie asked.

Jonas's eye twitched. "My old man was a hunter and wanted me to join in. I had an aversion to killing helpless animals for sport, but he crushed some of the bones to make a path to the door, and I thought that was cool. So I started collecting them and designing my own art."

Ellie's gaze caught sight of a canvas that had been turned to face the wall. Curious, she circled around to see what it was.

Dear God, he'd painted Hawk House and the woods surrounding the property.

Cord joined her, his jaw clenching as he realized what it was.

"That's not ready yet," Jonas said, hurrying over and covering it with a sheet. "I don't like to show things until they're finished."

Ellie's pulse raced. He was the right age to have been placed at the orphanage as a child.

And scars marred his hands. From working with the bones or digging for them? Or a crime? "You painted Hawk House," she said. "Were you there when you were a boy?"

He made an odd sound in his throat then shook his head. "No, I grew up in these parts. But that story and pictures of it have been on the news. It spoke to me so I did some research. Not illegal to paint a crime scene, is it?" he asked with a defensive bite to his tone.

"No," Ellie said, her gaze searching his. "But it is interesting that you replicated it and that you collect bones. We found numerous skeletal remains on the land. Some human, some animal."

A vein bulged in his neck. "I don't know anything about that."

"You said you grew up in these parts. Where did you attend school?"

"I was home schooled," he said bluntly.

"Where's your family?" Ellie asked.

His lips thinned into an angry line. "My family is none of your business."

Cord stepped up beside her and took her elbow. "Come on, Ellie, let's go."

She dug her heels in. "Do you know something about that place or the man who ran it?"

"No," he said. "I told you I collect from the woods around here."

"How about a man named Abel Crane?"

His nostrils flared slightly. "Never heard of him."

Ellie sensed he was lying. But she had nothing to base that on but a gut feeling. Maybe Landrum would turn up something else.

Cord coaxed her outside and she followed but whirled on him when they stepped away from the house. "Don't ever do that again, Cord."

"He could have been dangerous," Cord said. "Dammit, Ellie, I'm trying to protect you."

Ellie was seething. "I don't need your protection. I need you to let me do my job. If you can't handle that, maybe we shouldn't work together anymore."

His jaw hardened, anger palpable. But she ignored it and started back down the trail.

When she glanced back, she saw Jonas watching them through the window. His green eyes, the color of a feral cat, were watching.

The Native Americans had saved the bones of the dead and the drums were pounding. Soft wailing echoed around her as the mummification and the long period of mourning began. She heard screams as some claimed they saw the ghosts chanting by the fire.

Laney closed her eyes to shake away the image. Last night's storytelling had featured burial rituals of the Native Americans. She faintly remembered enduring the long mourning period when her grandmother had passed.

Inhaling deep, she straightened, opened her eyes and oriented herself for work.

But the sight of the bones on her table at the morgue sent her chest pounding. She'd met Dr. Chi to work on them, but the world blurred again...

Suddenly she felt a hand on her arm, someone shaking her. "Dr. Whitefeather, are you okay?"

Laney blinked, jerking around and saw Dr. Chi staring at her over her glasses, her face pinched with worry. Confusion warped her mind. She realized she was becoming enmeshed in the feelings of the children at Hawk House, and the descriptions Ellie had shared of the orphanage.

"Laney?" Dr. Chi said again.

The images slowly faded, but Laney still felt odd.

What was happening to her?

She'd heard of burn-out happening to medical examiners. Knew that some cases got into an ME's head worse than others. Knew that cases involving children were the most tormenting. She'd always been torn between modern medicine and the medicine of her people.

"You need to go home?" Dr. Chi asked.

Summoning her control, she forced herself to compartmentalize, then adjusted her glasses and face mask. "No, I'm fine."

She refused to give up on this. She wanted to see that the monster who'd murdered these children was caught. For that, she needed to focus and find something that would help her close the case.

83

SOMEWHERE ON THE AT

Ever since the story aired, he'd been thinking about Sugar. Sex with her had been amazing. Her screams and cries still rang in his ears at night.

He'd thought the picture he'd taken and left her would keep her quiet. After all, he knew she was married. That she had a secret life that she didn't want anyone to know about. That she had a young daughter, who wouldn't want to know what Mommy was up to.

But now that detective was asking people to speak up, Sugar might figure out who he was and come forward.

He could not let that happen.

Logging onto his computer, he sent her a note.

Can't stop thinking about you. Meet again?

He immediately received a message that he'd been blocked.

Fury made him shoot up from his desk, hurling his phone across the room. It bounced off the wall and hit the floor with a thunk. He paced the room, shoving his hands through his hair as he debated what to do.

You have to stop her from talking.

There was no doubt about that.

He grabbed his phone from the floor, checked to make sure the screen wasn't broken then jammed it in his pocket. Adrenaline surging through him, he rushed to his closet, dug out a black hoody, snagged his keys and headed to his vehicle.

Outside, thunder clapped and a cold gust of air caught his hood and flipped it up as if it was protecting him. Heart racing, he climbed in his car and drove to the trailer park where he'd left her.

Her Toyota was not in the drive, so he drove toward the Sweet Tooth where she worked. The place was crowded with customers. Kids and families rushing to satisfy their own cravings.

His hands knotted into fists as he spotted her through the door handing a little brown-haired girl a chocolate ice-cream cone.

It was too busy for him to go into the shop. But he had time today. He'd wait on her to get off work...

And when he was finished, he wouldn't have to worry about her ratting him out.

84

CROOKED CREEK

Gayle Wimberly glanced through the store window and saw the man in the black hoody still parked across the street. He'd been sitting there for hours, watching the door. At first she thought he was waiting on someone shopping in town, but he hadn't left his car and no one had approached.

He angled his head sideways and suddenly her breath caught. He... looked familiar.

A tap of the plexiglass case brought her attention back to work.

"I wants a strawberry cone," a tow-headed little girl said.

Gayle smiled at the elfin. "Coming right up, sweetie." She dug the metal scoop into the tub of strawberry and packed the cone full, adding an extra scoop just because it was the last cone of her shift. She handed the child the ice-cream, then pulled off her apron and stuffed it in her tote bag to take home. Her shoulders and feet were aching, and she was anxious to get back and soak in a hot bath before picking up her baby girl.

Worse, she knew the money she'd made today would barely pay her rent for the month. But she'd sworn not to sell her body again. She was still limping and scarred from that creep who'd dumped her at the trailer park like a dog. Bastard.

Her live-in Kenny had found her that night and been furious, but not at the man, at her. Told her she'd got what she was asking for. Then he'd hauled away in his Corvair, leaving her with the rent to pay and not even a carton of milk in the fridge for the baby.

Thank goodness her neighbor had the heart of an angel and agreed to keep little Tilly for free to help her out.

"Got a hot date tonight?" Rachel, the girl taking over her shift asked.

"Nope, learned my lesson about going out with strangers," Gayle said. She gestured toward the black sedan. "Do you know that man in the car?"

Rachel wrinkled her nose. "No, why?"

"He's been watching the store for hours."

Rachel tied her apron around her waist. "Be careful, Gayle. There's some creep out there killing women."

Gayle shivered. Rachel didn't have to warn her about the crazies.

Unnerved, she pulled her keys from her purse, grateful she'd bought mace. If that hooded man came after her, she'd be ready.

85

EAGLE'S LANDING

Jonas didn't like the fact that the cop and fed had shown up at his house. Thankfully he'd been able to close the cabinet containing his collection before they'd seen it.

Antsy from lack of sleep, he picked through the dozens and dozens of bones he'd collected after they'd left. Sorting them out took time, but he'd been taught to clean and identify each bone and place it in the proper category according to size, body part, animal or human.

The storm had blown through, tearing up fallen limbs and unveiling bones from carcasses scavenged by vultures, coyotes and wolves. The scent of death and blood clinging to them reminded him of his youth. Of the hunts he was forced to go on. Unpleasant but part of him now, whether he liked it or not.

When he'd stared at the bones spread out on the ground as a boy, he'd seen images of shapes and abstract art just like he saw shapes and animals in the clouds when he looked up at the sky.

Over the years, he had slipped up to that place and collected some.

But he couldn't go back to Hawk House to look for more bones now. It was too dangerous.

The large bones he'd chosen to use today had dried from the cleaning and bleaching. He put them in the crusher and watched as it created ivory fragments.

Then he returned to the canvas he'd started of the bone-yard. He'd painted the dark woods, a lone wolf hovering on the ridge. He used the browns, grays and greens of the plants and bushes and trees, adding sketches of pine cones, twigs and wild mushrooms. Driven by his memories, he scattered the bone fragments along the floor of the forest and hid them with more brush just as Blackstone had done.

His heart thundered just as it had back then. He'd slipped a human bone into the mix, a souvenir he'd been keeping for himself. A bone that could be used against him.

No one would ever know that inside the beautiful rendition of the Appalachian Mountains, he'd hidden the bone of a person who'd been murdered.

The wind picked up, battering the shutters where Leah lived on top of the ridge that overlooked Coyote Canyon.

Rubbing the kink from her calf, she hobbled to the bedroom then sank to her knees, pushing aside her nightstand and reaching inside the hole where she'd stowed her files. She dug out the box of articles she'd written, along with her research on Hawk House. Those kids deserved for the truth to be revealed. Watching Angelica Gomez on the news had reminded her why she'd loved journalism. The hunt for the truth, to expose people's dirty secrets and obtain justice for them had given her purpose.

She reached for the box, deciding she'd show it to Angelica, but the sound of the heavy front door opening echoed in the silence.

Knowing her husband would be furious again, she quickly shoved the box into its hiding place, then pulled the nightstand back in place. She flipped off the lamp and drew the curtains, pitching the room into darkness, then crawled on the bed and closed her eyes, pretending to be napping. If he woke her, she'd claim she had a migraine.

Footsteps shuffled closer. Heavy breathing reverberated in the quiet. A rancid odor filled the room. Then she felt a presence, ominous and threatening.

She opened her eyes then stared in shock at the shadowy figure standing over her. A scream lodged in her throat, and she raised her hands to fight, but he grabbed her by the hair and plunged the knife into her.

After Cord dropped Ellie off at the police station, Ellie teamed back up with Derrick.

She called Ogden again as she drove to Coyote Canyon where Leah Gentilly lived, but once again received no answer. Irritated, she left another message, then told Derrick about her meeting with Jonas Timmons.

"Interesting," he said. "Maybe he was at the orphanage and doesn't want to admit it because of the remains."

"If he was there, then he knows what happened and is covering it up," Ellie said. "He certainly is obsessed with bone collecting." She felt as if she was beating her head against the wall.

"I looked through Arm Candy's client list," Derrick said. "Nothing there so far."

"Keep digging. There has to be some lead there." Twisting through the mountain until she reached the turn off for the ridge, Ellie wondered why Leah Gentilly had moved to this isolated area.

"This reporter might be our best lead," Ellie said.

Derrick gave a little nod, then the two of them walked up to the house. The cottage was small, but the expansive view of the mountain was breathtaking. You could see for miles and miles, rolling hills, yellow and purple wildflowers dotting the landscape, steep overhangs which created scenic stops for travelers, and jagged peaks that rose like staircases.

The front door stood ajar, but Ellie knocked and called out. "Leah Gentilly, are you here?"

No answer. Just the sound of dripping water and the wind blowing through. Something didn't feel right.

Derrick held his weapon, and Ellie inched forward into the entryway. A quick glance at the tiny living area proved it was empty. Then a low moan erupted from down the hall. She veered toward it, Derrick acting as back-up, and crept past a bathroom to a bedroom. The moment she looked inside, she pulled her own service weapon.

A man in a green coat was leaning over the bed, his body shaking as he gripped a bloody pillow in his beefy hands. Below, lay a woman, body limp, her eyes staring lifelessly back at him.

88

"Police," Ellie said. "Put your hands up, sir, then turn around and step away from the bed."

He remained frozen, body trembling, while Derrick inched to the side. From her vantage point, Ellie couldn't see if the man was armed. Derrick motioned that he didn't see a weapon, but still Ellie moved cautiously.

"I said put your hands up and turn around, slowly," Ellie ordered.

Derrick moved to the side in the man's peripheral vision and cleared his throat. "Do what the detective says. Now."

Derrick's deep voice must have registered and slowly, the man dropped the pillow, then pivoted toward them. A glazed look clouded his eyes. "I... oh, God, she's dead." A wail escaped him, and he grabbed the bed to steady himself, leaving bloody fingerprints.

Ellie kept her weapon trained on him while Derrick crept forward, gun aimed in a warning. With a grim look, he pressed two fingers to the woman's neck. Ellie held her breath as she waited.

The man looked as if he'd been in the woods for days, with a scruffy appearance, long beard and shaggy, unkempt hair. His clothes were dirty, eyes bloodshot, complexion pasty. Was he high on something?

Derrick frowned and gave a small shake of his head, confirming the woman was dead.

Judging from the scene, she had to treat the man as a suspect. Ellie braced herself for the man to fight. Or run. "Who are you?" Ellie asked.

"Harold Dutton," he said in a broken voice. "That's... my wife, Leah. Who did you say you are?"

"Detective Ellie Reeves from Crooked Creek Police Department and this is Special Agent Derrick Fox, FBI." Ellie gestured toward her shield.

"What happened?" Derrick asked.

The man appeared to be in shock. "I... found her... like this."

His knees buckled, and Derrick grabbed him by the arm to steady him. "Come on, sit down in the kitchen. We're going to talk." Ellie phoned for the ME and a crime team as Derrick hauled Dutton from the room.

Had Leah's husband killed her?

Or... Pieces started to click together. She was certain that Yolanda Schmidt had been murdered because of her connection to Hawk House. And Leah Gentilly had investigated the orphanage years ago... It had to be the same killer.

The breaking news about the skeletal remains was the common thread between the two women.

She just needed proof.

Everything pointed to a cover-up, which meant whoever killed Yolanda and perhaps Leah knew they had information to share. Information that could explain the bodies that had been left at Hawk House for thirty years.

Working on instinct, she eased forward to study the scene. Her stomach clenched as she zeroed in on the blood around the woman's mouth and on her chin. Breath tight in her chest, she tugged on latex gloves and eased her bloody lips apart.

A curse rolled from her lips. Leah Gentilly's tongue had been removed just as Yolanda's had.

89

Ellie wanted to question Leah's husband herself, but if Leah was killed because of something she knew, she might have kept records.

She studied the scene. Leah was still dressed in sweats. No immediate signs of a sexual assault. No stab wounds or other visible injuries although if she'd fought her attacker, she might have bruises on her body beneath her clothing.

And evidence.

She turned in a wide arc and surveyed the room, looking for signs of an altercation, for something out of place, but nothing struck her as off. There was a chair in the corner, bedroom shoes by the closet door, no overturned lamps or blood anywhere. And the front door had not been locked.

ERT would be here soon. But she wanted to look around first.

She checked the nightstand beside the bed. Inside she found a mystery novel, along with a book of prayerful meditations, chap stick, and a comb.

Her foot hit something on the floor beside the bed, and she noticed indentations where the legs of the nightstand had been moved. Dropping to her knees, she pulled it away slightly and found a small opening cut into the wall.

Her pulse raced as she slid her fingers into the hole, removing a box. Lifting the lid, she saw there were numerous articles, a journal of notes and photographs inside.

On the outside of the small black notebook, Leah had written the words *Hawk House.*

90

Jaw clenched, Derrick gave Dutton a quick pat-down to confirm he wasn't armed then shoved him into a kitchen chair. The man's gruff exterior, chafed hands, and the rifle he'd noticed on the wall in the living room indicated he was a hunter.

"Tell me again what happened?" Derrick asked.

Dutton's eyes were unfocused, darting back and forth as if he was confused. Or trying to fabricate a feasible story to explain why he'd been caught by his dead wife's bedside with her blood on his hands.

"You'd better start talking, Dutton," Derrick said firmly. "What happened?"

Dutton jerked his head up as if the question finally registered, but his nostrils were flared, eyebrows drawing together as he scowled. "I don't know," he mumbled. "I... came in and found Leah like that. Dear God..." His voice cracked with what sounded like raw, real emotion.

Then again, he might be upset because he'd been caught.

"You said you came in. From where?"

He inhaled a shaky breath. "Me and Leah, we had a fight..." His eyes widened and he shook his head as if he realized his wording would make him look guilty. "I mean, an argument. I left for a while to clear my head."

"So where did you go?" Derrick asked.

"Huntin'," Dutton said. "Been out in the woods all night."

"Was anyone with you?"

Dutton jiggled his leg up and down then shook his head.

"Did you see anyone while you were out hunting?" Derick asked. "Someone who can verify your story?"

"I went by myself like I always do." Panic flashed in Dutton's pale brown eyes.

Derrick waited a minute to see if Dutton would elaborate, but he clamped his lips together as if searching for a response.

"So you and your wife fought. And then... what? You lost your temper? Killed her in a fit of passion?"

A muscle ticked in Dutton's jaw as he jerked his head up to glare at Derrick. "I told you I came in and found her. I called her name, but she was so still, then I shook her and she didn't move and then... I saw all that blood."

"If you simply came in, why do you have blood all over you?" Derrick pressed.

"Because I tried to save her... and then I saw what he did to her mouth... to her ... tongue... and then you showed up."

Derrick breathed out, debating whether or not to believe the man. "You mentioned that you two fought?"

Dutton released a long, winded sigh. "It was an argument, not a fight. I never got physical with Leah. I... loved her."

"What did you argue about?"

Dutton's stared at the blood on his hands. "Maybe I should have a lawyer present."

"Do you need a lawyer?"

"I didn't kill Leah," he said. "I loved her. I saved her life years ago and I've protected her ever since."

Derrick's pulse raced. "You've protected her from what?"

"From everything," he said, teeth snapping together.

Derrick heard footsteps and realized Ellie was at the door, a box in her hand.

"You said you saved her and protected her?" Ellie said sharply. "Did your protection have something to do with what's in this box?"

Dutton cursed. "Shit, I told her yesterday to get rid of that."

"Apparently she didn't," Ellie said. "It's her notes about Hawk House."

"Is that what you two argued about?" Derrick asked.

Dutton nodded. "She saw the news report about those bones, and she started talking about calling that reporter Gomez."

Derrick and Ellie exchanged looks. "And you didn't want her to?" Ellie pressed.

"Hell no," Dutton mumbled. "I told her if she spoke up, she'd get herself killed."

91

Ellie raised a brow. "That sounds like a threat, Mr. Dutton. Let me guess what happened. You warned her not to dig the story up again, but she said she was going to. You argued and the argument became physical." She folded her arms across her chest. "Maybe she tried to leave and you caught her and pushed her onto the bed. You lost your temper and you grabbed a knife and killed her to keep her from talking."

"That's not what happened," he growled. "I warned her not to speak up because I loved her and was afraid she'd get hurt if she did."

"What would make you think that?" Ellie asked.

He looked down at the floor, his boot tapping on the floor.

"Answer the question or we're going to throw the book at you," Derrick ordered.

Dutton cursed again. "Because someone tried to kill her thirty years ago when she was doing a story on the man who ran the orphanage."

Ellie's heart thudded. "Go on."

"You obviously knew this or you wouldn't have come," he

said in a low voice. "But years ago, she was attacked and left in the woods for dead."

"She told you that?" Ellie asked.

"No. I found her," he replied. "I was out hunting and saw her lying in the weeds at the bottom of a ledge. I managed to get her up and carried her here."

"Why not call 911?" Ellie asked.

"Because she begged me not to," he said. "She came to and told me someone tried to kill her, and she was afraid they'd come back for her if they knew she was alive."

"She could have gotten police protection."

"I know," he said with a pained sigh. "But she was scared and disoriented, and she couldn't remember the details of what happened. She begged me to keep quiet until she got back on her feet."

"That was thirty years ago," Derrick pointed out.

"It took her months to heal and overcome the trauma. She'd injured her leg, had bruises and a concussion, and would barely speak. Then there were the horrible nightmares, and for a while she was terrified to go outdoors."

"If someone tried to kill her, why would she trust you?" asked Ellie. "You were a stranger, right?"

"I was. But almost immediately we connected. She was so vulnerable and scared that I promised to protect her. I had a spare room and lived off the grid, and she wanted to lay low for a while." He hesitated, tears raining down his ruddy cheeks. "She thought the police would figure out what happened at that place, then she could come out of hiding."

Ellie still couldn't imagine Leah trusting a stranger enough to stay with him. But perhaps this big gruff guy was telling the truth and had a tender side.

"She was a reporter," Ellie said. "Didn't she feel the need to finish the story?"

"We watched the news. Kept up with it, but a few weeks

after I found her, the story died. Sheriff claimed he'd investigated, that the headmaster had abandoned the orphanage and the kids had been placed elsewhere. Said there was no proof of foul play."

Back to Ogden, Ellie thought.

"Did Leah tell you what she'd learned about Hawk House?" Ellie asked.

He shook his head. "She said the less I knew the better. That knowing would put me in danger." His voice cracked, and he blinked against another onslaught of tears. "All this time, and now she's dead."

"Did she ever mention a woman named Yolanda Schmidt?"

He furrowed his brows. "Who?"

"Yolanda Schmidt?"

"I never heard of her." His tormented gaze met Ellie's. "What does she have to do with Leah?"

"She worked at Hawk House," Ellie said. "And she was murdered just like Leah."

He dropped his head into his hands, releasing another sob. His anguish sounded so real that Ellie believed him. Even if he'd wanted to keep her quiet, cutting out his wife's tongue was over the top. He couldn't have copied the crime either because she hadn't released that detail to the public. And if he didn't know Yolanda, he had no motive.

A car engine reverberated outside, and Derrick stepped to the door to greet the ME and ERT.

Ellie glanced at the box where Leah had stored her notes. The manner of death was the same as Yolanda Schmidt. Which meant someone was killing everyone who had information about what happened back then. If Leah's suspicions and interviews had gotten her killed, hopefully there would be a lead in that box.

"One more question," Ellie said to Dutton. "Two people associated with Hawk House are dead now. If you two have stayed off the grid up here and Leah hadn't contacted anyone about the story, how did the perp know where she was?"

"I have no idea," Dutton said. "But he's obviously smart enough to stay in the wind for years. How the hell will you find him?"

Ellie folded her arms. It was a good question, and one she didn't know the answer to yet. But whoever committed these murders must have kept tabs on anyone who could expose him.

Which meant he might not be finished.

92

Derrick met the ERT to get them started while Laney performed an initial exam on Leah. Her face went ashen as she realized that Leah's tongue had been removed just as Yolanda's had.

Ellie pulled Derrick to the side while Dutton sat stewing in the chair, still handcuffed. "Let's hold him until we process the house and look into him more," Ellie said. "His story about saving her could be feasible, but I'm still on the fence as to why she'd trust him."

"Love at first sight?" Derrick suggested sardonically.

Ellie rolled her eyes. "You don't believe that and neither do I. He could have been a plant, watching her for whoever killed those children. Maybe he kept her up here to make sure she didn't talk."

Derrick's eyes darkened. "That's possible. Or we've all heard of Stockholm Syndrome."

"Right," Ellie said, "kidnap victims attaching themselves to their abductors because they rely on them."

Derrick shrugged. "I'll look into him."

"See if he had an alibi when Yolanda Schmidt was murdered."

Ellie motioned toward the box containing Leah's notes. "Maybe the answers are in there. Let's take Dutton to the station. With what we have now, we can hold him for twenty-four hours without booking him."

She glanced back at Dutton and saw him swiping at his eyes with the back of his hands. His grief seemed real, but she'd dealt with psychopaths before.

Laney lifted the woman's hand and indicated her short stubby fingernails. "If she fought back, maybe she got DNA."

"Compare it to the husband's but look for other DNA, too," Ellie said quietly.

Laney gently laid Leah's hand over her stomach and patted it tenderly. "I do have a small update about the bones," Laney said.

Ellie perked up. "Tell me."

"We know some of the bones belonged to children," Laney said. "I have more on the bodies in that second pit."

Ellie tensed. "Go on. Male? Female? Age? ID?"

"Both. Dental records confirm the female was Henrietta Stuckey."

"And the male?"

"IDed him as Willard Buckley. He was a janitor at—"

"Hawk House," Ellie said, putting it together in her mind.

Laney wrinkled her nose. "There are striations on the bones as if hit hard with a sharp instrument. Whoever killed them was violent, sadistic, and chopped the bodies into pieces before scattering the bones."

A shudder coursed through Ellie. Had Blackstone killed the children, the teacher and the janitor?

Was he still alive and now killing anyone who could reveal the monster he was?

93

CROOKED CREEK

While Derrick put Dutton into a holding cell at the station, Ellie phoned Ogden again. This time he picked up.

"What is it now, Detective?" Ogden said, his tone irritated.

"We found Yolanda Schmidt, the cook at Hawk House."

Ellie waited for a reaction, but Ogden was calm when he spoke. "Oh, yeah, now I remember that was her name. She was a sweet lady. Could she help you out?"

"She was murdered," Ellie said bluntly. "Viciously stabbed to death in her home. Tongue cut out. My guess is to keep her quiet."

"Holy moly. You got any idea who did it?"

"Not yet. But considering the breaking news about the orphanage, it's most likely related. Yolanda knew something and she died because of it. And now the reporter who worked the case was killed in the same manner."

"What?" Ogden blurted. "Sweet Jesus, Detective. You got bodies piling up left and right."

Ellie contemplated whether his shock was real or fake. "You must have spoken with the cook when you visited the orphanage."

Ogden inhaled sharply. "I guess I did, but she didn't say much. Kept to herself and stayed in the kitchen."

"We know her daughter was ill with MS. Did she mention her?"

"Don't remember, but then again, it was thirty years ago. Details are fuzzy now."

"Did you talk to Leah Gentilly, the reporter who was investigating the story?"

"I did. Now listen to me, Detective, I know you're trying to make a name for yourself, but I did things by the book. And I told that reporter everything I knew."

"Really?" Ellie's patience was wearing thin. "You were supposed to protect the people in the county, yet you turned a blind eye to the child abuse and did nothing. That makes you an accessory."

His angry breath punctuated the air. "You think pushing people will get you what you want. But you're wrong. If I say I didn't find anything, I didn't."

"I don't believe you," Ellie said.

"Your daddy should have taught you to respect the law, especially the ones who enforce it. If you want to talk to me again, go through my attorney."

Ellie knew he was stonewalling her. "I do respect honest lawmen. But not those who hide behind it for their own reasons. And trust me, I will find out what you're hiding and why you covered it up."

Without waiting for his response, she hung up and sent a text to Deputy Landrum:

Dig into the former sheriff, Edgar Ogden. Look at his financials and living situation during the time Hawk House was open and after it shut down. Look for any connection between him, that orphanage and Blackstone. If he covered up the crimes, I need to know his motive.

94

CROOKED CREEK

He was getting antsy now. Sugar had lingered too long talking to the other woman in the Sweet Tooth, then walked to that crystal shop and now he'd watched her go into the Corner Café.

Dammit, it was risky to take her in broad daylight, so he'd broken into her car and now, with the sun setting and more storm clouds darkening the sky, memories bombarded him.

His first kill. The sight of the blood. The thrill of listening to his victim draw a last breath.

He stared at his hands and in his mind saw the blood beneath his fingernails. Tonight, it would be Sugar's. He couldn't wait much longer.

It was all Ellie Reeves' fault. If she hadn't made that hooker out to be an innocent victim, he wouldn't have snapped like he did and killed again.

Hell, he used to be able to purge the rage eating his soul by sinking himself into a woman's body.

Ellie Reeves had ruined that, too. Now only the kill fired his blood.

The café door opened, and Sugar emerged, carrying a bag of food in her arms. She glanced around her as if she knew he was watching, and a smile curved his mouth. The terror on her face drove him mad with lust and the need to end her right here. Right in town.

He hovered low in the floor of the back seat and held his breath as she slipped inside. Then she turned to set the food on the back seat and saw him. She opened her mouth to scream, but he was too fast for her.

"Goodbye, Sugar."

The mean man who'd brought her here had come back today. She'd heard them talking outside the door to the bone room where he'd locked her.

His voice boomed so loud she heard it through the crack in the door. A tiny sliver of light wormed its way through the bottom where the floor didn't quite meet the door edge. She clung to that sliver, grateful not to be totally swallowed by the dark.

"No one can know about her," he said.

"Don't worry. So far she hasn't said a word," the other man barked a laugh. "But if she tries to talk, I'll cut out her tongue."

The big meany clapped his hands. "Perfect. But we have another problem."

"What kind of problem?"

"The ole biddies in town are talking, spreading rumors about this place."

"Shut them up," the man who'd barked said.

Footsteps hammered near the door, and she held her breath, terrified he'd open the door and kill her. He paused and she felt as if his eyes were boring through her.

"There's more," the meany said. "A reporter asking questions. She said she's coming out here to talk to you."

"I'll handle her," the barker said. "Now get out of here and keep your mouth shut, too."

"No problem." The footsteps pounded again. Two pairs of them. The light coming from the other room faded. Then a door slammed. And darkness was all around her.

Closing her eyes, she finally let the tears fall. Maybe the lady who was coming would find them. Maybe one of the other kids would tell.

But if they did, he'd kill them.

She thought of the boy in the basement. Saw his fingers reaching beneath the door. Heard him whimpering.

How long had he been locked down there? And why did he keep him away from the others?

Picking up one of the bone slivers with her shaky fingers, she began to scratch on the wall above the bed. She'd been marking the wall with lines to count how long she'd been here.

She wondered if she'd be like the boy and be locked up forever.

DAY 5

Morning sunlight poured through the window of the Corner Café as Cord stopped by for coffee. Work was calling and so was his need for food. Lola made the best country ham and red-eyed gravy he'd ever tasted.

Lola burst through the double doors leading to the back with a terrified expression. "Cord! Come here! Hurry!" At the sound of the panic in her voice, he raced after her. "What's wrong?"

She hesitated at the back door, her voice trembling, "I went to take out the garbage... b... but I think there's a body in the dumpster."

Cord's heart pounded. "What?"

Tears filled her eyes, and she pointed to the door. "B... back there."

Cord squeezed her arm gently. "It's okay. Stay here and I'll take a look."

She nodded, her chin quivering, and he rushed outside. The dumpster was halfway in between her place, the Cat Café next door and the Sweet Tooth. He pulled gloves from his pocket, then a flashlight, scanning the alley as he strode toward it.

The acrid odor of garbage filled the air, made stronger by the wind hurling through the alley. The lid on the dumpster was partially closed, the end of a black garbage caught in the metal edge.

He shined the flashlight around the ground, searching for signs of trouble. A red heel lay wedged in the ground to the side, and a rat skittered back behind the dumpster.

A bad feeling seeped through him. When he reached the dumpster, he slowly raised the cover. His light illuminated garbage bags piled inside. He smelled rancid food and saw disposable containers poking through the bags, then... a hand protruding from the one caught in the metal.

Damn. Lola was right.

Knowing better than to touch it, he stepped away and called Ellie.

97

Running on little sleep the last few nights, Ellie slugged down her coffee as she drove to the station. Hopefully Deputy Landrum had found some helpful information. Maybe today they'd catch a break.

Her phone rang, Cord's ringtone.

She punched Connect. "Good morning," she said, striving for optimism.

"I'm afraid it's not," Cord said. "I'm at the Corner Café, El. There's a body in a garbage bag in the alley dumpster."

Ellie's breath quickened. "I'll be right there."

She pressed down on the accelerator as she hung up then called Derrick. His phone went to voicemail, so she left a message, slowed through the traffic light, then veered into the café's parking lot.

Cars from the breakfast crowd filled the area, families bundled up against the wind as they hurried inside. She swung into a space and parked, forgoing her siren so as not to panic the customers.

As always, she scanned the area for anything suspicious, although if the body was another murder victim which seemed likely, she doubted the killer had stuck around or even dumped it in broad daylight.

She walked around to the alley behind the café, where a metal tin can lid rattled in the wind and a rancid odor hit her in the face.

Covering her mouth with her hand, she hurried toward the dumpster where she saw Cord waiting. She braced herself as she rushed to him, then pulled her flashlight.

"Lola spotted the bag when she came out with the trash," Cord said.

Poor Lola. She would be traumatized by that.

Standing on tiptoes, Ellie looked inside and saw the torn garbage bag, with a woman's hand jutting through the plastic.

"Bastard threw her away like she was trash," she muttered. Her mind was already taking leaps, wondering if this murder was related to the others this past week. Although why leave this woman in town and carry the other one into the woods?

The body would tell.

She stepped down and called Laney.

98

While ERT roped off the alley and went to work, Ellie headed inside to speak to Lola. She'd already hung a 'Closed' sign on the door and the crowd had cleared out.

She looked shaken and nervous, flitting around the café, storing the baked goods to save for the next day. Cord looked uneasy as if he didn't know what to do.

"Sit down, Lola," he said quietly. "Let the other girls close up for you."

Lola turned tear-filled eyes toward him then Ellie. "Who was she?"

"I don't know yet," Ellie said. "We're recovering her body now and the ME is here."

Lola pressed her hand to her mouth, a tear trickling down her pale cheek. "No one is going to come back here now."

"Sure, they will," Cord said. "Look at all the crimes that happened the last two years. The people in this town are used to it."

Which they shouldn't have to be, Ellie thought. "Lola, were you the first one here this morning?"

"Yes," she said, a tremor in her voice. "I got here about five to make the pastries and biscuits."

Ellie offered her a sympathetic smile. "Did you see anyone hanging around outside?"

Lola shook her head. "No, it was quiet like usual."

"Were there any cars around?"

"Just the produce delivery guy. He dropped off the fresh vegetables for the day."

"How about a noise out back?"

"No, nothing," she said, her voice agitated. "I got my turnovers ready and the biscuits in the oven, then prepped some vegetables. We usually take the trash out at night, but I found a bag someone missed so went to take it out and that's when I... saw the bag poking out of the dumpster."

"Did you hear anyone in the alley? Or a car engine taking off?"

"I told you I didn't." Lola paced behind the counter.

Ellie traded a look with Cord. "Cord, why don't you drive Lola home?"

Relief that she'd given him a task flitted across his face. "Sure. Lola?"

She rubbed her arms with her hands. "Okay," Lola said, going to get her purse and keys to lock up.

"If you don't mind, I'll keep the keys and we'll look around in here just in case the killer came inside. I'll lock up and get the keys back to you," Ellie said.

Lola shivered but agreed, then she and Cord left through the front door. Ellie hurried back outside and found Laney stooped by the body. She was cutting the bag as Ellie approached.

"Female, mid-twenties," Laney said. She pulled the bag all the way open, and Ellie's pulse jackhammered.

"Multiple stab wounds to the chest and torso," Laney confirmed.

Similar to Kelly Hogan's injuries. "I know who she is," Ellie said as Laney thumbed dark hair away from the woman's face. "She works at the Sweet Tooth." Ellie swallowed hard. "Her name is Gayle Wimberly. Any idea TOD?"

"Judging from rigor and liver temp, I'd say sometime last night." Laney shined her light down the body, then twisted Gayle's leg to the side.

Ellie swallowed forcibly. "The killer marked her with the same symbol as Kelly."

Laney twisted her head to look up at Ellie. "You're dealing with the same perpetrator."

"Yeah," Ellie said under her breath. "And he's escalating. But leaving her body in town was risky."

Mistakes like that could get him caught.

99

Nerves knotted Mandy's shoulders as she went to look out the window. The sun was trying to peek through the heavy clouds, and the trees in her backyard swayed in the relentless wind rolling off the mountain. Even the birds seemed to be disturbed, chirping noisily and fluttering from tree to tree, as if they sensed something was wrong.

Her phone pinged with a text, and she took a deep breath and checked it.

Sherry: *Check out this new gaming site, BONE HUNTERS. Pretty dope. It's like the inventor was at Hawk House.*

A shudder rippled through Mandy. She didn't want to think about that horrid place. But she couldn't stop the scary thoughts from coming.

Inhaling a deep breath, she clicked on the link Sherry had sent. A second later, the screen was filled with images of dark thick woods just like the ones surrounding that orphanage. Then pinpoints of light broke through the cracks between the trees. Everywhere she looked, she saw eyes staring back as if they were monsters hidden in the forest.

A directive appeared in the window of a house that looked haunted.

YOU ARE INVITED TO PLAY THE GAME – THE BONE HUNT – can you find them before it's too late? If you don't, you will die.

Stomach clenched with nerves, she chose an avatar and clicked to begin the hunt. Suddenly she was moving through the woods, digging in the dirt, following a trail of bones scattered on the forest floor.

Shadowy spirits drifted between the rows of trees and rose from a pit in the ground. Screams of horror came from the house, and when she looked at the window, she saw the ghost of a little girl staring out the window.

Chilling her to the bone, Mandy shuddered and clicked out of the game.

100

It was only ten a.m. and Ellie was already exhausted as she left the Corner Café and returned to the station. Laney had the body transported to the morgue for the autopsy.

Calling Bryce, Ellie filled him in. "See if Gayle has family, and canvas the employees at the Sweet Tooth. See if someone was bothering her."

"Will do," Bryce said.

"I'll get Agent Fox to check if she belonged to that escort service. That may have been how her killer chose her and Kelly."

"My fake profile on Arm Candy worked. I have a meet-up set up tonight. Maybe this woman knows something."

"Good. Did you ever talk to your father?"

A tense second passed. "Not yet."

"What's the hold-up?" Ellie asked, annoyed that he was dragging his feet.

He huffed. "I told my folks about Mandy but they don't want anything to do with an illegitimate child."

"But she's their granddaughter," Ellie said, appalled.

"They don't see it that way. They don't want me telling

anyone," he said gruffly.

She'd never liked his parents. Now she detested them. "I'm sorry, Bryce. That's not fair."

"Doesn't really matter. Mandy wants nothing to do with me." He cleared his throat. "I thought you were going to stop and see her. Why haven't you?"

Ellie went still, guilt setting in. "In case you haven't noticed, I've been busy with all these murders," she said, although she knew it wasn't an excuse. Maybe she just didn't know what to say to the teenager.

"If you don't intend to do it, then don't say you will," he said. "That's not fair."

Well, wasn't Bryce acting like the parent now? Good for him. "You're right," she replied, hating she had to agree with him. "I'll stop by today."

"Good. I'll let you know what I find on Gayle."

Ellie thanked him, her mind returning to the case, struggling to make a connection between the recent crimes. Numerous skeletal remains – several belonging to children and two adults, Henrietta Stuckey and Willard Buckley.

Then the recent murders – a sex worker, Kelly Hogan. Yolanda Schmidt, the cook at Hawk House. Leah Gentilly, the reporter who'd originally investigated the story. And a woman named Gayle who worked at an ice-cream shop.

All within a few days.

Her head was spinning.

What was she missing?

A knock sounded at Ellie's office door and her captain poked his head in. "Angelica Gomez is here to see you."

"Thanks. Give us a couple of hours to review what's in the box I found at Leah Gentilly's, then I want everyone to convene in the conference room. If we don't get a handle on this, more people are going to die."

"I'll set it up," the captain said.

Questions needled Ellie. But Angelica appeared at the door, eyebrows lifted in question. "Did you find something?"

Ellie nodded. "Leah Gentilly was murdered."

Angelica gasped, the wheels obviously turning in her mind. "Because of what she knew?"

"Has to be. Off the record – her tongue was cut out just like Yolanda Schmidt's was." Ellie grabbed two bottles of water and carried them to the table, then seated herself. Angelica claimed the chair across from her. "We brought the husband in for questioning, but I don't think he's behind this. He claims someone tried to kill Leah years ago and he saved her. She went into hiding for fear her attacker would find her."

"I figured she didn't just drop the case," Angelica said.

Ellie indicated the box. "I found this at her house hidden in the wall. She kept notes and articles." She reached for a Manila envelope tucked inside. "I thought you might want to help me look through it."

A fire flamed in Angelica's voice when she spoke, "Thanks for including me, Ellie."

"Sure, I can use your insight." Pulling the notebook from the box, she handed it to Angelica. "Read through there while I dig into the contents of the envelope."

Angelica eagerly began to thumb through it while Ellie uncovered three articles Leah had written about Hawk House. The first one described the history of the orphanage. The old house had been passed down in the Blackstone family, and Blackstone himself had decided to turn the facility into a home for wayward boys. Two years in though, and he also accepted girls. The staff included the cook Yolanda Schmidt, teacher Henrietta Stuckey and janitor Willard Buckley. Children were placed there by parents or court ordered.

It had been open for five years at the time allegations of misconduct were reported.

Leah quoted Sheriff Ogden: *The sheriff stated that Black-*

stone is taking the allegations seriously. If the abuse is confirmed, arrests will be made.

Yet no charges were ever filed, no arrests made. What the hell had happened?

"Anything yet?" Ellie asked Angelica.

Angelica looked up from the notebook, a fraught look on her face. "Leah used shorthand, I'm sure for privacy. It looks like Pitman's shorthand, the type taught years ago in school for secretaries where you substituted symbols for words. Some called it speed hand. It's mostly disappeared in schools, although you can take classes to learn it. Can I use your computer?"

"Sure." Ellie retrieved her laptop and set it on the table. While Angelica dove in, Ellie turned back to the next article.

Leah wrote: *Sheriff Ogden insists he interviewed all employees at Hawk House. They claim Blackstone is a tough disciplinarian but that the kids need it. He enforces strict rules and expects the kids to comply. But none admit that abuse is taking place.*

Article three said: *Today, I requested an interview with Mr. Blackstone who refused to speak to me or answer the allegations. The janitor describes the school as having a military-type atmosphere that shaped the boys and girls into stronger adults.*

The fourth article stated that Leah spoke with Abel Crane's mother. Her story matched the one Ruth Crane had given Ellie.

Ellie rubbed her forehead in frustration then removed another envelope from the box. This time when she opened it, she found photographs.

Her chest throbbed as she looked at images of the exterior of the orphanage. Then candid shots of children Leah had spotted outside the place. She flipped the pictures over and found names scribbled on the back.

Hope flared in her. This was what she needed. And probably what had gotten Leah killed.

"I found photos of some of the children who were placed at the orphanage," Ellie said.

"So terrible," Angelica said. "But at least it's a lead."

Derrick rapped his knuckles on the door. "Ellie, the sheriff and everyone else is filing in for that briefing."

"Thanks." She stood. "Bring the book with you and you can keep studying it while I fill everyone in," she said to Angelica, who nodded.

Setting the photos and articles back in the box, Ellie carried it with her, Angelica on her heels. Captain Hale loped in, popped a mint into his mouth and took a seat. Shondra and Deputy Landrum followed, and Derrick joined her at the front of the room.

"Everything okay?" she asked in a low voice.

"Fine." He cut his gaze away from her. "Did you find something?"

"Hopefully. Let's get started." She gestured toward the whiteboard where she'd placed photos of the pit where the bones had been discovered. "This is our initial crime scene. We're still waiting on forensic reports, autopsies and IDs from the medical examiner. I did speak with Dr. Whitefeather yesterday and she has determined that two sets of remains belong to adults, one male, one female. Female was Henrietta Stuckey, the teacher who worked there, and male was the janitor, Willard Buckley."

Ellie placed a photo of each of them on the board. "At this point, Blackstone is a prime suspect in the murder of each child found on the property, as well as the adults."

"I may have some insight into Blackstone," Derrick said. "He grew up in the mountains with a father who worked in zooarchaeology."

"What is that?" Landrum asked.

"It's also known as faunal analysis," Derrick answered, "a branch of archaeology that studies remains of animals from archaeological sites. Faunal remains are the items left behind when an animal dies. These include bones, shells, hair, chitin, scales, hides, proteins and DNA."

"Sounds like he had an interest in his father's work," Shondra said.

Derrick nodded, then went on, "As a teen, he got into trouble a few times, then joined the military where he was on the frontline in Vietnam. Took some shrapnel to the brain which he actually survived, but he was discharged due to erratic violent behavior. Then he returned to the area and later turned his house into a home for wayward boys."

Ellie absorbed that information.

"Any idea where he is now?" Landrum asked.

"My partner is searching but so far has found nothing," Derrick answered. "No renewal of his driver's license, employment history, property rental or ownership, not even a bank account."

"He can't have just disappeared into thin air," Shondra said.

"It's possible he created a new identity," Derrick replied.

"He could be living under an assumed name with an entirely new life."

Ellie drummed her fingers on the table. "If that's true, and he was a child abuser, then it's hard to believe he could just stop." She snapped her fingers. "Deputy Landrum, start looking at reports of abuse from teachers or leaders at other schools. He was described as running the orphanage in a military style so look at military schools."

"Copy that," Heath agreed.

Ellie added a picture of her father and the storage units. "My father was assaulted when he went to this storage unit to retrieve the files from the original investigation into Hawk House."

Next, Ellie added a photo of Kelly Hogan and Gayle Wimberly along with crime scene images of where they'd been found. "At this point, we have no connection between Ms. Hogan, Ms. Wimberly and Hawk House. We are exploring an escort site Kelly worked with. Sheriff Waters is looking into Gayle and her family and canvassing her coworkers."

She attached Yolanda Schmidt's visual onto the board next. "Yolanda worked as the cook at Hawk House. She was found brutally murdered, her tongue removed." In the middle of the board, she placed a picture of the orphanage then drew a line connecting it to Yolanda.

Chairs squeaked as everyone reacted, recognition of the connections and depth of violence rumbling through the room.

Next, she posted a photo of Leah Gentilly and drew a line to Hawk House. "This woman investigated the orphanage thirty years ago then disappeared and went into hiding. She was found dead in the same manner as Yolanda Schmidt, tongue removed."

"He wanted to keep them from talking," Shondra said.

"Which means he's getting desperate," Ellie said. "Any word from the lab on the crime scenes?" she asked Landrum.

He consulted his notes. "Forensics did find DNA at the storage unit. Matched the former sheriff, Ogden."

Ellie twisted her mouth in thought. "Could have gotten there when he stored the files." So that was a dead end.

"They're still analyzing forensics from Hawk House, and the other crime scenes. Those outside barrels held old clothing, but chemicals and fire destroyed them to the point they couldn't retrieve DNA. A couple of barrels also held animal remains."

At least there were no more human bodies. "We finally have a lead," Ellie said. One by one she posted photographs of the children she'd found in the box and listed their names. Murmurs of sorrow and disbelief drifted through the room.

Ellie massaged her temple where her headache was gaining momentum. "I know, it's horrible. This boy, Abel Crane," she said. "Agent Fox and I tracked down his mother Ruth. She claims her son ran away from the orphanage, that she has no idea where he is and she doesn't care."

"What kind of mother would just give their child away like that?" Heath asked.

Shondra grunted. "Happens more than you'd think."

Ellie took a beat to let the group settle. "Agent Fox and I will track down the kids listed here. Meanwhile we'll request their medical records for DNA comparison to the remains." She glanced at Derrick. "Anything else from Leah's husband?"

"No. He said she didn't share details about what she'd found out, that she said it was safer that way."

"Hmm." Ellie wasn't sure she believed that, but she let it slide for now. "Angelica has been looking through Leah Gentilly's notes. Angelica?"

The reporter stood, brushing her black pencil skirt into place. "Leah kept her notes in shorthand. I still have more to decipher, but she was definitely on to something. According to her notes, she bought a camera with a high-powered night lens.

She hid in the woods by the property and watched children being led outside and ordered on a scavenger hunt in the dark."

Ellie had a bad feeling about where this was going. "What were they hunting?"

"Bones," Angelica said. "Blackstone hid them in the yard and forced the kids to find them and identify them." A bead of perspiration dotted her forehead. "One night she watched and heard screams. She saw Blackstone throw one of the boys into the pit. She ran to call for help."

Ellie's lungs strained for air as the horrific images flooded her. Leah's husband's story fit.

"But Blackstone or someone working with him must have seen her and tried to kill her," Ellie said. "That's the reason she went into hiding."

Now she was dead anyway.

102

"Let's talk about the children," Ellie said. "First, these boys' names appeared in Leah Gentilly's notes." She pointed to the pictures as she spoke.

"One: nine-year-old Ralph Lawrence. Father sent him to Hawk House after he was caught beating another child to death.

"Two: twelve-year-old Jerry Leeks. Social worker placed him there after his father was incarcerated for murder. Mother died two years earlier.

"Three: nine-year-old Thaddeus Cornerstone. Placed there after his parents died in a housefire.

"Four: Abel Crane."

Ellie paused and shook her head. "Ten years old. His mother was the one we talked to. Sent him there to get him out of her hair. He supposedly ran off and was never heard from again.

"Five: Jonas Timmons." Her heart thundered. "Jonas is an artist who uses bones in his work." She and Derrick traded looks. "Agent Fox and I talked to him. He claims he'd never been to Hawk House."

"Then he lied," Captain Hale said. "Find out why."

"I will. There's more. Three girls. Nine-year-old Tristen McElroy, placed there after charges of parental abuse were confirmed."

"Poor kid went from one devil to the next," Shondra muttered.

Ellie grimaced. "There are two others. Eight-year-old Wanita Weathers. Placed there after her parents abandoned her.

"And one more. Like Jonas Timmons, this name is one we've seen before." She pointed to the photo of the small dark-haired girl with the big brown eyes. "Willow Rodgers. She runs the site Arm Candy, the one our escort Kelly Hogan belonged to." Now she had a loose connection between the sex worker and the orphanage. "Both Timmons and Ms. Rodgers have to know something."

"I'll send deputies to bring them in," Captain Hale said.

"Timmons lives off grid. Have Ranger McClain lead your deputy to his place." That would allow her time to get this to Laney. Now they had names, the process would be easier.

"Ellie," Angelica said with a wave of her hand. "Leah mentioned one social worker's name repeatedly, a woman named Theresa Lumpkin."

Ellie snapped her fingers. "We'll bring her in, too." There was no way the social worker was innocent in all this. She was supposed to protect children, find them better homes.

Not throw them to the wolves.

103

"Interesting that Jonas Timmons and Willow Rodgers both are in the area now instead of living away." Adrenaline surged through Ellie. "Deputy Eastwood, search NCEMC data bases for the names of the ones we haven't accounted for. Check within a year prior to and after Hawk House shut down and see if you can learn where they went from there. Also, text Dr. Whitefeather these names so she can request their dental and medical records. Then we can compare with the remains."

Shondra gave a nod and opened her laptop.

"Meanwhile Agent Fox and I will search for the remaining children," Ellie continued. "First though, let's talk to Timmons and Ms. Rodgers. They might be able to fill us in."

Having tasked everyone with their assignments, Ellie dismissed the team so they could get to work. But the faces of the little children haunted her. Jerry with his red freckles, Abel with his front teeth missing, Jonas with his big eyes and skinny frame, Willow as an innocent girl before she grew up to run an escort service. And Wanita, a tiny dark-haired girl with the biggest saddest brown eyes she'd ever seen.

Ellie started researching the names of the children on the

list. As far as she knew, Abel Crane could be anywhere. If he'd run away from Hawk House, she doubted he'd return. Although Willow and Jonas were in the area.

Derrick had already run Abel Crane's name and found nothing.

Next, she ran the name Ralph Lawrence, but she found no information on him other than his birth certificate. His father Hal had died twenty years ago with no mention of his son in the obit. She found no record of an adoption. Maybe the social worker could tell her where he was placed.

Her search into Jerry Leeks and Thaddeus Cornerstone yielded similar results.

Jerry's father died in a prison fight two years after he was incarcerated. No other relatives listed. And Thaddeus Cornerstone, whose parents had died in a housefire, had been placed at Hawk House, was reported as a runaway just as Abel Crane.

Had they run away or were they among the skeletal remains?

"I found Theresa Lumpkin," Derrick said, cutting into her thoughts.

"Where is she?"

"She died in a car accident a few months after the orphanage closed. Although there were suspicions surrounding it. Report stated that her brakes failed."

Ellie's mind churned. "She could have been murdered to silence her."

Most everyone associated with that place was dead. Or... if she didn't figure out who was behind this now, they would be soon.

104

HAWK HOUSE

Thirty years ago

She was trying hard to remember her mommy's voice. But it was gone. Lost somewhere in the dark and the days that had run into each other.

Lifting her throbbing hand, she raked her fingers across the scratches in the wall. So many of them now that she couldn't remember the sun outside on her face or the feel of the rain splattering her cheeks.

Cold seeped all the way through her, and she closed her eyes and tried to see her mommy in her mind. She was forgetting what she looked like, too. Forgetting the way she'd held her at night when she had bad dreams of monsters. Forgetting the smell of the sweet perfume she dabbed on her neck.

"There's no such things as monsters," Mommy would whisper as she stroked her hair. *"You're safe, honey."*

But Mommy was wrong. She wasn't safe.

There was a monster in this old house. And another monster who'd brought her here.

There were monsters everywhere.

Lindsey was calling again.

Derrick didn't know what to do. He needed to be here working, yet she needed him, too. Guilt consumed him, rattling his conscience and making his heart pummel with worry.

"I need to take this," he said, standing.

Ellie looked confused but didn't push. "I'm going to run over and check on Mandy. Meet you back soon. Maybe by then Bryce's deputies will have Jonas Timmons and Willow Rodgers here."

He gave a quick nod, but his heart was back in Atlanta, and he was already heading to the door. He knew he was being evasive, that he didn't have his head into the case as he should, but he couldn't help himself.

The past month back in Atlanta had changed everything. He should be there now.

As soon as he finished tying up this mystery, he'd go back and face Lindsey. Then they'd figure out what to do together.

Ten minutes later, Ellie stopped at Mandy's house.

"How is she?" she asked Trudy.

"She's been hovering in her room, afraid to go out. She won't eat and I don't know if she's sleeping. Her friends call and want to come over, but she refuses to see them." Trudy twisted her hands together. "Bryce stopped by but it didn't go well. She said some pretty awful things to him, and he hasn't been back."

No wonder he was so upset. "No teenager should have seen what she did. It haunts me every day." Ellie signaled toward the stairs. "Mind if I go up and talk to her?"

"Please do," Trudy said. "I just hope she lets you in."

So did Ellie... Worried about the girl, she climbed the steps then knocked on her bedroom door. "Mandy, it's Ellie. Can I come in?"

"No just go away."

"I'm not going away until I see you," Ellie said. "So either open the door or I'll open it myself. I'm pretty good at picking locks."

That brought a loaded silence. A minute later, she heard shuffling and Mandy eased open the door. The frightened, wary look in her big eyes tore at Ellie's heartstrings. She was still wearing her pajamas, her hair was a rat's nest, and it was clear she hadn't been eating. Her T-shirt hung on her, her cheeks looked sunken, and her complexion sallow. "Can I come in, honey?"

Mandy gave a little nod, then motioned her in. Posters of the US soccer team and a country rock band hung on the walls, and clothes had been tossed onto a chair in the corner.

"Did you come about the gaming site?"

"I came to check on you. Bryce and your aunt and I are all worried about you."

Mandy sank onto the red and black quilt on her bed in front of her open laptop. A UGA blanket lay on her pillow.

"I don't know what to say to anybody," Mandy whispered. "I know you all want me to be fine, but I can't stop thinking about that pit and every time I close my eyes, I see dead bodies, and I wake up thinking I'm covered in bones."

"Ahh, baby." Ellie wrapped her arm around Mandy. "I know how you feel. It was scary."

"But you're not scared," Mandy cried. "You're not scared of anything."

Ellie gently tucked a strand of Mandy's tangled hair behind one ear. "That's where you're wrong," Ellie said softly. "I'm scared every day."

"You're just saying that to make me feel better," Mandy replied.

"No, it's true. When I was little, I got trapped in a cave. After that, I was scared of the dark. I still sleep with a light on."

Mandy sniffled, her brows crunching together with a frown. "Really?"

"Really," Ellie said. "I've gone to counseling to talk about it. And with each case I work, I get spooked. I'm scared of the awful things I see like those bones."

Mandy gave a tiny nod.

"But you know what I'm most afraid of?"

The girl tugged her lip with her teeth. "What?"

"I'm most afraid of not getting justice for the victims. I'm afraid I'll fail."

Mandy's gaze met hers for a long, pained moment. "But you can't save everyone," she murmured.

Ellie offered her a small smile. "I know. But I want to try."

Mandy swiped at a tear. "I hate what happened to those kids. They never got to grow up and have a life."

"No, they didn't. And that's tragic." Ellie gestured to the sun peeking through the window. "But you can't stop living now because of it. You deserve to have a happy life, Mandy. To play soccer and have friends and dates and go to college."

Many picked at a loose thread on her pajama bottoms. "I said awful things to Bryce," she admitted. "I told him I wished he'd died instead of Mama."

Ellie's breath stalled. Poor Bryce. "Maybe you meant that, maybe you didn't. And it's okay. You miss your mother. That's natural."

"But he's really not so bad," Mandy whispered. "I mean he's awkward, and he knows nothing about good music, but... I guess he's trying."

Ellie bit back a chuckle. "Then give him a chance."

"He probably hates me," Mandy muttered.

"No, honey. He loves you and is worried about you. He was mad at me for not coming out here sooner."

Mandy studied her, blinking as if she was considering what Ellie had said.

"Now, what did you mean when you asked if I'd come because of some gaming site?"

Mandy scooted her laptop over and opened it. "It's a new online game called *Bone Hunters*."

Ellie wasn't into gaming, but she didn't like the sound of that.

"Watch. It's like the guy who made the game replicated that old house." She angled her computer so Ellie could see. "You pick your avatar and then go on a scavenger hunt for buried bones on the property." She trembled, wrapping her arms around herself. "Some are easy to find and some are hanging from the trees. Others are buried deep in the forest. There are multiple pits covered in brush just like the one I fell in. And then inside the house there are bones hidden in the basement." She pressed a few keys and a series of dark stone steps led from the crawl space into a tunnel that wound beneath the ground. The setting was morbid, dark and spooky, with music and sound effects that chilled Ellie.

Mandy was right. Whoever had invented this game had replicated Hawk House and the woods surrounding it. Although animated, it was so vivid, and captured the area so well that the designer must have been on the premises.

The question was – was it created before or after the discovery of the bones?

"It's so freaky," Mandy whispered, her eyes wide with fear. "It's like he was there and knew exactly where that pit was."

Perhaps he had been, Ellie thought.

"Thanks for showing this to me," Ellie said. "Now I want you to turn off your computer and go outside and kick the soccer ball around. Or call your friends to come over. You need to be around people right now."

Mandy clenched her hands together. "But what if that killer comes after me?"

Now they were getting to Mandy's real fears. "Honey, there's no reason for him to come after you. You may have found those bones, but you don't know who put them there so you're not a threat to him. And we never released your name of any of the other teens' names to the public." Ellie playfully tugged at the girl's hair. "Now get a shower and wash your hair. And eat something," she said with a smile.

"Okay, okay." The girl wrapped her arms around Ellie, who hugged her tightly.

Ellie didn't think Mandy was in danger, but they were dealing with a serial killer. On the way back to the station, she phoned Bryce and filled him in.

"We should probably have a deputy conduct drive-bys. I think she'll feel safer that way."

"I already set it up," Bryce agreed. "And I talked to Gayle's coworker at the Sweet Tooth. She said Gayle was nervous yesterday and thought someone was watching her."

"Did she say who?"

"No, Rachel said they were busy and she didn't notice anyone. But a few days ago, Gayle had bruises and when she asked about it, Gayle got all jittery and didn't want to talk about it."

Ellie's mind raced.

"Rachel thought the man was parked across the street yesterday," Bryce continued. "I looked for street cams, but the one facing that direction wasn't working."

Ellie ran her fingers through her hair. They needed better security and cameras around town.

Hanging up as she reached the police station, Ellie found Angelica and Laney waiting along with Derrick.

"I questioned Leah's husband again," Derrick said. "His story is the same and there's no proof that he killed Leah. With her death similar to Yolanda Schmidt's, we have to release him."

"I agree," Ellie said. "I just saw Mandy. She showed me a gaming site called *Bone Hunters* that all the kids are playing. It's eerily similar to our crime scene at Hawk House."

"I'll take a look and track down the inventor," Derrick said, striding to her office.

Ellie walked over to Laney and the ME filled her in on the results she'd found. Now they had names and IDs, it felt even more devastating to Ellie. "We'll let you give the official report," Ellie said, too shaken to speak. "But we aren't releasing any information about Gayle Wimberly's murder yet. The sheriff is trying to locate family for notification now."

Laney nodded, her notes trembling in her hand. Yet anger hardened her voice, "Of course. I want you to catch this animal and put him away for what he did."

Angelica then introduced herself to camera and the segment. "Dr. Whitefeather, our resident medical examiner, has determined identities for the bones discovered this week at Hawk House. I'm going to let her fill you in."

Laney took the mic. "With the help of a forensic anthropologist, we've completed results of the autopsies on the remains, two of which belong to adults Henrietta Stuckey, a teacher at Hawk House, and the janitor Willard Buckley. Both were stabbed multiple times and left in an underground pit where they were buried in brush, dirt and debris." Laney paused, her voice catching. "The remainder of the bones belonged to children, three male, one female.

"Males include nine-year-old Ralph Lawrence, twelve-year-old Jerry Leeks and nine-year-old Thaddeus Cornerstone. Then a nine-year-old girl, Tristen McElroy. After careful examination, we've concurred that all four children were severely mistreated. There was evidence of starvation and dehydration along with signs of physical abuse." Perspiration beaded Laney's forehead. "Evidence also indicates that the children were alive when left in that underground pit."

She swayed slightly and breathed out, rubbing her finger around the silver circle necklace she always wore. Ellie had the strongest urge to save her from the interview, but the ME finished and stepped away, her face pale.

Ellie stepped up next. "We also learned the names of two other children who are unaccounted for. A boy named Abel Crane who we were told ran away from Hawk House. And a girl named Wanita Weathers. Both would probably be in their late thirties, maybe forties by now. If anyone has information regarding those two individuals, please call the police." She steeled herself to remain professional. "If you're out there, Mr. Crane, or Ms. Weathers, we desperately need your help. We also are still in search of Horatio Blackstone. If you have information regarding his whereabouts, please call my office any time day or night."

She turned the mic back over to Angelica who recited the contact numbers. When she looked up, Laney was gone.

The faces of the other children he'd met at Hawk House stared back at him from the news report. Jerry was the geek with the red freckles and a squeaky voice. Everyone picked on him and called him Mouse. Blackstone especially. He'd tried to make him into a man.

He'd failed. Jerry had cried like a baby.

They all had at one point. Except for him. He was as mean as Blackstone.

The memory of how he'd ended up there played through his head. But first the images of his mother...

He'd loved her. He'd hated her. He wished he could forget but he couldn't.

"Murderer."

His mother's cruel accusations echoed in his ears as she dragged him from the rattletrap blue station wagon. The big gray house looked like some kind of haunted house from the movies. A wild animal howled from the dark woods beyond and shadows clung to the corners and floated in front of the grimy windows.

"I don't wanna stay here," he said.

"Shut up, this is where boys like you go," his mother snarled.

He dug his sneakers into the graveled drive. "I'll be good, I promise. Just don't leave me." His voice sounded tiny and lost in the rustling of leaves and the groan of his own heartbeat thumping wildly.

He'd heard about this awful house – Hawk House – they called it.

Heard bad children were sent here and never came back.

"You have to be taught a lesson," his mother said coldly. Then she pushed him toward the front door.

Giant cement hawks were perched on each side of the stone walkway, talons bared as if ready to swoop down and tear into carrion. The black metal gate swung back and forth, screeching. He tugged against his mother's hand to get free and run, but she jerked him along the stone path, then shoved him up the steps. He stumbled, a cry tumbling from him as cold fear engulfed him.

She made a sound of disgust. "Go on, cry baby." She tapped the heavy gold door knocker that was shaped like the wings of a falcon and a gong echoed through the old building. The sound of raptors grunting as they dove for food made him look up and he saw a dozen black hawks flapping and swarming above as if to welcome him – or give him a warning.

Then the door squeaked open, and a big hairy man peered down at him with eyes the color of coal and a beard so thick he looked like a wild animal.

He jerked free of her and took off running. He was only ten, but he was fast and maybe if he made it back down the long hill to the road, someone would help him.

The bitter wind chafed his face. The clouds rumbled and opened up, and rain began to pelt him. They'd driven so far up that long, graveled drive that the road seemed miles away. With the storm clouds, he couldn't see any lights below. Couldn't make out the stars, only shadows that looked like wolves hiding behind the trees. Teeth bared, snarling.

His calves ached as he jumped over broken branches that had fallen. His breath panted out. Voices shouted at to him to stop.

But he kept running. Around the bend. Over another hill. Past a sharp ridge.

He cut through the woods, thinking it was a shortcut. Briars clawed at his legs through his jeans. Rain soaked his shirt and ran down his face. A scream echoed behind him – was it an animal or another boy?

Something rotten and rancid filled the air, then he realized he'd stepped in a puddle of blood. His stomach lurched. He jerked his head away from the carcass of an animal, heard the buzzing of insects swarming it. The screech of vultures above as they swooped down for their next meal.

He bolted again, blindly running. Then his foot hit a slick spot and he flailed his arms as he realized he'd come to a steep drop off. Terrified of falling over, he backed up a step, his legs shaking.

"Gotcha," a harsh voice bellowed. "You can't escape."

He jumped sideways to escape, but the man grabbed him by the arms and dragged him back toward Hawk House. He struggled and sunk his sneakers into the ground, but the man was too strong.

His feet dug into the muddy ground as they hauled him up the hill. Tree branches slapped him in the face.

A car engine rumbled and his mother's station wagon flew down the dirt drive.

His lungs ached for air, and he screamed for her to stop. But she sped away and disappeared.

The man tossed him up the steps and then hauled him inside. The heavy door clanged shut. Then he saw the bars on the windows and the giant winding dark staircase.

Someone screamed from upstairs.

He jerked back to the present, his body teeming with tension. He'd hated his mother.

The dark fantasies swept over him, consuming him with need and desire and unforbidden lust. Willing women were waiting. This one's name was Catarina.

His heart battered his chest, as he imagined punishing her, watching her blood spill onto his hands and drip from his fingers. He could already taste it.

110

CROOKED CREEK

Dread wrapped its tentacles around Jonas as the deputy escorted him into an interrogation room in the police station.

Dammit, his hunt would have to wait.

He knew what they wanted from him. To know what happened at that horrible place. But he'd sworn years ago to keep quiet. They all had.

And there was no way he'd break his word.

He had no regrets.

The door to the room slammed shut, and silence echoed around him. The clock ticked. Seconds turned into minutes. Minutes into half an hour.

He wasn't stupid. They were leaving him to stew and worry. Tormenting him with the wait.

A chuckle bubbled in his throat. Waiting here in an empty room was nothing compared to the hours he'd endured at Hawk House. Here, they had rules.

Blackstone had none. No restrictions on what he did to them. No one cared. No one had noticed. Even those who should have helped them turned away as if the innocent children deserved it.

He closed his eyes, allowing his mind to travel to a distant place and block out his surroundings just as he had back then. It was the only way he'd survived.

He felt the bones and pine needles jabbing at his knees as he knelt on the brush-covered ground. Saw blood dripping from his fingertips as he clawed at the dirt to unearth them. Felt the sting of fire ants nipping at his hands and arms.

Then the piercing pain as Blackstone buried his face in the bones.

111

As Ellie entered the interrogation room, she sized up Jonas Timmons. Hat ramrod-straight, his scarred hands on the table, fingers curled into the metal.

A text came in before she began the interview.

Heath: *No record of Blackstone at another school, including military ones. And nothing more on Timmons' father.*

Damn.

"Mr. Timmons, thanks for coming in," she said as she seated herself across from him.

"I didn't realize I had a choice," he said flatly.

So he was on the defensive. "You know why you're here then?"

He nodded, gaze level with hers. "I've already answered your questions."

Ellie set her file on the table. "You did, but you lied to me before."

A twitch of his eye was his only reaction.

"You said you'd never been to Hawk House, but I know

differently. You see, we learned that a reporter named Leah Gentilly was doing an investigative piece on Hawk House before it was shut down. She was threatened and assaulted and went into hiding, abandoning the story."

"I don't know her or anything about her."

Ellie sighed. "Maybe not. But she knew about you and the other boys. And she was just found murdered. I believe because of what she'd discovered." One by one, Ellie removed the children's pictures from the folder. "She believed Blackstone was abusive and she snuck onto the property. She captured pictures of the children outside."

His Adam's apple bobbed as he swallowed, but he simply gave her a blank stare.

"We've identified each of the children in the photographs." One by one, she tapped the pictures and named them. "This one, Mr. Timmons, is you."

Eyes steady, he clenched his jaw.

"You were there when you were a child," Ellie said calmly. "What I don't understand is why you lied about it."

His breath tumbled out. "Because I've spent my entire life trying to forget it."

Ellie gave an understanding nod. "I saw the dorm room where you slept, the chains on the walls, and we found the secret room behind Blackstone's office with the cot and restraints. It's obvious that he kept one or more of you inside."

His fingers curled tighter into his hands. "He called it the bone room," he said in a distant voice. "It was the ultimate punishment. He spread bones on the bed and covered you with them, then closed you in the room in the dark."

A shudder coursed through Ellie. "I'm sorry," she murmured. "Why didn't someone tell the social worker?"

His lips creased into a frown. "Because that would have only made things worse," he said. "He was always listening."

"You never had a chance to speak to her in private?"

Jonas shook his head.

"What about Sheriff Ogden?" Ellie asked. "Did you talk to him?"

Jonas shrugged, then lifted his head and his expression closed. "No."

Now she had Timmons talking, she pushed for more. She pulled a chicken bone from the ones she'd found in the basement of the orphanage and laid it on the table. "We found these in the basement. A jar of pulley bones. What did he do with them?"

Jonas stood. "I'm done here." His mouth twitched at the sight of the bones, as if they'd triggered a bad memory.

"You may not have been able to speak up back then, but you can now, Jonas. The cook at the orphanage was murdered to keep her quiet. So was the reporter. Do you know who killed them?"

A seed of rage flared in his eyes then disappeared quickly before he flattened his hands on the table and stared at them. "I don't know. Now unless I'm under arrest, I have nothing else to say."

112

Ellie had no evidence that Jonas Timmons was a killer. But she'd sensed some deep-seated rage against Blackstone. Still, he seemed too controlled to commit such violent crimes.

Although he definitely had motive.

She'd heard pain in his voice, and he'd ended the interview abruptly. Because talking to her dredged up his painful past.

She had a feeling he knew more than he was saying. But she couldn't prove that either. Not yet.

She joined Derrick and explained about the interview.

"Blackstone was some kind of bastard," Derrick muttered.

Ellie couldn't argue with that.

"I tracked down the inventor of that gaming site, Mason Dirks. Let's go have a talk with him."

This time, Derrick drove. The wind gusts were gaining in intensity, thin pine trees swaying, leaves and twigs scattering across the road like tumbleweed. Gray clouds rolled across the sky, no sign of the sun in sight, adding to the eerie chill in the air. They whizzed past farmland and side roads leading up to Bear Mountain, past camping grounds, and toward cabins that bordered the riverbank. Dandelions and other wildflowers fought to stay alive in the wake of the harsh winds and weather.

Fifteen minutes later, Derrick wove down a narrow, pebbled drive to a secluded rustic cabin with towering trees shadowing the front exterior. Ellie saw a kayak leaning against the garage and an ATV parked beneath a detached carport.

The shadows from the trees hung over the cabin, the sharp ridges of the mountains jutting out over the river. When Ellie climbed out of the car, she heard the sound of the river rushing over the rocks, rippling downstream. Smoke curled from the chimney, a sign the man was home.

This area had been dubbed Blackwater Cove because blackbirds flocked here in droves, adding a mystery to the rugged setting. As a child, she used to sing the nursery rhyme about four and twenty blackbirds baked in a pie.

The blackbirds were singing now, a loud and warbling flute-like melody, but as they approached, the trees rustled and they emitted a noisy chatter at being disturbed.

Derrick led the way and knocked. A minute later, a muscular man, in loose jeans and a flannel shirt, opened the door, a beer in his hand. His hair looked rumpled, his eyes slightly bloodshot, his clothes wrinkled as if he hadn't changed them in days.

Derrick identified them and Dirks' brows shot up. "What's going on?"

Ellie pushed past him into the foyer. "We need to talk."

Dirks tunneled his fingers through his shoulder-length wavy hair. Ellie guessed his age to be late thirties, the right age to have been a child at Hawk House. Although Leah Gentilly hadn't listed his name in her file.

"About what?" Dirks asked.

"Your gaming site," Derrick said. "You invented *Bone Hunters*, didn't you?"

Dirks' mouth cut into a smile. "Yeah, everyone's into it. Biggest success I've had so far."

People were drawn to the macabre, Ellie thought. "May we sit down?"

"I guess so," Dirks said. "Although why are the cops interested in my game? I copyrighted it so I own all the rights."

Ellie walked into the den where she saw his set up – the entire back wall was filled with computer equipment, story boards and sketches of the images in the game.

"You did this yourself?" she asked.

Another proud smile. "Yeah. It's been fun. But why are you asking about my game?"

"Because it closely resembles the boneyard discovered at Hawk House this week."

He sank into his work chair. "I know. I was working on a scavenger hunt game to go along with the stories about the Native Americans in the mountains when that news story aired. Interest is high for paranormal right now, so I decided to take advantage of it."

"And it's paying off for you," Derrick commented.

"Most popular game I've invented yet." He indicated a shelf lined with several other games. Ellie walked over and studied the titles. All of them were paranormal or sci-fi.

"Mr. Dirks," she said as she turned back to him. "The images on your game are drastically similar to the real crime scene. Which leads us to believe that you were there at some point."

His jaw went slack. "Look, I know the sign said no trespassing, but I didn't mess with anything. I just slipped up there to take some pictures for inspiration."

"You realize that's a crime," Ellie pointed out.

"I had to be creative," he said. "Besides, the cops had already searched it and were gone. You're not going to jam me up for that?"

Ellie sucked in a breath and ignored the question. "When were you there?"

"The night the story aired," he said. "I took pics then came home and stayed up all night sketching and putting the site together."

"Was that the only time you'd been to the property?" Derrick cut in.

Dirks rocked back in his swivel chair. "Yeah. Although I heard about it when I was a kid. Grew up around here. Everyone talked about that place."

"Are you certain that's the only time you were there? You weren't sent there as a child?"

Surprise flitted across his face. "No. My uncle raised me. This cabin belonged to him. He died last year and left it to me."

He sounded sincere. "Is there anyone who can verify your story? Did you go to Hawk House alone?"

Silence stretched between them for a heartbeat. "Yes. But I told my partner I was going."

"We're going to need a name?"

"He doesn't like folks to know we're together. We try to be discreet."

"His name?" Ellie pressed.

Dirks released a weary sigh. "Jonas Timmons. He's a—"

"Bone artist," Ellie finished. "We know who he is." If the two men were together, it was hard to believe that Jonas hadn't talked to Dirks about his past at the orphanage.

113

SOMEWHERE ON THE AT

He dragged the woman into his cabin, the sight of the chains and whips sending his blood pulsing hot through his veins. But he couldn't erase the image of his dirty mother from his mind. Or the fact that Arm Candy offered up such services. There were so many to choose from. This one was especially pretty.

"Down on your knees," he ordered.

She whimpered and fell to the floor, wriggling at the ropes securing her hands behind her back.

"Please," she said. "I won't tell anyone who you are."

He jerked her head back by her hair, enjoying her yelp of pain. "What makes you think you know who I am?"

A sob rumbled from her. "You're the Judge. I heard about you from some of the other models. That you liked to play games."

It wasn't good they were talking about him. He might have to do something about that. "I do like games," he responded. "What else did you hear?"

The woman clamped her teeth over her bottom lip to stifle another whimper.

He clenched her hair so hard that she sucked in a sharp breath. "What else?" he barked.

"That you're handsome and smart and you pay well," she said, her voice quivering.

He went still. "That's why you agreed to meet me?"

"Yes," she said, although the nerves in her voice told a different story.

"You're lying," he ground out. "What else?"

Her labored breathing echoed in the air between them. He wanted her. Wanted her to please him. Make him feel something.

Something other than the rage and disgust he felt with his mother's angry words in his ears.

Catarina's face disappeared into a blur, her screams distant as he threw her back to the floor and traced the knife over her face. Slowly, he stripped away her clothing, shredding it with the blade. His heart thumped wildly as he imagined piercing her skin, saw the blood flowing down her breasts.

He muffled her scream with one hand as he raised the knife.

114

BLUE SKY

The police had called Willow again. They wanted to question her further. Did they know something or were they making guesses?

That call triggered her panic – she'd packed her suitcase and raced to her car. She had to run again. Get away from his godawful place and the memories.

Her tires squealed as she raced around the switchbacks toward Blue Sky, a resort of remote cabins where she'd worked when she'd first escaped the madam who'd taken her in. She didn't like the fact that someone had killed one of her girls. She'd tried her best to protect them, but dangers came with the job. God knows, she'd walked the line dozens of times when she'd first gone into the business herself.

She tried not to think about those early days when she'd escaped Hawk House. About the things she'd seen there. And the things she'd been forced to do.

Her fingers automatically brushed over the scar on her ankle where she'd received the marking.

No one knew about that except for the ones at Hawk House. Surviving back then had been all that mattered.

It was all that mattered now.

She could do without the business if they shut her down. And she did not want to talk about that time in her life. Or how she'd escaped.

She called them the dark days.

Memories of the boy who'd saved her flitted through her head. He was mean. Tough. Not afraid of anything.

She'd owed him back then, but things had happened so fast and he'd yelled at her to save herself. And she had.

Kelly had not been at Hawk House. But her death was connected to Willow.

And she felt responsible.

She spotted a quaint coffee shop called Dark Beans next to an outfitters store at the fork in the road and swerved into the parking lot. Snagging her computer and purse, she battled the winds, bumping into two hunters, as she rushed inside.

The warm little cottage smelled like chicory and chocolate, and posters advertising the scenic drop-offs and best areas for kayaking and hiking adorned the rustic walls. Willow walked to the coffee bar, ordered a mocha latte then carried it and a chocolate croissant to a small round table in the corner, situating herself so she could watch the door.

Keeping one eye on the entrance in case someone was following her, she booted up her laptop and logged onto Arm Candy. Heart hammering, she accessed the client list.

Maybe she could figure out who'd killed Kelly. Then she'd decide what to do with the information.

115

RATTLESNAKE RIDGE

Cord and his crew had been hunting for a lost hiker for hours. Finally, they stumbled on a ravine where three small trees had been ripped from the ground by the ferocious winds early this morning. Now here he was at Rattlesnake Ridge, an area known to be infested with the poisonous snakes.

His dog Benji paused, sniffing, then suddenly barked and broke into a run. Cord jogged after him. He trusted Benji more than any person on earth. Well, except for Ellie.

The barking grew louder as Benji trotted down the hill toward the fallen trees and brush, and Cord braced his feet as he descended the steep hill. His boots skidded over sticks and loose rocks, and he practically skated down, the wind pushing him with its force.

He shouted the missing man's name, but his voice died in the wind. A vulture soared above, its loud caw echoing through the trees.

Benji was barking wildly, sniffing at the brush and pawing behind a big rock. The vulture dipped down, talons bared, wings whooshing in the air, but Benji started running in circles jumping in the air as if to chase it.

Cord loved his dog with a vengeance. Dogs were smart. Devoted. They loved you no matter what.

He loved Benji even more so now because all he wanted was a belly rub, a bowl of food and water. He didn't have to pretend to be someone he wasn't.

Racing forward, he slid down the rest of the way until he reached the bottom, gaze darting in all directions as he searched for a bed of snakes. Wind beat at the trees and him, knocking him sideways and carrying a fetid scent through the chilly air. He grabbed a tree branch to maintain his balance, a limb flying past his face.

Slowly he approached the boulder, pushing the brush and limbs aside where Benji was pawing and howling. "I got it, buddy," he said as he patted the dog's back. "You did good." Senses alert, he eased closer, shining his flashlight across the mangled brush. He instantly froze when he spotted what Benji had been barking about.

It wasn't the man he was looking for.

This was a woman.

Cord dropped to his knees and with gloved hands.

Using a stick, he moved away enough weeds and saw a black garbage bag which had been ripped open by small critters.

A bag just like Kelly Hogan and Gayle Wimberly had been found in.

116

Another call from Cord. A third body dumped in a garbage bag.

They were now officially dealing with a serial killer.

Ellie was still pondering her conversation with Dirks as she, Derrick and Laney hiked to Rattlesnake Ridge to meet Cord. Derrick had pushed the inventor of the gaming site to explain why Timmons wouldn't have told him about his life at Hawk House, and Dirks admitted he didn't know. He claimed Timmons was quiet and sometimes seemed fragile. He didn't like to discuss the past and he and Dirks had left it at that because they were in love.

Her phone buzzed. Bryce.

"Gayle has no family except a baby," he said, when she answered. "The neighbor babysits for her. I called Family and Child Services and they came to take the child to foster care. Neighbor said a few days ago Gayle was all bruised and banged up. When she asked her about it, she clammed up. Rachel at the Sweet Tooth said the same thing."

"Maybe she'd met our guy and he let her go the first time. But with the news airing he could have gotten spooked and was afraid she'd put two and two together."

"Possible," Bryce said. "I canvassed the neighbors, but no one remembers seeing a man hanging around."

"Thanks, Bryce. We have another victim. Agent Fox and I are on the way to the scene right now." She hung up and filled Derrick and Laney in. They picked up their pace as they trudged through the hills.

"Keep an eye out for snakes," Ellie said as she hacked at weeds.

"I hate this place," Laney said in a raspy voice.

"You've been here?" Ellie asked.

Laney shook her head. "No, but my grandmother used to tell me the Native American tales. One of them was the Rattlesnake's Revenge. I had bad dreams about them crawling in my bed at night."

"People don't realize how scary stories affect children, do they?" Ellie asked.

"No. But she had other stories of wisdom."

"You grew up on the reservation?" Ellie asked.

Laney nodded. "She believed that the hearts of children were pure. That the Great Spirit told them things that older people would miss."

"I can see that," Ellie said. "And it's our job to protect them. Only no one protected those poor kids at the orphanage."

They came to a fork and Derrick halted. "Which way?"

"Northeast," Ellie said.

They fell silent as they plowed their way through more overgrown weeds and hiked past a creek overflowing with lichen. By the time she, Derrick and Laney reached the ridge, forensics was already combing the area. Cord waved them down into the hollow, and they picked their way over fallen trees and brush, the occasional hiss of a snake nearby making them pause to search the ground as they hiked.

At the sight of the black garbage bag, Ellie's stomach

recoiled. Laney shined her light around the body as if searching for the snakes before she stooped to examine the remains.

"What brought you out here?" Derrick asked Cord.

"Search for a missing hiker," Cord said brusquely. "The team split up. Just got a call that he was found. Busted knee but he's on his way to the hospital."

"How did you spot the body down here?" Ellie asked as she surveyed the distance from the top of the ridge to this hollow. "You couldn't have seen it from up there."

Cord rubbed Benji's back. "I didn't. Benji did."

Ellie stopped and patted the dog's thick coat. "You're the hero, buddy."

"That he is." Cord smiled, an unusual occurrence that warmed her as the wind picked up around them. She wondered if Cord meant Benji had saved him, too.

Meanwhile, Derrick circled the boulder, looking up then down at the site where the body lay.

Anxiety coiled inside Ellie. She wondered if the woman had the same symbolic marking on her ankle as Kelly.

Ellie had to press her hand to her mouth to stifle a reaction as the CSI ripped open the bag to reveal the mangled body of the woman. With Kelly, the killer had focused on her body, multiple stab wounds on her chest and torso. If this was the same killer, he hadn't stopped there this time. He'd slashed her face.

Which meant he was escalating. Growing more violent.

"Any ID?" she asked the crime investigator.

"Haven't found any."

The woman was naked just as Kelly Hogan and Gayle Wimberly had been, bloody gashes covering her chest and torso.

"Signs of bondage or restraints," Laney said, her expression schooled as if mentally distancing herself to keep her emotions at bay.

Ellie pushed at her hair. "I need to know what other injuries she sustained."

Laney's body tensed. She knew what Ellie was asking.

Grim-faced, she focused on the lower part of the victim's body.

"No sign of sexual activity, but..."

"I see it," Ellie said, her stomach roiling as Laney turned the victim's leg sideways to examine her ankle. "He marked her with the same symbol as Kelly."

Which confirmed they were dealing with one killer.

By the time Ellie and Derrick reached town, Laney had an ID on the victim. Her breast implants had led them to the manufacturer and were traced back to her.

Her name was Catarina Hamilton. She was twenty-three years old, single and worked as a nail tech at a local salon by day. She also worked for Arm Candy and stood in Judge Karmel's court on solicitation charges, given a warning then released.

He seemed to be a common denominator.

Ellie phoned Willow Rodgers again. When she didn't answer, she left a message. "Ms. Rodgers, another one of your models Catarina Hamilton was murdered. Please warn your girls someone's preying on them. Call me or come to the station ASAP."

If she didn't, Ellie intended to issue an APB for her.

Now that he had warrants for Arm Candy, Derrick confirmed that Gayle Wimberly also was a model for them.

Next, he checked Catarina's profiles and calendar. "You aren't going to believe this," Derrick said. "She was seeing someone who called himself the *Judge*." He cross-checked with

Kelly's and Gayle's correspondence and saw that each of them had referenced seeing the Judge as well.

Her mind spinning, Ellie phoned Bryce again. "Have any of the models mentioned someone called the Judge?"

"No, they're not saying anything. In fact, the minute I asked about their clients, they block me."

118

MAGNOLIA PARK

Ellie called ahead to the manager for the apartments where Catarina Hamilton lived to request access to her apartment.

As Derrick drove, she wondered how the three victims had gotten into business with Arm Candy.

Had Willow Rodgers recruited the women online? Or did she go out and find them under the guise of turning them into models?

Another question for Ms. Rodgers.

Catarina Hamilton had lived in a modest apartment complex with tiny balconies that overlooked the mountains behind. Magnolia trees dotted the property, adding a touch of southern charm which was ruined by the exterior of the units. Except for the dark green trim, everything was beige.

A few cars were parked here and there, and a young woman carried her baby to her sedan as Derrick parked in front of the manager's place. More heavy winds were blowing in rain clouds, casting a dismal gray over the mountain ridges.

Ellie battled the force of the gale as she and Derrick walked up to the manager's office and knocked. The man looked to be late forties although who could tell from his smoker's leathery skin? His hair looked mussed, and so did his flannel shirt which barely covered his paunch as he opened the door. His breath reeked of nicotine and beer.

"You know who killed Catarina?" he asked, his voice slurring slightly.

"We're working on it," Ellie said. "That's why we're here. To search her apartment."

"How well did you know her, Mr. Ingram?" Derrick asked.

Ingram shrugged, the aluminum can collapsing in his fist as he crushed it. "Not very well. She seemed like a nice girl. Real pretty. Always had flashy nails and clothes."

"What else can you tell us?" Ellie asked.

"Paid her rent on time. Told me she wasn't going to renew her lease in June. Guess she found a better place. I can't believe she's dead."

"It is sad," Ellie agreed. "Did you notice any men she dated or anyone hanging around who looked suspicious?"

He tossed the empty can into a trash receptacle by the door. "No. Not that I was watching her or anything. But some of the tenants come and go. They have parties. I get complaints. Catarina never did. Her place was usually quiet."

Because she met her johns away from home. Ellie wanted to know exactly where that was.

"We need to look in her apartment," Derrick said.

"Sure." The man pulled a set of keys from a wall hook and stepped outside. He locked his own door then led them across the parking lot to the next building, and up a flight of stairs. "Had an end unit on the main open when she came here but she wanted upstairs. Said it'd be safer." His voice cracked slightly. "Fat lot of good that did, huh?"

"Yeah, fat lot," Ellie muttered as he opened the door and waved them in. "Just lock up when you finish."

They agreed, and he shuffled down the steps toward his

own place. Ellie entered first and checked out the layout while Derrick went straight to the desk in the small living room.

In the kitchen, Ellie found it stocked with health food items. She shook her head sadly.

A woman who chose the second floor for safety and ate like a health nut wanted to live.

"No cell phone," Derrick said. "Her computer is password-protected. I'll have to send it to the lab."

"Killer probably took her phone and tossed it," Ellie said. "Check under the desk. Maybe you'll find her password."

He stooped to search, and she headed toward the woman's bedroom. The room was neat and tidy, with a queen bed covered by a purple comforter, decorative pillows and a chair in the corner where she'd draped a chenille robe. She checked the closet and found athletic wear, running shoes, and a row of casual shirts and jeans. Another section held more risqué sexy dresses.

She returned to the living room and Derrick stood. "According to applications I found, she had plans for college. Her bank accounts indicate she had hefty savings."

"So she could get out of this lifestyle," Ellie said, her heart aching for the young woman as she recalled Willow's statement.

She'd had no idea that her date the night before would be her last.

DAY 6

Ellie was still stewing the next morning when she and Derrick met up. Kelly, Gayle and Catarina all worked for Arm Candy. All three had been arrested for solicitation and seen Judge Karmel in his courtroom.

She wanted to talk to him and see his reaction.

Ellie and Derrick entered the courtroom along with a handful of spectators. Catarina's mangled body replayed in her head as they seated themselves. It was not likely that the client called the Judge was actually a real judge but at this point, Karmel and Arm Candy were the only two connections between the women.

Judge Karmel had an appealing face and charm written all over him. Although definitely not Ellie's type, he probably seduced women left and right. He was late forties, with short brown hair neatly styled, an angular jaw, and bronzed skin as if he liked the outdoors. He also had an air of confidence about him as if he knew he held power and liked women to yield to it.

The next case on the docket was a restaurant owner charged with money laundering.

The judge cited bail at one-hundred thousand, and the bailiff escorted the defendant from the courtroom.

Ellie noted the court reporter tapping away, his eyes darting toward her and Derrick as if he knew who they were. They had been on the news, she reminded herself.

They sat through two more cases, then the judge called a recess for lunch and disappeared into his chambers.

Ellie and Derrick rose, heading toward the bailiff. "We need to talk to Judge Karmel. In private."

He gave a clipped nod. "I'll inform him."

They waited while he went to talk to the judge, and five minutes later were escorted to the judge's chambers. He'd removed his robe and was sipping a coffee.

When they introduced themselves, a muscle twitched in his cheek. "Detective? Special Agent Fox? What can I do for you?"

"Where were you last night?" Ellie asked bluntly.

His charming smile diminished in an instant. "What's this about?"

Ellie scrutinized his facial expression. "We're here about a murder. Actually, three murders."

He tugged at his red power tie. "I don't understand."

"Last night a woman named Catarina Hamilton was found dead in the woods in a similar manner to two other murder victims," Derrick said. "She was in your court a while back."

Judge Karmel simply stared at them. "Dozens of people are in my court every day. You can't expect me to remember all of them."

"This woman faced solicitation charges but you let her off," Ellie pointed out. "Just as you did Kelly Hogan and Gayle Wimberly."

"We've heard you do that a lot, that you're easy on sex workers," Derrick added.

Karmel's lips curled into a frown. "I do because the laws here are antiquated. Most states and counties don't make arrests for solicitation or prostitution anymore. And," he said with a finger raised to make a point, "I'm trying to give these young girls a break. Encourage them to pursue their educations and make a better life for themselves."

"So you care about them?" Ellie said.

His green eyes flashed. "Yes, is that so hard to believe?"

"Each of these women belonged to an online modeling site called Arm Candy," Derrick cut in. "Do you belong to that site?"

"No." Judge Karmel squeezed the stress ball on his desk then stood. "Now I don't appreciate where you're going with this."

Ellie stepped closer to him. "Your name is a common denominator with three murder victims."

"As I said, I see a lot of people in my court," he ground out. "Do you think I murder them all?"

"No," Ellie said. "But maybe you pressured these women for sex in exchange for letting them off and things got out of hand."

A seething warning sparked in his eyes. "That's ridiculous."

"Is it?" Ellie asked. "We know that the night before each victim died, she met a man through Arm Candy who called himself the Judge."

He scoffed. "I'm not the only judge in Georgia. And if I was going to commit a crime, you really think I'm stupid enough to use my title?"

Ellie arched a brow. "I think you're so arrogant that you didn't think anyone would suspect you. But perhaps you connected with them, then took it too far and one or both of them threatened to expose you. You snapped and killed them to keep them quiet."

He leaned toward her and clenched her arm. "You are making a big mistake, Detective."

Derrick stepped forward to intervene, but Ellie shook her head. In one fast movement, she jerked the judge's hand from her arm, flipped him around and twisted it behind his back. "No, you made the mistake by touching me." Disgust laced her tone. "But that's what you do, isn't it? You take advantage of women by using your power." Ellie pressed harder, trying to goad him. "And you prefer rough sex, don't you?"

"If you want to know how I like it, I'll show you," he said with a smirk.

Ellie shoved him away from her. "Just try it, and you'll either find yourself on the other side of court or buried. Your choice."

He rubbed at his wrist which was red from her grip then jutted up his chin in challenge. "Is that a threat?"

Ellie shot him a sadistic grin. "No, sir, that's a promise. And if you killed those women, I will find the proof and put you away. I wonder how the prisoners you locked up will like having you as their cell mate?"

His eyes bulged. "Watch out, Detective. I'm still a judge in this county."

"Not for long if I have anything to do with it." Seething, she turned and strode from his office. She didn't stop until she reached the outside, where she could breathe.

120

BLUE SKY

Just breathe. Just breathe.

Ever since Willow escaped Hawk House, she'd told herself that. If she simply breathed, she could get through it. The pain would pass. The torture. The minutes. The hours.

And then she'd be free.

Back at the orphanage, she'd drawn the short end of the pulley bone and failed at the tests, so Blackstone had dragged her to the pit. She'd screamed and fought, but she was only ten and tiny against his mountainous frame.

Then he was there. The boy who led them all. Their hero because he showed no fear.

He fought for them. Took punishments in their place. Taught her to lie perfectly still so she wouldn't feel the bones jabbing into her back and legs and arms as she was forced to lie on the bed of bones.

"I see the way the boys look at you. You deserve to be punished," Blackstone had said.

Now three of her girls were dead. Murdered. Marked with Blackstone's symbol for being a temptress just as Blackstone had marked her. The son of a bitch blamed women for everything.

Quoted the Bible and how Eve tempted Adam with the apple from the forbidden tree. Said all women lured men into sin.

The killer couldn't be the same boy who'd saved her, could he?

He'd been her hero. After all this time, she'd assumed he'd made something of himself. Had pictured him in a powerful position. Saving the weaker. Punishing the ones who deserved it.

She felt the walls closing around her just like they had when she'd been locked in that room.

Then he'd stepped in to prevent Blackstone from throwing her into that hole and told her to run and... everything had happened so fast. Blood and screams and shouts and... then the shovels were passed out.

Her hand shook as she stared at it and remembered digging as he'd told her to do. No one would ever know, he said.

Then they would all be free.

But she'd run in a blind panic. And freedom was the last thing she'd found when she'd escaped.

121

CROOKED CREEK

Rage steamrolled through Derrick like an out-of-control freight train. No one manhandled a woman on his watch. Especially Ellie.

"You touch her again, or bother her, Judge, and I'll come after you. Then that robe won't be worth the cloth it's made of." Leaving the cocky asshole with his pride split open and worrying about the threat, he strode from the room, hoping they did find some evidence against the man.

His temper exploded again when he saw Ellie pacing by his vehicle. He knew how damn stubborn she was, and her pride had to be smarting from what had just happened. Karmel might have thought he was putting her in her place, but he'd just pissed her off.

Him, too.

He took the steps from the courthouse two at a time, welcoming the stiff wind to cool the angry heat burning through his veins. By the time he reached Ellie, he told himself to chill. But then he couldn't help himself.

"You okay?" he asked. "That bastard—"

"Don't." She threw up a hand and motioned to get in the

car. He did, starting the engine as she spewed, "You think I haven't had to take that crap before? Because I have. First in high school and then the academy." She whirled on him. "And I don't need you saving me. I can damn well save myself."

His fingers curled around the steering wheel and he silently ordered himself to keep his mouth shut. But he wanted to save her. Wanted to pound the ass wipe's brains in and lock him up.

"You know I'm not like that."

She jerked her head toward him, and for a moment he thought anger sizzled in her eyes. Then something else. A softer look.

"If you were, I wouldn't be working with you."

Her breathing quickened. His did, too. Suddenly he wanted to pull her to him. Kiss her. Wipe away the darkness in both their lives.

But he couldn't do that, not under the circumstances. So he forced himself to drag his gaze from her. To break the moment.

"Good. Glad we got that settled." He pressed the accelerator and backed from the parking spot. "Where to now?"

"You saw how he deflected our question about his whereabouts last night. Let's talk to his wife."

"Ex," Derrick said he pulled away from the courthouse. "Wife filed for a divorce six months ago."

Ellie smiled and tugged on sunglasses. "I have a feeling we both know the reason. But I want to hear her story."

Deciding not to allow Judge Karmel time to call his wife for an alibi, Derrick drove straight to the wife's house. He'd already looked at the couple's social presence and financials and knew at one point Barbara Karmel had enjoyed the status her husband's job afforded, especially the country club life.

His partner phoned, and Derrick put him on speaker. "Some news," Bennett said. "Searched all three victims' phone records. All received calls from the same number."

"Who does it belong to?" Derrick asked.

"Judge Alexander Karmel. He's—"

"In town. Yes, we just spoke to him," Derrick said. "But he lied about having personal contact with the women."

If he'd lied about that, he might have lied about killing them.

122

"I knew he was hiding something," Ellie said. "Is he so narcissistic he thought we wouldn't find out? Or does he think *I'm* stupid?"

"Narcissistic," Derrick said flatly. "But if he's behind these murders, we'll find proof and nail him to the wall."

Ellie nodded and they lapsed into a strained silence. Despite herself, her mind strayed to the tension between them earlier. She'd been so pissed at Judge Karmel that she was fuming. Then Derrick had assured her he didn't hold the man's sexist beliefs and she'd nearly kissed him.

She knew he was nothing like that bastard Karmel. Otherwise, she never would have slept with Derrick on their first case. Since then, they'd managed to keep things on a professional level. But he was tempting, she couldn't deny that...

Remembering he had a woman named Lindsey in his life, she checked her desires. If he had a girlfriend back in Atlanta, she didn't intend to be the *other* woman. And until she knew, she'd keep her hands to herself. End of story.

They passed farmland, speeding along a curvy road until they reached the polo fields. Gated communities housing million-dollar mansions with manicured lawns and outdoor pools were spread in the area. Just as Derrick turned down the long winding drive to the estate where the judge's wife, Barbara, lived, Deputy Landrum texted.

Checked into Ogden. Moderate but steady income from position as sheriff during his office. Pension enough to retire when he did. Note: thirty-two years ago he donated ten-thousand dollars to a charity, but I can't find a record of the name of it.

Ellie drummed her fingers on her thigh. She sent a return text.

A one- time donation?

Heath: *Yes.*

Interesting. If that charity had something to do with Hawk House, why wouldn't he have mentioned he'd helped them out? Or if he'd covered for Blackstone, she would have guessed the headteacher had paid Ogden to keep quiet, not the other way around.

Another message came in from Heath, just then.

Studied NCEMC's data base – no records of Abel Crane, Willow Rodgers or Wanita Weathers being reported missing. Also researched adoption records. None on the three of them. And no record of their placement after leaving Hawk House.

Ellie sighed. Willow had survived. But how? Had she lived on the streets? Found someone to take her in? More questions she'd have to ask when they located her.

123

CUMMING, GEORGIA

Ellie refastened her ponytail after the wind had ripped it apart while they waited on Barbara Karmel to answer the door. Her antebellum home looked like something you'd see in Southern Living magazine. White with giant columns and wide porches. A manicured sprawling lawn with a garden full of colorful flowers. A Mercedes parked in the circular drive.

When Mrs. Karmel answered the door, Ellie noted the interior was just as elegant as the exterior. Marble floors, a two-story foyer, a crystal chandelier. Wide rooms with fourteen-feet-ceilings. From the foyer, she could see rich brown leather furniture and a picture window that overlooked a pond in back.

Mrs. Karmel looked elegant in a pale pink pant suit, her platinum-blond hair fashioned in a chignon held back by a pearled clip. But she was so thin that her cheekbones jutted out and her arms looked frail.

"Mrs. Karmel," Ellie began then she and Derrick identified themselves.

"I know who you are, and you can call me Barbara," she said. "I watch the news. You're investigating those bodies found at that horrible-sounding orphanage."

"Yes, and three other murders. May we come in?"

Her gaze flitted between the two of them then she gestured for them to follow her to the living room. An expensive oil painting of horses hung above the fireplace. "Nice place," Ellie said.

"Thanks." Barbara indicated a silver coffee set on a cherry buffet. "Coffee?"

Ellie and Derrick both declined, then the wife seated herself on a velvet settee and they claimed the wing chairs facing her.

"I'm not sure why you're here. I don't know anything about those bones you found," Barbara said with a wince.

"Actually, we've come about the murders of Kelly Hogan, Gayle Wimberly and another woman named Catarina Hamilton," Ellie said.

Barbara simply crossed her legs and looked at them. "That's awful, but I don't understand how I can help you."

"Where were you last night?" Derrick asked.

Her lip curled into a frown. "Excuse me?"

"Where were you last night?" Ellie repeated. Although she couldn't imagine this sophisticated woman stabbing someone multiple times then having the strength to carry the body into the woods.

"Having dinner with three of the ladies from the club," Barbara said. "Now, why are you asking me about those women?"

Ellie and Derrick exchanged a look, then Ellie spoke. "They belonged to an escort service called Arm Candy," Ellie said. "We also have reason to believe your husband knew them personally."

"Ahh, I see," Mrs. Karmel murmured. "For the record, Alexander is my ex. And before you ask, I divorced him because he was cheating. And yes, with a hooker. Multiple hookers."

She fanned her face. "It was downright humiliating. We had a good life, but he had a wandering eye."

"So you were aware of his affairs?"

"Of course. I'm not a fool. But I'd hardly call them affairs," she answered. "That might have been better. But he was into porn and call girls and said I shouldn't mind because they meant nothing to him." She sighed as if she was bored.

"I'm sure you were angry," Ellie said. "Maybe you wanted to get back at him. Hurt him."

Barbara chuckled. "Frankly, I stopped caring a long time ago. And if you think I killed those women out of jealousy or revenge, you couldn't be farther from the truth. He is not worth ruining my life over. That's the reason I left him."

She leaned forward, smoothing a wrinkle in her slacks. Her eyes crinkled as if the wheels were turning in her head. "Do you think my ex had something to do with their deaths?"

Ellie breathed out. "We believe he's connected with all three victims through that site. And he lied about that."

Derrick crossed his arms. "Do you think he's capable of murder?"

"I honestly don't know. He had gotten into rough sex. I know because he came home with scratches and bruises sometimes. And..."

"And what?" Ellie asked.

"He loves the power of sitting on that bench and doling out judgments." Her voice was steady when she spoke. "And he'd do anything to protect his reputation."

Ellie wondered if that included murder.

124

While Derrick drove them back to the police station, Ellie made a phone call to request warrants for the judge's phone and computer.

"You really suspect Karmel of murder?" Judge Thorndyke asked, hesitation in his voice.

"I don't know if he committed the crimes, but he lied about knowing the victims personally. His wife admitted that she caught him cheating on her with sex workers and that he liked rough sex. We also found a connection between both women and a client they called the Judge."

"That's a stretch," Thorndyke said. "But... that man is a disgrace to the bench. I'm going to issue the warrants, but only because my own clerk worked for him and resigned because of sexual harassment."

Ellie's temper resurfaced and Derrick's hands tightened around the steering wheel. "Did she file charges?"

"No, I encouraged her to, but she has children and just wanted away from him and to put it behind her."

The very reason these men got away with it, Ellie thought in disgust.

"I wish she had spoken up," Ellie said. "You know she wasn't the first and won't be the last."

"Yes, I know. Karmel needs to be shaken up. And if he hurt those women, I'd enjoy sending him to prison myself."

Ellie grinned, sensing she had an ally. Even if Karmel wasn't guilty of murder, maybe she could put a stop to his bullying. Getting him thrown out of office would be even better.

Warrants in hand, she and Derrick drove to the courthouse next. Judge Karmel had finished the cases on his docket and was about to leave. But they caught him just in time.

"What the hell are you two doing back here?" Karmel growled.

"Taking you in for questioning," Ellie said with a smile.

"You can't do that. I'm a goddamn judge."

Derrick laid the warrants on the judge's desk. "This says we can. Now, sir, we need your phone and computer."

"What?" His eyes bulged with anger. "You little bitch. How dare you come to my court and—"

Derrick cut him off. "Shut up before I arrest you for threatening and harassing an officer."

"You'll pay for this, Detective Reeves," Karmel said in a menacing tone.

Derrick crossed his arms, demanding. "Now, your phone and computer. And you are going with us to the station until we clear this up."

Judge Karmel cursed a blue streak, then yelled at his assistant to call his attorney. Ellie smiled to herself as Derrick escorted him from his office while his coworkers watched in stunned silence.

125

While Judge Karmel stewed in a waiting area, Ellie and Derrick dove into his phone and computer.

Karmel's attorney showed up, a silver-haired lawyer in his fifties with a southern twang. "You have nothing to worry about, Alexander," Jed Wheaton said. "They're just fishing."

Karmel reluctantly agreed, but anger radiated from him in palpable waves.

"I'm being set up," Karmel declared. "You won't find anything because I'm innocent."

Ellie folded her arms. "That's not what I've heard, Judge. I heard you like sex workers and you used your power against women."

His lips turned blue he was so mad. "You must be dumber than I thought if you believe everything you hear."

"Kelly Hogan's name, Gayle Wimberly's and Catarina Hamilton's are in your phone," Derrick pointed out.

The judge stood, hair ruffled where he'd run his hands through it. "That can't be true."

"The evidence doesn't lie," Ellie said.

"Then someone is setting me up," Karmel insisted.

"Why would someone frame you?" Ellie asked.

"I deal with criminals on a daily basis," Karmel said. "I make enemies. It comes with the job."

"You handle misdemeanor cases," Ellie pointed out. "Who would be angry enough about whatever minor sentence you gave them to frame you for murder?"

His breath wheezed out. "Do your job and tell me. Run background checks on the defendants who've come through my court. Maybe one of them has an obsession with sex workers and a history of violence. Or a vendetta against the law and they're using me as a scapegoat."

Ellie glanced between the attorney and the judge. "I'll do that. Meanwhile make a list of anyone you can think of who crossed you." Ellie would bet the majority were women. Maybe one of them had found a way to get back at him.

"Your computer records also indicate meet-ups with the women," Derrick said. "How do you explain that?"

Karmel's eyes flared with panic. His attorney saved him from responding with a quick shake of his head. "We've answered your questions." He checked his watch. "Now get this cleared up before we press charges against the police department for harassment and defamation of character." His gaze pinned Ellie. "And you, Detective Reeves, will be the focus of that complaint."

Ellie spun around and left the room. Derrick followed, boots clicking on the floor.

"I'll have Deputy Landrum look at each and every case that asswipe has presided over," Ellie said. "He can send the list of females to Shondra, and she can start questioning them."

"I'll look into staff and employees he might have crossed," Derrick said. "If there's something there, we'll find it."

Ellie nodded. She wanted the judge to be guilty. But something nagged at her. It almost seemed too easy and tidy – that the killer had called himself the Judge. And all three women's numbers had been in his contacts. His in theirs.

Judge Karmel might be a narcissistic bastard. But if anyone knew how to cover their ass, he would.

What the hell was she missing?

126

HAWK HOUSE

Thirty years ago

She clapped her hands over her ears to drown out the sound of the other girl crying. He'd moved her into the dorm room, he called it, but it was almost as scary as the bone room.

She searched for a way out from where she lay chained to the bed, but there were bars on the small windows. It was dark and dreary and smelled like pee. The sound of mice skittering across the old wooden floor made her hunch into a ball against the wall.

The chains clanked as she tried to turn her back against the door.

Sometimes he checked on them at night. Sometimes he left them for hours and hours.

She closed her eyes, squeezing them so tight she thought her eyeballs would bulge right out.

The other girl sobbed harder.

She had no idea who she was. But the girl slapped and kicked at him when he came for her. Then he dragged her from the room, and her ear-splitting screams filled the house.

A clock ticked the minutes away. Thunder boomed outside. Rain pinged the tiny windowpane, the glass rattling. Lightning streaked the room in jagged lines that lit up the ceiling.

The cracks looked like the bones she'd seen in jars in his basement.

Shivering, she closed her eyes and tried to block it all out.

The sound of the boys across the hall drifted to her. "The new girl is dumb. She can't talk," one of them said.

"Weirdo," another one called her.

"She'll never make it," said another.

Her body shook with fear. She didn't know if she'd make it either.

127

All the pieces were falling into place. They'd arrested Judge Karmel. The pig was finally going to get what he deserved.

But the others... He'd been watching them all and he was getting nervous. Willow had disappeared from her house. She didn't want to be found.

But she couldn't hide for long.

Jonas might a weak link. Except... the boy owed him. He'd been so frail back then, like a thin sheet of glass that could shatter if the wind rattled it too hard. And Blackstone had come down on him like a funnel cloud during tornado season.

The boy's daddy had sent him to Hawk House. Said Jonas wasn't normal. Told Blackstone to beat the gay out of him.

Disgust rolled through him in waves. Jonas was who he was. No amount of beating or threatening or punishing had made him any different. Except he had learned from the bone hunts. Ironically, he'd turned those gruesome games into an artform. The bone windchimes were especially mesmerizing.

No, Jonas wouldn't talk. He didn't want to go to prison. He wouldn't last there a day.

Still, he wanted Jonas to know he was watching.

He went to his work room, shut the door then walked to the shelf of bones, setting one of the jars of assorted bones on his workspace. Then he pulled a canvas from the drawer and drew an open door in the center. Emulating the room where they'd been kept, he fashioned a bed of bones. Then he painted a long hallway that led to another door, this one closed. Above the doorway he used the tiny bones of a bluebird to write the word *Shh*.

He smiled to himself as he finished. Jonas would know exactly what it meant. Raising his hands, he stared at the crisscross scar on the underside of his wrist. It symbolized the promise they'd all made.

Jonas would keep the promise or he knew what would happen.

128

LAKE LANIER

While Heath investigated the cases Karmel had presided over and Shondra questioned employees who worked with him, Ellie and Derrick drove to the judge's house.

Ellie expected another mansion, but Karmel had moved into a rustic home on Lake Lanier in Gainesville, GA. His work commute was over an hour, but she supposed it was worth it for the privacy and magnificent lake view. Built of logs, the ranch house sat on a deep-water cove with a private boat dock. Mountains rose in the distance to meet the clouds. Ruby slippers, Lynwood gold forsythia shrubs and purple creeping verbena plants added color to the lush greenery. A flock of gulls swooned over the surface of the serpentine water.

Tales that the lake was haunted abounded in the area, saying angry spirts called people to submerged graves below the surface. Although partygoers and boaters didn't let that deter them from flooding the lake each summer. Today she could see sailboats and ski boats dotting the water.

"Looks like he enjoys the single life," Ellie commented. "Wonder how many young girls he's brought here."

"It is secluded," Derrick said as he turned in a wide arc to survey the wooded property. "He could do whatever he wanted, and no one would hear."

"The jerk planned it that way," Ellie said. Fishermen floated along in canoes, casting lines and enjoying the quiet. In spite of the beauty, Ellie imagined women being forced to do unspeakable things in the basement of the ranch-style home, a house so secluded with vegetation and set in an isolated cove so no one could hear if they cried out for help.

"Let's check out the inside." Before they'd left the station, Derrick had managed to convince the judge to give him his house key. Karmel insisted there was nothing incriminating inside but still balked. Derrick emphasized that if he was innocent, it was the best way to clear himself.

Unlocking the oak front door, Derrick revealed an open foyer that led to an impressive cathedral ceiling and deep mahogany leather furniture. Deer heads and antlers adorned the walls, indicating Karmel was a hunter or collector. Behind the suit, lay a mountain man.

"Let's divide up," Derrick said. "I'll take the kitchen and study."

"I'll check the bedrooms. We'll search the basement together." Chill bumps skated up her arms. If they found anything incriminating, she sensed it would be downstairs.

While Derrick swept the kitchen, checking drawers and cabinets, she headed down the hall. A guest room to the right held exercise equipment and a mirrored wall. She quickly checked the closet but found only a stack of weights.

Moving on, she found the master bedroom at the end of the hall. A king-sized oak bed, black walls and a gold bedspread. She searched his closet and found neatly laundered suits and shirts, polished Italian loafers and an array of designer ties. Expensive colognes, body washes and shampoo promising to increase hair growth lined the marble vanity.

Ellie rolled her eyes. The items fit.

She rushed back to find Derrick shaking his head. "Nothing in here. In his desk, were personal business files, bank statements and such, but I looked through them. He has some savings but also paid his wife a chunk in alimony and gave her the house. If he paid off any women to keep them from filing sexual harassment charges, he knew how to cover it up."

Ellie gestured toward the hall door leading to the basement. "Let's see what's down there."

A frown marred Derrick's forehead as he led the way, and Ellie flipped on the overhead light as she went. At the base of the steps, lay an entertainment room with a plush sofa, a fully stocked bar and a surround system that piped music from a Bluetooth set-up.

Mirrors lined one wall and a pole was featured in the center. She imagined Judge Karmel forcing girls to lap dance for him in this very room and her stomach turned.

Across the room, Derrick located a set of double doors leading into an area cast in pitch black. He shined his flashlight around the space and Ellie's breath caught.

Chains hung from the metal hooks from the ceiling and whips were strung around the room. Candles lined the shelves, and sex toys filled the tables. A hint of musk and sex and other body odors swirled around her.

How many women had he brought here? How many took money for sex or to keep quiet?

And why kill Kelly, Gayle and Catarina? Because they threatened to expose his dirty secrets?

Derrick called her name. "Come here, you have to see this."

She'd been so lost in thought she hadn't realized he'd disappeared into another room. Pulse hiking, she ducked into the dark space. Twinkling lights flickered across the interior and Derrick shined his flashlight into a shiny black metal shelving system. The doors stood open revealing a wall of photographs of dozens of women indulging in sex, bondage and S & M. Bile rose to her throat at some of the graphic images. Women being whipped, their bloody backs exposed. Women on their hands and knees, blindfolded, begging to be let go. Women crawling to escape.

"Dear God," Ellie whispered. "He's more perverted than I imagined."

"Our three victims are here," Derrick said, his voice thick with disgust. "And look at this."

He opened another door and Ellie gasped. There were more photos, this time of Kelly, Gayle and Catarina lying dead, their blood-soaked bodies being stuffed into a trash bag.

Then there was a photo of those body bags left in the woods.

129

"We've got him."

"The evidence is damning," Derrick agreed. "I'll call a forensic team. If Judge Karmel brought the women home for his sex games, then killed them down here, maybe they'll find evidence."

Ellie phoned for a crime team, then she and Derrick snapped photos of the wall of horrors.

"I wonder why none of these women came forward," Derrick said.

"You know how sexual assault cases go. Defense attorneys put the female under the microscope and tear her apart. She dressed too provocatively, she chose to drink, she chose to get in the car with the guy. She agreed to sex. Then she decided she didn't like it and cried rape."

"I can't imagine anyone consenting to this type of S&M," Derrick muttered.

"I don't understand it myself, but it does exist," Ellie said. "And once a woman agrees to participate, she's caught in a trap just as women who are sexually harassed are. If they come forward, their reputations get destroyed. They often lose their jobs and are blackballed from employment elsewhere. The system sucks."

Derrick remained quiet as he walked around the room searching for other evidence. "True. And with a powerful man like Karmel, she would be even more intimidated."

"It's possible that Kelly, Gayle, and Catarina threatened to talk and that's why he killed them."

Ellie's phone buzzed. It was Shondra so she put her on speaker. "I may have something," Shondra said. "Two of the clerks who work with Karmel admit he sexually harassed him. When they threatened to speak up, he claimed he'd fire them and that they came onto him."

"Despicable," Ellie murmured.

"There's more. I got the name of a young woman who quit her internship three weeks in. She claims Karmel threatened to blackball her professionally if she made allegations against him. He also threatened to make it look like she attempted to black-mail him."

"I hope you assured them that wouldn't happen if they came forward."

"I tried, but all three women were extremely nervous," Shondra said. "Tell me you have something to nail him with. That would make it easier for them to speak up."

"I do," Ellie replied, describing what they'd found.

"That no good scumbag," Shondra said. "I hope he rots in prison."

"First we have to make sure the case sticks. Anything else from other employees?"

"Not yet. The bailiff didn't offer much – said he kept his head down and did his job. The court reporter, Shamus Dorton, said Judge Karmel was cocky and treated the staff like they were below him, but that's about it."

Ellie wasn't surprised at the comment, but that didn't prove

Karmel was guilty of anything but being arrogant. "Keep digging."

"I will. Deputy Landrum has names of other women who faced Karmel in court. I'll talk to them."

"Thanks. Keep me posted. Meanwhile, we'll keep Karmel in holding. And ask Bryce for help. He can arrange protection for those women."

"Will do."

The doorbell rang and Ellie hung up, then hurried to greet the ERT. She quickly explained what they'd discovered in the basement. "The main floor appears clean. The basement is what's interesting." She showed the team down the stairs and gave them time to absorb the shock of their findings.

"Holy mother of God," the woman said.

The young man pulled a hand over his face. "He was into some kinky shit, wasn't he?"

True, but Ellie realized it was all circumstantial evidence at this point. Damning, but she wanted more. "Go over this place with a fine-toothed comb," Ellie said. "Look for prints, DNA, blood, semen, anything that can connect Karmel to the victims."

"Copy that," the guy said.

"And this is confidential as always." ERT was sworn not to reveal details of cases they worked, but she still issued a reminder. During pillow talk or drinks, sometimes people's tongues got loose. And incriminating a judge with sex crimes and murder would be a juicy topic.

The female's gaze swung to Ellie's, disapproval flaring across her features. "Don't worry. We won't do anything to jeopardize this case."

"Just find me something," Ellie said. "A hair. Blood. DNA. Something that can't be disputed."

Something that would confirm Judge Karmel was a murderer.

130

EAGLE'S LANDING

Jonas's lungs strained for air as he stared at the message written in bones. The old house, the forest of bones, the scents of blood and animal decay, the bleach… the smells and sounds and hideous reminders of the past that had been meant to shape him into the man his father wanted.

None of it had worked. It had only made him more determined to fight for who he was.

"Why didn't you tell me about being at that orphanage?" Mason asked, dragging him from the memories.

Jonas quickly tucked the message beneath a stack of sketches he'd drawn for his latest creations. Taking a deep breath, he faced his partner. "Because it was a long time ago. I've tried to forget that time in my life."

Mason's dark blue eyes raked over him, questioning. The moment he'd met Mason he'd felt a connection. As if he was the one person in the world who'd understand him. Who'd get him.

Still, he had his secrets to keep.

"You want to talk about it now?" Mason asked softly.

Yes, he wanted to shout to the world what that sadistic

monster had done to all of them. Let the world know that he deserved to go to Hell.

But that meant exposing innocents. Answering questions he'd sworn a long time ago to never answer. At least not with the truth.

"Jonas, listen, man. I'm here. I saw the news about those poor kids' remains." He picked up one of the necklaces Jonas had crafted with a wolf's teeth. "Rumors in town say the headmaster was cruel and abused the children. Is that true?"

Sweat beaded on Jonas' upper lip, and he dug his fingers into his palms. "Yes. But I don't want to talk about it."

"That's how you got those scars on your back and arms, isn't it?" Mason asked.

"I said I don't want to discuss it," Jonas said sharply.

Mason moved toward him, lifting Jonas's hand and studying his fingers. "You have scars on your fingers, too."

Panic built in his chest to the point he thought he might explode.

"Do you know what happened to those kids?" Mason pushed. "Because if you do, you can tell me. We can go to the police together."

"I'm not going anywhere," Jonas ground out. "Now drop it or get out."

For a second, hurt flared in Mason's expression and Jonas felt like a heel. But the message he'd just received rang loud and clear.

Years ago, he'd made a promise. They all had. Then they'd gone their separate ways. Agreed not to look for each other or make contact. That it was too dangerous.

But one of them was back. One of them was in town and knew where he was.

Jonas had no doubt he'd end up in the grave if he talked.

That day had ended the way it should have. No one had helped them when they were there.

Why should he help *them* now?

More gray clouds were forming as Ellie and Derrick returned to the police station, faint red, orange and yellow streaks shimmering through the gray. She'd phoned Willow Rodgers again, and left her a voicemail. Now that she knew Willow had been at Hawk House as a child, she assumed the woman was intentionally avoiding her. Landrum was trying to locate her.

Could she possibly have killed her own models? If so, why?

Her frustration with Judge Karmel intensified. She was sick and tired of men using their power. Blackstone. Karmel.

Even Ogden who'd been avoiding her.

Once she finished here, she intended to confront him again. If he knew where Blackstone was, she had to make him talk.

Armed with the photographs forensics had collected, she and Derrick ordered Karmel to be brought to the interrogation room again. Fury radiated from the man's every pore, and he stabbed Ellie with a venomous look. His lawyer placed a hand on Karmel's arm as they sat, a silent warning to control himself.

"You said you had no personal contact with Kelly Hogan, Gayle Wimberly or Catarina Hamilton," Ellie began. "But you lied, Mr. Karmel."

"It's Judge," the man ground out.

Not for long, Ellie thought. "As I stated earlier, we know that you connected with them on Arm Candy. Maybe you recognized their profiles and after letting them off easy, you decided to take advantage of that."

"I did not take advantage of them," he said. "Besides, if I'd wanted sex with them, I wouldn't have needed that site."

"That's right. You knew their contact information from the arrests," Ellie said. Which his attorney could use to punch a hole in her theory.

Derrick cleared his throat. "Give it up, Karmel. We were just at your house. In your basement."

Ellie watched as Karmel fidgeted.

Stone faced, she laid the disturbing pictures of the women on the table. He blanched, his mouth working from side to side. "Those are not mine," he said through clenched teeth. "Someone must have put them there."

"Good try," Ellie said. "But I don't believe you." She placed the booking photo of Kelly Hogan on the table, followed by Gayle Wimberly's and Catarina Hamilton's.

His olive skin turned a pasty white. He opened his mouth to speak but his attorney pressed a hand to his arm again and shook his head.

"And then look at these." Ellie stood, towering over him as she laid the graphic photos of the women's mutilated bodies in front of him. "You couldn't help yourself, could you? You killed them in a fit of rage, then you took pictures as souvenirs before you dumped their bodies."

Karmel's hands balled into fists. He lurched up, his eyes bulging with outrage. "You little bitch. You planted those—"

His attorney grabbed his arm. "Sit down, Alexander, and be quiet."

"But—"

"I said sit down," his attorney barked.
Ellie simply folded her arms.
They had him.

132

"One case solved, now we can focus on the Hawk House investigation," Ellie said as she and Derrick left Karmel in lock-up. "With the evidence against him, hopefully bail will be denied." Although she'd still like to get a confession from him. Maybe with some pressure and a few nights in jail, that would come.

Derrick grimaced. "Hopefully. Although we don't know who owes him favors or how deep his pockets go."

"True, but let's enjoy the victory for now. At least he's off the street so the sex workers and other women will be safe tonight." She rubbed her neck where it ached. She could use a good night's sleep. "But there's no proof of a connection between him and Hawk House." Which meant that if he hadn't killed Yolanda Schmidt and Leah Gentilly someone else had. There were also the remains of the teacher and janitor they'd found on the property along with the children's remains.

She rolled her shoulders, exhaustion tugging at her muscles. "Feel like dinner?"

Derrick took a peek at his phone, his expression unreadable again. "Sorry. I need to make a call."

Ellie wanted to ask if that call involved Lindsey but refrained.

He left, and Ellie yanked on her jacket, then headed to her Jeep. Dusk had come and gone while she was inside, and the sky was a dull gray. Thunder rumbled, the winds from the bowing trees reminding her of the tornados that had torn up the area last year.

She spotted Cord's truck at the Corner Café and started to stop in, but he would be busy with Lola, and she needed to talk to Ogden. A light drizzle of rain seeped from the clouds as she drove toward Quail Ridge.

A streak of lightning zigzagged across the treetops and the clouds unleashed, rain pummeling the windshield. She slowed and turned on the defroster and wipers, but it was coming down so fast and hard that she could barely see the road.

Suddenly, bright lights blinded her from behind and she looked up to see a vehicle roaring toward her. She pushed on her flashers in case he didn't see her, but he sped closer, swinging the car around her to pass.

Ellie was tempted to turn on her siren, force him to pull over and cite him for dangerous driving. Instead, she clenched the steering wheel in a white-knuckled grip, slowing so he could move on.

As the vehicle veered up beside her, rainwater spewed from his tires, and she heard a ping. Instantaneously, the window on the driver's side burst.

She swung the Jeep sideways. What the hell? The driver had shot at her! Glass shattered and the wind blew rain in pelting her.

She swerved, tires churning through the deluge of water, but the road was slick and she skidded.

A second later, another bullet pinged the side of her Jeep and the SUV – or was it a truck? – swerved sideways and slammed into her, sending her car careening toward the ditch.

She grappled for control but lost it and her Jeep raced headfirst into the gulley, then rolled.

Her heard pounded as it flipped to the side and skidded into the ditch. Her air bag exploded, knocking the breath from her, and the seatbelt jerked tight. Pain shot through her neck, shoulder and chest.

Worried the shooter was going to come after her, she shoved at the air bag, pulled a knife from her pocket and punctured it, then cut the seatbelt. Breath rasping out, she retrieved her weapon and gripped it at the ready as she glanced through the shattered window. She expected to see someone there and braced herself to shoot, but the heavy rain blurred her vision.

Then he *was* there. A shadowy figure loomed over her.

133

Heart thrashing, Ellie raised her gun and aimed at the shadow, but the rain was coming down so hard she couldn't discern a face.

But he must have seen her weapon because suddenly he was gone.

Her chest ached with each breath, and she kept alert in case he returned. Then she heard the sound of an engine roaring to life, and the vehicle racing away.

Shaking with anger, she fumbled for her phone. Her hands were so wet she dropped it and had to reach to the floor to retrieve it. Water was pouring into the car, soaking her and the seats, but she snagged her phone and managed to find Derrick's number.

With trembling fingers, she called him, picking glass from her hair as she waited. "Come on, Derrick, answer," she whispered as she waited. Four rings and he finally did.

"Derrick, someone shot at me. Car crash. Ditch," she rasped. "Need help."

"Where are you?" he asked gruffly.

She gave him the location.

"I'm on my way. Do you need an ambulance?"

"I don't think so."

"I'll be there ASAP."

She hung up, then stuffed her phone into the inside of her jacket and her gun in her holster. She shoved at the car door to open it, but it was jammed shut. Another three tries and she gave up, then pulled her jacket sleeve down to cover her hand. Using her covered fist, she smashed the remaining bits of glass, careful to guard her face and eyes with her arm. Glass flew, shards falling inside and other bits flying outside, caught in the wind and rain.

When she'd cleared the space, she rolled to her knees and pulled herself through the window. Thunder roared and the trees were shaking all around her, the rain pounding in heavy sheets. She could barely see the ground for the downpour but managed to clear the window before falling into the ditch. Her hands sank into the mud as her knees hit the soggy ground.

Shoving her wet hair from her face, she looked up in search of the man or another car, but saw no lights, only the fog of rain and darkness. For a moment, she simply sat there on her hands and knees, struggling to recover.

As her adrenaline waned, she pushed herself up from the muddy ground. The wind and rain battered her, making it hard to stand, but she put one foot in front of the other and began to climb from the ditch. Her ribs ached with every step she took, and she slipped twice, sliding downward on the slippery slope, but she pushed on, instincts alert in case the shooter returned.

As she reached the top of the ditch, she peered over the edge, crouching low until she could make out her surroundings. A car whizzed by, followed by another, but then there was nothing.

Battling tears of frustration, she tried to recall details of the vehicle, but it had been too dark to see the color or model. Her mind raced to who would want her dead.

She'd pissed Judge Karmel off earlier and he'd warned her she'd be sorry. Had he sent someone to kill her?

134

Worry knotted Derrick's belly as he sped toward Ellie. He should have stuck with her. But with Karmel in jail, he'd thought they had a reprieve tonight and he'd have time to talk to Lindsey.

You still have the Hawk House case. Something was nagging at him about the dead sex workers and the discovery of the bones. There were still too many unanswered questions. Too many loose threads.

Like where was Willow Rodgers? Why didn't Jonas Timmons admit he'd been placed at Hawk House? And what was Ogden hiding?

The downpour slowed him as he sped along the mountain road, and he searched left and right for Ellie's Jeep, slowing around a curve. Car lights blinked through the haze of rain, the thunder clapping above him.

Another mile and he slowed again as he approached a bend in the road and spotted a ditch to the right. Easing to the shoulder so he could see, his headlights illuminated the area.

Then he saw Ellie staggering toward him.

A cold knot of fear gripped him in its clutches, robbing him of breath. A second later, he jerked himself into action, cut the engine, pulled on his rain jacket and hood, then jumped out and ran toward Ellie. She was limping, fighting the wind and rain to stay on her feet, and he saw blood trickling down the side of her face.

She called his name although it sounded faint, and he sprinted to her, then grabbed her gently and lifted her chin to look at her. "You're bleeding."

"Just some cuts from the glass," she shouted over the roar of the thunder. Her teeth chattered, and she was shaking violently so he wrapped his arm around her waist and slowly helped her to his car. He opened the passenger side and she slid in, and he jogged around to the rear of the sedan, opened the trunk and grabbed a couple of blankets. Tucking them beneath his jacket, he raced to the driver's side, then wrapped one of the blankets around Ellie and drew her up against him.

She was still shivering so he rubbed her arms and back with his hands to warm her and steady both their nerves.

"What happened?" he asked in a raw whisper.

"I was going to Ogden's," she said. "A vehicle roared up behind me. I slowed for him to pass but then he shot at me. Shattered the driver's window. Twice. I lost control and flipped into the ditch."

Anger railed inside him. "Did you get a look at the vehicle?"

"Not a good one. It was raining too hard and dark." She burrowed against him. "But it was some kind of SUV. Or no... a truck, I think."

"How about the driver?"

Ellie clutched at the blanket. "Didn't see his face. But after I rolled in the ditch, he came down and looked in the broken window. But the rain was beating in my eyes, and I couldn't make out his face. When he saw my gun aimed at him, he disappeared."

Derrick silently cursed. The squeal of a siren broke through the deafening thunder and the ambulance approached. He reluctantly released Ellie, then got out and met the medics.

"Detective Reeves was shot at and crashed her Jeep into the ditch. She appears to be okay but has some minor lacerations. Take her to the hospital for a check-up," he said.

"I don't need to go to the hospital," Ellie argued.

"You're going," he said in a tone that brooked no argument. "Besides, I'll know you'll be safe there and I can hunt for those bullet casings."

He knew that Ellie didn't like to take orders. But she clamped her lips together and he helped her from the vehicle. She winced and pressed her hand over her chest, a hint her ribs were either bruised or cracked. Another reason she needed to be examined by a doctor.

"Come on, ma'am," one of the medics said. "Let's get out of the storm."

"All right. But Derrick, be thorough. I want to find the bastard who tried to kill me."

"Don't worry, so do I," Derrick said, his mind racing. She'd pissed off Judge Karmel. Had he contacted someone to scare or hurt Ellie?

Ellie seemed to swallow her pride and allowed the men to assist her to the ambulance. Derrick watched them go, then phoned Deputy Landrum and explained about the attack on Ellie.

"Is Karmel still in lock-up?"

"Yeah. He's being arraigned in the morning."

"Has he had any contact with anyone since we left?"

"Just his lawyer."

Surely to God the attorney hadn't arranged for someone to come after Ellie. Although the judge could have paid him to do so. If Derrick checked into the man's financials, no doubt the attorney would claim whatever money Karmel had received was payment for representation fees.

"Send an ERT," Derrick said. "Meanwhile I'll look for bullet casings." He hung up, grabbed his flashlight and dug his heels into the soggy ground as he went into the ditch.

The sight of Ellie's Jeep on its side, rain filling the interior through the shattered window roused his temper.

Who other than Karmel would have shot at Ellie?

Three names circled back in his mind. Willow Rodgers, Edgar Ogden and Jonas Timmons.

Had one of them ambushed Ellie?

135

SOMEWHERE ON THE AT

Heavy rain pounded the roof like nails. Willow had run away just like before, all those years ago when she'd abandoned him. He'd needed her back then. Had sacrificed for her. But she'd betrayed him.

Enraged, he chose a bag of bones from his collection and crushed them with his fists. Slivers flew in all directions, stabbing his fingers and drawing blood.

The memories looped through his mind like a horror film. He had to find her.

Hoping to draw her out through her website, he left the pile of brittle bones scattered everywhere and logged onto the Arm Candy site.

His dark urges rose like the devil inside him, beckoning him to kill another. He scoured the site in search of the perfect one for tonight, but a message popped up and he clicked to read it.

The killing has to end.

Excitement zinged through him. It was from Willow.
He replied instantly:

If you want it to end, meet me.

Willow: *Where?*

You know where.

His heartbeat thrummed, exhilarated at the idea of meeting her back where it had all begun.

136

BLUE SKY

Willow's pulse jumped as she read the message. She had a good idea who this was. They'd all lived that nightmare together.

Although disbelief still made her question it was him.

The past rolled back to haunt her. She could live with what they'd done years ago. But the women who worked for her did not deserve to die, especially such violent deaths.

She had to stop him. If that meant meeting him tonight, then so be it.

Once they'd all shared a strong bond. Survival had meant everything.

If it was who she suspected, she owed him. Despite everything, she didn't want to expose him. But the killing had to cease.

Nerves skittered along her spine, and she packed the .38 special she kept in her nightstand. Years ago, she'd thought escaping Hawk House meant freedom from danger. But living on the streets had brought another set of challenges. And then she'd met the woman who'd introduced her to the business. At first, she'd done what she was told.

But eventually she'd broken away from her, too.

All those life lessons had taught her to fight.

She tucked her pistol in her jacket pocket and headed to her car. She hoped she didn't have to use it tonight.

But she would if she had to.

As she buckled her seatbelt, she entered Detective Reeves' phone number and put it on speed dial just in case he had the same plans for her as he had her girls. If he did, he wouldn't get away with it.

137

CROOKED CREEK

"I told you I didn't need to see a doctor, my ribs are just bruised," Ellie said as Derrick drove her home from the hospital.

"You were in a bad accident and looked like hell, so stop complaining."

Ellie gritted her teeth, but she let it slide. At least the doctor had prescribed pain pills if her sore ribs kept her awake tonight. "Did you find the bullet casings?"

"Yes, they're on the way to the lab," he said as he parked at her house. "They look like they came from a .45."

Ellie took a deep breath against the sharp pain in her chest as she opened the car door. She'd traded her soggy, muddy clothes for a pair of scrubs they'd given her at the hospital and Derrick had wrapped a dry blanket around her before they'd left the hospital. Thankfully the earlier downpour had slackened to a drizzle.

He came around the side of the car with an umbrella and offered his hand. Ellie accepted it only because her legs still felt shaky from the accident. Together they walked up to her front door, and he used her key to let them inside.

Although she'd left the kitchen light burning as usual,

Derrick flipped on the living room lamp as they entered. "Let me go through the house," he said, gesturing for her to wait.

Ellie tensed at being given orders but knew he was right. Someone had just tried to kill her. They could easily have come here to finish the job although getting past her alarm would be difficult.

While he checked the bathroom and two bedrooms, she stared through the glass doors to the outside. It was so dark and rainy she couldn't see the woods, but they were there, the tree limbs drooping under the weight of the rain. Leaves and debris floated through the air as the wind hurled them around.

Teeth chattering, she hugged the blanket tighter around her.

"It's clear," Derrick said.

Ellie nodded, exhaustion wearing on her. "I'm still half covered in mud. I'm going to take a bath."

"How about I make us something to eat? Do you have eggs? I can whip up an omelet."

Ellie offered him a smile. "That sounds great."

A small grin curved his mouth, and he poured her a finger of vodka into a tumbler. "Take this to the bath with you. You deserve it."

"Thanks." Comforted by his presence, she breathed out as she headed toward her bedroom. Although as he opened the refrigerator and began pulling out ingredients, she realized it felt odd to have him cook for her.

Nice, but odd. And intimate. Something she tried to avoid...

Carrying her vodka to the bathroom, she ran a hot bath, pouring in bath salts. After stripping, she sank into the hot water hoping it would assuage her achy body. She sipped the vodka, closed her eyes and laid her head back, grateful not to be alone right now.

But thoughts of nearly dying ran rampant through her head.

138

Mandy paced her bedroom, her nerves raw. She was sick to death of everyone online talking about ghosts and the *Bone Hunter* game and those bodies at the old orphanage.

She shivered, the walls closing around her. Even though she'd been a brat to Bryce, he'd called to check on her although she hadn't talked to him. He probably hated her anyway.

Aunt Trudy kept encouraging her to go outside and kick the soccer ball, and Ellie had said the same, but every time she considered it, her knees locked up and she felt like she'd hurl.

There were bad people out there. One of them had killed her mama. Another had killed those poor orphans. Would she be next?

She paced to the window and peeked through the blinds, craving fresh air. Outside, she saw a dark SUV drive by. Her throat clogged with fear.

She was sure she'd seen that same SUV drive by a couple of times the last few days.

Ellie said a deputy would be doing drive-bys but this was no police car.

The car turned around at the end of the street and started back by her house, slowing by her drive. The windows were tinted, but it came to a near stop, and she swore whoever it was, was looking right at her.

139

HAWK HOUSE

A shudder rippled through Willow as she parked at Hawk House, horrifying memories overwhelming her.

The first time she'd laid eyes on Horatio Blackstone with his coal-black eyes. The other children staring up at her with wide frightened looks. Some angry, some challenging, as if they assumed she was too weak to make it here.

Then there was little Wanita with her chocolate-brown eyes and long brown hair with hints of auburn woven in.

Wanita who'd never spoken while they were there.

Until that last day when it had all happened. Wanita's screams had wrenched the air with the sinister kind of chill that still haunted Willow in her sleep.

The sky was black with storm clouds, the moon and stars lost, casting an eerie feel over the property that made Willow question her judgment in coming here.

If you want the killing to stop, meet me.

How could the boy who'd saved her and protected the others have grown up to be a cold-blooded murderer?

Maybe she was wrong. She hoped she was.

But her instincts screamed this was a set up.

Fingers trembling, she snagged her phone from her pocket and pressed the number for the detective. The phone rang four times then went to voicemail. Panic splintered through her, and she left a message. "It's Willow Rodgers. Meet me at Hawk House."

She slid the phone back into her pocket, turning in a wide arc to look at the property. Was he hiding somewhere waiting to ambush her?

The crime scene tape flapped in the harsh wind, the storm having torn it from the trees. Debris had fallen during the heavy deluge and droplets of rain stung her cheeks as they fell from the quivering trees.

She scanned the property for another vehicle but didn't see one. Maybe she'd beaten him here.

Fear thundered through her as she walked toward the rotting structure that had once been her prison. As a child, the house had seemed gigantic but now it looked small, pitiful in its dilapidated state. Gravel crunched beneath her shoes, and the scent of damp grass mingled with the metallic odor of blood lingering in her memory as she approached. Then she heard the screams echoing from within.

In her mind, she saw the bones scattered across the forest floor, saw them hanging from the tree limbs and poking through the soil. Felt them stabbing her knees when she was forced to crawl across them. Jabbing her back on the bed where he'd spread them in the punishing room.

As she'd lain there, she'd wondered what was wrong with her. Why her parents hadn't loved her. Why she'd been left there to rot and suffer.

Brush crackled and twigs snapped behind her. Suddenly a familiar smell wafted toward her. Sweat. Musk.

Going still, she started to turn around, but she felt the sharp jab of a knife at her back.

Terror shot through her, and her feet slipped on a muddy

spot, but he caught her arm, gripping her firmly. Remembering that he'd stabbed Kelly, Gayle and Catarina multiple times, she knew she had to stall.

"Let's talk," she said, her voice shaking.

"Just walk toward the pit."

She itched to reach for her gun, but his fingers dug into her arm, pushing her. The bodies of the children who'd died were gone now, but in her mind she saw their faces and heard their cries. Remembered Blackstone dragging her toward it.

He pushed her down beside it, and she spun toward him, her voice bitter. "Have you turned into Blackstone now? Are you going to push me down there like he did?"

He circled around her, a menacing figure. He'd been tall as a child, bigger than the others, but now he was even bulkier. In spite of the evil vibrating from him, his face was pleasing, his hair neat, his boyish face having blossomed into a handsome man.

He didn't look like a killer.

"You abandoned me," he said in a rumbling voice.

Willow's throat thickened with emotions. "You said we had to run. To save ourselves." She swallowed hard. "We all agreed not to contact each other."

"I thought you'd go with me," he said. "I thought you understood that."

"I'm sorry," Willow said. Although she'd sensed he wanted them to go off together, she'd been almost as terrified of him as she was of Blackstone.

"Get up," he ordered.

Panic clawed at her. Was this it? Was he going to push her into the pit? She rose on shaky legs, her stomach roiling.

Then he motioned for her to walk toward the house, and panic seized her. What was he going to do? Take her back to the room with the bed of bones?

"I said move it." He shoved her toward the door, and they

climbed the steps then entered the dark house. Willow's mind flipped back to the first time she was brought her. To the fear emanating in the cold rooms and the cries she'd heard from upstairs.

The familiar smell of mold and death permeated the air. Dust motes swam in the humid air. Just as she feared, he pushed her toward Blackstone's office.

"Why are you doing this?" she cried as she spun toward him.

"How could you turn into a whore after I saved you?" He paced back and forth in front of her. "Why? I risked it all for you."

Willow slowly slid her hand into her pocket. Her fingers glided over the smooth butt of the gun, and she began to pull it from her pocket.

"I thought you were better than that. Stronger." He halted in front of her, eyes condemning her. "But you're no better than she was."

"Who are you talking about?" Willow whispered.

"*Her!*" he shouted as if she should know. "She was a tramp. She made me watch the men going at her, and then one night that man got rough with her and I saved her, just like I did you. I saved her and she left me at Hawk House, just like you left me and became a whore, too."

Willow curled her fingers around the trigger then slowly slipped the gun from her pocket. She jerked her hand up and stepped back, pointing it at his chest.

The minute he spotted the weapon, he lunged at her. She didn't have time to pull the trigger before he slammed her arm so hard her wrist snapped, and the gun flew from her hand. She cried out in pain, and he dragged her toward the room. She tried to rally and fight, dug her heels in and screamed, but he slapped her across the face so hard her head flew backward.

Cursing like a madman, he threw her on the bed of bones and slammed the door.

Willow screamed, but her cries reverberated off the walls and she knew there was no one there to hear her.

Ellie inhaled the omelet Derrick had cooked, along with three slices of bacon and buttered toast with homemade peach preserves she'd picked up at the farmer's market. She couldn't remember when she'd last eaten or when food had tasted so good.

He seemed quiet again, studying her.

"Thank you for the meal," Ellie said as she wiped her mouth.

"You're welcome," he said softly.

She pushed away from the table and carried her plate to the sink. He followed, pressing a hand to her waist. "Go lie down. I've got this."

"You cooked. I can clean up."

"Stop being stubborn," Derrick said. "You were in a major accident and were shot at tonight. Put your feet up and relax for once."

Her shoulder was starting to throb along with her ribs, so Ellie conceded. She poured a second vodka and carried it to the sofa, then noticed a voicemail message on her phone. How could she have missed this?

She quickly retrieved the message, listening to the fear vibrating in the woman's voice. "It's Willow Rodgers. Meet me at Hawk House."

Ellie pushed the vodka away and stood. "Derrick, we have to go. Willow Rodgers left a message for me to meet her at Hawk House."

"You stay here. I'll go."

"No way. Give me a minute to get my shoes." She stuffed her feet into her boots, then grabbed her jacket, wincing as she pulled it on. Her weapon came next.

Derrick was waiting at the door when she finished, although he didn't look happy about it. "Did she say why she wanted you to meet her?"

"No, but she sounded nervous," Ellie said. "Maybe she's finally decided to talk."

Freezing rain fell as they hurried to Derrick's car, and he drove them toward the old orphanage. As they sped through the mountains, the sound of Willow's shaky voice played over and over in Ellie's head. The woman had refused to talk before.

What had changed?

The tires churned over the slippery road slowing Derrick and reminding Ellie of her own Jeep spinning out and rolling into that ditch. She'd seen her life flash before her eyes.

Her adopted parents. Mabel, her birth mother who was still practically catatonic. Cord. Derrick.

The little girls she'd saved three months ago. A child of her own.

She stiffened, wondering where that thought had come from.

She had no time for a family. She didn't even have a love life.

"This could be a set-up," Derrick said, drawing her back to the present.

Ellie laid her hand over her weapon. "I know." She scoured

the land as they drove, checking to make sure they weren't being followed.

Her ribs ached as she took steadying breaths, and Derrick veered into the drive to the orphanage. His headlights beamed through the rain, illuminating the tattered crime scene tape, and she spotted Willow's silver Lexus parked in the drive.

141

HAWK HOUSE

Willow crawled away from the bed of bones and pressed herself against the wall. A tremble had started deep inside her, the terror and memories of being locked in here as a child consuming her.

Fight through them. You have to save yourself. Find a way out.

Pushing through the fear, she felt her way along the wall toward the door. There had to be a way to open it from the inside. She hadn't found it as a child, but she'd been too afraid to look back then.

Her fingers brushed over more bones, the brittle bits cracking beneath her weight. She'd thought the police had confiscated all the bones at this place. *He* must have put more here just to torment her.

Tears blurred her eyes, but she blinked them away. She wasn't a scared little girl anymore.

But he was going to kill her. Or leave her here to die.

Biting back a sob, she felt up and down the edge of the door, the sharp edges of the metal pricking her fingertips. There was no doorknob. No latch.

Panic shot through her. No way to get out.

142

He paced Blackstone's study, fury eating at him. He hated Willow for leaving him.

But he'd forgotten how she could cast a spell on him. Make him do anything.

Just like Blackstone said, women were temptresses. He'd thought she'd be different after what she'd been through. After he'd saved her.

But not only had she turned into a whore just like his mama, she was raising another generation of them.

He had to put an end to it, or they would ruin more men for life.

Her screams catapulted back to the past when she'd been locked inside. He'd come to her rescue then. He wouldn't this time.

He clenched the knife in sweaty hands. He was so angry his lungs strained for air. He should just leave her there to die in the bone room.

As he started toward the front door of the old house, an engine rumbled outside. Running to the front window, he spotted that dark sedan the fed drove. That detective was with him.

Did they know he was here? How could they?

Then it hit him like a knife to his heart, ripping his inside out. Willow had called them...

Rage tore through him, and he stormed across and jerked the door open. She was cowering against the door, tears streaking her cheeks. "Please let me go," she whimpered.

He waved the knife at her face, pulling her to her feet. "Make a sound and I'll slash your throat right here." Her eyes opened wide in terror, but she clamped her mouth shut and he hauled her toward the back of the house and the door to the basement. He opened it, pushed her down the steps, took a step further in and closed the door behind him. Then he dragged her into the dungeon.

Blackstone had kept bones down here. His torture chamber. Another dark hole where no one would hear them scream.

He shoved her past the room then eased the bookshelf hiding the door aside, opened it and pushed her inside. She quaked with fear, clawing at his hands to get free, but he threw her down the stairs. Then he closed the door, pitching them into a dark abyss.

She was whimpering and trying to get up when he reached the bottom, but her leg was twisted at an odd ankle, and he smiled as he realized it was broken. She couldn't run away now.

She made a strangled sound, but he straddled her and covered her mouth with his hand just like he had years ago when they'd hidden from Blackstone.

Willow's face floated through his mind. They'd been young. Friends in a cruel world. Had bonded over their hatred of being thrown away, their self-pity.

"Snap the pulley bone in two and play chicken," Blackstone had ordered. "Whoever gets the short end gets a head start to find the bones."

Then the lessons had begun. Lessons Blackstone said he'd learned in his own childhood. Lessons that had made him into a man.

Hunt and uncover the bones. Sort them and name them one by one. They'd been studying them for weeks in that old hag Stuckey's class, learning their names, how to determine what bone came from which animal.

He saw the charts in his mind. He had memorized them instantly. Had felt the sharp sting of the jagged points as he was forced to his knees on the bed of bones when he gave the wrong answer.

He saw Willow on her hands and knees digging in the dirt. Heard the ping of bones in the pail as he collected them.

She was weak though and couldn't keep up. Her bucket was practically empty.

Her screams tore through the night like an injured bird, screeching and boomeranging off the mountain ridges, as she was dragged toward the pit.

He had to save her.

His calves throbbed as he ran after her. Brush and briars tore at his legs. Loose limbs slapped him in the face, and the hiss of the rattlesnakes circling the pit echoed from the thickets of overgrown weeds.

He'd learned to play the game. Could run like the wind. And he'd caught the bastard and grabbed at her to save her.

The monster turned with venomous eyes. "You want to save her? Fine, then in you go."

The monster flung the girl aside. She screamed, hitting a boulder. He clawed at the ground to keep from falling into the pit, rattlesnakes hissing and lunging at him.

Then his fingers slipped...

She'd betrayed him years ago and now again. She didn't deserve to live.

His mother's face flashed behind his eyes. He should have killed her.

Adrenaline firing his blood, he raised the knife and jabbed it into Willow's chest.

143

HAWK HOUSE

Thirty years ago

"Remember what I told you," the monster said. "Make a sound and I'll cut out your tongue."

She curled into a ball as he closed and locked the door, shutting her in the dark bone room again.

Tears clogged her eyes and nose and she buried her face in her hands to keep from crying out loud.

She heard footsteps in his office again. Was the big mean man back?

Then a woman's voice. Not the teacher or cook. She kept hoping one of them would help her, but they seemed scared of the monster, too.

"My name is Leah Gentilly, I'm a reporter."

"I know who you are," the monster said.

"Some believe you're abusing the children here," the lady said. "What do you have to say about that?"

"Those old biddies in town like to gossip," he said in a cold voice. "I run a tight ship, but the children here are well fed and taken care of. Just ask my staff."

"I intend to," the lady said.

Hope jumped inside her. Maybe Ms. Stuckey or Ms. Yolanda would tell her what was going on.

Hope died a second later. No, she knew they wouldn't. They were scared of him, too.

"I'd also like to look around the house."

Then she'd see the chains in the bedrooms. And maybe the bones in the basement. Maybe she'd even find this dark room and save her.

"No," he snapped. "Now I've answered your questions. You need to leave before I call the sheriff."

She curled her fingers into the palms of her hands. She wanted to scream, make some noise and let the lady know she was locked in here.

But the monster's warning made her bite her tongue. A minute later, she heard the footsteps again then the door of the office close.

And then she was all alone again.

144

Ellie called Willow's name as she and Derrick approached the house which looked even more formidable tonight with the wind banging the shutters. A window had been shattered – either from an intruder or the recent storms. Scanning the area, she saw footprints marring the mud that looked the size of a woman's. Another pair were larger, a man's boots, raising the hair on the nape of Ellie's neck.

Had Willow met someone here? Or had she been followed?

Derrick lifted his gun and so did she, then they crept up the mud-splattered steps. The door was ajar. Pausing to listen for voices, she waited seconds before she entered. The wind stirred around her. Rainwater dripped from the door awning and slashed at the porch.

Derrick shined his flashlight to illuminate the entry and she glanced left and right. Other than their breathing, an eerie silence swept through the frigid air.

If Willow was in danger, where would her assailant take her?

As she remembered the layout of the house and the study with the secret room, her instincts urged her to go there. Derrick motioned that he'd check the upstairs, and she veered into Blackstone's study. The room appeared just as they'd left it. Fingerprint dust still dotted everything in sight and drawers hung open where they'd been searched.

Gun at the ready, she went straight to the bookcase, and found the door unlocked. Holding her breath, she peered inside. The room was dark and cold, making Ellie shiver.

Willow was not inside.

Shining the light around, she spotted fresh droplets of blood on the floor.

Knowing Willow might be injured, Ellie rushed back to the entry and met Derrick. He shook his head. "She's not upstairs."

"Or in the study or that room," Ellie said, then headed toward the basement door. It was closed but locked. Derrick motioned for her to step back, and he kicked it in with one hard swift movement. As they walked down, Ellie lit the way to guide them down the steps, moving slowly and as quietly as she could. But the steps creaked, and the walls seemed to rattle with the force of the wind outside.

The jars of bones had been confiscated by forensics, but she could still see them in her mind and smell the acrid odor of bleach and blood emanating from the dingy walls.

"Where are they?" she whispered. "There was blood in the bone room. Willow may be hurt." She shined the light across the floor and spotted a few drops leading toward the back wall.

Derrick ran his hand over it. "In that *Bone Hunter* game there were tunnels where more bones were hidden," he said. "Maybe there's one down here just like there was a secret room on the main floor."

Ellie jumped on the idea. "Willow?" Ellie called. "Are you here?" Or had he taken her somewhere in the woods?

Silence was her only response. A second later, Derrick called Ellie's name. "Over here. I found a door." Gun braced, he eased it open and shined his light inside.

Ellie eased behind him and heard a whimpering sound from downstairs. Footsteps pounded somewhere below.

Derrick inched down the steps, then called to her. "She's here."

Ellie rushed down the steps, shining her light over the woman who lay in a pool of blood.

"Stay with her. I saw a man running away," Derrick said, then disappeared into the dark tunnel.

Ellie knelt beside Willow. "Hang in there. I'll get help."

Willow gasped for a breath. "He... was... here." Ellie pulled off her jacket, balled it up and pressed it over the stab wound, applying pressure. Quickly, she grabbed her phone from her belt to call an ambulance. Dammit, she had no cell service.

"Willow, I have to leave to make the call."

Willow clutched at her arm. "Please... stop him... Blackstone's... down here..." She gurgled up blood, then her body jerked and her eyes rolled back in her head.

145

Derrick darted through the tunnel, shouting for the man to halt. The beam of his flashlight revealed dust and dirt, and he smelled dead rats and animal feces as he gave chase. Footsteps hammered ahead of him, and he caught sight of a man dressed in all black. Slight build, brown hair, about his height.

He rounded a curve, then his foot hit something and crunched beneath his boot. Pausing to see what it was, he aimed his light on it and froze.

A partial skull. Human. Large enough to be a man's. Or a woman's. Dr. Whitefeather would have to determine that.

Catapulting himself back in motion, he raced ahead, careful not to step on the remains. Another few feet and he saw the man escaping. He fired a round, shouting for him to halt again, but the man ducked into the shadows.

Breath panting out, he ran ahead and caught the perp just as he reached an opening which must lead to the outside.

"Give it up!" Derrick shouted as he raised his weapon and aimed it again.

The man suddenly lunged at him like a wild animal.

Derrick felt the sharp jab of his knife blade tear his jacket as the man propelled him backward.

His finger pressed the trigger and a bullet pinged off the rocky wall but missed his attacker. Kicking Derrick in the stomach, the perp turned and dove for the door.

Anger engulfed Derrick and he raced forward and caught the man's legs just before he could escape.

He yanked him so hard they both fell backward and hit the floor. The man fought back, swinging his knife wildly. The blade pierced Derrick's arm through his shirt. Pain ripped through him and he felt blood oozing. His hand went numb and he dropped his weapon.

The perp dove for it and almost snagged it, but Derrick kicked his hands away. They traded blows, the knife jabbing into Derrick's shoulder and his right arm went limp. His attacker took advantage, jumped up and raised his foot to stomp Derrick's shoulder.

Reacting on instinct, Derrick grabbed the man's foot and flipped him to his back. The man grunted and rolled sideways, raising the knife again with a feral growl.

Derrick fired his weapon. Blood gushed and spattered from the bastard as he clutched his belly, doubling over. His knife clattered to the floor.

A second later, he screeched like a madman again and rushed Derrick, but Derrick shoved him backward. Then he threw himself forward on top of his assailant and jammed his knees into his stomach. Blood gushed. Then the killer wrapped his hands around Derrick's throat and began to choke him.

146

Willow was so still Ellie didn't know if she'd make it. But she felt for a pulse and finally found one.

Nerves tightening her shoulders, she ducked back upstairs, called for assistance then rushed back down the stairs. The woman was unconscious but still breathing. "Ambulance is on its way, Willow," Ellie murmured.

Remembering that Willow said Blackstone was in the tunnel, she clenched her weapon in her hand. Panic at being closed in underground swept over her, but she fought its dangerous pull and darted down the tunnel. If Derrick was in trouble, he needed her.

Dirt and rocks covered the floor, and a rancid odor circled around her. A rat skittered in front of her feet, and she yelped, jumping back. Then she heard the crunch of bones.

Dead God... Someone else had died here.

She swept her light across the ground and saw bone fragments strewn across the dark floor. The empty eyes of a skull stared back at her. Who did these belong to? Abel Crane?

She shouted Derrick's name, but he didn't respond. Gripping her gun by her side, she inched forward. Footsteps shuffled somewhere in the dark. Then a menacing howl echoed in the tunnel, and she began to run. A few feet, a few more.

The flashlight caught two shadowy figures – Derrick and a dark-haired man rolling on the ground. The son of a bitch was choking Derrick. Blood was everywhere. All over Derrick's chest. Dripping from the killer.

Anger snapped Ellie into action, and she raised her gun and crept forward. "Release him. Now," she screamed.

But the man didn't seem to hear her. He squeezed at Derrick's throat shaking him. Derrick punched his attacker in the belly, more blood spurting. Ellie crossed the distance, then knelt and pressed the barrel of her gun to the bastard's head.

"Release him or your brains go everywhere."

Her threat must have finally registered, because he finally went still, slowly dropping his hands. His breath panted out, and Derrick rolled sideways, rubbing his throat, keeping his eyes on the killer.

Ellie aimed her light on the man's face. It wasn't Blackstone. This man was younger. Angular face, short brownish hair. She recognized him. The court reporter who worked for Karmel. Shondra said he'd acted odd when she'd questioned him. His name was Shamus Dorton.

And now she was looking directly into his eyes, she saw the resemblance to the photograph of one of the missing boys. The one they'd been looking for.

"You're Abel Crane, aren't you?"

His lips curled into a twisted smile. "I knew you'd figure out the truth."

"You killed those women," Ellie said. "Why?"

"They deserved it," he snarled. "They were whores just like she was."

"Like who?" Ellie asked, her gun still pointed at his face.

"Like *her*," he yelled. "My mother. She opened her legs for all these men, then she threw me away. She left me here because I killed the man who was beating her." Disgust hardened his voice.

"What about Willow? She was one of Blackstone's victims," Ellie said. "Why try to kill her?"

He heaved a breath and Derrick staggered to a standing position gripping his arm where the blood was flowing.

"I saved her," he shouted. "Then she abandoned me. After I took her punishment for her, saved her from being thrown into the pit, she left and then became just like Mama. A whore raising other whores. Just like Blackstone said, they're witches, tempting men with their bodies." He huffed. "Just like Eve in the Bible. And just like Blackstone's mother. She ran a whorehouse and his daddy killed her. Blackstone drilled into us that his old man taught him how to identify the bones and how to be a man just like he was teaching us."

That was the reason he'd marked the women with that symbol. "You framed Judge Karmel," Ellie said, putting the pieces together in her mind. "Because he let them off easy."

"He thrived on his power," Abel said. "Looked down on me like I was below him because I worked for him. Hell, he treated those sex workers better than he did me." He pounded his chest with his fist. "It was my time to be the judge."

His demented mind had its own logic.

But his breath became labored, his body started shaking, his eyes fluttering closed. He was losing a lot of blood, and fast.

Derrick dropped down and pulled off his jacket, wincing as his arm hung limp, then pressed it over Abel's wound adding pressure.

"You killed Yolanda and Leah to keep them from talking?" Ellie said, needing to hear him say it.

Abel shook his head instead.

Then his mouth slackened, his body jerking.

"We found more remains in the tunnel," Ellie said. "Who do they belong to?"

But Abel's breath only rattled, and then there was silence.

147

Ellie bit back a curse. Damn, Abel Crane had just died. Now they might never know what else he'd been hiding.

Derrick stood but staggered slightly, and she rushed forward. "You're bleeding."

"He got me with the knife, but I'm fine," he said although his skin was pale and his teeth clamped as if fighting the pain.

Ellie slipped her arm around his waist to support him. "An ambulance is on the way. I called the ERT, too. Willow said Blackstone was down here. Did you see him?"

"No."

He dragged in a breath and Ellie heard voices above. She helped Derrick toward the steps and called out to inform the team of their location. The medics ran down and she indicated for them to treat Willow.

"Special Agent Fox has been stabbed," Ellie said. "I'll help him upstairs if you two will bring the woman. There's also another man in the tunnel. He's dead."

Derrick gripped the handrail with one hand while she gave him support and they made their way upstairs. Laney and the ERT team had just arrived and she filled them in.

Laney blinked, her brows drawn. "Who's down there?"

"Willow Rodgers, the woman who ran Arm Candy. And Abel Crane, one of the children who lived here. He stabbed Willow and killed Kelly Hogan, Gayle Wimberly and Catarina Hamilton."

Laney gripped her medical kit and shivered as if the thought of going into the basement unnerved her.

It unnerved Ellie, too. The closed-in space was full of death.

The medics brought Willow up and one of them hurried to Derrick, pulling blood stoppers from his kit to stem the blood flow from his injury. The other medic looked up from Willow. "We need to get her to the hospital."

"I know. Go with them and get stitches," Ellie told Derrick.

"I'll go after we tie things up here," Derrick replied tersely. "Show the ERT and Dr. Whitefeather Crane's body."

Ellie didn't have time to argue. "Send another bus," she told the medics. They would need one to transport Crane.

She motioned for the ERT and Laney to follow and she led them down the stairs. "Watch out for the blood at the bottom of the step," she said. "We need to preserve forensics."

Laney nodded, and they all stepped around the area where Willow had lain. As they passed the skull and scattered bones, Laney halted, her breath raspy.

"Laney?" Ellie gently touched her arm.

Laney shook her head, her voice a croak. "I... can't do this." With a low moan, she turned and fled, swaying as she made her way back.

"Follow the tunnel and you'll find the man's body," Ellie told the ERT.

Then she ran after Laney. They'd worked countless cases together, had seen some of the most gruesome murders imaginable, but Laney had never let them get to her. Not like this.

By the time Ellie reached the landing, Laney was staggering

toward the steps leading from the basement to the main floor. Ellie followed her into the house then out the front door. Then Laney slumped on the steps and dropped her head between her knees, her ragged breathing reverberating through the air.

148

Ellie sank down beside Laney, stroking her back. Thankfully the rain had died off, although the wind was wild, indicating another storm was headed their way. "What's going on, Laney?"

A moment passed, then Laney looked up at her with big dark eyes. "I don't know, I got dizzy in there. I tend to get vertigo when I haven't slept."

"Maybe you should see a doctor," Ellie suggested.

"I am a doctor," Laney said wryly.

"You know what I mean. Have a physical." Ellie offered her a sympathetic smile. "You may be coming down with something."

"Maybe so," Laney murmured.

They sat in silence for a moment while the second medic team arrived. She asked them to check Derrick, then explained about the body and they rushed into the house.

"Why is this case getting to you?" Ellie finally asked Laney.

Laney blotted perspiration from her forehead with the back of her hand. "I honestly don't know. Maybe because there were children here. Or this time of year when they have the Native American festival, I always feel off. Have nightmares about the

Trail of Tears. And I think about all the old stories and the children who died so cruelly."

"Just like now," Ellie murmured. "That was horrible."

"My people were taught not to fear death, but children are so innocent. They should be protected."

"True." Ellie squeezed Laney's shoulder. It's late. We'll have Crane's body transported to the morgue for autopsy, along with the remains in the tunnel. Go home and get some rest." Ellie rubbed her own bleary eyes. Now the adrenaline was wearing off, her body was throbbing from her earlier accident.

Was Abel Crane behind that?

Dammit, he'd died before she could ask.

"Thanks. I think I will." Laney stood, holding her medical kit in one hand as she walked toward her SUV.

Just then, Sheriff Waters arrived and Ellie filled him in. "Dead man's name is Abel Crane. He killed Kelly Hogan, Gayle Wimberly and Catarina Hamilton and stabbed Special Agent Fox. Fox shot Crane in self-defense. Details will be in our report."

Per protocol, Derrick's gun would have to be examined, the number of bullets verified and matched to the casings or bullets lodged inside Crane.

"Are you okay, Ellie?" Bryce asked. "Chief Hale said you had an accident earlier."

"It was no accident. Someone fired at my car and caused me to crash." Irritation flooded her. "But Crane died before I could confirm that he was the one who did it." She glanced at Derrick who was looking paler by the minute. "Agent Fox needs stitches."

Bryce's mouth twitched. "Then take him. I'll stay here and cover this."

"Thanks."

Rolling her aching shoulders, she hurried inside to Derrick

and found him arguing with the medic. "I don't need an ambulance."

"Now, who's stubborn?" she said. "Come on, I'll drive you to the hospital myself." She glared at him. "And that is not up for debate."

Derrick hissed between his teeth, but she ignored him and jerked her thumb toward his car. "Let's go. I would like to see my bed sometime tonight."

His gaze met hers, and he gave a clipped nod. He was silent as she drove to Bluff County Hospital.

When they arrived, questions still ticked through her head as he was wheeled back for treatment. She wanted everything tied up in a nice red bow.

But there was a knot in that bow. And she wouldn't give up until she unraveled it.

149

CROOKED CREEK

The man with no face was after her again. He'd been storming her nightmares the last week, just like he had when she was a little girl

You're next. You're going to die.

No! she cried. But no one heard her. And no one was coming. She'd be dead like Mama next.

"Run, hide, don't make a sound," Mama had whispered, just before she was killed.

A booming voice roared around her, and she saw her mama push the man away. "Just leave. No one will ever know," Mama cried brokenly. "I promise."

She peered through the crack in the doorway.

"You're damn right you'll be quiet." The shadowy figure's voice thundered, and he swung the kitchen knife at her mother.

The he snatched Mama's hair, shaking her so hard the air whooshed around her. Terrified, she dug herself deeper into the box of Goodwill items Mama had collected and hid beneath them. She covered her ears and her mouth. Rocked herself back and forth. Prayed he'd go away.

But the door swung open, and a cold blast of air hit her. He grabbed her and dragged her from the closet.

She screamed and kicked at him, but he hauled her across the rough gravel and threw her into the back of his car. The trunk door slammed shut. Darkness sucked her in like quicksand.

She sobbed but no sound came out. The engine roared to life. Tires screeched. She clawed at the floormat and cried, but silent tears rolled down her cheeks and soaked her hands.

The car bumped over ridges. Spun around curves that made her so dizzy she pressed a hand to her mouth to keep from throwing up. Another spin, and the awful smell of gas hit her. She couldn't help herself. Her Cheerios and milk came up, spewing all over her hands and the floor.

He hit a bump and she bounced, her head hitting the top of the trunk. Pain made her dizzy and she closed her eyes, more tears leaking out as he sped up. Another rough bump, and she hit her head so hard that stars danced behind her eyes.

She raked her hand sideways, and her fingers touched Mama's hair. Hair so wet with blood that her fingers came away sticky and red.

She sobbed into the hot floor of the trunk then scooted closer to her mama. She lay perfectly still. Curled on her side.

The air stopped moving. The heat surrounded her. The smell of blood and death.

She lifted her mama's hand and arm, but it felt like dead weight. Then she crawled closer, and let it fall around her.

DAY 7

Ellie hadn't expected to sleep, but with Derrick on her couch, nursing his own injury, and her body aching from her accident and the ordeal of catching Crane, they'd both passed out.

Morning came too early, and she was stiff, sore and cranky as she showered and brewed coffee. She had answers but still more questions. She had no car and had to rely on Derrick.

She didn't like relying on anyone.

He looked equally annoyed about his injury as he sipped his coffee, and she drove him back to his cabin to shower. A planned press conference was set for ten.

Listening to the shower run and knowing Derrick was naked beneath the spray stirred desires she couldn't pursue. She paced his living room, trying to outpace the thoughts, until he emerged. Her mind spun, trying to tie up all the loose ends of the case. Willow said Blackstone was in the tunnel. But Derrick had only seen one man, or so he thought. Could Blackstone have been there and escaped? And what about those bones? Whose were those?

She phoned the hospital to check on Willow. She might be able to fill in the missing pieces.

"I'm sorry, but Ms. Rodgers hasn't regained consciousness yet," the nurse informed Ellie.

"Please call me as soon as she does," Ellie said. She had to talk to the woman. She might hold the answers.

Moments later, Derrick emerged from his room, his damp hair combed back, his expression troubled. He winced as he tugged on his holster and jacket.

She avoided eye contact, reminding herself not to jump to his rescue. He might be headed to his lover after the press conference.

He reluctantly allowed her to drive, the silence thick with tension. Ellie couldn't seem to forget the scent of blood as they entered the police station. But Angelica was already waiting with her cameraman, poised for action.

Captain Hale pulled her aside before she started the interview. "Judge Karmel and his attorney are in my office. We have to cut him loose for those murders."

Ellie hated to eat crow, but he was right. Dammit, that man deserved to go to jail for being a sexist pig. Knowing that wouldn't happen though, she simply nodded.

Reining in her temper, she stepped up and waited while Angelica introduced the segment.

"As most of you know, police have been investigating remains found at Hawk House, along with a string of murders including three local females Kelly Hogan, Gayle Wimberly and Catarina Hamilton." She turned the mic toward Ellie. "Detective?"

"Yes, last night we had a break-through in the case. Special Agent Fox and I tracked one of the surviving members of Hawk House, Willow Rodgers, to the former orphanage where she met with a man named Abel Crane, who also was placed at Hawk House as a child. Both were survivors who suffered abuse at the hands of the headmaster Horatio Blackstone. Mr. Crane admitted to murdering Kelly Hogan, Gayle Wimberly, and Catarina Hamilton." Ellie forced her hands to be still and control her nerves. "During his arrest, he was shot to death."

"Go on," Angelica pressed.

"During the pursuit of the killer, we also discovered the remains of another body in a tunnel below the house. Those remains are with the medical examiner now to be autopsied. We hope to have results soon." Ellie paused. "There are also a couple of loose ends to tie up. We are still looking for a woman named Wanita Weathers who may have more information on this case. If you're out there, Ms. Weathers, please give us a call."

Interest sparked in Angelica's expression, and Ellie stepped away and headed toward her office. Judge Karmel and his attorney appeared, and Karmel gave her a look of smug satisfaction.

"I told you I didn't kill those women," Karmel snarled. "And you, Detective, will regret arresting me."

Refusing to give the judge the pleasure of intimidating her, Ellie schooled her reaction. She had no doubt he could be vindictive. And he certainly had ties to criminals, someone he could pay to hurt her.

Shondra burst into the room, her eyes lit with fire. "Wait," she said, arms outstretched, "you can't release the judge yet."

Karmel and his attorney were almost to the door but halted. The judge started forward, angry lines slashing his face, but the lawyer pressed a hand to his client's arm and shook his head. "Let me deal with this."

Shondra strode toward Ellie, pulled her to the side and lowered her voice. "The news of the judge's arrest triggered a wave of phone calls. Those women I told you about decided to come forward. They're filing complaints against Judge Karmel. Everything from sexual harassment to assault."

Ellie's heart skipped a beat. "You think they're legitimate?"

"Oh, yeah and they'll stick. The women claim they have written communication between themselves and Karmel. I think they have a case. They're on their way here now."

"Good work, Shondra." She crossed to Karmel and his attorney. "Judge Karmel, we are not releasing you today."

"You can't keep me here," he hissed. "You already proved I didn't murder those women." He angled his head toward his lawyer. "This is harassment. I want you to file charges against the detective for maligning my character."

Ellie lifted her chin. "Actually, you're not leaving. We'll be filing new charges against you."

The door opened then and, as Shondra stated, three women entered, all young, all angry, with a fierce determination in their eyes.

Shondra rushed to meet them. "Come this way, ladies. I'll take your statements." Karmel's nostrils flared as he shot Ellie a menacing look. Tonight, he'd be sleeping in a cell with some of the very people he'd put away.

She grinned at the thought.

152

QUAIL RIDGE

Ogden slammed his fist on the kitchen table, rattling dishes and sending coffee sloshing over the rim of his mug.

Damn that Detective Reeves.

She'd found the bones in that tunnel. And Abel Crane. Not that he cared about the boy, but he hoped to hell he hadn't spilled everything.

The detective wasn't satisfied yet. He heard it in her voice. She was still looking for that girl Wanita. And she wasn't going to quit until she finished digging up the truth.

Morning sunlight splintered through the dark rain clouds, shafts of it streaking the old wood floor that was gummy with dirt and mud. Outside, the wind swirled pine straw across his backyard.

So much had gone wrong back then. So much he couldn't fix.

But he could prevent the truth from being revealed. He'd taken too many chances, just to go down now for mistakes that happened three decades ago.

Decision made, he strapped on his pistol, pulled his jacket

on over it and snatched his keys from the keyring by the door. Then he strode outside and climbed into his vehicle.

BLUFF COUNTY MORGUE

Laney was shaking so badly she had to hold onto the door for support as she climbed from the shower. Last night she'd had nightmares of that orphanage. A case had never tormented her sleep like this one.

Today she had to autopsy more remains found at that orphanage. Only she felt sick to her stomach and dizzy again.

Maybe Ellie was right, and she should see a doctor.

Blinking the room back into focus, she towel-dried her body and dressed in scrubs, preparing for work. A quick run of a brush through her hair, then she braided it and wound it into a bun at the base of her neck. On her first case she'd made the mistake of leaving it loose and she'd ended up with blood in the strands.

A rattling sound came from outside. Probably another storm. March seemed as fraught with turbulent weather as the town did with violent crimes, as if the two walked hand in hand.

She glanced out the window to see where the noise came from and saw a cat streaking across her tiny yard.

The clock chimed, indicating she was already late and she fought to settle her anxiety. Ellie wanted answers about those remains and curiosity made Laney want to know, too. To put this case to bed at last so she could sleep again. Not that she slept that well anyway...

Ever since she was little and she'd attended her first festival, she'd wake up in a sweat, screaming and hiding in the closet. Her grandmother said she was an empath. That she felt too much for others. But the thought of children dying on the trail had haunted her sleep.

Just like those poor children at Hawk House must have felt helpless when they'd been left to that madman Blackstone.

Except she had the faintest memory of tiptoeing to her mother's bed and crawling inside with her. The poor orphans didn't have that.

"Shh, baby," Mama whispered. "It's all gonna be all right." Then her mama had sung to her in their native language.

But later... A few months passed that she couldn't remember. Only that Mama was gone and she'd missed her and... the days were blank.

Then after a while, she was back at the reservation with her grandmother, her Ensi. Ensi had grown sad when she mentioned her mother. Whispers rippled around their people that her mama had abandoned her. That she was never coming back. Warnings were hushed that they mustn't speak about her.

Now, Laney squeezed her eyes closed and pinched the bridge of her nose. She hadn't thought about that time in forever. But the case... that feeling of her mama leaving her. The kids at Hawk House must have felt that way, too.

The best way she could help them was close the case. She stuffed her feet into comfortable shoes, hurried to the kitchen for her keys and raincoat.

Ten minutes later, she parked at the morgue and hurried inside. Already the morning sun was losing its battle to the clouds, and a gray fog shaded the building. Dread gnawed at her as she walked down the hall to the autopsy room.

Back when she was little, she'd watched the Medicine Man heal her people using herbs and plants from nature, and Laney had been drawn to medicine. Intrigued, she'd decided she wanted to be a healer so she'd learned the names of each herb and plant and how they could be used to help make people well.

Then one summer the body of a young girl was found on the reservation, and she'd watched the investigation with an intense curiosity that changed her thinking. The details of the dead told the story. They had brought a killer to justice.

Inspired, she'd decided to become a medical examiner instead of a Medicine Woman.

Although she was accustomed to the cold hallways and smells in the morgue, today the pungent odors made her stomach turn. The hall seemed darker than usual, the hollow emptiness echoing with the padding of her footsteps.

The room housing the children's remains beckoned her, but she veered into the cooling room where the metal drawers held remains awaiting autopsy.

Abel Crane, in drawer one. Ellie had filled her in on the details, so she knew manner of death, but she'd have to follow protocol to confirm COD.

Drawer number two held the remains found in the tunnel. Ellie wanted an ID on those. Her stomach churned as she opened the drawer then the bones began to blur, and she was back at that house. Walking across the dirt floor. Bones scattered in the tunnel. Rats skittering through the dark, gnawing on the bones.

The lights in the room suddenly flickered off and she startled. The floor squeaked.

She clenched the edge of the drawer to steady herself. Maybe Dr. Chi? Lord help her, she had to get it together. She couldn't allow her nightmares to keep her from doing her job. The children needed her.

Yet she was sure she heard the low sound of breathing... Another squeak. Then a musky odor swirling around her. Someone was definitely in the room.

Not Dr. Chi.

She pivoted slightly. Then, the silhouette of a big man appeared in the shadows.

Terror gripped her, and she opened her mouth to scream, but he lunged at her and threw her against the drawer. She caught the edge with her hands to keep from falling, but pain shot through her chest.

Then she felt a hard whack on the back of her head, her chin hitting the edge of the metal drawer as she collapsed. Darkness swallowed her.

Cord let himself in his dark house, knowing he needed time to himself after the long grueling hike earlier. They'd rescued a small boy who'd fallen into a ravine, and thankfully he was going to be okay. His mother had been hysterical though, and he had a feeling she'd be fretting over the accident for a while.

But all he could think about while he watched her hug and comfort her son was Ellie. He thought about her constantly. Worried if she was safe. Trapped by another killer.

He even wondered what kind of mother she would be. But he dismissed that thought quickly. He didn't have to wonder. Ellie would be loving and kind and amazing just like she was at everything else.

But he couldn't think about her like that.

Still, he liked working with her so he could protect her. Whether she wanted it or not.

He remembered the one night they'd spent together years ago, how he'd pushed her away the next day when she turned on the light in the bedroom.

He didn't want her to see his scars. Was afraid she'd run.

So far he'd managed to keep most of them hidden from

Lola, too. She'd felt a couple on his back but he'd insisted on lights off to spare her.

He grabbed an IPA from the refrigerator and carried it to the bathroom, then stripped his shirt and stared at himself in the mirror. The jagged ridges and puckered skin had faded slightly but still remained a testament to his upbringing.

He'd gotten what he deserved, the asshole of a foster father had said.

In the end, so had the asshole.

Images of that day passed behind his eyes, and a smile curved his mouth. But when he opened his eyes, he saw the rage still burning in them. Then he stretched his hands out in front of him, hands that were as battered and rough as the hell eating at him, and knew he had to keep Ellie in the dark.

155

CROOKED CREEK

The fact that they still hadn't found Blackstone or Wanita Weathers bugged the hell out of Ellie. She walked to the conference room and stared at the whiteboards covered in pictures and theories.

Derrick rubbed his injured arm which was secure in a sling. "You did good, Ellie," he said. "You solved it."

Then why did she feel so unsettled?

His phone buzzed, and a frown marred his face. "I have to get this."

While he stepped aside to make the call, she studied the board again. Crane had confessed to killing the three sex workers.

She hadn't had a chance to ask him about the teacher and janitor but most likely either he or Blackstone had murdered them. But if Blackstone was alive, he most likely murdered Yolanda Schmidt and Leah Gentilly.

Derrick returned, his expression troubled. "Ellie, I have to go."

"Is something wrong?"

"I... just have to leave," he said, his tone short. Running his hands through his hair, he turned and hurried from the room.

Ellie sighed, wondering if he was going to Lindsey. The fact that he refused to tell her about the new woman in his life hurt.

He doesn't owe you. You're just coworkers.

Still contemplating the case's loose ends, she touched the children's pictures one by one. They'd all looked so innocent years ago. But Abel had been traumatized to the point of becoming a killer himself. And Willow... She'd survived but look what it had cost her.

Then there was little Wanita. The tiny little girl, the youngest of them all. Those big haunting eyes. That olive skin. Black hair with streaks of red...

Her heart began to pound. The glazed look of fear in her eyes, the slope of her nose... Her skin tone and high cheekbones...she looked mixed heritage. Maybe Native American.

Dear God. It couldn't be.

But she'd seen that same look, just yesterday at Hawk House. Those same brown eyes.

Shock pounded through her. She knew that little girl...

Wanita Weathers was Laney Whitefeather.

156

Confusion clouded Ellie's brain. Why wouldn't Laney have said something? She'd been working the case but hadn't once hinted that she'd lived there as a child.

Laney also knew they were looking for Wanita. If Blackstone was alive, he would be looking for her, too.

Sweat beaded her neck as she pulled her phone and called Laney's cell number. But the phone rang and rang, going to voicemail. "Laney, call me ASAP," Ellie said. "I think you're in danger. We have to talk." She hung up then called the main number for the ME's office.

One of the assistants answered. "Bluff County Morgue."

"This is Detective Reeves. Is Dr. Whitefeather there?"

"No, I haven't seen her. In fact, Dr. Chi was looking for her, too. But she's not answering her phone."

Ellie's stomach plummeted. Laney hadn't felt well when she'd left the crime scene last night. Maybe she'd just slept in. Or if Blackstone was alive, he might have found her.

She rolled her shoulders where a kink had begun in her neck, then grabbed a key to one of the squad cars.

Deputy Eastwood drummed her fingers on her desk. "Ellie,

you asked me to let you know when the lab analysis for the bullets in your car came in. They did. Casings match the ones fired at that storage shelter."

Ellie went still. "What kind of gun?"

".45. I can do even better. I know who it belongs to."

"Who?" Ellie didn't have time to play guessing games.

"Ogden."

Ellie's pulse thundered. Ogden had shot at her and her father? Ogden hadn't wanted those files to be found. She'd sensed he was hiding something all along. That he'd covered for Blackstone.

Maybe it went deeper than that.

"Shondra," said Ellie, "I think Dr. Whitefeather's in trouble. She didn't show up at work and she's not answering her calls. Drive to her house and see if she's home." Her keys jangled in her hands. "I'll find Ogden. And this time he's damn well going to talk."

157

Derrick hated leaving Ellie. And lying to her. Well, he hadn't actually lied but he hadn't confided the truth either.

Because Eternity Chapel was the last place he wanted to be. He paused at the entrance, dreading the next hour with every fiber of his being. Needing courage, he sucked in a breath, but Ellie's face flashed behind his eyes. He'd done nothing but think of that damn woman for the last three months, ever since their last case. She was tough and tenacious and tenderhearted, a contradictory but irresistible combination.

The door to the chapel opened as another couple entered, and soft gospel music flowed from inside.

Better get it over with. He'd run from his past long enough. Had shared it with no one, including Ellie.

Especially Ellie.

The moment he entered the chapel, his gaze was drawn to the photo display honoring his friend Rick. "Amazing Grace" echoed through the room. The pews were filled with veterans who'd come to mourn Rick's loss, yet because of the circumstances an awkwardness vibrated in their restless movements.

Rick had taken his own life.

Rick's wife Lindsey sat quietly crying on the front row with their two children, both huddled close and leaning into her. A stern reminder of the reason he'd shied away from pursuing a family of his own.

Guilt for not staying closer to Rick made Derrick's chest ache, but it had been too difficult to see his friend sink deeper and deeper into depression the last few months and to not be able to help him.

"I don't want to talk to you, man," Rick had yelled the last time he'd seen him. "You remind me too much of that day. Our mistake."

Derrick had understood. He felt the same way, although he'd been a glutton for punishment and tried again and again afterward to reach him. Each time Rick became more and more vocal. Eventually his wife had finally asked him to stop calling.

Until this last week. She'd made repeated calls, telling him she was worried. But he'd been too busy with the case in Bluff County to go home. And now it was too late.

He swallowed against his emotions. The anniversary of the day that had haunted them had been two days ago. They'd followed orders and blown up a village of insurgents. But innocents had died in the mix because their information had been incorrect. Derrick could still see the charred bodies.

Lindsey walked to the casket, pressed a kiss to her hand then laid it on top of the gray polished surface where the American flag lay draped. A flag to honor Rick's service.

Then she turned and looked at Derrick with a mixture of pain, grief and anger. Derrick knew she blamed him. There were dark days where he blamed himself, too.

Days like today when he couldn't hide from the truth either.

158

QUAIL RIDGE

Siren blazing, Ellie swung the squad car up the narrow road leading to Ogden's.

Her phone buzzed. Shondra.

"Hey," she said, answering quickly.

"Dr. Whitefeather is not at home. Neither is her car," Shondra said. "I peeked through the windows and nothing looks out of place."

Dammit. "Go by the morgue. Dr. Chi said she didn't show up but see if her car is there."

"Copy that. And Ellie, be careful."

"Always. You, too." She turned off the siren, tires churning over the muddy drive as she flew along. She spotted smoke ahead and pressed the accelerator. As she got nearer, she realized something inside the shed was on fire.

She pulled her weapon as she parked, scanning the property. Instincts alert, she looked all around her, listened for voices, a scream. Anything to lead her to Laney if she was here. But why would Ogden take Laney?

Because he knew she'd been at Hawk House and he'd covered for Blackstone?

She inched closer and peered into the small outbuilding. The fire had started in an old barrel but were shooting toward the ceiling. Tools hung on one wall. A worktable sat along the far wall. Fishing equipment occupied one corner. And cans of paint thinner and a gas can.

Slowly, she turned around and used her flashlight to look for footprints. She found a man's boot prints then drag marks, following them toward the woods. Brush rustled and leaves crackled beneath her shoes. The sound of the river gurgling echoed in the silence, the scent of wildflowers blending with the acrid smoky odor.

She wove around bushes and trees, following the indentations in the soil. A quarter mile in, she heard a voice. Grunting. Taking cover behind the trees, she inched closer and peered around a pine until she spotted Ogden. He was breathing heavy, cursing and shoveling dirt.

Panic nipped at her as she scanned the area.

Fear tore through her. Laney was lying on the ground. Hands and feet bound. Mouth gagged. Eyes closed.

Please don't let her be dead.

Raising her Glock, Ellie tiptoed through the weeds, weaving toward him until she was so close she could see perspiration streaming down the bastard's ruddy face. He piled shovel after shovel full of dirt to the side, pausing every now and then to catch his breath and wipe sweat from his face with the back of his arm.

Ellie glanced at Laney again then saw her eyes flicker open slightly. Terror filled them and she began twisting her hands to break the ties.

"You're not going anywhere," Ogden yelled at Laney. "I should have killed you back then, too." He lumbered over and poked at the grave with the shovel. "Now you're going to be with her forever. And no one will ever know."

Laney's cry of terror bled through the gag.

"Shut up," Ogden shouted. "Your mother deserved what she got. When she got knocked up, she wanted me to leave my wife for her. But I couldn't do that. I couldn't tell her I had an illegitimate child."

Ellie stepped from behind the tree, piecing the truth together. Now she understood why he'd covered for Blackstone. "You killed Laney's mother, then left Laney at that orphanage."

He jerked toward her in surprise then pulled his gun from his belt. Ellie was ready though and released a shot, but he dodged the bullet and fired back at her. Jumping sideways to avoid being hit, Ellie pulled the trigger again.

But Ogden moved quickly and she missed, then he yanked Laney up by the hair and dragged her in front of him. Terror streaked Laney's eyes as Ogden pressed the barrel of his gun to her temple.

"Don't do it," Ellie said. "If you hurt her, I will kill you."

"You're not taking me in," he howled. "Not now. Not after all this time."

Laney whimpered as he gripped her tighter, so tight she hung like a rag doll in his beefy hands. Knowing she had to stall, Ellie tried to get him to talk.

"Why hurt Laney? She was just a kid back then."

He cut his eyes toward Laney who was wiggling and squirming to free herself.

"Because I knew you'd keep looking and figure it out. And when she analyzed the bones in the tunnel, she would remember."

He dragged Laney toward the grave. "Move and I'll shoot her in the head," he warned.

Ellie gritted her teeth. He was going to kill them anyway. Her gaze met Laney's. She shifted her eyes, sending Laney a silent message to duck. A second later Laney elbowed Ogden, then went limp, sagging. Ellie took advantage of the split second and fired her weapon.

The bullet caught Ogden in the shoulder. He bellowed in shock then snatched Laney again and yanked her toward the grave. With one shove, he pushed her inside. Laney screamed although it was muffled by the gag, and Ellie pounced. She raised her gun to hit him with the butt, but he swirled around and knocked it from her hand.

Then his hands closed around her throat. Ellie clawed at his eyes and face, but he squeezed so hard she couldn't breathe. She fought wildly, but the world began to swirl and inky spots danced behind her eyes.

Dammit, she didn't intend to die here and let him kill Laney.

She held her breath, letting her body go limp until he released her. Grunting with the effort, he snatched her legs and dragged her toward the grave.

Gathering a deep breath, Ellie glanced around for her gun, but it must have flown into the bushes. Summoning her energy, she kicked him with both feet, sending him flying backward. His head hit a boulder and blood spurted, then he passed out.

Ellie jumped up, kicked his gun into the bushes then rushed to Laney. She was crying, clawing at the dirt and side of the grave to escape. Her panic ripped at Ellie, and she dropped to her knees, grabbed Laney's arms and dragged her over the edge to the ground.

Laney was shaking, her body shivering in shock. Ellie quickly pulled the gag from her mouth, then untied her hands and feet, and Laney collapsed into a heap of sobs.

A loud howl rent the air, and Ellie spun around and saw Ogden had come to. Yanking her knife from her pocket, she flipped it open and this time when he charged her, she stabbed him in the thigh. He collapsed, writhing in pain.

"Come on," Ellie said. She helped Laney up. "Let's get you to the car." She coaxed Laney back toward the house and heard Ogden cursing and shouting.

"You won't get away!"

She wanted to retrieve her back-up weapon from her car, but just as they reached the yard, Ogden was on their heels.

"Run!" Ellie yelled, urging Laney forward. Ellie raced behind her but as they passed the shed, it exploded, bursting into a ball of fire. Metal and glass sprayed the yard and rained down.

Ellie threw herself over Laney to protect her as the force threw them to the ground.

A scream burst through the air and when she looked back, Ogden was staggering wildly, his body engulfed in flames.

Smoke clogged Ellie's vision, and heat scalded her skin.

Ogden spun around, flames eating at him as he collapsed, his screams renting the air.

Laney was shaking, her skin clammy. Ellie helped her up and they ran to the squad car. Grateful she'd parked a safe distance from the shed, she opened the passenger door for Laney and coaxed her inside. Then she grabbed a bottle of water from the trunk and a blanket, wrapping it around Laney.

Laney gripped the bottle with dirt coated fingers then uncapped it, taking a long sip. Shock glazed her eyes as she stared at the rising ball of fire lighting the sky.

Ellie took a sip of water and called Shondra. "I found Laney. Get an ambulance and crime team out to Ogden's ASAP."

"Copy that."

Ellie ended the call, then soothed Laney. "Hey, you're okay now," Ellie whispered. "It's over."

A heart-wrenched sob escaped Laney then she turned those big, haunted eyes toward Ellie. "He... killed my mother."

Ellie sucked in a breath. "I know that now. She was in that grave?"

Laney nodded, brushing at tears. "I... didn't remember. I mean, I've been having nightmares lately, horrible ones about those bones. But I thought it was just the case getting to me."

"You didn't remember being at Hawk House or your mother's murder?" Ellie said.

"No. I... knew I had some blank spaces in my childhood but no one would tell me why." Laney shook her head. "But ever since you found those remains, I've been having bad dreams. I... They must have been memories." She dragged in gulping breaths. "I only have a few fleeting memories of my mother when I was really young. Then there's a time that's missing." She stared at Ellie. "That must have been when I was at the orphanage. Later I remember living on the reservation, but no one wanted to talk about my mother."

"You repressed the memories because of the trauma. That's the reason you didn't come forward," Ellie said. "That's understandable."

Laney swiped tears away, her expression tortured.

"You're Wanita Weathers, aren't you?" Ellie asked as everything fell into place.

She shook her head, massaging her temple as if the memories were still coming at her. "Oh my God. Ogden told them that was my name when he took me to Hawk House and dumped me there so if anyone looked for me, they wouldn't find me." She bit her lip. "How did you know?"

"I didn't," Ellie said. "But when I saw your face yesterday, your haunted look when you saw the bones in that tunnel, then I looked at the picture of Wanita on the murder board, I realized it was you." Ellie lowered her voice. "Tell me what happened, Laney."

Laney clenched the blanket tighter and rocked herself back

and forth. "I don't recall everything. But it's coming back in jumbled fragments."

Ellie waited, giving Laney time to process what she might be remembering.

Laney blinked several times, her eyes glassy, expression tormented. Finally, she cleared her throat. "One night... he... Ogden was at the house, and I heard him yelling at my mother. She told me to run and hide so I snuck in the closet, but then... he... he killed her." Another sob was ripped from her throat.

"I'm so sorry, Laney, that must have been horrible."

She nodded miserably. "I was so scared. Then Ogden found me, and he dragged me to his car and locked me in the trunk." Her breath rushed out. "The next thing I knew he left me at Hawk House." Her lower lip quivered. "I was so terrified. I... didn't speak for a long time..."

Compassion for Laney filled Ellie. "That's the reason you reacted so strongly at the crime scenes."

"It must have been." Sniffling, she glanced back at the fire. "I think Ogden came out to Hawk House a few times," Laney said. "I heard them talking, when I was a kid there, and Black-stone said he'd cut out my tongue if I talked."

Ellie cringed. They had literally terrorized her.

"Ogden made it appear like he gave money to a charity, but it must have been his way of paying Blackstone to keep you there," Ellie said. "They made a deal to protect each other." Two devils in cahoots.

Laney lifted her pained gaze. "And I didn't tell anyone. I was too scared of Blackstone. He was cruel and twisted. The teacher made us learn anatomy and the names of all the animal bones. Then Blackstone made us play games, made us hunt them," Laney murmured. "He collected them and made us sleep on a bed of bones, and he punished the losers by throwing them into that pit." Her voice grew stronger, anger taking root. "He... left them to die in that hole without food or water. Said life was about survival of the fittest and that if they were meant to live, they'd find their way out. That weakness could not be tolerated."

"Because his own father didn't tolerate it," Ellie said. "You haven't had time to autopsy the remains we just found in the tunnel, have you?"

"I don't have to," Laney said shakily. "I know who they belong to." Laney dragged in another deep breath. "Blackstone."

Ellie had her suspicions. "He didn't just run off, did he?"

Laney shook her head. "Abel saved Willow then Blackstone shoved him toward the pit and... Abel fought back." Her voice cracked and she leaned her head over, dragging in huge gulps of air. "Oh, God, Ellie, then... then I remember Blackstone was dead. His body hacked into pieces. But... the details are blurry."

Ellie couldn't blame Crane for killing him. To the others, he was probably a hero. "Now that you've opened the door to the memories, more may come back to you. But at least we know Blackstone is dead and you're safe now."

Derrick's throat thickened with grief as he stared at the coffin where his former buddy lay.

If the dead could talk, what would Rick say right now? Would he regret taking his life and leaving his family behind?

Although somewhere deep inside, Derrick understood Rick's need to end the constant suffering his guilt caused. They both should have died that horrible day instead of those people in that village.

But he couldn't take the easy way out himself. He'd spent the last few years trying to atone for that one unforgiveable deed. Worse, he couldn't abandon his mother, not after all she'd lost.

Derrick received a frosty look when he stopped to offer his condolences to Lindsey. Her soft crying shredded his composure. And those kids... Rick had loved them. But he'd been so lost... "I'm so sorry for your family," he said sincerely. "Please let me know if there's anything I can do for you or the children."

Lindsey pursed her lips. "You've done enough." She snatched her children's hands and coaxed them over to a group who appeared to be family, turning her back to him.

Grief robbed his breath as he stepped outside of the tiny chapel. The air was chilly with a light drizzle of rain adding to the day's gloominess. Head lights dotted the parking lot as the attendees made their way to their vehicles. Car engines revved up and Lindsey's family began to exit.

Suddenly Derrick felt very much alone.

He didn't want to be alone tonight.

As he climbed in his sedan, he turned on the news. Angelica Gomez was reporting.

"In another twist in the homicide cases in Crooked Creek, Detective Ellie Reeves discovered that former Sheriff Edgar Ogden covered up for Horatio Blackstone who brutalized the children at Hawk House. Blackstone's remains were found in the tunnel below the house. Tonight, Detective Reeves took down Ogden at his home where he'd buried the body of a woman he killed years ago."

Derrick's chest clenched. He should have been there as back-up for Ellie. Just like with Rick, he'd let her down.

Dammit, the urge to see her seized him though. The city with its beautiful skyline, traffic and thousands of people was loud and noisy. Plus, Ellie wasn't there.

He didn't belong here.

He started the engine and headed toward the mountains.

"See, it's over," Aunt Trudy said as she clicked off the television. "Ellie said they caught the man who killed those women, and the man who killed those children are dead, too."

Mandy nodded, relieved. After Ellie's visit, her aunt had insisted she come out of her room for dinner.

"I need to run to the drug store," her aunt said. "I'll be back in a few minutes." Mandy didn't want her to leave, but she knew she'd been acting like a baby. Ellie was right. She had to face her fears.

But as her aunt left, Mandy glanced through the window and saw the dark SUV pass by her house again. She'd seen it a half dozen times this last week.

Her aunt said she was imagining it. Thought she was just paranoid.

But there it was again. Slowing as it passed the house.

The hair on the nape of her neck prickled, the news segment replaying in her head. Ellie had shown a photograph of the killer.

She closed her eyes, willing herself to make out the face of the man she'd seen at Hawk House through the window. An image slowly took shape in her mind – a tall lanky man about Ellie's age. Thin. Sharp angular face. He saw her...

But the man she'd seen wasn't the man on the news tonight.

Stomach knotting with fear, she glanced out the window again, but the SUV was gone.

Still nervous, she ran toward her room to lock the door, her phone in her hand. She punched Ellie's number but got her voicemail. "Ellie, call me. I saw someone else at the orphanage that night..."

She halted in the doorway, panic zinging through her. The window in her bedroom was open, the curtains flapping. She turned to run to the front door, but the floor creaked, then she heard breathing...

EAGLE'S LANDING

Jonas's chest felt as if a weight had been lifted from him as he watched the latest breaking story revolving around Hawk House. The detective had closed the case.

Blackstone's body had been found.

Well, most of it.

A chuckle started in his belly and erupted from his throat.

"You knew him, didn't you?" Dirks said as he flipped off the news.

Jonas nodded. "He got what he deserved."

"And the man, Abel Crane? You knew him, too?"

"He was there when I was," Jonas admitted. "Believe it or not, all the kids looked up to him. He was fearless and stood up to the old man."

"What happened to Blackstone?"

Jonas had vowed never to speak of it, and he refused now. But he was launched back in time with the memory of that night. He saw it all happening as if it he was in the moment.

Blackstone dragging Willow toward the pit. Abel chasing after him with a shovel, arguing for Blackstone to let her go.

Blackstone whirled on Abel, his evil laugh boomeranging off the mountain. "Then you go in." He shoved Willow to the ground where she fell in the dirt, trembling and terrified. Abel ran to her to make certain she was okay.

But before he reached Willow, Blackstone grabbed Abel and hauled him toward the pit. Abel kicked and shouted, beating at the man with his fists and kicking with all his might. Blackstone tossed him to the ground near the pit and raged toward him, kicking Abel in the stomach and pushing him closer to the edge.

Jonas and the others stood watching, wanting to help. Too afraid to move.

Then Abel got a burst of energy and pulled a knife from his pocket. With one quick lunge, he jabbed it toward Blackstone. A second later, Blackstone was screaming. "You're dead, boy. And I'm going to make it painful."

Then out of nowhere, an animal-like screech came from behind Blackstone. It wasn't Abel... But the wild creature pounced on Blackstone...

"Jonas, talk to me," Dirks murmured, shaking him gently. He held a gin and tonic in his hand in offering. "You look pale. Are you all right?" Jonas dug himself from the past and accepted the drink, then a smile slowly formed. "I am," he murmured.

He looked down at his hands and saw the blood that had soaked his skin that night as he and the others had helped carry Blackstone's body parts to the tunnel.

The girls cleaned out Blackstone's belongings and they made a bonfire, shouting and crying happy tears as the embers burned and ashes floated into the muggy air.

But Jonas had wanted a keepsake. Some of Blackstone's bones.

Now, he turned up his drink and took a sip, then glanced at the painting he'd done of Hawk House, the one hiding the bones.

Yes, some of Blackstone's bones were missing. He'd taken a few for himself. He'd used them in his art and the windchimes. Now, every time the bones tinkled, he remembered the punishments that had been meant to shape them into men.

Then Blackstone's own scream as he'd met a painful death.

163

CROOKED CREEK

Mandy had called.

Ellie clicked to hear the message, hoping Mandy was feeling better than the last time they'd spoken.

But her voice sounded panicked. "Ellie, call me. I saw someone else at the orphanage that night…" The message was cut off mid-sentence.

Ellie called Mandy's number, but it went to voicemail.

Concerned about her, she rushed outside to her rental Jeep, then jumped in and called Bryce as she sped toward Mandy's. His voicemail answered as well. Dammit. "Bryce, it's Ellie. Mandy just called. She sounded scared. I'm headed to her house now."

She hung up, punched the accelerator, and flipped on her siren. Mandy's words echoed in her mind. When Mandy had first fallen into the pit, she said she'd been running because she thought she saw someone. If it had been Abel, she should feel safe after seeing the news today.

But the message said Mandy saw someone else there. Had she remembered their face?

With the Native American festival closing down for the

year, traffic was thinner tonight and the town seemed eerily quiet. The Nor'easter had passed and the winds had died down, but she felt chilled as she approached Mandy's street.

She flipped off her siren and her lights, then slowly drove down the street, scanning left and right for trouble. Trudy's car was gone, but she spotted a black SUV a couple of blocks away.

Lights burned inside the house and through the window of Mandy's room she saw the shape of a man. Ellie swerved to the curb, parked and slid from her vehicle, drawing her weapon as she crept up the driveway.

Just as she reached the house, she heard a noise inside. Mandy scuffling with her attacker.

Ellie inched to the door, opening it enough to ease inside. A scream sounded and she heard footsteps in the kitchen, then the sound of scrapping. "Let me go!" Mandy cried.

Creeping toward the kitchen, Ellie pressed herself against the wall as she peeked inside. There was a muffled cry then footsteps across the floor as the man dragged Mandy. Mandy tugged at his hands and kicked at him as he shoved open the back door.

Ellie slid closer, then raised her weapon. "Police. Let her go. Now."

The man turned toward her, a knife glinting in his hand as he wrapped his arm around Mandy's neck. "Move and she dies."

His voice was gruff and shaky. She quickly assessed him. Thin. Sharp angular features. Pale brown eyes. He limped as he dragged her another step away.

"I said, let her go," Ellie ordered. "No one has to die today."

"It's too late for that." He waved the knife at Mandy and Ellie saw red. She could not lose this girl.

A siren wailed. Bryce was coming. Her fingers clenched the gun, and she fired a bullet, catching him in the shoulder. He jerked with the impact and released Mandy. She stumbled toward Ellie, and Ellie grabbed her and stepped in front of her.

The front door burst open, and Bryce's boots pounded the floor. "Ellie? Mandy?"

The man in front of her turned to run and she pushed Mandy toward Bryce. As Bryce pulled his daughter into his arms, she broke into sobs, while Ellie chased after the intruder.

His injury and limp slowed him, but he staggered across the yard. Ellie sprinted after him, running past the red tips bordering the properties, and caught him just before he reached the SUV. He was reaching for the door handle, but she jumped him and ripped him away. Whirling around, he hit her, and her head jerked backward, then he punched her in the stomach, knocking the breath out of her.

Groaning, Ellie fired her gun again and this time hit him in the chest. He bellowed, shock flaring across his face as his body hit the ground. Ellie gripped her weapon tighter as she straddled him.

"Why did you come after Mandy? Who are you?"

His body convulsed as blood gushed from his chest.

Then Ellie looked into his eyes and saw something familiar. Blackstone was dead, but the picture she'd seen of him... His nearly black eyes... That high forehead. *My God.*

"You're Blackstone's son, aren't you?" Ellie asked the truth dawning. "No one mentioned he had a son."

"Because no one knew about me," he spat. "He made sure of that."

Ellie raised a brow. "Your father did?"

Rage flared on the man's lean face. "He locked me away from everyone. Kept me in a room in the basement because he was ashamed that I was weak." Pain and rage radiated from him. "But I showed him in the end."

Ellie swallowed hard. "You killed Blackstone? It was you, not Abel Crane? You hacked your father into pieces."

A smile curved his mouth. "He got what he deserved."

Ellie couldn't argue with that. "Then you killed everyone who could tell."

"Not the kids. I set them free."

The pieces slid into place. Abel killed the female escorts because of his mother, and Ogden went after Laney because he was afraid she'd remember that he killed her mother. But the others... "You killed Henrietta Stuckey and Willard Buckley, didn't you?"

"They should have helped the children," he muttered angrily. "But they stood by and did nothing. They just left us at his mercy."

"What about the cook?"

"She ran before I could get to her. Told me she'd never tell. She was too scared." He rasped a breath. "But when you found those bones and plastered it all over the news, I thought she might speak up."

So he'd killed her and Leah.

Sympathy for Blackstone's son and what he'd endured didn't justify what he'd done. "You are under arrest," she said then started to read him his Miranda rights, but he cut her off.

"I can't go to prison," he cried. "I left there once. I won't go back."

"I'm sorry," Ellie said. She glanced over her shoulder and saw Mandy hovering in Bryce's arms. "But I can't let you go free either."

She pulled her phone and called an ambulance. Too many people had died during this investigation.

Blackstone's son would not be one of them.

164

While they waited on the ambulance, Ellie secured Blackstone's son and pressed towels to his wounds to stem the blood flow. "What's your name?" Ellie asked.

"Norman," he muttered.

"Why was your father so mean?" Ellie asked.

"He said it was how he was taught," Norman said, teeth gritted in pain. "He hated me because I had a bum leg. And I think he hated himself because he was a failure." He groaned in pain.

"Why do you say he was a failure?"

"He wanted to be like his old man, continue his study of animals and archaeology but he was rejected from grad school. After I killed him, I found letters saying he was denied because of psychological issues. He applied to vet school, but he was turned down from there, too."

So he took his rage out on the children and the cycle of abuse continued.

The ambulance careened up, lights twirling. Ellie went to talk to them and passed Mandy and her father, who had his arm around her protectively.

"I'm sorry for what I said, I didn't mean it, Daddy," Mandy said in a choked whisper.

"Shh, it's okay, you really are safe now, honey," Bryce said gently.

Ellie saw tears in Bryce's eyes, then smiled to herself. Those two were going to be okay.

"Do you need to see the medics, honey?" she asked Mandy.

Mandy shook her head, clinging to Bryce. "No, I'm okay now."

"Good," Ellie said gently. "Stay with her, Bryce, and wait on the ERT. I'll accompany our prisoner to the hospital." Bryce agreed then ushered Mandy back into the house just as Trudy pulled in the drive. Eyes wide with alarm, she rushed from her vehicle toward Ellie. "What in the world is going on?"

"Sorry, Trudy, but everything's okay now," Ellie said. "Bryce is here with Mandy and can fill you in."

Trudy hurried inside, and Ellie guided the medics to Blackstone's son. He was fading in and out of consciousness as they checked his vitals.

"Will he make it?" Ellie asked in a low voice

"He should," the man answered. "But we need to get him to the hospital."

"He's in my custody," Ellie said. "I'll ride along." There was no way she'd let the man escape. He might have been a victim in his young years, but now he was a cold-blooded murderer.

165

Two hours later, Blackstone's son was secure with a guard at the door. He would survive and was in stable condition. Ellie had dropped by and checked on Willow who was recovering and was shocked to learn that Norman Blackstone had resurfaced. Willow had asked about charges, but since she hadn't actually aided Crane or Blackstone's son in the recent crimes, and had in fact called Ellie to report Crane contacting her, Ellie applauded her courage.

She called Laney on the way back to the station and updated her.

"I knew there was another boy at the house that never came out," Laney said. "He was locked in the basement. I saw his fingers beneath the door and heard him whimpering."

Ellie grimaced at the image.

"He was the one who charged Blackstone that night," Laney continued, her voice trailing off with the memory. "He had an ax and saved Abel..."

"And all the other kids helped carry his body to the tunnel," Ellie said.

"We burned his clothes and belongings so everyone would

think he ran off," Laney admitted. "Oh, God. That makes us all accomplices."

Ellie's heart thundered. "You were all just innocent children, victims," Ellie said. "And since you had nothing to do with these recent murders, no judge is going to hold you responsible. In fact, we could argue that you acted in self-defense."

"Are you sure?" Laney asked.

Ellie didn't intend to ruin Laney's reputation, not when she'd helped so many families with her work. And Willow and Jonas had kept quiet to protect the boy who'd saved them. "I'll handle it," Ellie promised.

"But you're going to tell the judge, aren't you?" Laney asked.

"I don't need to," Ellie said. "Norman Blackstone confessed and took full blame. And I don't have a shred of evidence against any of you." If she did, she'd bury it. They'd all suffered enough.

Laney thanked her, but she still sounded shaken and worried. Ellie assured her she'd take care of her. She hung up as she reached the police station.

Angelica was waiting inside. "Ready, Ellie?" Angelica asked.

This was one report she was glad to give because it meant the case was finally over. Clearing her throat, Ellie took the mic. "We now have the full story behind what happened at Hawk House thirty years ago," she said. Ellie went on to explain about Blackstone's son. "The residents of our county are once again safe and can rest peacefully knowing that the case is solved."

When she looked up from the press room, she saw her parents entering. Vera looked shaken and was clinging to Randall whose expression looked closed as his gaze met hers.

"Thanks, Angelica," Ellie said.

Angelica squeezed her hand. "I'm glad you're safe, Ellie."

Bracing herself for another dressing down by her mother,

she attempted a smile but her cheek was throbbing from the punch Blackstone's son had delivered. Dammit, she should have applied makeup before the interview.

"Are you okay, honey?" Vera asked in a small voice.

Ellie softened immediately at the strain in Vera's eyes. "Yes, Mom, I'm fine."

"You look like hell," Randall said.

Ellie chuckled. "Thanks, Dad. You know how to turn a girl's head."

His scowl turned to relief at her wry comment. "I'm proud of you," Randall said.

Ellie wasn't so sure her mother was.

"Your mom and I talked," he said. "And I don't want to worry her anymore."

Vera pressed a hand to Randall's arm. "Let me."

Ellie inhaled, waiting.

"We decided, well, that we'd rather know what's going on than be kept in the dark." She fluttered a hand to her cheek. "The things that go through my mind are scary, but it's... almost worse not knowing. So..." Her mother's chest rose and fell with a deep breath. "You can talk to Randall about the cases. That way if you need his help, or back-up, I guess you call it, at least we'll know you're safe."

Ellie smiled slowly. "Sandwich?"

It was a saying, a game, they'd played as a child. Her parents would both hug her, and she'd call out that she was the cheese in the middle and they were both the bread.

Vera and Randall laughed surrounded her with their arms. Ellie rested her hand against them for a moment, grateful they'd taken her in years ago. The kids at Hawk House hadn't been so lucky.

Cord shifted on the bar stool at the Corner Café, his gut tightening as the news segment ended. Ellie had been shot at, had an accident, fought with a serial killer and then was attacked by the former sheriff. Then she'd saved Mandy Morely from Blackstone's son. He could hardly wrap his mind around it.

"Glad that case is over and folks around here can relax." Lola pushed a beer toward him. "Now maybe you can enjoy a break from work for a while."

Yeah, the case was over, and people were safe because of Ellie.

But her face looked like she'd been in a boxing match. He itched to see her for himself. Make sure she was really okay, that no more animals were lurking or going to come out of the woodwork to try and kill her. He knew damn well that judge she'd arrested had it in for her.

Karmel had connections, too.

Worry made him anxious as Lola flipped the TV to another channel and leaned over the counter. She smiled and traced her finger over his hand. "I was thinking, Cord. Things have been going good with us, haven't they? Maybe we could take a little vacation together."

Cord tried to bridge the gap in his mind between Ellie's battered face and Lola's flirty eyes. "I guess a vacation would be okay," he muttered. "Maybe we could go camping."

"Camping?" Lola scoffed. "I was thinking something more romantic." She squeezed his hand. "It could be the start of something new. Maybe we should take our relationship to another level," she said softly.

His heart skipped a beat, a seed of panic setting in. "But things are fine the way they are."

"Sure. But I was thinking that you could move in with me. Or I could move into your place." She lifted his hand and kissed his fingers, making him squirm. "Then we wouldn't have to go back and forth."

The news reel replayed in his head. Ellie with the bruised face. Ellie who was strong and independent. Ellie who didn't need him. Ellie who didn't want commitments.

Ellie who he couldn't get out of his damn head.

"Cord?"

Lola's soft voice brought his gaze toward her. Lola was kind and sweet. She wanted him. She made him feel good about himself. He cared about her and didn't want to hurt her.

She pressed a kiss to his cheek. Tempting him. A reminder of how tender she could be. "What do you think?"

Cord swallowed hard. His life flashed behind his eyes. He was just like those kids at Hawk House. No one had loved him. He'd done bad things. He had dark thoughts. Nightmares he refused to share with anyone. Secrets...

Suddenly he couldn't breathe. Felt as if his lungs couldn't find air.

He'd be a fool to say no to Lola.

"Let me think about it," he said.

A smile lit her eyes, and she cupped his face in her hands

and kissed him. Her wet lips felt soft against his. A silent offering.

But when he closed his eyes, he saw Ellie.

Lola ended the kiss, and he tugged his jacket off the bar stool. "I have to go. Take care of something. Then... I'll be back."

He didn't know if he would, but he couldn't commit to Lola until he talked to Ellie.

167

Another storm raged through Atlanta as Derrick had left. Tornado warnings were spread far and wide across the South. But he kept driving, hoping to outrun it and reach Ellie's before it ripped through the mountains, destroying trees and homes and trailer parks.

He told himself a hundred times to turn his car around and head back to Atlanta. To give himself time to move past the day. Deal with his guilt.

Not to involve Ellie. She had enough problems of her own.

But the car kept going and he kept seeing her battered face and her fierce determination and her stubbornness that made him want to lose his mind.

And here he was.

Back in Crooked Creek. Pulling into her drive.

The lights were dim in the house, but he knew Ellie kept at least one on to sleep. Affection and admiration for her welled inside him. Her childhood had triggered her fear of the dark and closed in spaces. He understood. He never wanted her to be in the dark alone again.

The wind died down as he pulled in her drive, and he

noticed a black Jeep. She must have gotten a rental while hers was in the shop.

Another reminder that she could have died in that crash. And that he'd never told her how he felt.

Rational thoughts intruded.

Don't. It can't go anywhere.

Mixing personal lives and work never meshed.

He started to back from the driveway, but again he didn't listen. He saw Rick in that coffin, his family crying for him.

He'd had love and yet he'd thrown it away in his own despair.

Wiping sweat from his brow, he climbed out and walked up to the door. Wind ruffled his hair as he rang the doorbell, bringing the smell of wild honeysuckle, then the door opened and Ellie was there.

168

Ellie tugged her bathrobe tighter around her. She'd showered off the day's grime, but the memories tainted her.

"What are you doing here?" she asked, surprised.

"I heard about what happened with Ogden," he said, his voice thick. "I'm sorry I wasn't here for back-up."

Ellie ran her fingers through her damp hair and decided to be direct. "It's fine. I realize you've been seeing someone in Atlanta. Lindsey's her name, right?"

His throat tightened. "It's not like that." Maybe he could get away with a half-truth. "Lindsey was my friend Rick's wife." His voice caught. "We served in the military together. He's been suffering from PTSD and depression and... she called me for help."

Ellie could see the pain in his eyes, hear it in his voice. "I'm sorry, Derrick. You never mentioned him."

"I know." He closed his eyes, as if to control his reaction then just spit it out. "It's been hard to talk about."

She let a beat pass. "What happened?"

"He couldn't live with the guilt anymore." He jammed his hands into his pockets. "We... worked together on a mission a few years back. People... innocent people died because we had wrong intel and... the government covered it up."

Understanding dawned. "So you and your friend have had to harbor that secret," Ellie said, sympathy in her voice. She understood his reticence to talk now. "I hope you were able to help him when you were back in Atlanta."

His eyes dulled to black, and he looked down at his feet "He committed suicide two days ago. I just came from the funeral. His... kids... They're devastated."

Sorrow for Derrick, for his friend and his wife engulfed Ellie. "I'm so sorry, Derrick. How awful."

"It w-was," he said, his voice breaking.

Ellie didn't know what to say. Except he was suffering and he was here, so she reached for him. He fell into her arms and buried his head against her for a long moment. She felt his chest rise and fall. His labored breathing bathed her neck. She inhaled the woodsy scent of his cologne and felt his body shudder.

169

Cord clenched the steering wheel in a white-knuckled grip as he approached Ellie's. Uncertainty nagged at him. He should have gone home and showered. But he'd had to see Ellie tonight. Had to talk to her. Rip off the band-aid and let her see the scars.

He glanced at the sunflowers on the passenger seat. Ellie loved sunflowers. Had once said they reminded her of sunshine and hope. That's what he saw when he looked at her – sunshine and hope for his life.

But dammit as he reached her driveway, he saw Fox's car in the drive.

For a second, he felt paralyzed. Had something else happened with the case? Had Karmel come after her?

He slunk low in his truck like some kind of stalker, not wanting her or the agent to see him as he slowed a couple of houses down from hers.

His gaze locked on them.

Ellie inviting Fox inside. The door closed then he watched them through the window. Ellie pulled the fed into a hug, and he lowered his head and kissed her.

Knocking the flowers to the floor with one hand, Cord sped

away. Lola was waiting for him at her house. Waiting on his answer.

His heart began to race, his lungs tight with the need to breathe.

The mountains loomed ahead, tall, ominous and unforgiving. But they were home to him.

Tonight, he couldn't face Lola. He needed to go home and lose himself in the wilderness.

A LETTER FROM RITA

Thank you so much for returning to the world I've created with Detective Ellie Reeves as she explores the dark and twisted case in *Hidden Bones*! If you enjoyed *Hidden Bones* and would like to keep up with all of my latest releases, you can sign up at the following link. Your email address will never be shared, and you can unsubscribe at any time.

www.bookouture.com/ritaherron

The moment my editor suggested the title *Hidden Bones*, my mind started spinning with ideas and images. I pictured an abandoned orphanage set in the wilderness of the Appalachian Mountains where long kept secrets and horrors had gone undiscovered for thirty years. There, among the untamed land, nestled deep in the mountains, lay bones that had been scattered in the woods and buried on the property, bones of the innocent children who'd been abandoned by family.

Children who had had no one to speak for them.

But as always Detective Ellie Reeves was determined to do just that and risked everything to find the answers and get justice for the innocents.

I hope you enjoyed the twists and turns of the story and this case as much as I enjoyed writing them. If you did, I'd appreciate it if you left a short review. As a writer, it means the world to me that you share your feedback with other readers who might be interested in Ellie's world.

I love to hear from readers so you can find me on Facebook, my website and Twitter.

Thanks so much for your support. Happy Reading!

Rita

www.ritaherron.com

facebook.com/ritaherron
twitter.com/ritaherron

ACKNOWLEDGMENTS

A special thanks to my amazing editor, Christina Demosthenous, who pushes me to the limits to make my story better! Her amazing insights, guidance, support and fabulous titles always spark my creativity and inspire me to write more of Ellie!

As always, a huge gratitude to the Bookouture team for creating such great covers, branding the series and providing promotional support!

I love being part of this fabulous team!

Printed in Great Britain
by Amazon

20122961R00263